Thinking Skills

K & UP

Spatial Reasoning

Table of Contents

To parents:

Spatial Reasoning

In this section, your child will learn spatial reasoning skills as such as spatial judgment and visualization of objects from multiple perspectives. This section contains activities like tracing, mazes, coloring, jigsaw puzzles, matching shapes, comparing heights, and others. By completing this section your child will gain the ability to thinking about objects in relation to space and to draw conclusions based on the information gained from each activity.

Each skill is introduced in a step-by-step manner that allows your child to master it without frustration. Over the course of the section, the difficulty level of these activities increases as your child gains confidence in his or her spatial reasoning ability.

1 Missing Pieces

Level One

Name

Date

■ Choose the piece that fits. Write a check mark (✓) above the picture.

To parents
Guide your child to write his or her name and date in the box above. Do the exercise along with your child if he or she has difficulty.

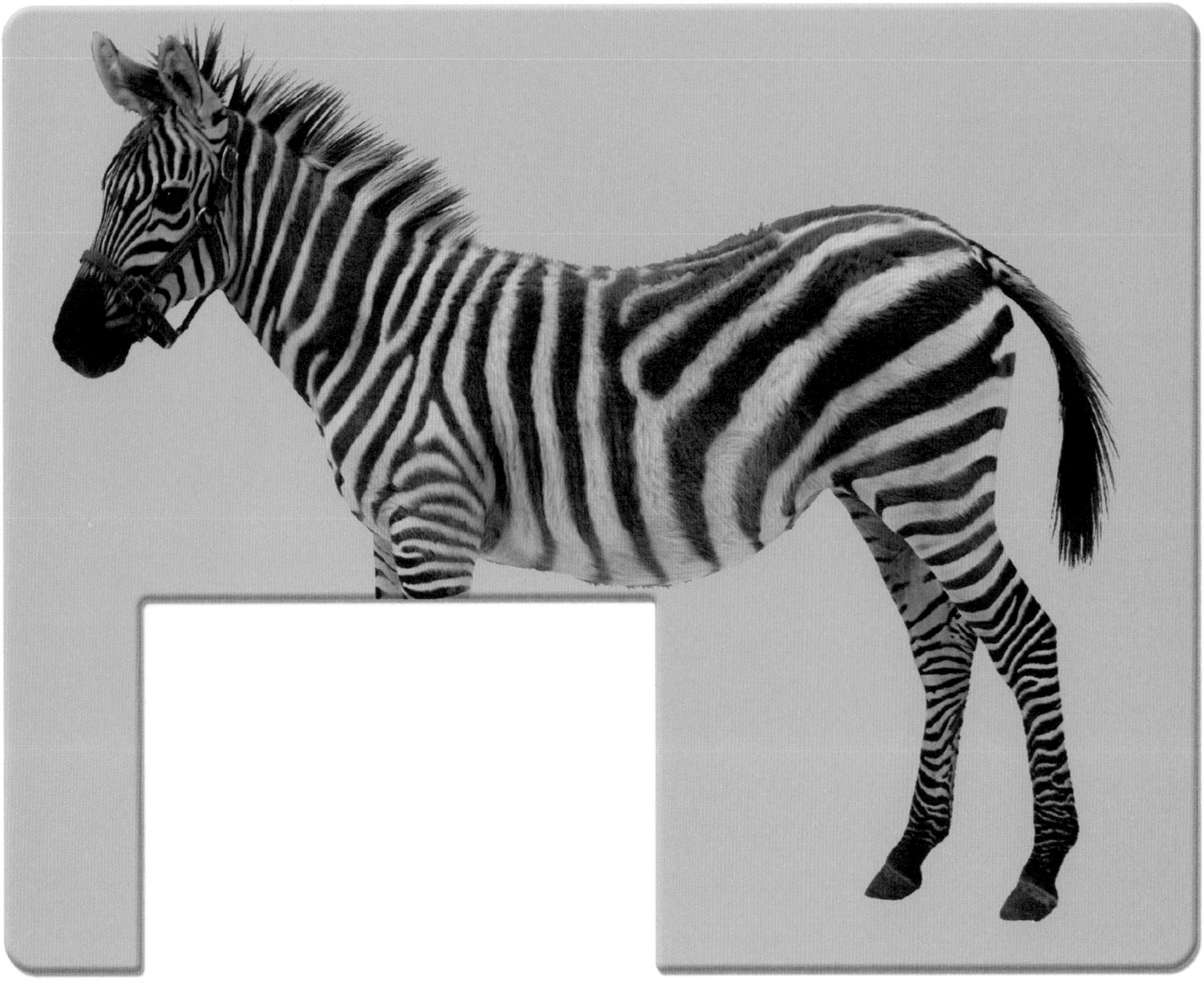

( )

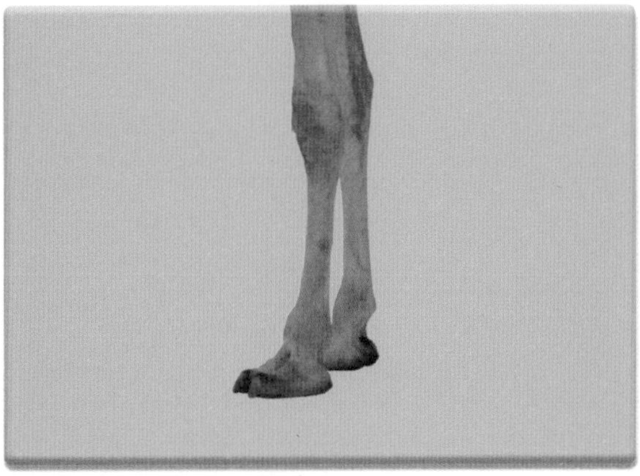

( )

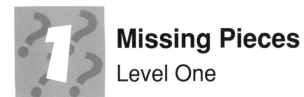

■ Choose the piece that fits. Write a check mark (✓) above the picture.

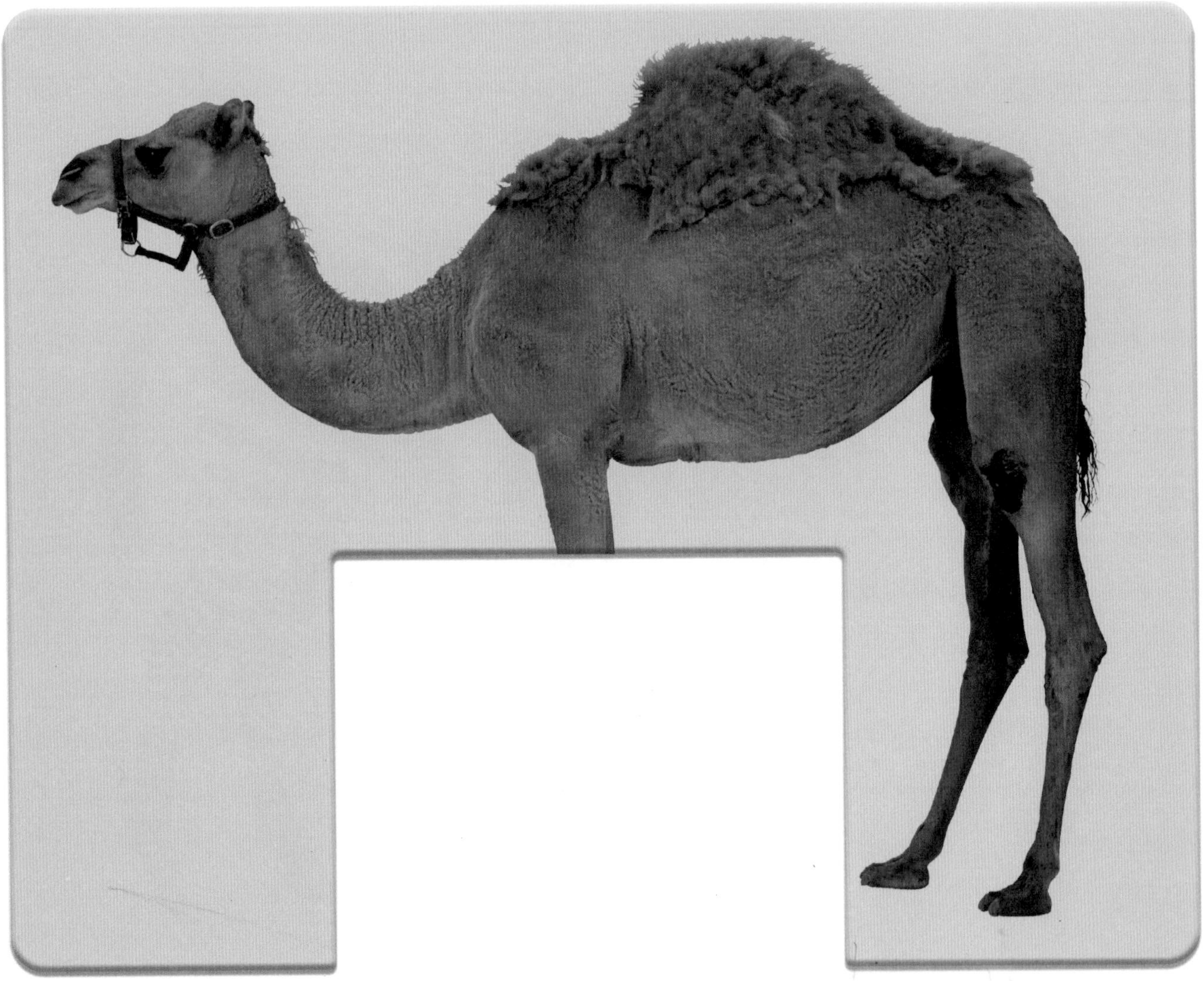

( )

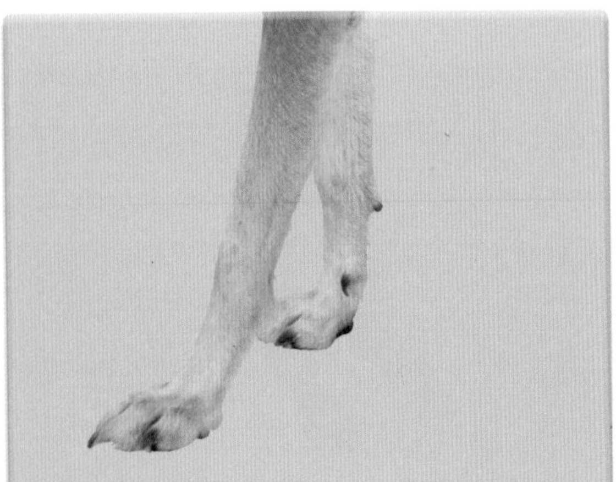

(✓)

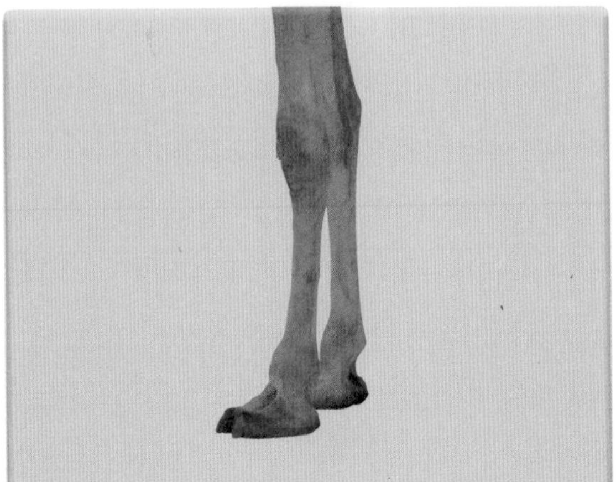

2 Missing Pieces
Level Two

Name

Date

■ Choose the piece that fits. Write a check mark (✓) above the picture.

To parents
Encourage your child to look carefully at the shapes of the pieces.

( )

( )

■ Choose the piece that fits. Write a check mark (✓) above the picture.

(✓)

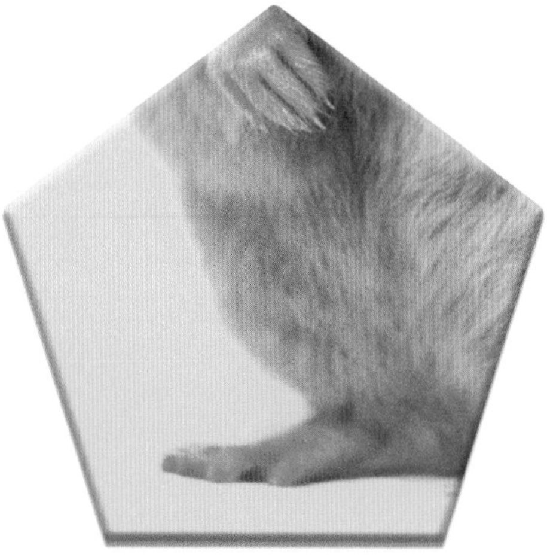

( )

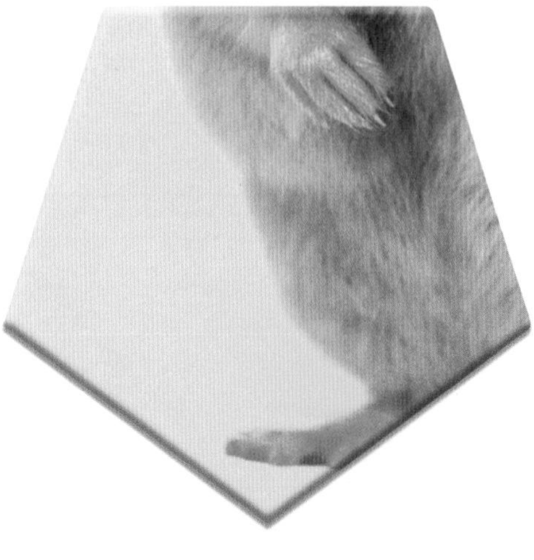

3 Missing Pieces
Level Three

Name

Date

■ Choose the piece that fits. Write a check mark (✓) above the picture.

To parents
Encourage your child to look carefully at the pictures on the pieces.

( )

(✓)

( )

■ Choose the piece that fits. Write a check mark (✓) above the picture.

( ) ( ) ( )

4 Missing Pieces
Level Four

Name

Date

■ Choose the piece that fits. Write a check mark (✓) above the picture.

To parents
Encourage your child to look carefully at the shapes of the pieces.

( ) ( ) ( )

■ Choose the piece that fits. Write a check mark (✓) above the picture.

(✓)

( )

( )

( )

5 Missing Pieces

Level Five

- Choose the piece that fits. Write a check mark (✓) above the picture.

To parents
If your child has difficulty, encourage him or her to describe what the missing part of the picture might look like.

Name

Date

( ) ( ) ( ) ( )

■ Choose the piece that fits. Write a check mark (✓) above the picture.

(✓)　　( )　　( )　　( )

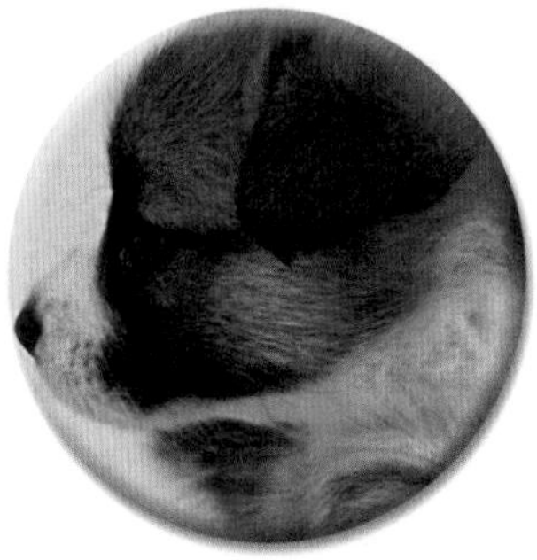

6 Missing Pieces
Level Six

Name

Date

■ Choose the piece that fits. Write a check mark (✓) above the picture.

To parents
Counting the sides of each piece will help your child find the correct piece.

( )	(✓)	( )	( )

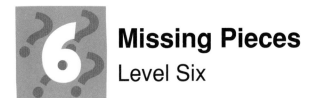

■ Choose the piece that fits. Write a check mark (✓) above the picture.

( )   ( )   (✓)   ( )

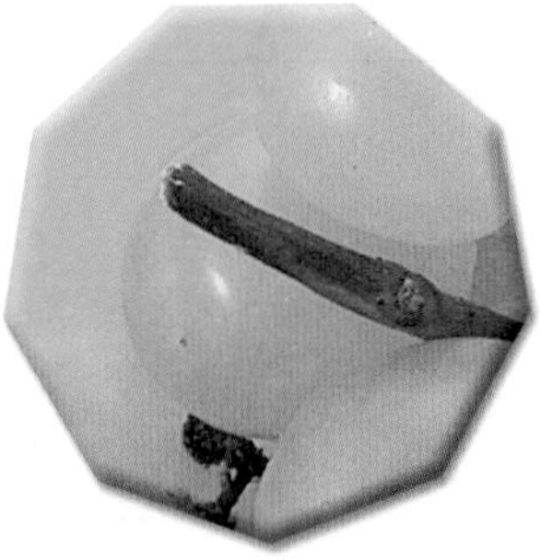 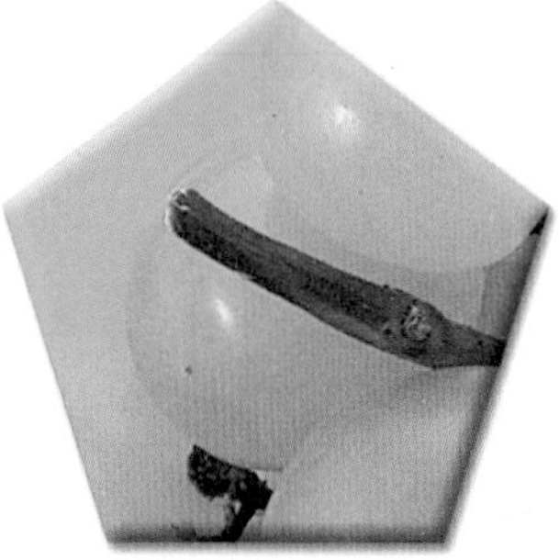 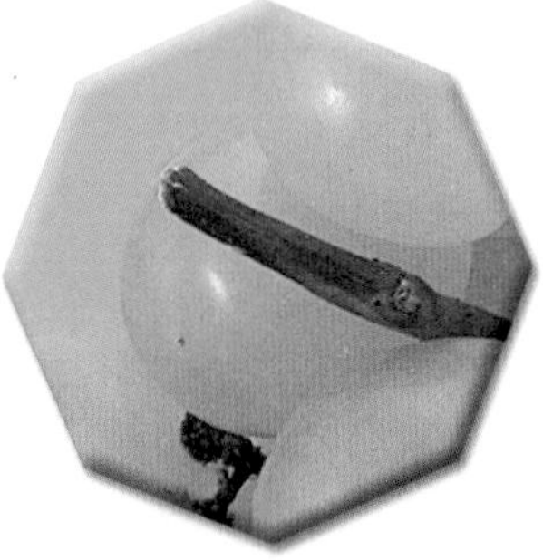 

Missing Pieces
Level Seven

Name

Date

■ Choose the piece that fits. Write a check mark (✓) above the picture.

To parents
Looking at the shapes of the pieces carefully will help your child find the correct piece.

() () () (✓)

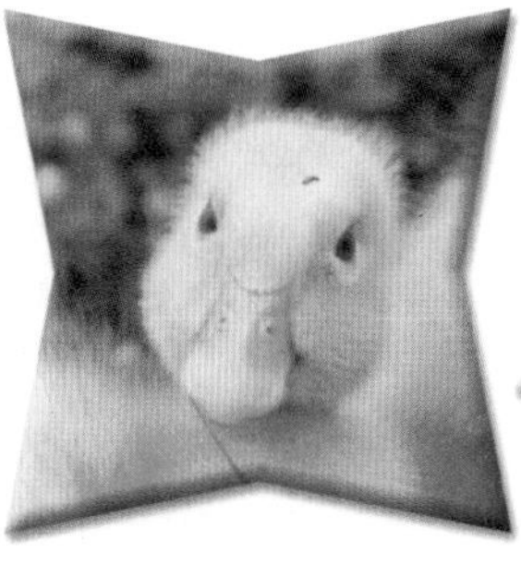

■ Choose the piece that fits. Write a check mark (✓) above the picture.

( ) ( ) ( ) ( )

8 Missing Pieces

Level Eight

Name

Date

■ Choose the piece that fits. Write a check mark (✓) above the picture.

To parents
If your child has difficulty with this activity, look at the shape of each puzzle piece with your child. Together, describe the shapes that you see.

( )

( )

( )

( )

( )

( )

■Choose the piece that fits. Write a check mark (✓) above the picture.

() () ()

() () (✓)

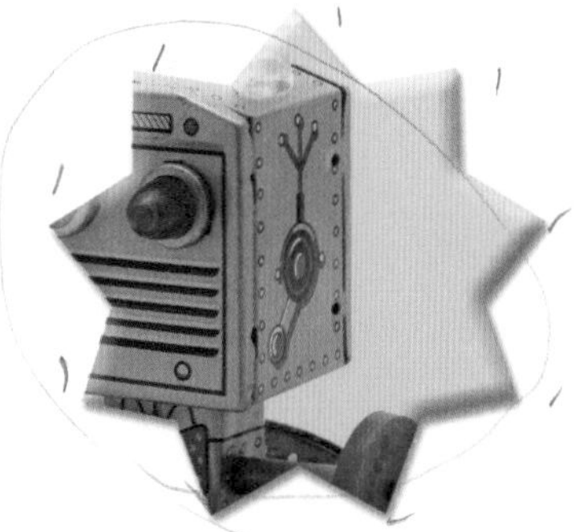

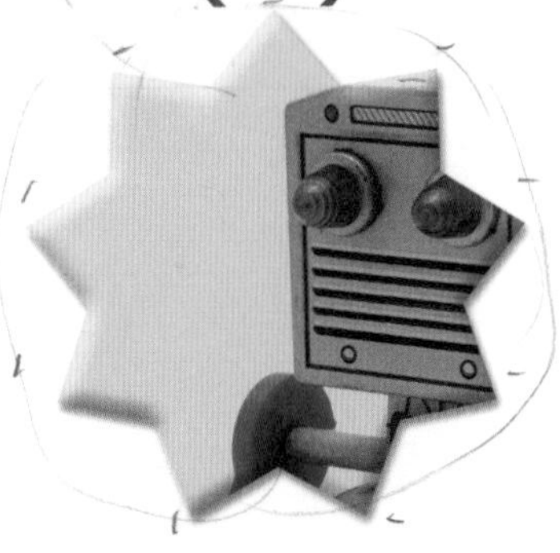

9 Jigsaw Puzzles
Level One

Name

Date

■ Draw a line to the piece that fits.

To parents
Looking at the illustrations will help your child match the correct pieces.

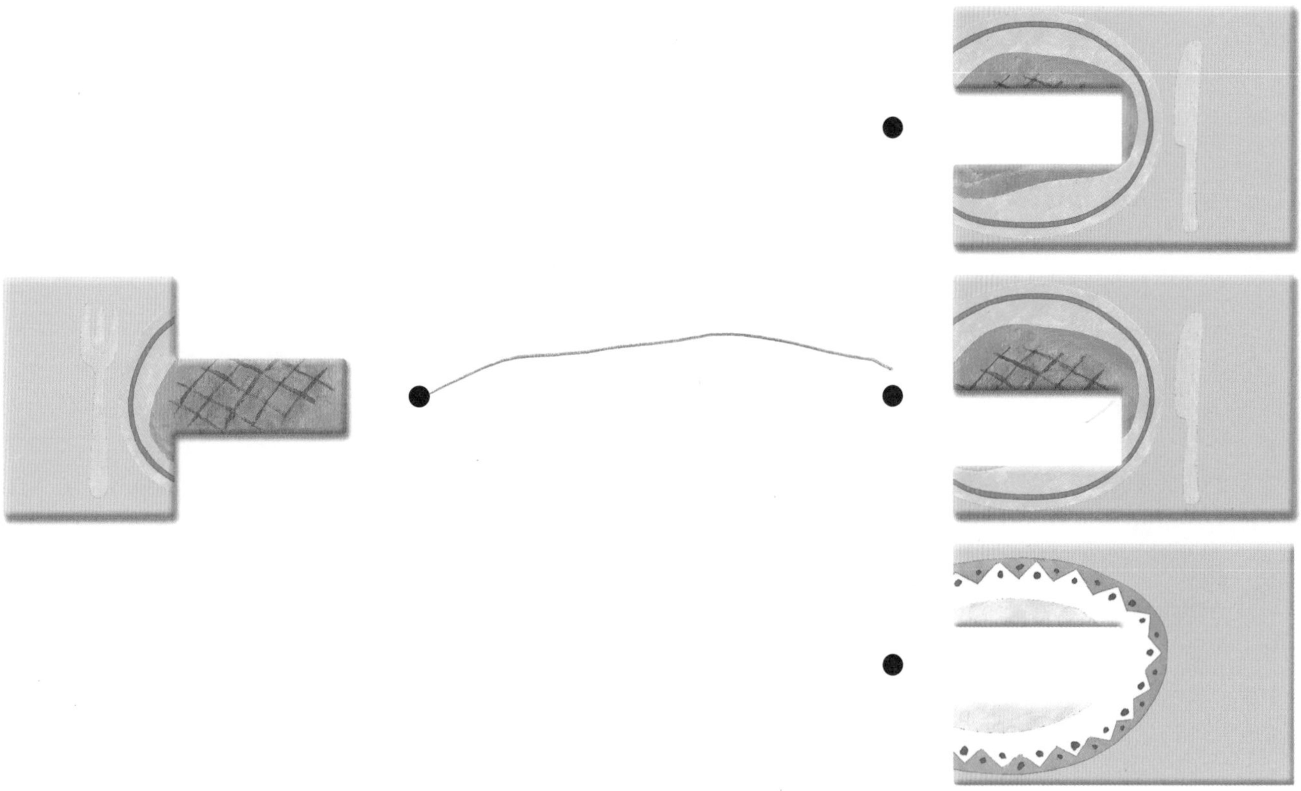

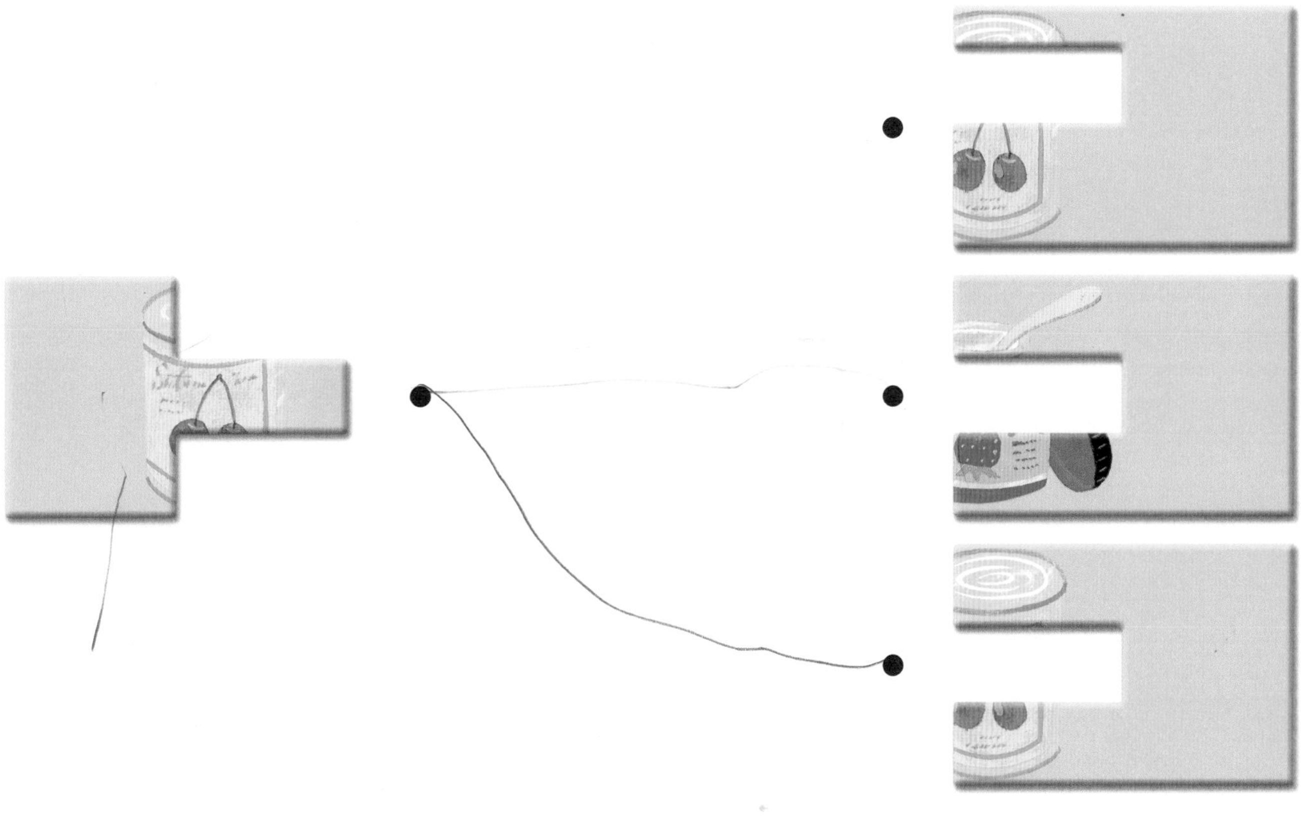

■ Draw a line to the piece that fits.

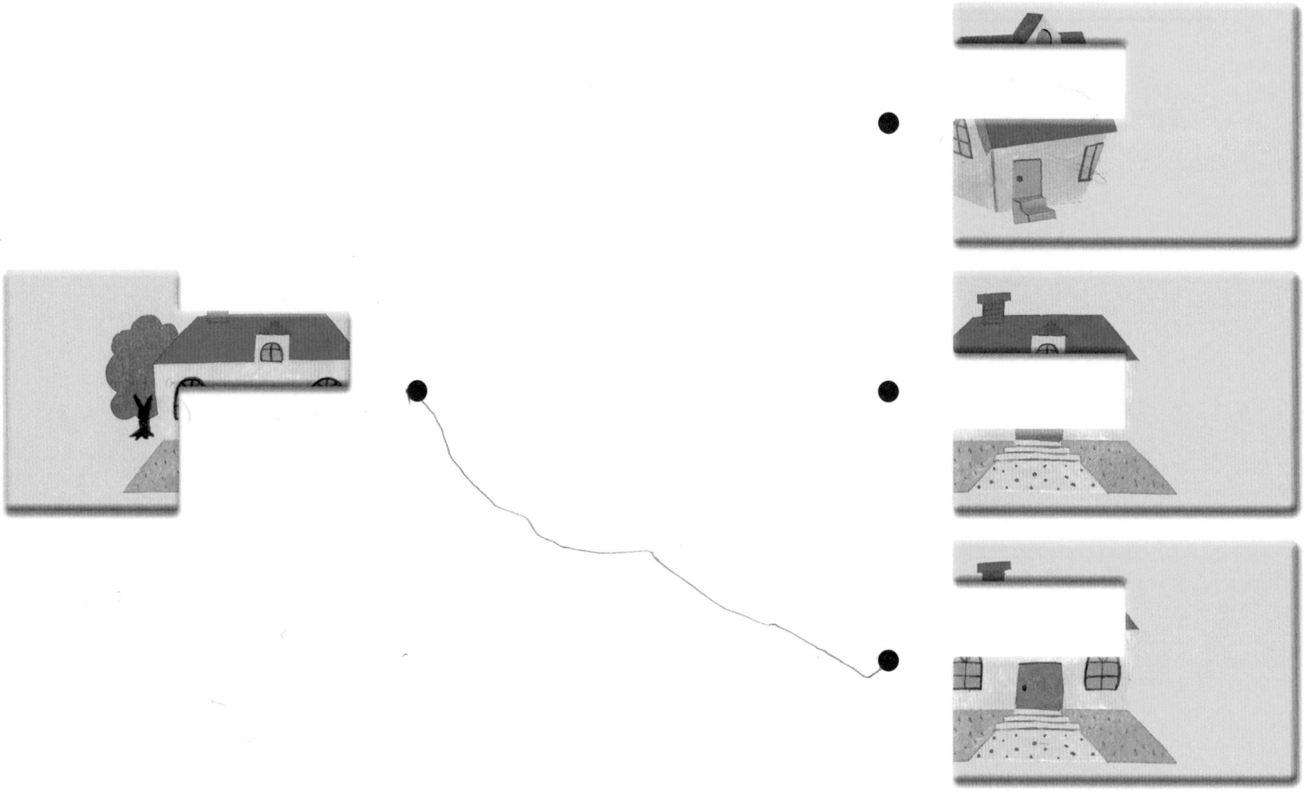

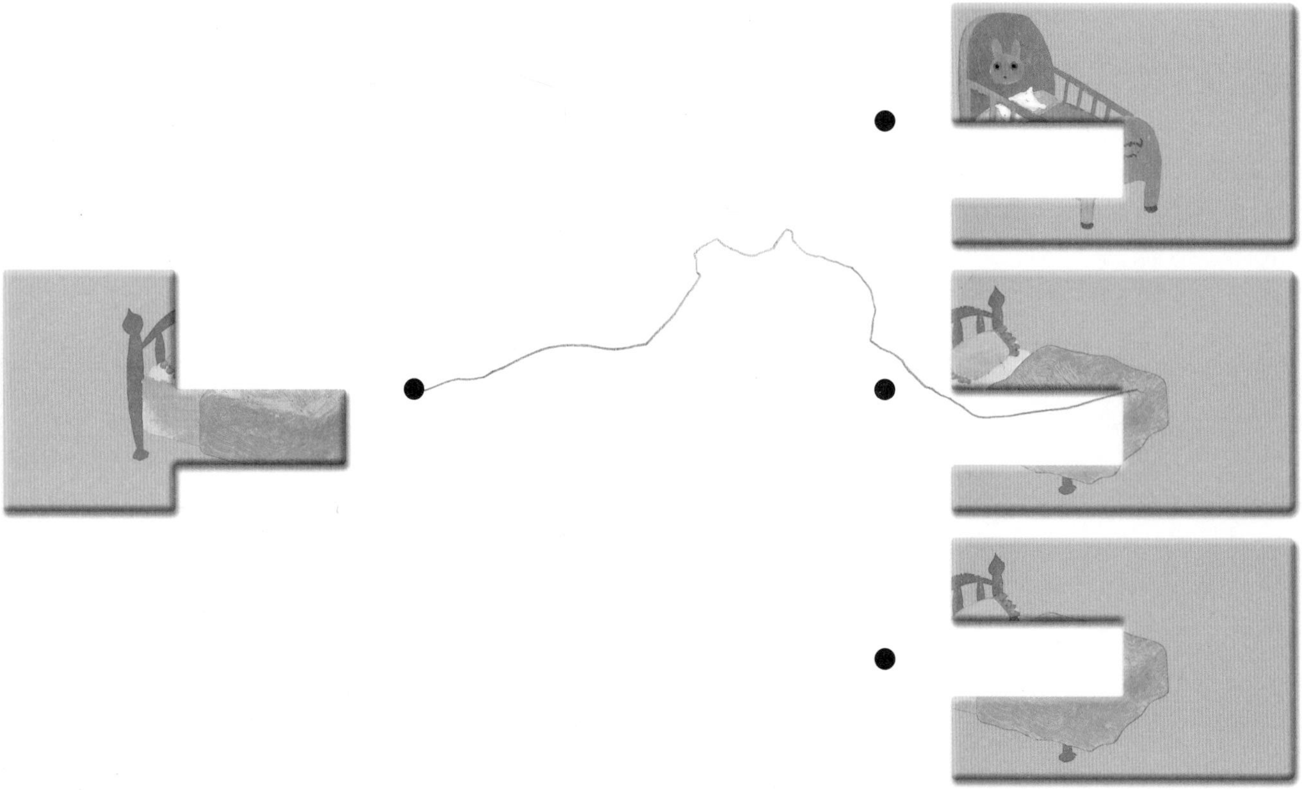

10 Jigsaw Puzzles
Level Two

Name

Date

■ Draw a line to the piece that fits.

To parents
The three puzzle pieces in the right column have the same illustration. Encourage your child to look at the edge of each piece.

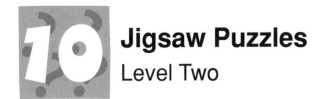

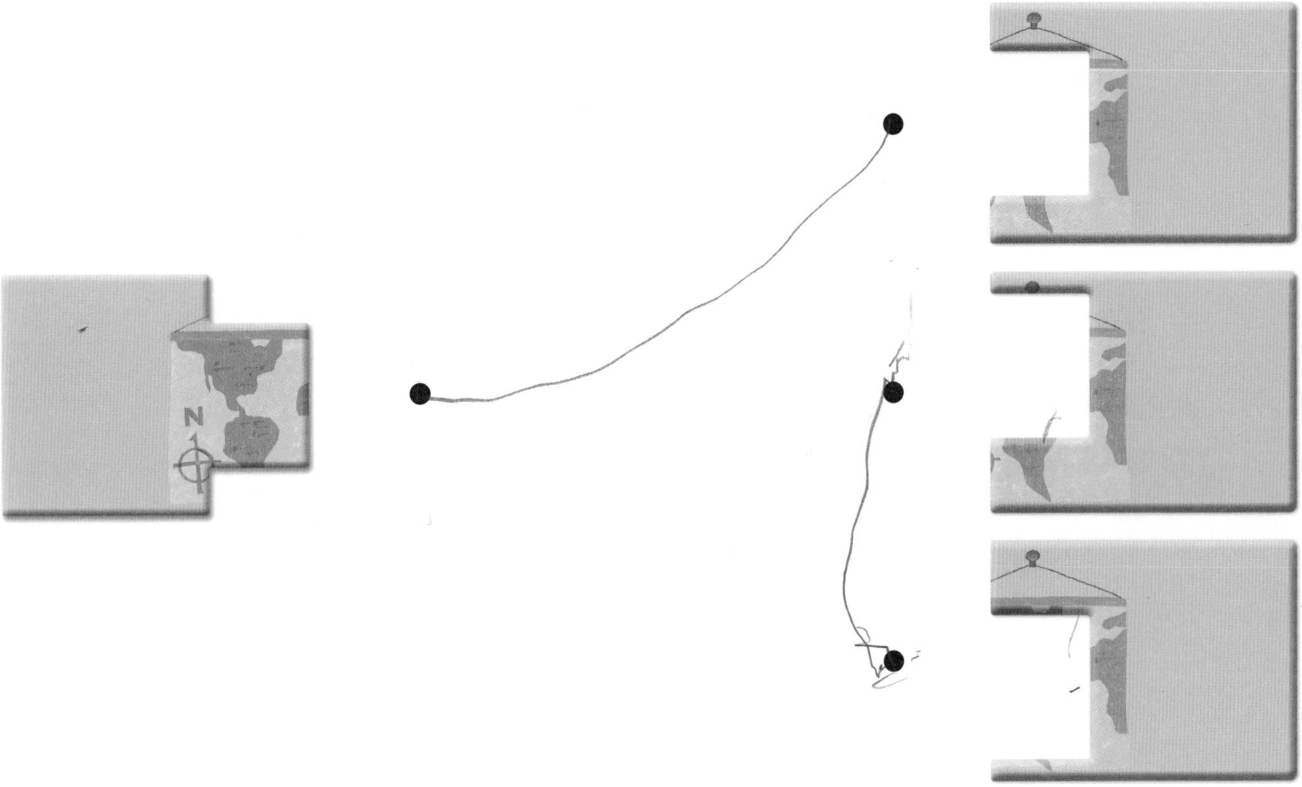

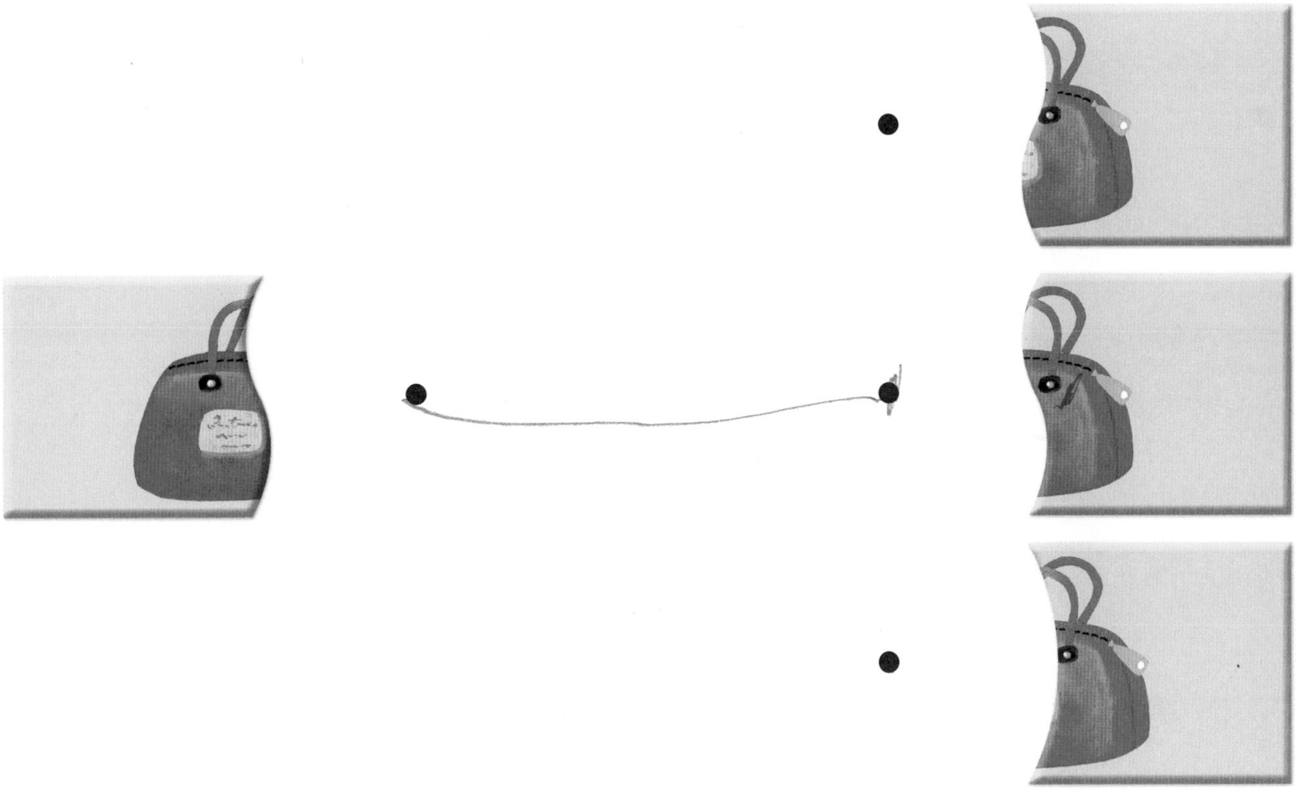

■ Draw a line to the piece that fits.

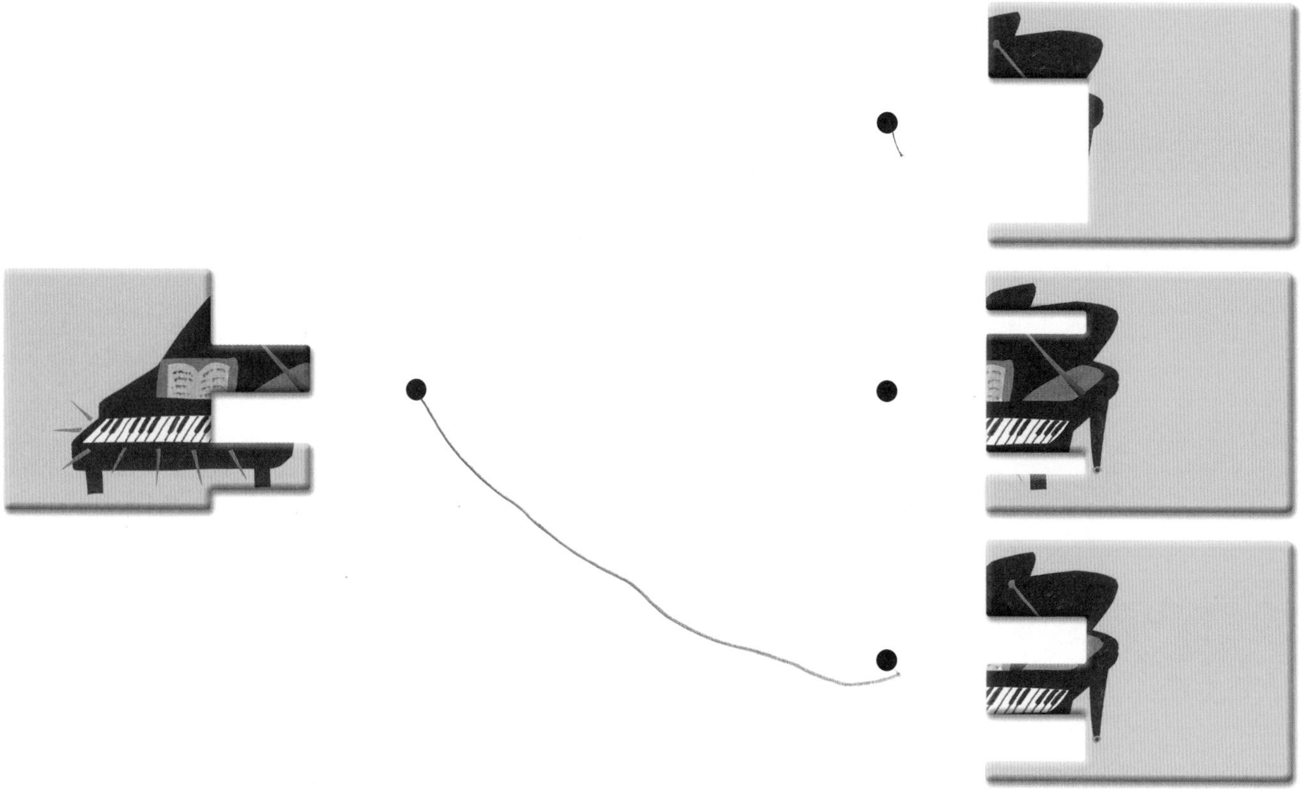

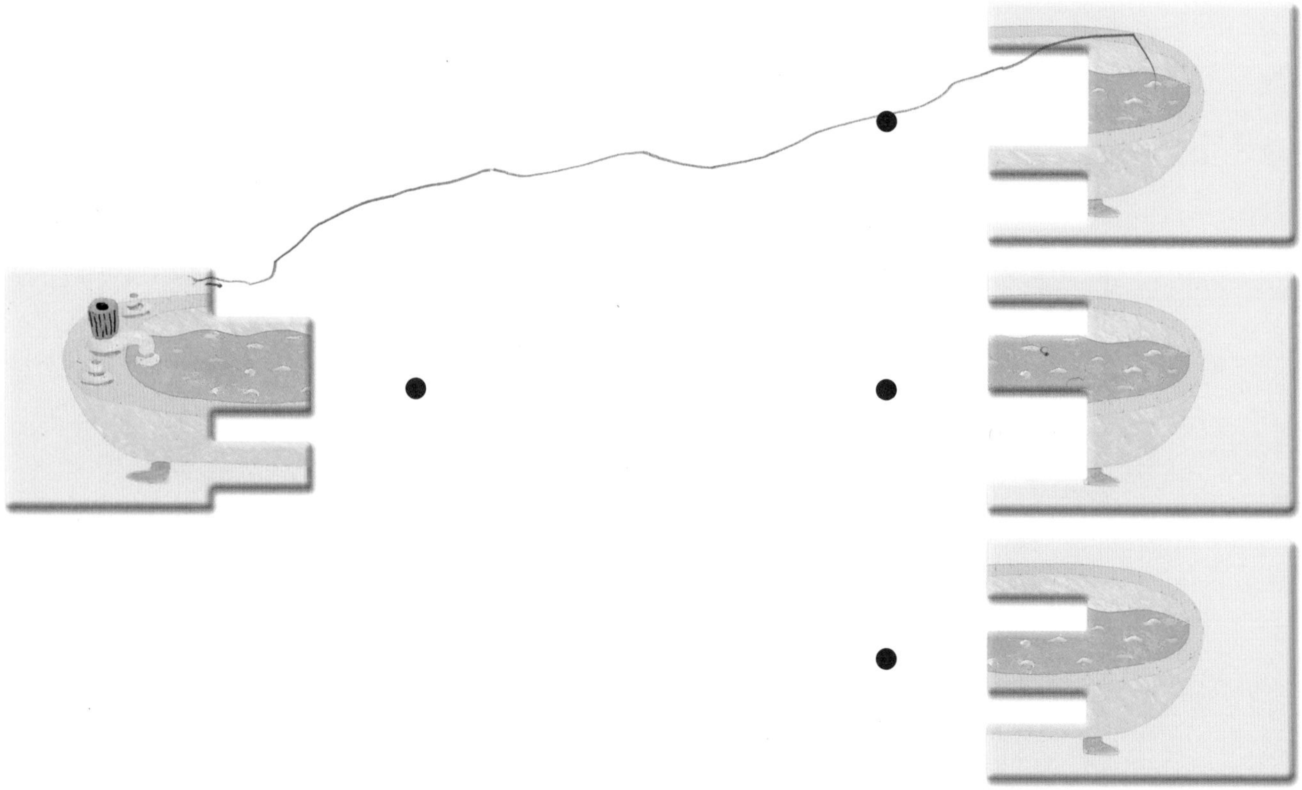

11 Jigsaw Puzzles
Level Three

Name

Date

■ Draw a line to the piece that fits.

To parents
The number of puzzle pieces has increased. Encourage your child to look carefully at each piece.

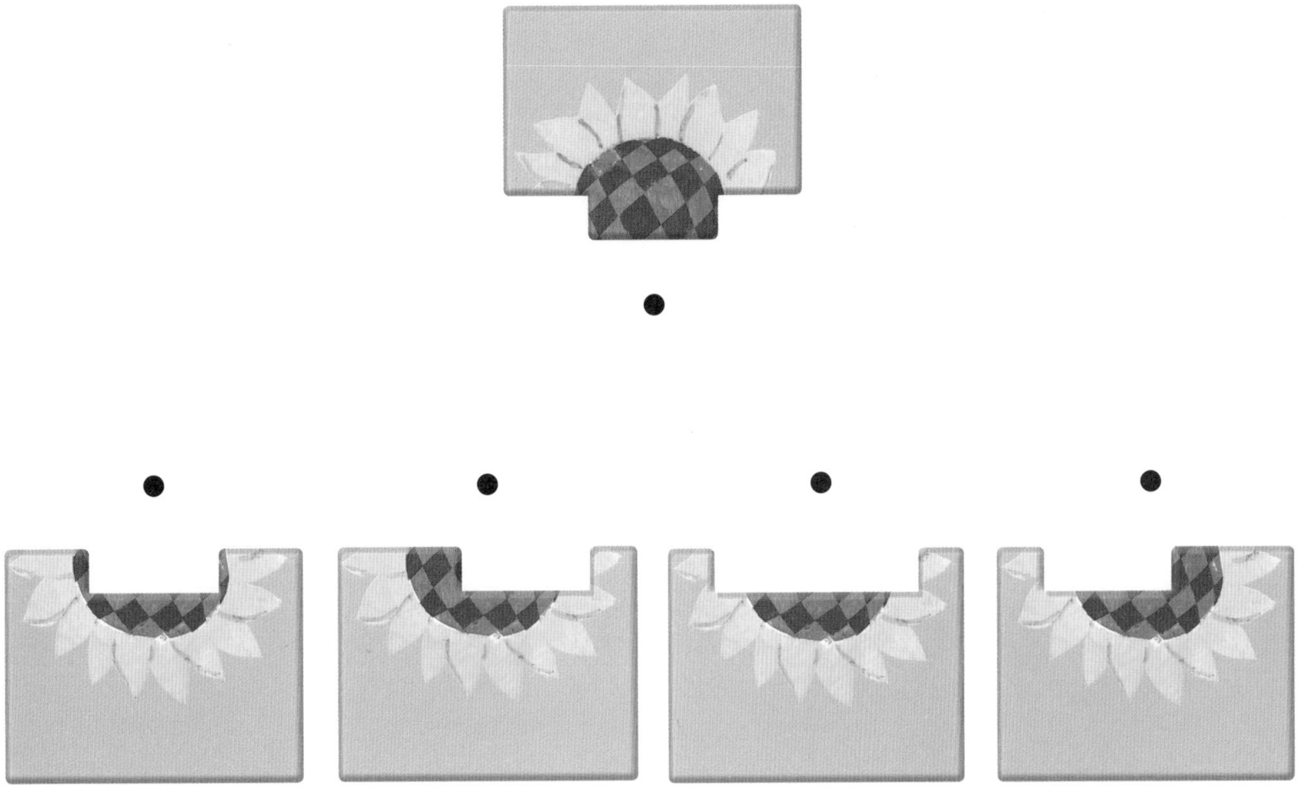

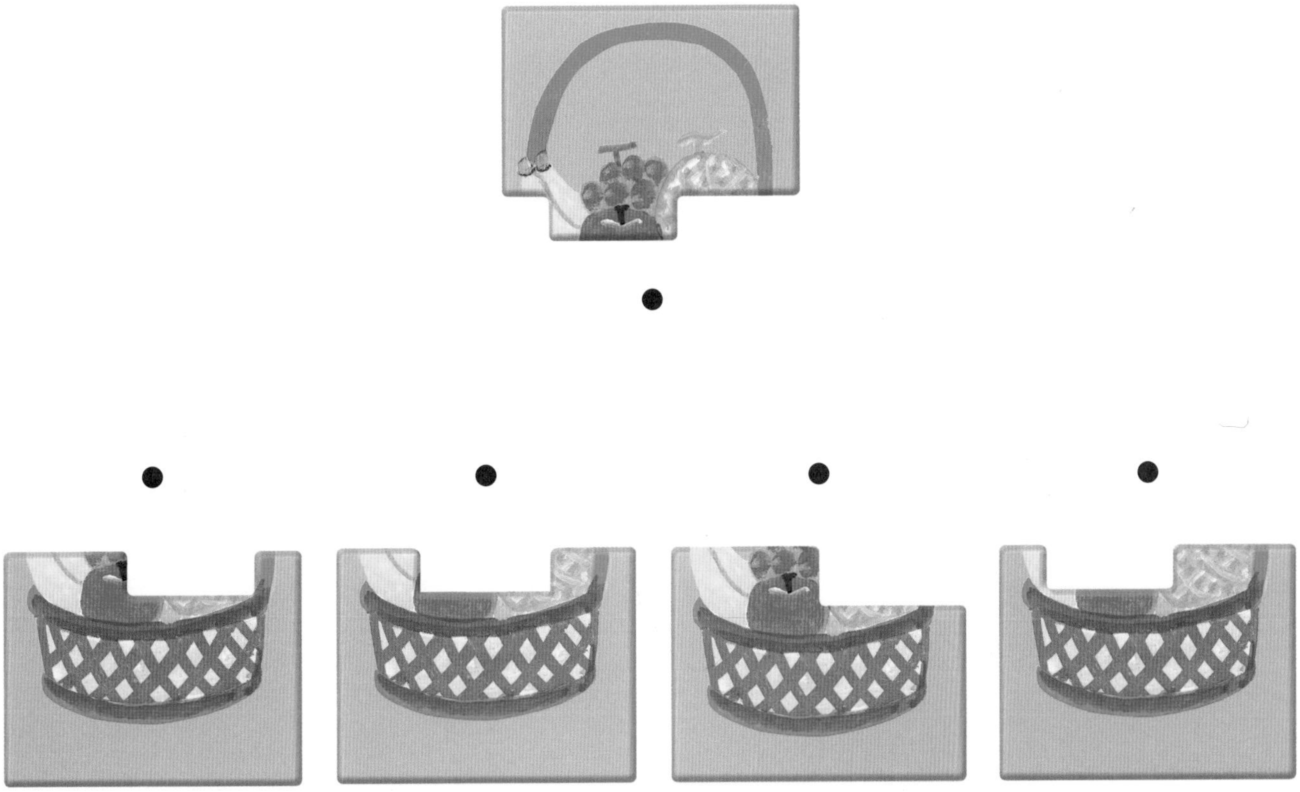

■ Draw a line to the piece that fits.

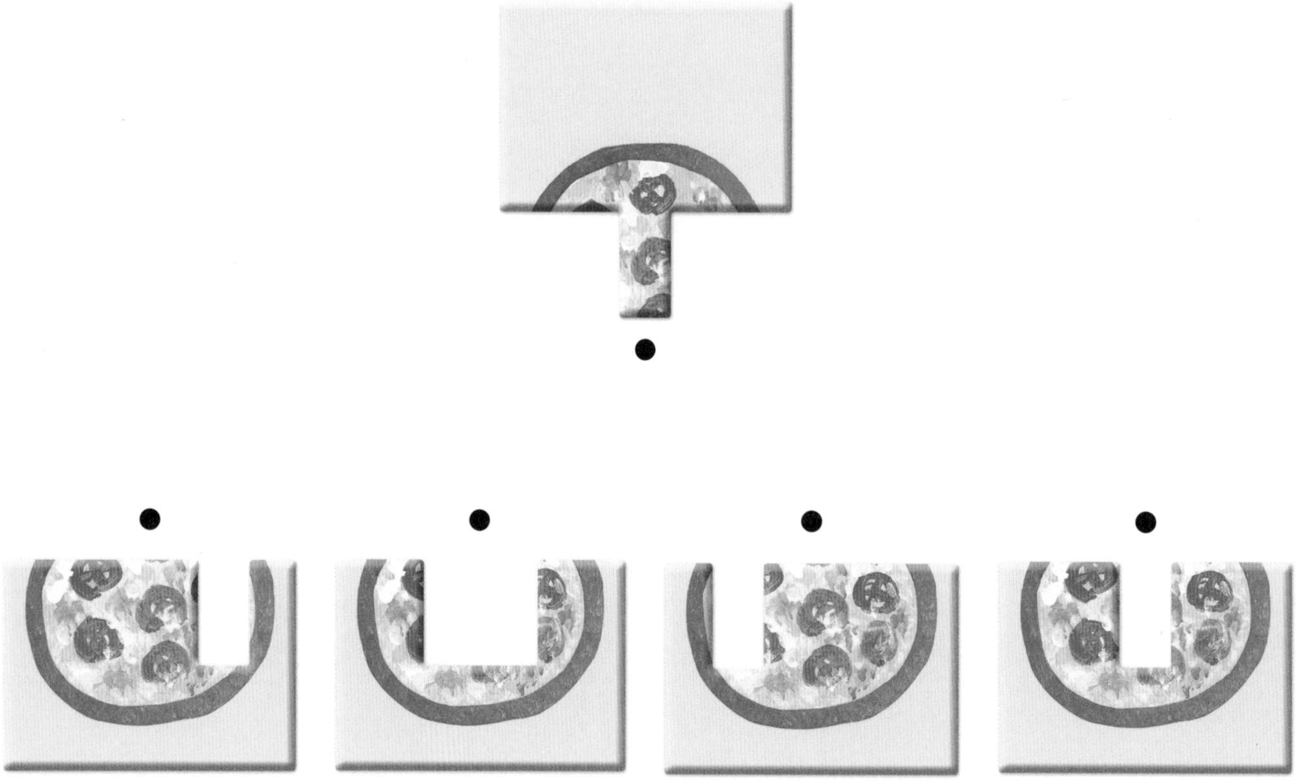

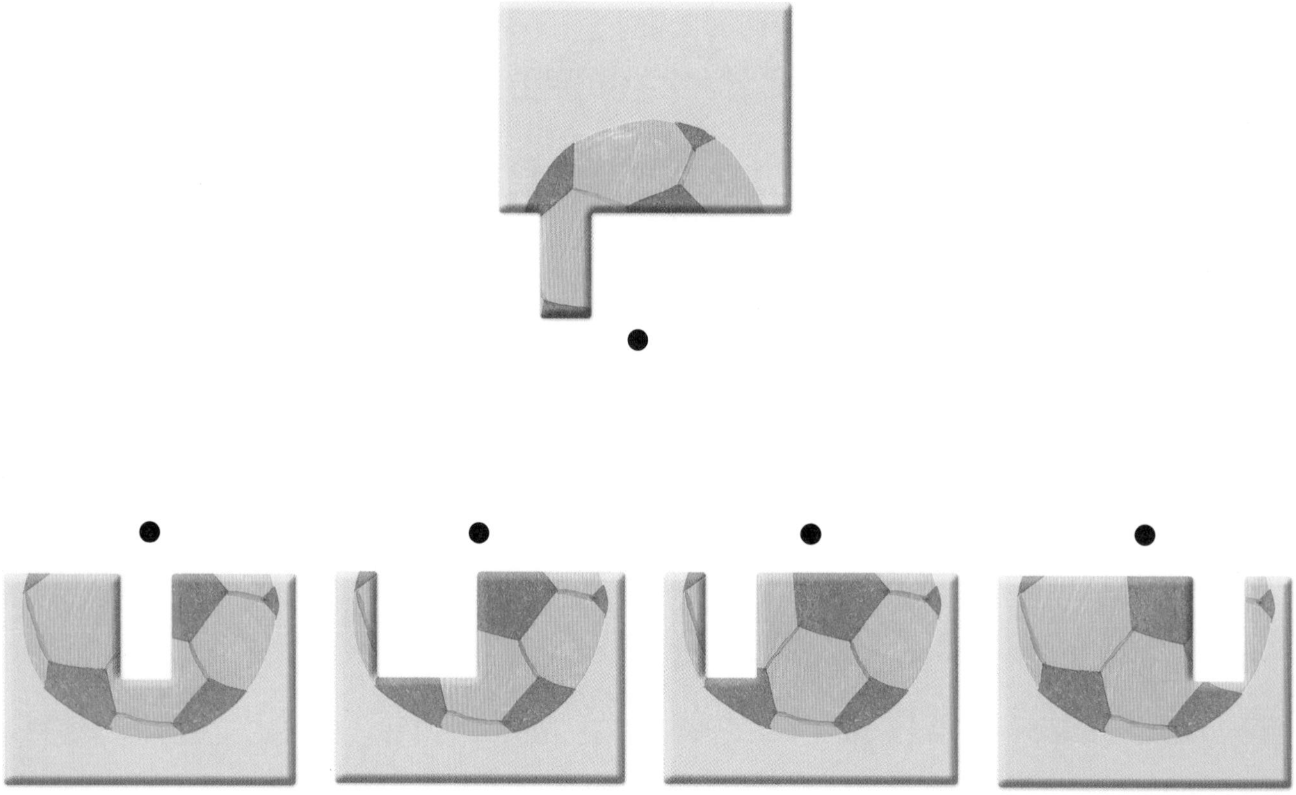

12 Jigsaw Puzzles
Level Four

Name

Date

■ Draw a line to the piece that fits.

To parents
If your child has difficulty with the activity, look at the edge of each puzzle piece with your child. Together, describe the shapes or patterns that you see.

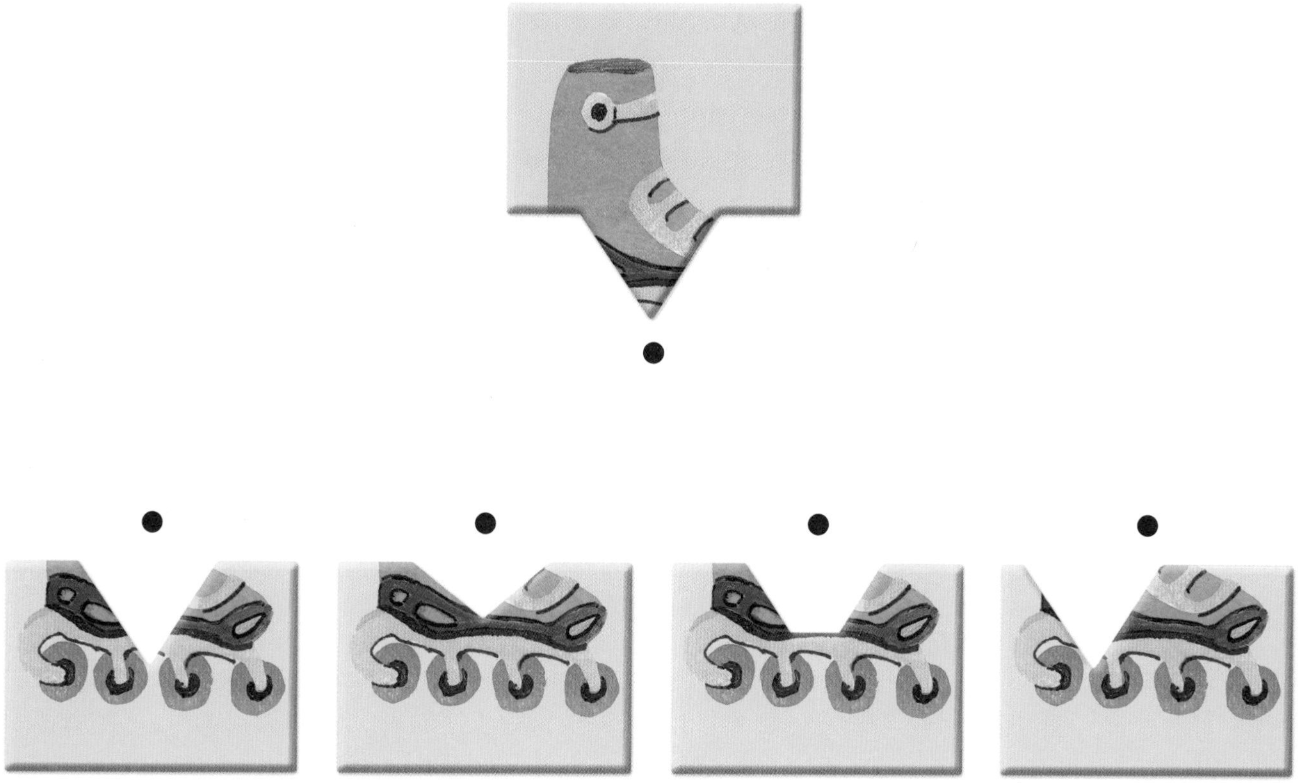

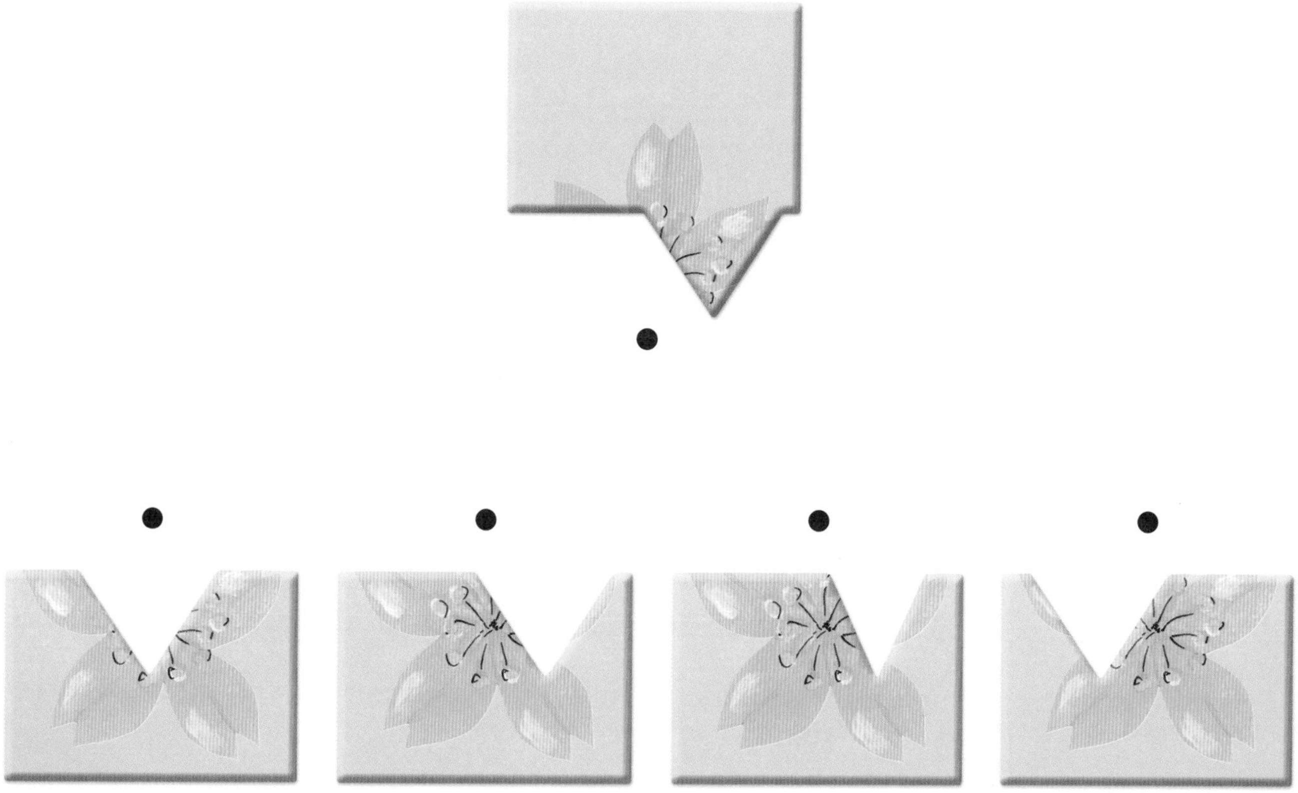

■ Draw a line to the piece that fits.

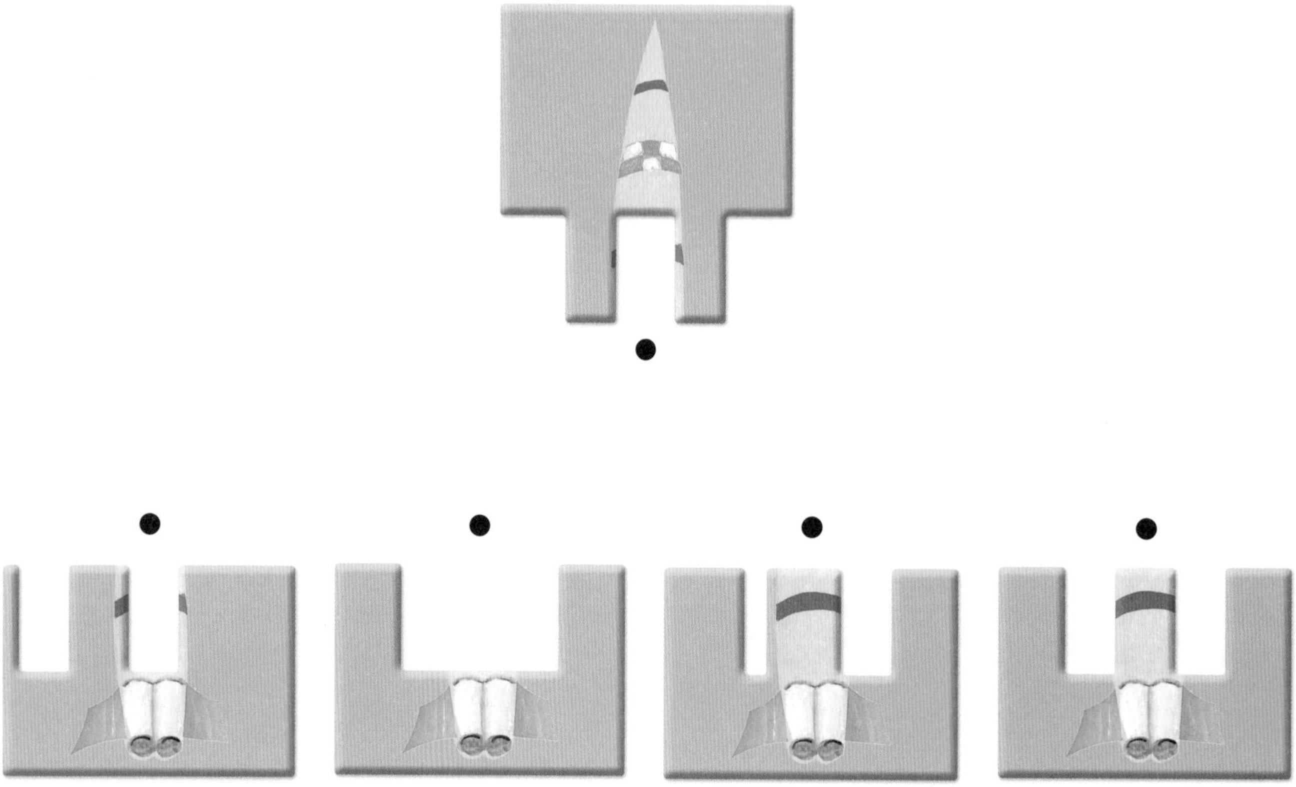

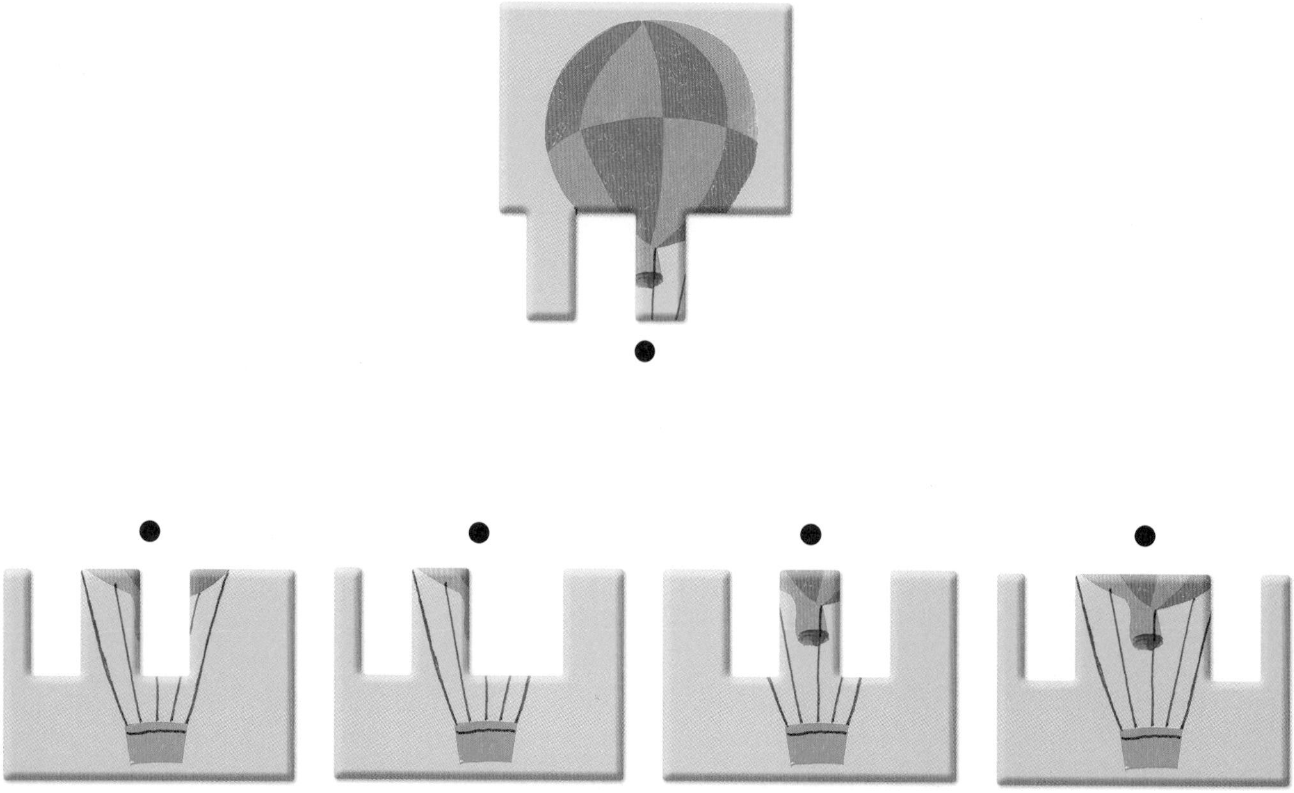

13 Matching Figures
Level One

Name

Date

■ Write a check mark (✓) above the matching animal.

To parents
If your child has difficulty with the exercise, look at the silhouette together. Ask your child to describe the features he or she sees.

( ) ( ) ( )

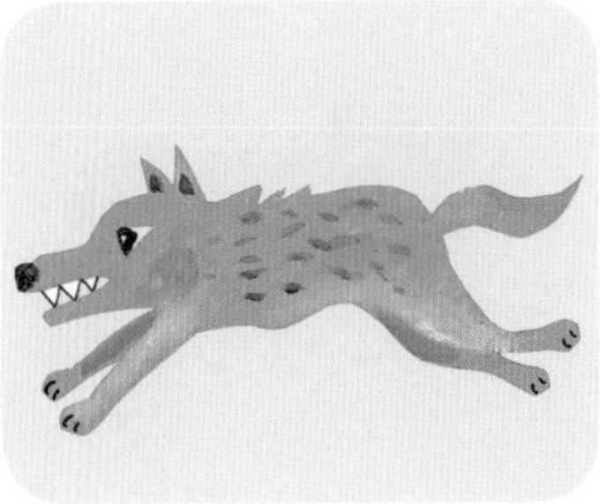

( ) ( ) ( )

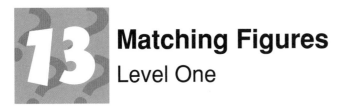

■ Write a check mark (✓) above the matching animal.

( ) ( ) ( )

( ) ( ) ( )

14 Matching Figures
Level Two

Name

Date

■ Write a check mark (✓) above the matching animal.

To parents
When your child has completed the exercise, you may wish to have him or her explain how he or she chose the matching picture.

( ) ( ) ( )

( ) ( ) ( )

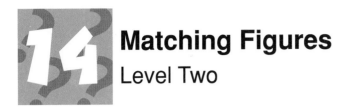

 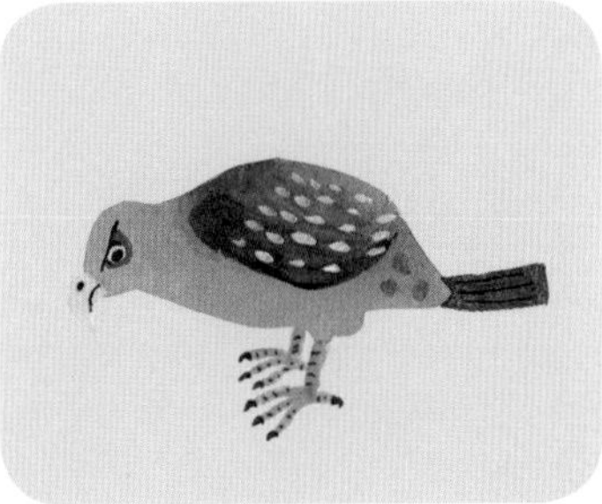 

■ Write a check mark (✓) above the matching animal.

( ) ( ) ( )

( ) ( ) ( )

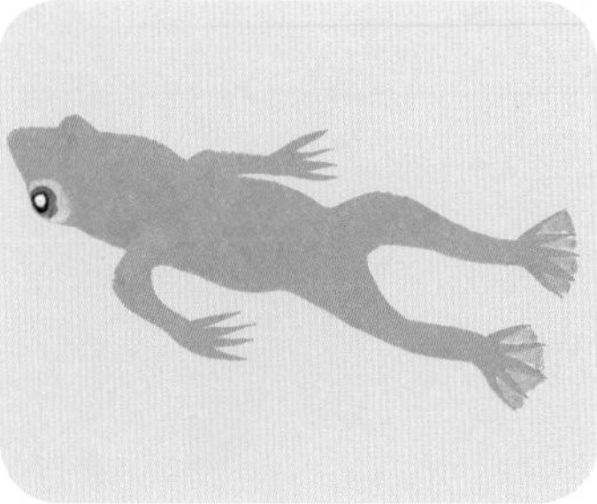  

15 Matching Figures
Level Three

Name

Date

■ Write a check mark (✓) above the matching animal.

To parents
The number of illustrations in the bottom row has increased. Encourage your child to look carefully at each illustration.

( ) ( ) ( ) ( )

( ) ( ) ( ) ( )

■ Write a check mark (✓) above the matching animal.

( ) ( ) ( ) ( )

( ) ( ) ( ) ( )

16 Matching Figures
Level Four

Name

Date

■ Write a check mark (✓) above the matching animal.

To parents
Encourage your child to notice the details of each silhouette.

( ) ( ) ( ) ( )

( ) ( ) ( ) ( )

■ Write a check mark (✓) above the matching animal.

( ) ( ) ( ) ( )

( ) ( ) ( ) ( )

17 Copying Shapes
4 × 4 Dots

Name

Date

■ Draw the same shape.

To parents
Your child can start drawing from any dot he or she likes. The shapes in this section can be drawn without picking up the pencil, if your child would like to try.

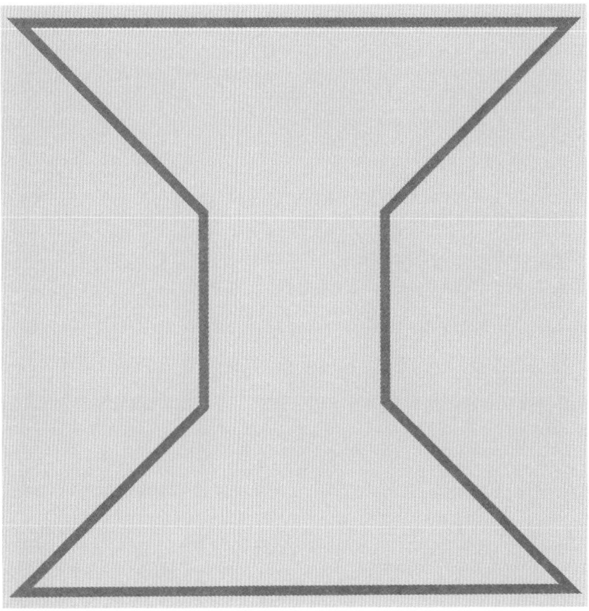

■ Draw the same shape.

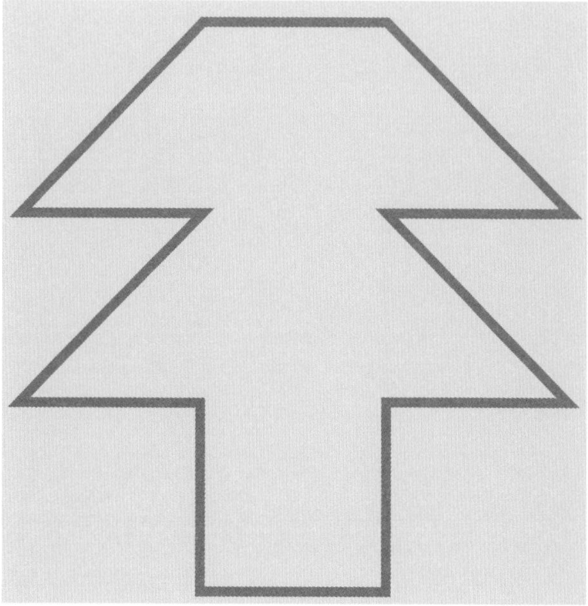

18 Copying Shapes

4 × 4 Dots

Name

Date

■ Draw the same shape.

To parents
If your child draws any of the lines incorrectly, encourage him or her to erase only the incorrect lines and to try again.

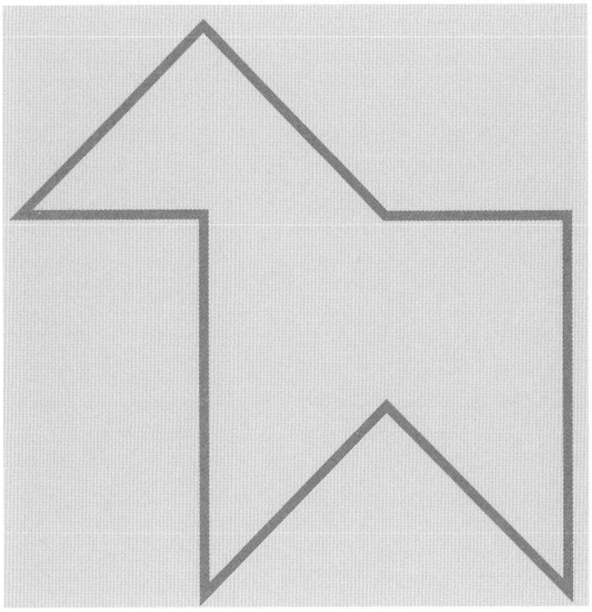

■ Draw the same shape.

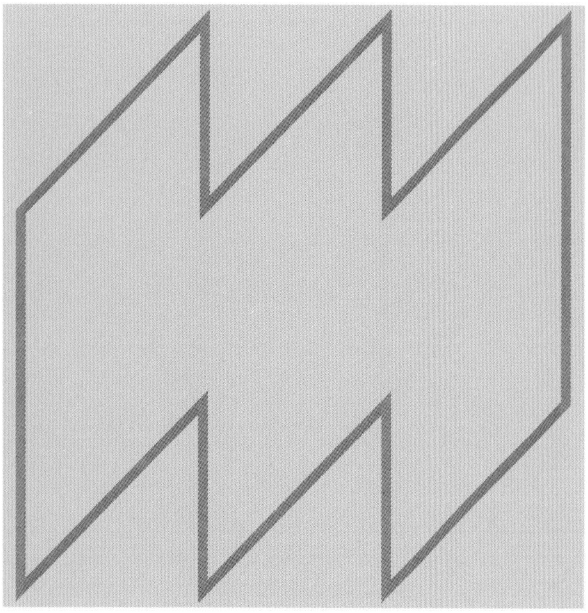

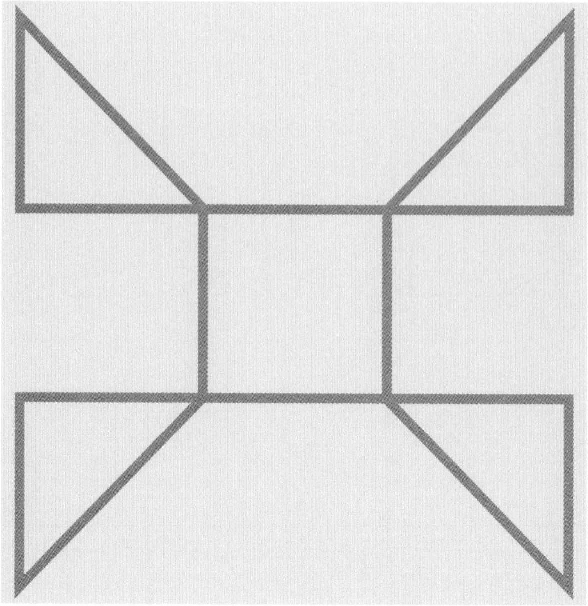

19 Copying Shapes

5 × 5 Dots

Name

Date

■ Draw the same shape.

To parents
The number of dots in the grid has increased. Guide your child to look carefully at the shapes before starting to draw.

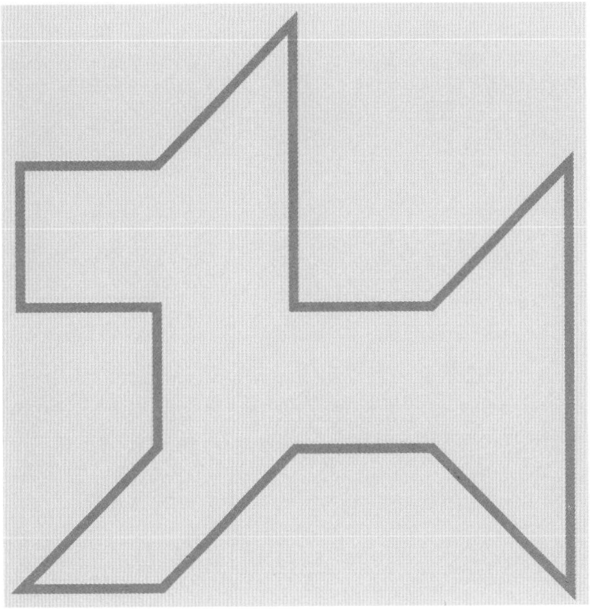

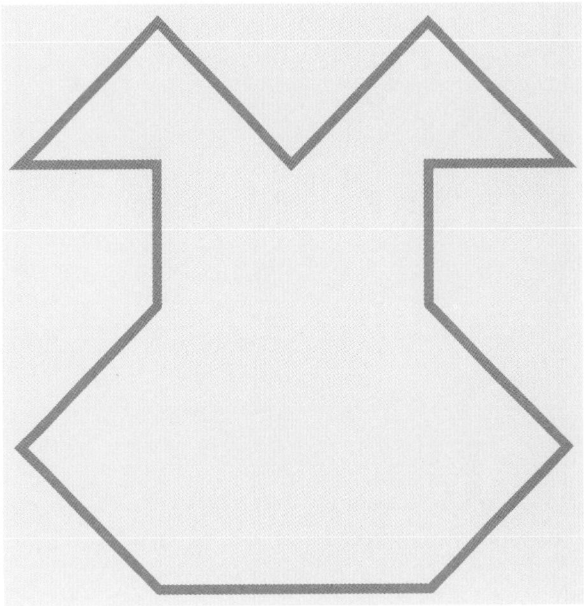

■ Draw the same shape.

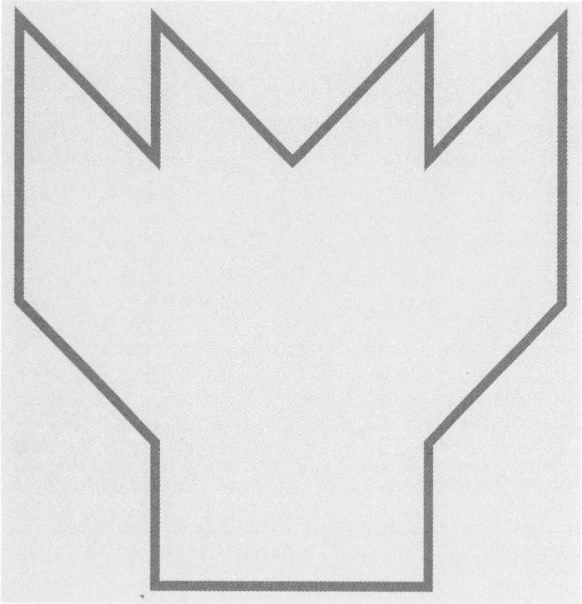

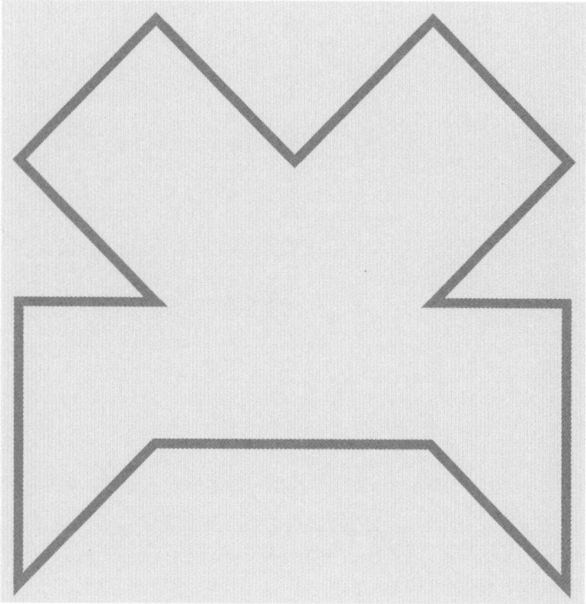

20 Copying Shapes

5 × 5 Dots

Name

Date

■ Draw the same shape.

To parents

From this point on, the shapes become more complicated. Give your child a lot of praise for his or her effort when your child finishes drawing.

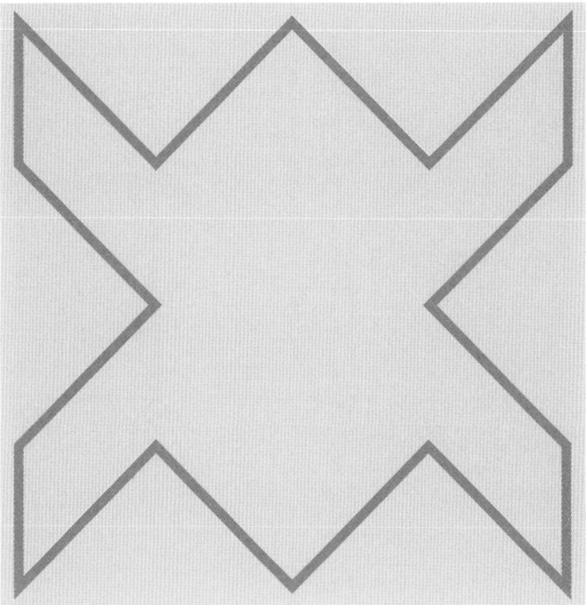

To parents
The shape in the right column on this page cannot be drawn without picking up the pencil.

■ Draw the same shape.

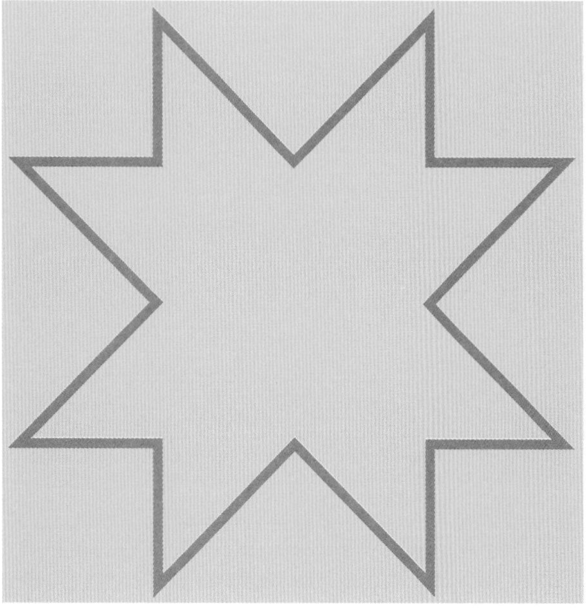

21 Above and Below

Level One

Name

Date

To parents
Before beginning this activity, you may wish to help your child recognize the words "above" and "below."

■ Which animal is above the flower?
Write a check mark (✓) beside the animal.

above

below

(✓) 

( ) 

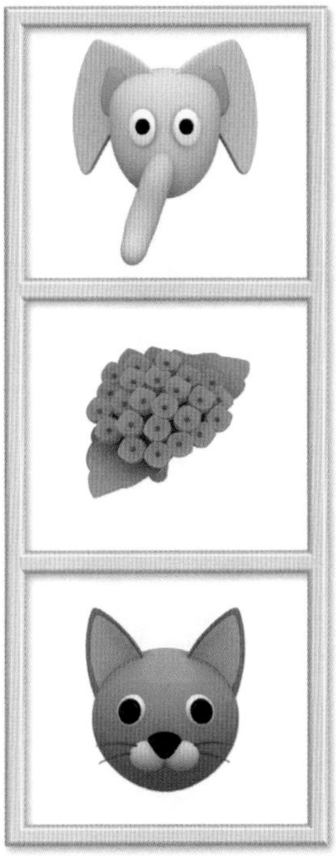

( ) 

( ) 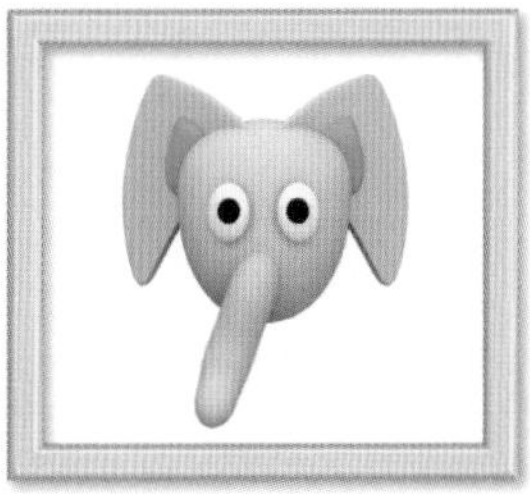

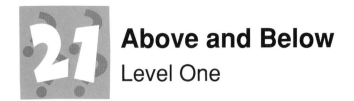

■ Which animal is below the fruit? Write a check mark (✓) beside the animal.

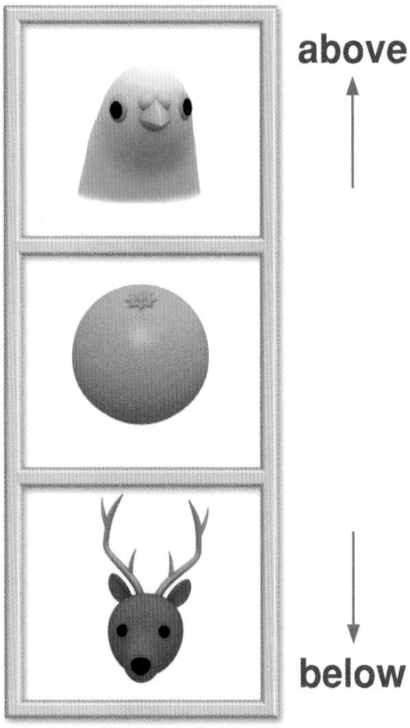

( ) 

(✓) 

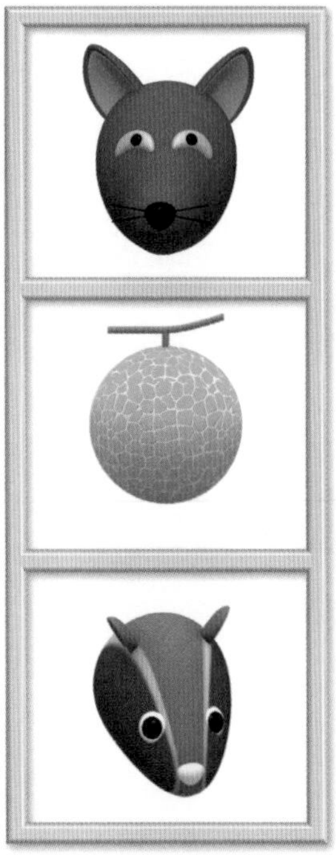

( ) 

( ) 

22 Above and Below
Level Two

Name

Date

■ Which animal is above the flower?
Write a check mark (✓) beside the animal.

To parents
The activity now includes pictures on all sides of the flower. Encourage your child to choose the correct animal.

( ) 

( ) 

( ) 

( ) 

( ) 

( ) 

( ) 

( ) 

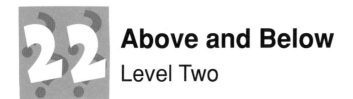

■ Which animal is below the fruit? Write a check mark (✓) beside the animal.

( ) 

( ) 

( ) 

( ) 

( ) 

( ) 

( ) 

( ) 

23 Above and Below
Level Three

Name

Date

To parents
If your child has difficulty, help him or her understand the activity is similar to pages 41 and 42.

■ Which animal is right above the flower?
Write a check mark (✓) beside the animal.

( ) 

( ) 

( ) 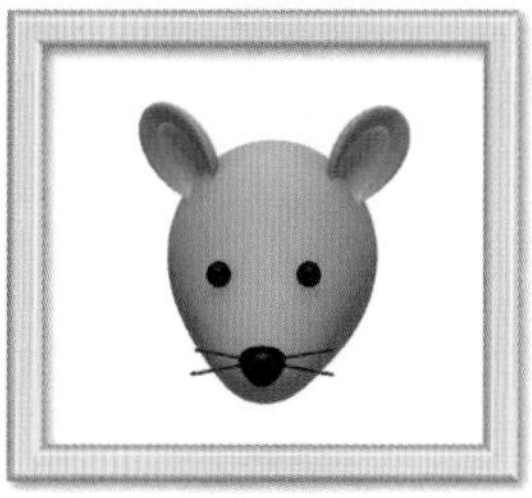

( ) 

( ) 

( ) 

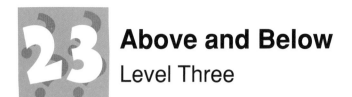

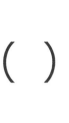

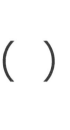

■ Which animal is right below the food? Write a check mark (✓) beside the animal.

( ) 

( ) 

( ) 

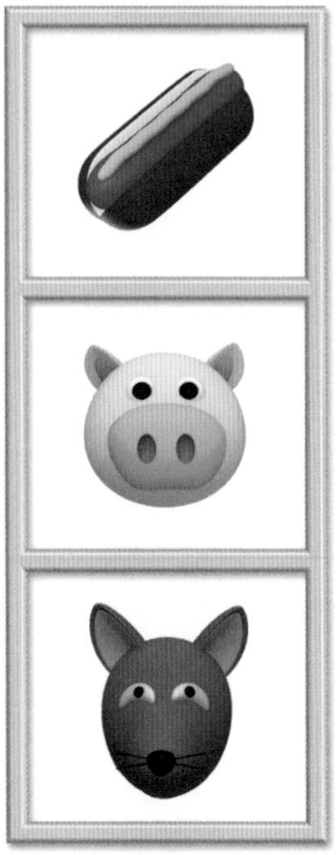

( ) 

( ) 

( ) 

24 Above and Below
Level Four

Name

Date

■ Which animal is right above the flower?
Write a check mark (✓) beside the animal.

To parents
If your child has difficulty with the exercise, work with him or her to describe the animal above the flower.

( ) 

( ) 

( ) 

( ) 

( ) 

( ) 

( ) 

( ) 

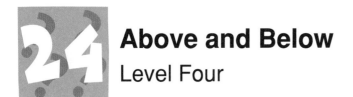

■ Which animal is right below the fruit? Write a check mark (✓) beside the animal.

( ) 

( ) 

( ) 

( ) 

( ) 

( ) 

( ) 

( ) 

25 Right and Left
Level One

Name

Date

■ Which animal is to the right of the flower?
Write a check mark (✓) beside the animal.

To parents
Before beginning this activity, you may wish to help your child recognize the words "left" and "right."

( ) 

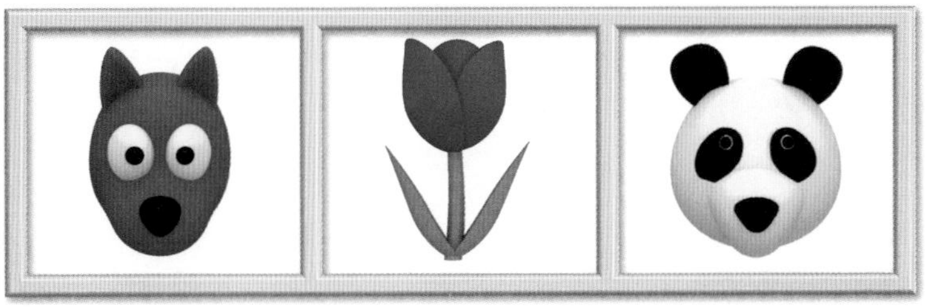

left ← → right

(✓) 

( ) 

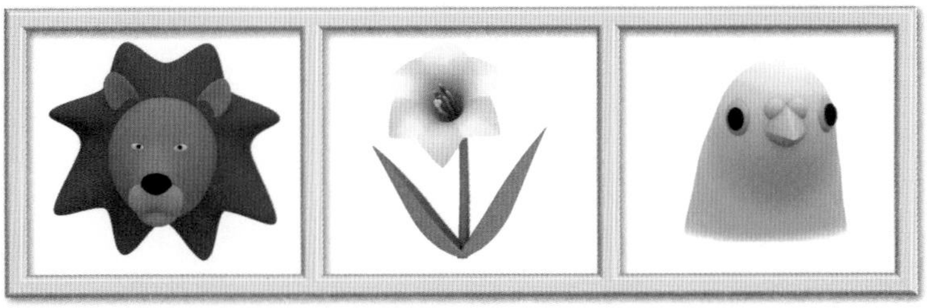

( ) 

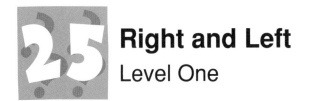

■ Which animal is to the left of the fruit? Write a check mark (✓) beside the animal.

left ←—— ——→ right

(✓) 

( ) 

( ) 

( ) 

26

Right and Left
Level Two

Name

Date

■ Which animal is to the right of the flower? Write a check mark (✓) beside the animal.

To parents
The activity now includes pictures on all sides of the flower. Encourage your child to choose the correct animal.

( ) 

( ) 

( ) 

( ) 

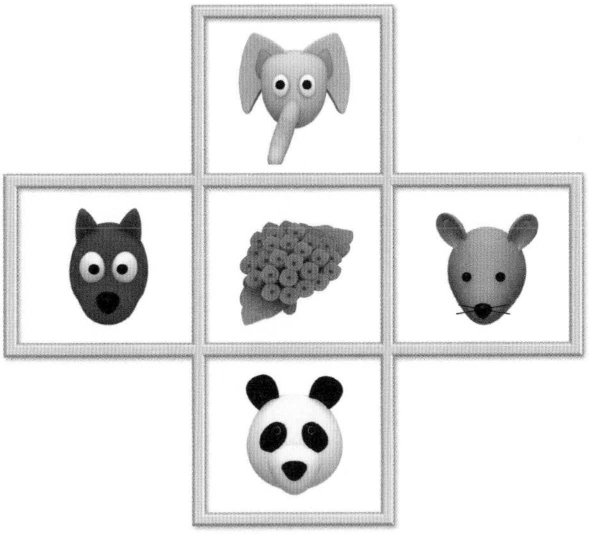

( ) 

( ) 

( ) 

( ) 

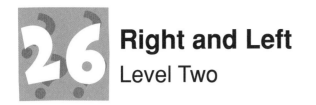

■ Which animal is to the left of the fruit? Write a check mark (✓) beside the animal.

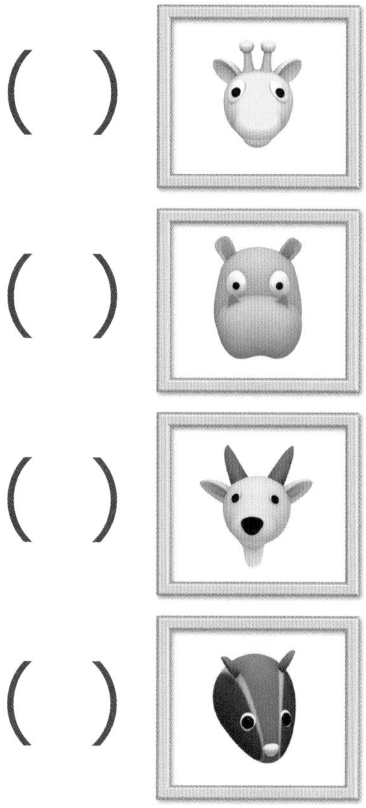

27 Right and Left
Level Three

Name

Date

■ Which animal is to the right of the flower? Write a check mark (✓) beside the animal.

To parents
If your child has difficulty, help him or her understand the activity is similar to pages 49 and 50.

( ) 

( ) 

( ) 

( ) 

( ) 

( ) 

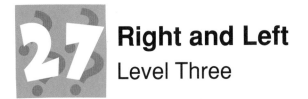

■ Which animal is to the left of the food? Write a check mark (✓) beside the animal.

( ) 

( ) 

( ) 

( ) 

( ) 

( ) 

28 Right and Left
Level Four

Name

Date

■ Which animal is to the right of the flower?
Write a check mark (✓) above the animal.

To parents
If your child has difficulty with the exercise, work with him or her to describe the animal to the right of the flower.

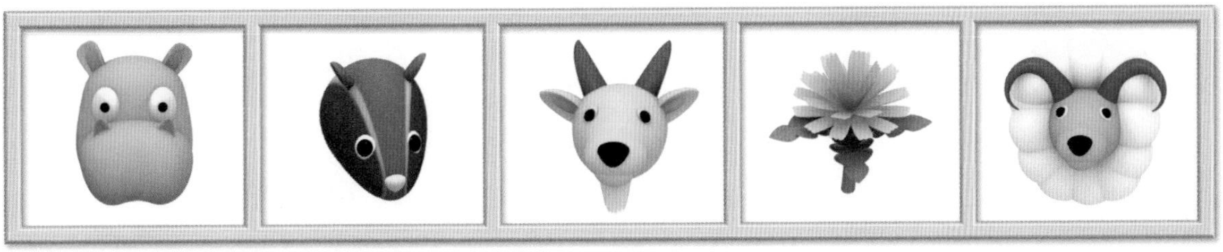

( ) ( ) ( ) ( )

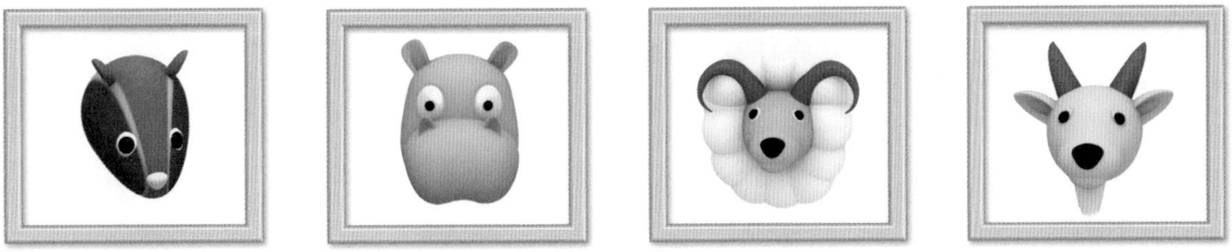

( ) ( ) ( ) ( )

■ Which animal is to the left of the fruit? Write a check mark (✓) above the animal.

( ) ( ) ( ) ( )

( ) ( ) ( ) ( )

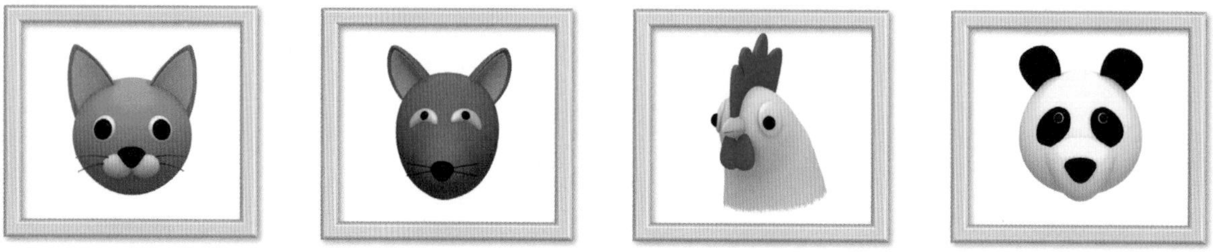

29

Comparing Length

Level One

Name

Date

To parents
Encourage your child to find the answer by looking closely at the pictures.

■ Look at the pictures. Then write a check mark (✓) above the object that is longer.

( )

(✓)

( )

( )

■ Look at the pictures. Then write a check mark (✓) above the object that is longest.

( )

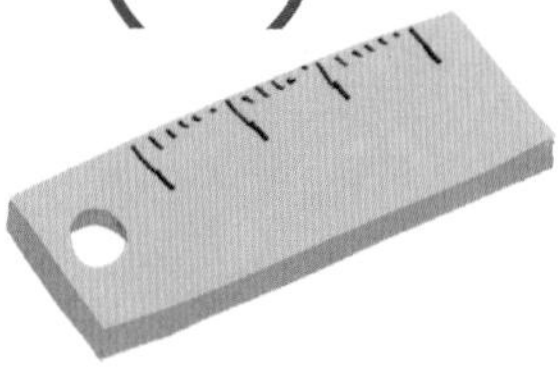

( ) ( )

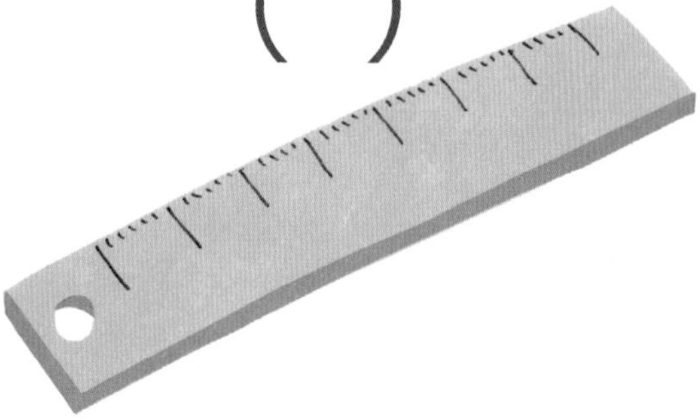

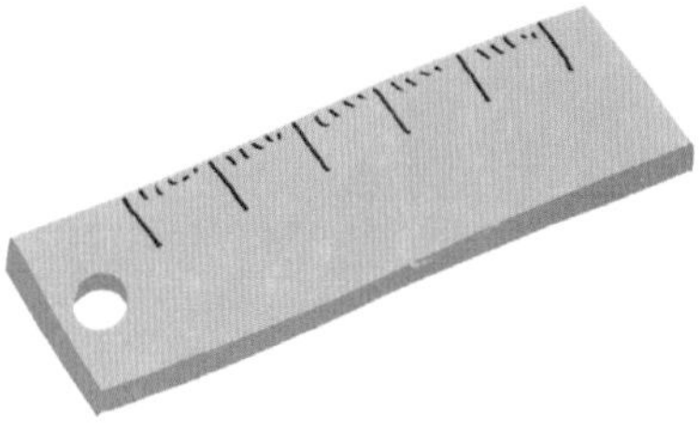

( )

( ) ( )

30 Comparing Length
Level Two

Name

Date

To parents
The number of pictures has increased. Encourage your child to compare all of the pictures.

■ Look at the pictures. Then write a check mark (✓) above the object that is longest.

( )

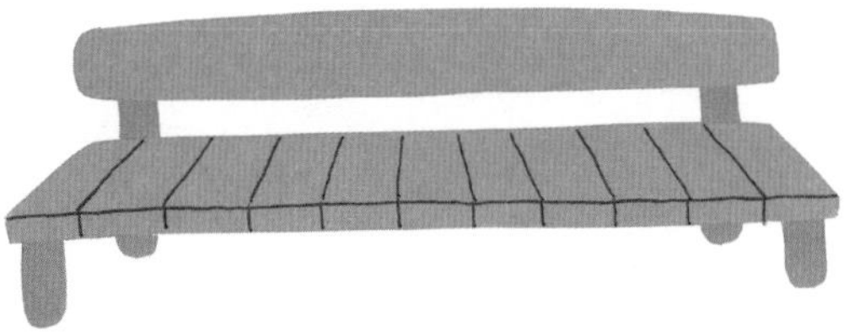

( )

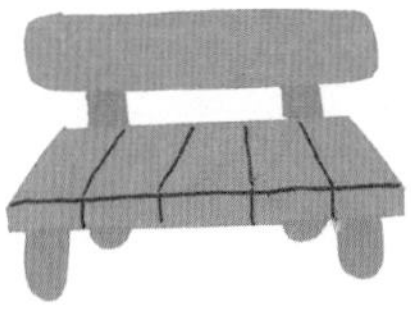

( )

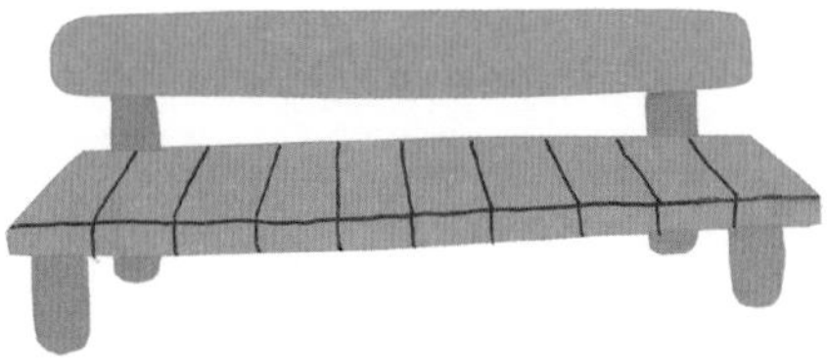

( )

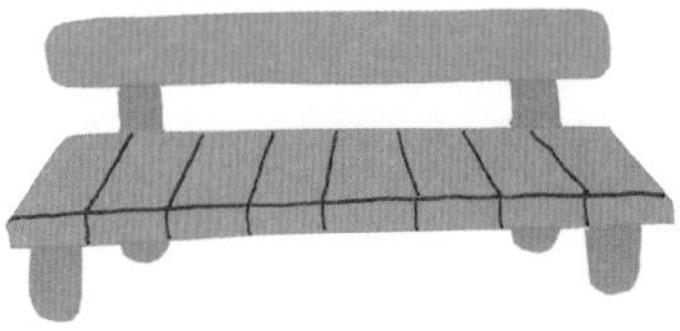

( )

( )

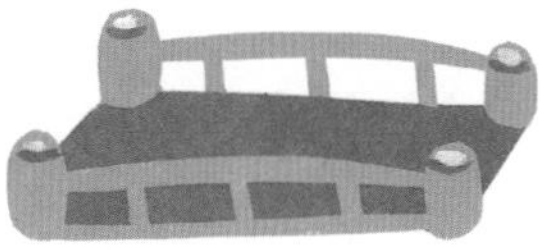

( )

( )

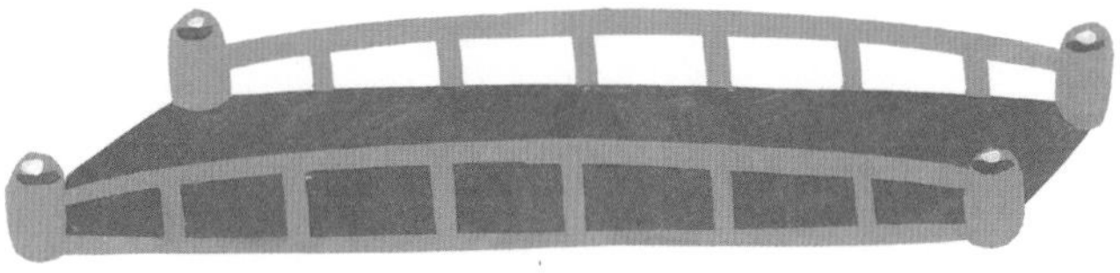

■ Look at the pictures. Then write a check mark (✓) above the object that is longest.

( ) ( )

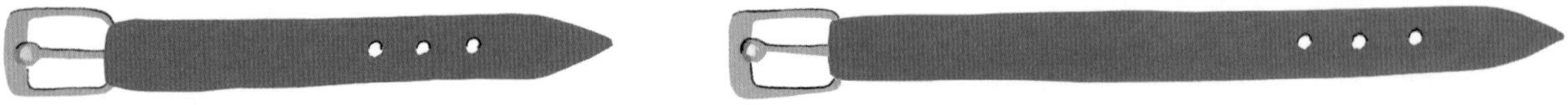

( ) ( )

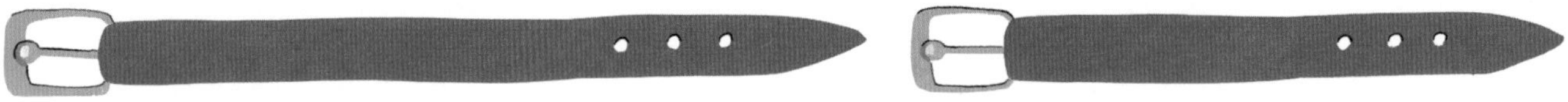

( ) ( )

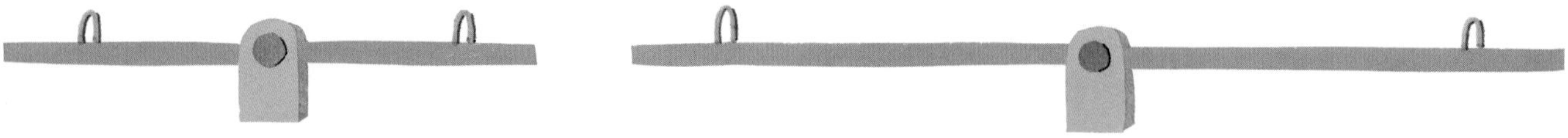

( ) ( )

31 Comparing Length
Level Three

Name

Date

To parents
Encourage your child to think how long the objects would be if they were stretched out straight.

■ Look at the pictures. Then write a check mark (✓) above the object that is longer.

( )

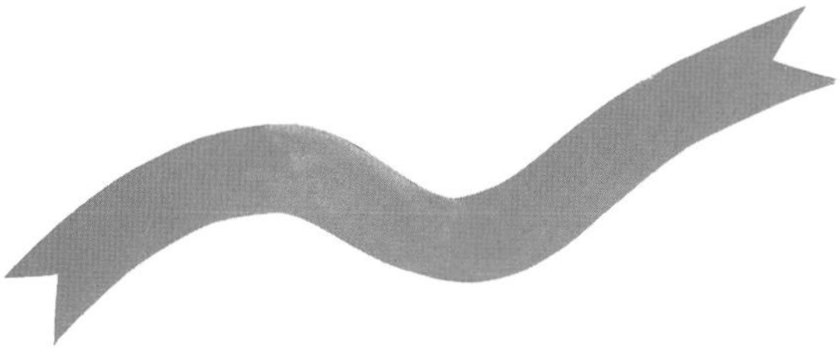

(✓)

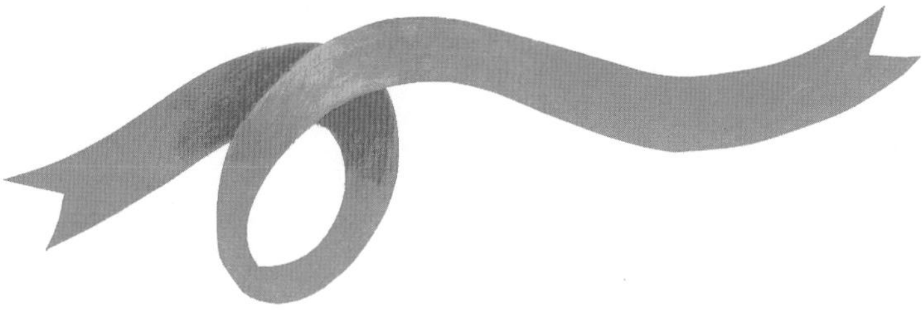

( )

( )

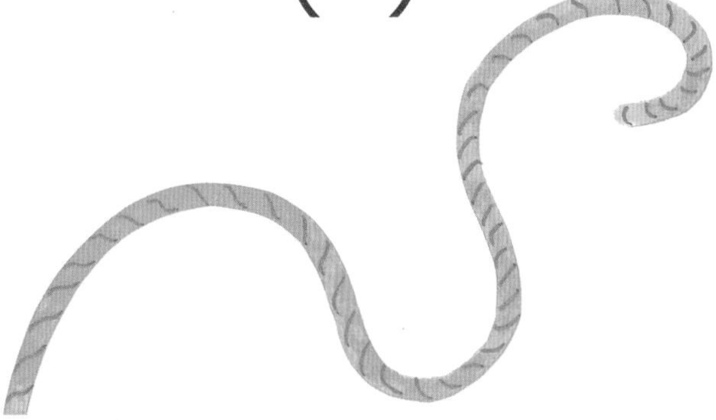

■ Look at the pictures. Then write a check mark (✓) beside the object that is longest.

32

Comparing Length

Level Four

Name

Date

To parents
Give your child a lot of praise when he or she finds the right answer.

■ Look at the pictures. Then write a check mark (✓) under the object that is longest.

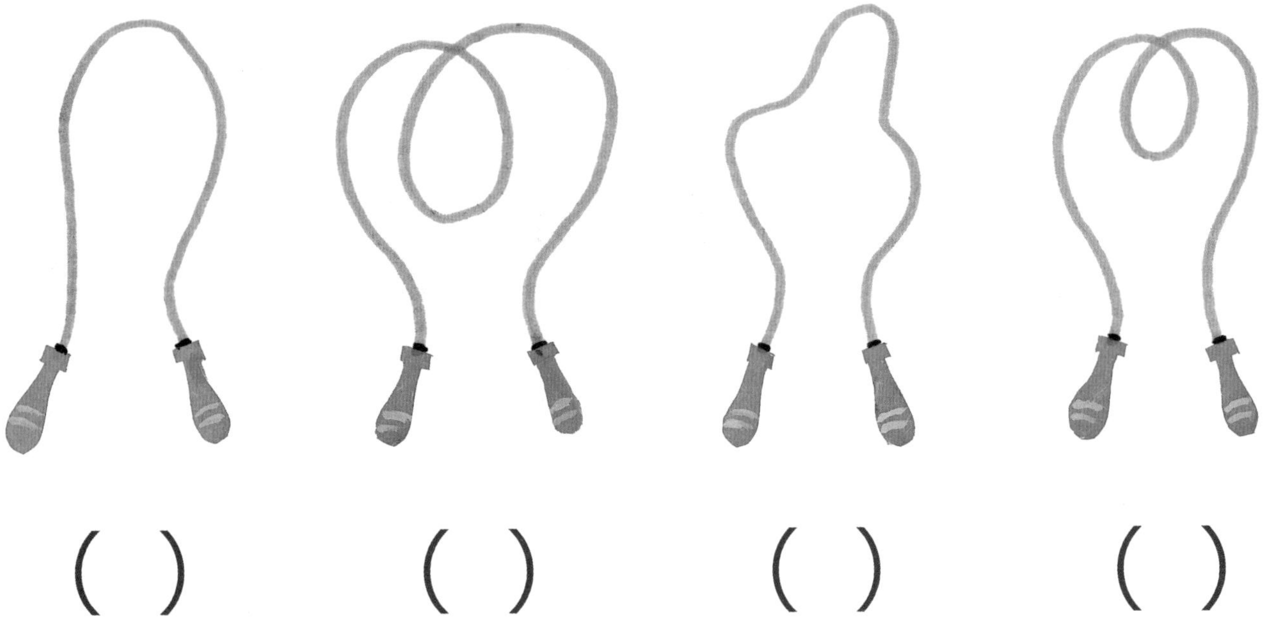

■ Look at the pictures. Then write a check mark (✓) above the object that is longest.

( ) ( ) ( ) ( )

( ) ( ) ( ) ( )

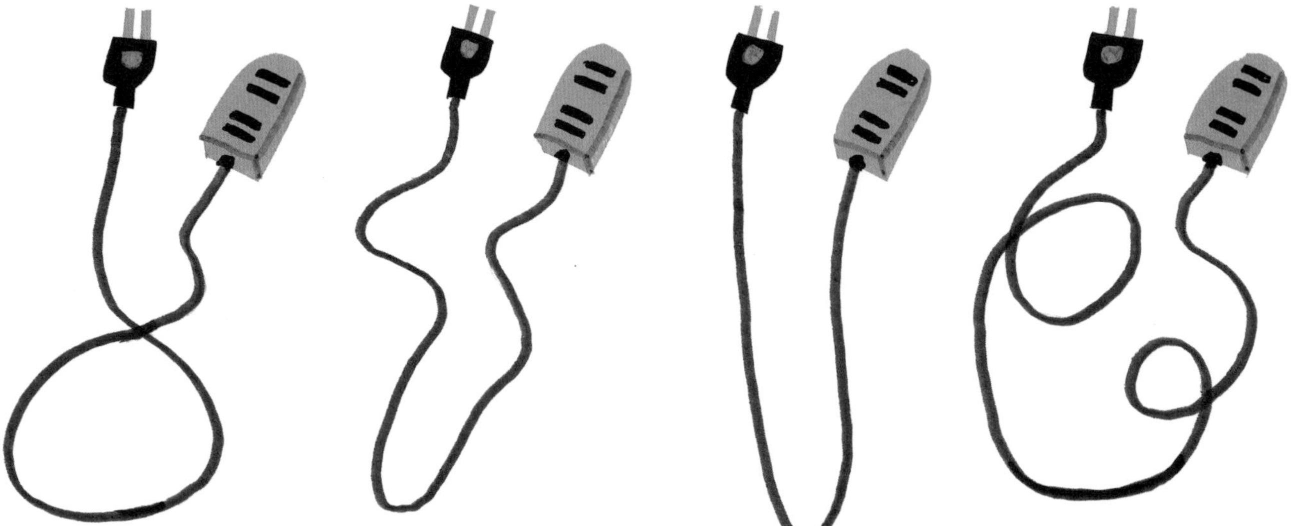

33 Coloring Patterns
Four Colors

Name

Date

■ Color each pattern with the correct color.

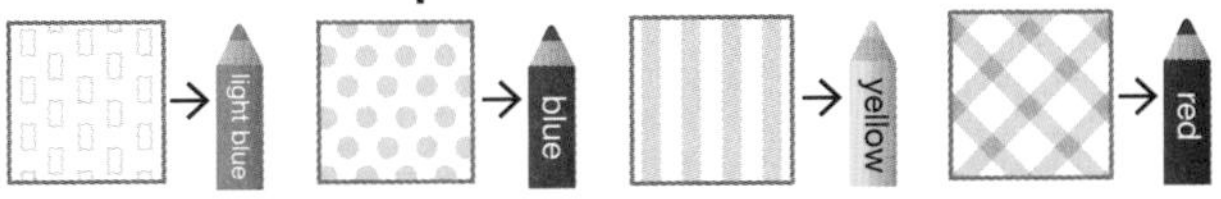

To parents
From this page on, your child should use colored pencils. Give your child the colors listed in the instructions.

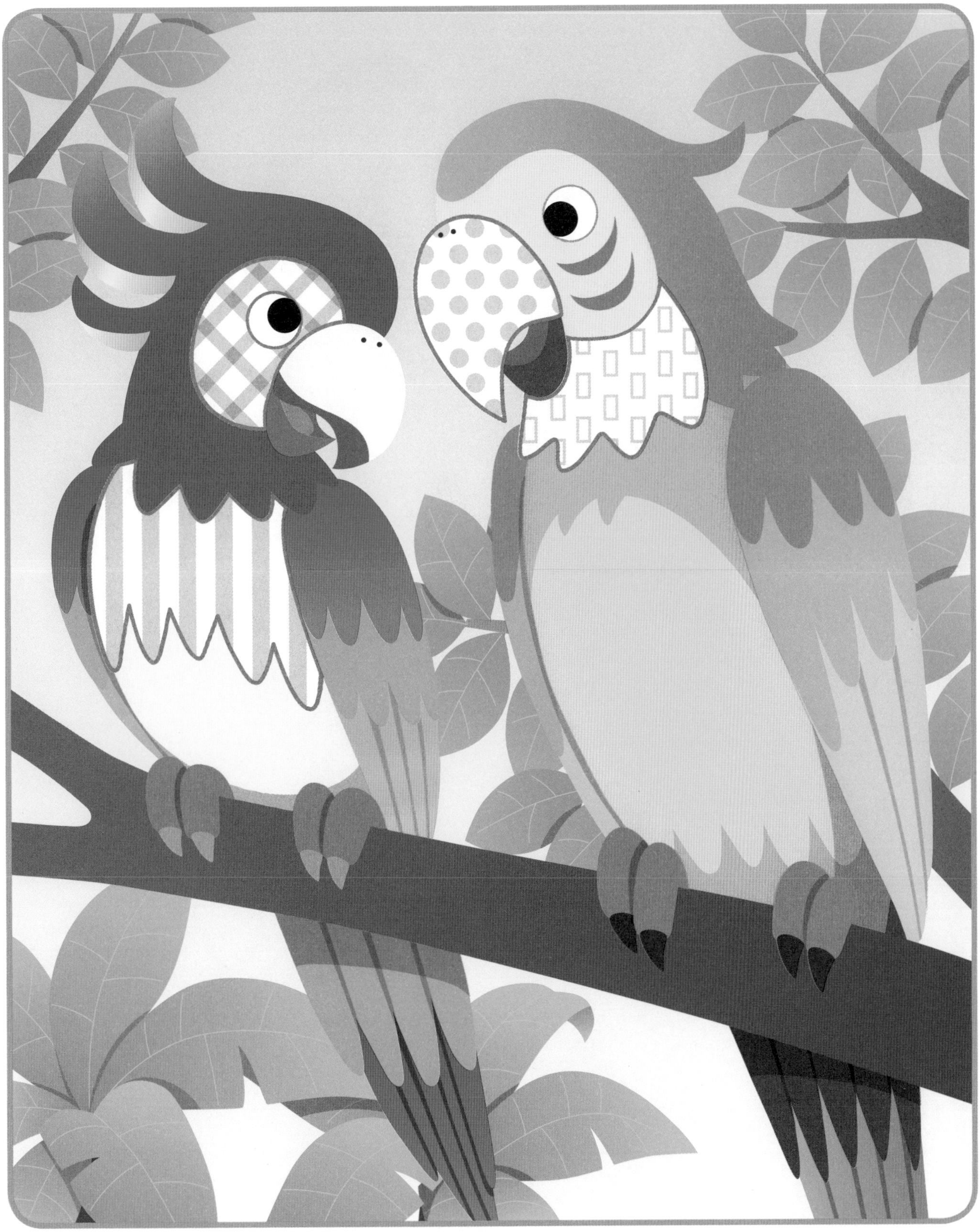

■ Color each pattern with the correct color.

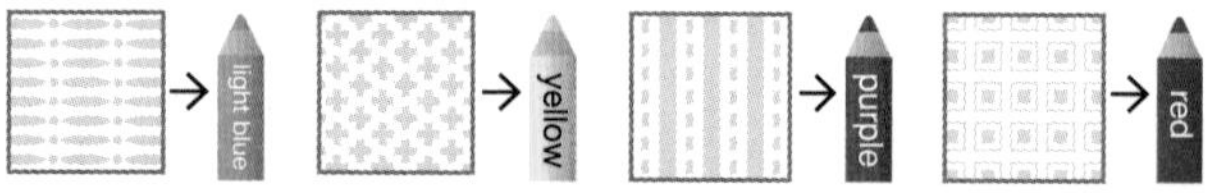

34 Coloring Patterns
Five Colors

Name

Date

■ Color each pattern with the correct color.

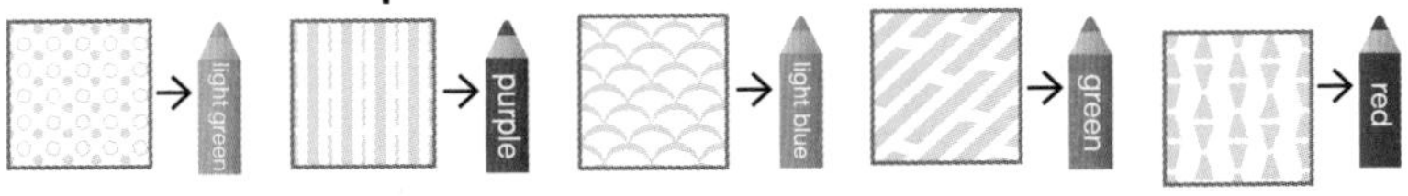

To parents
Encourage your child to color the patterns in the picture, using the colors indicated.

■ Color each pattern with the correct color.

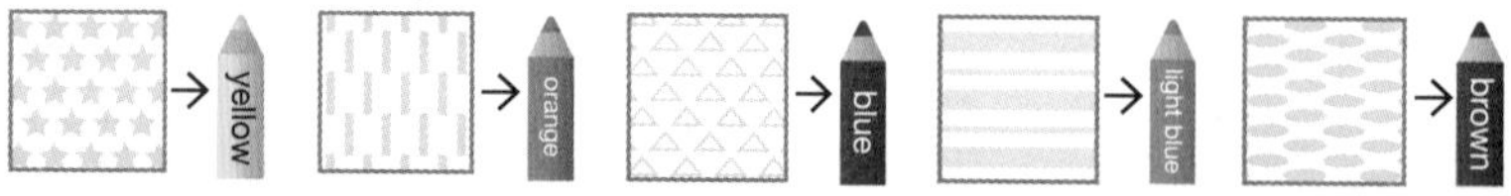

35

Coloring Patterns

Five and Six Colors

Name

Date

■ Color each pattern with the correct color.

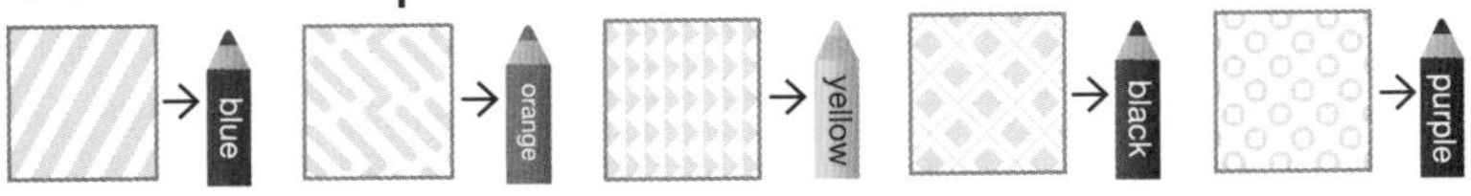

To parents
Encourage your child to color in each patterned area completely.

■ Color each pattern with the correct color.

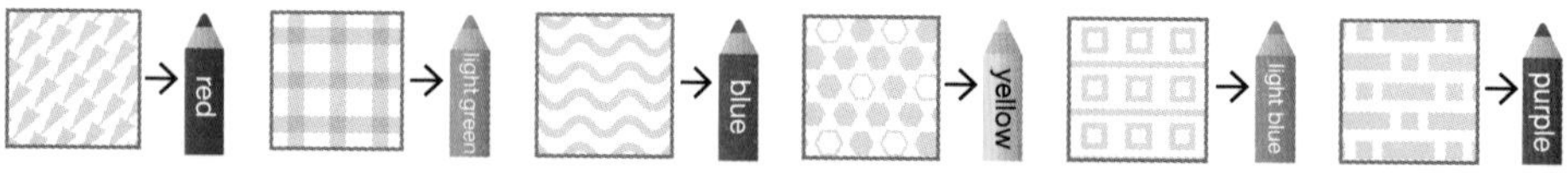

36 Coloring Patterns
Six and Seven Colors

Name

Date

■ Color each pattern with the correct color.

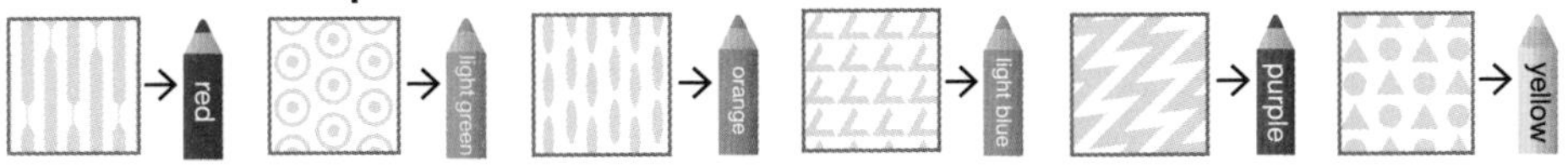

To parents
Help your child use the instructions to match up each pattern with the correct color.

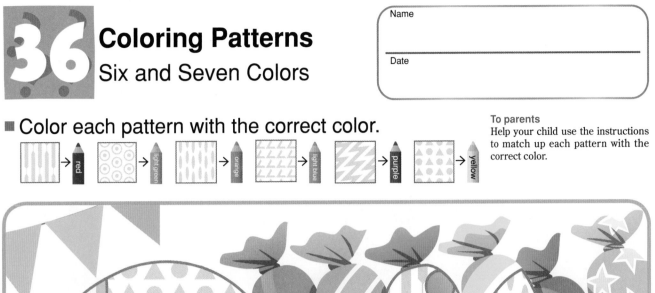

To parents
This is the last exercise of this section. Please praise your child for the effort it took to complete this workbook.

■ Color each pattern with the correct color.

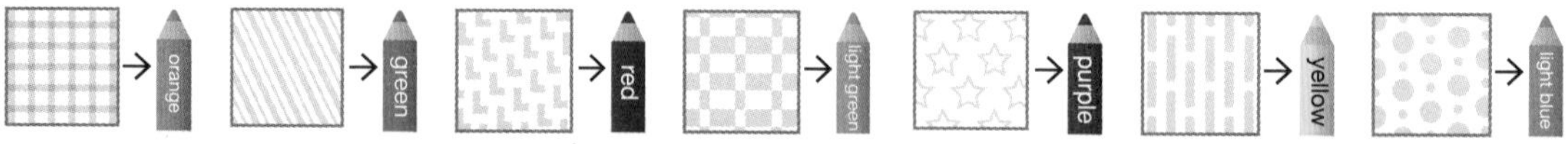

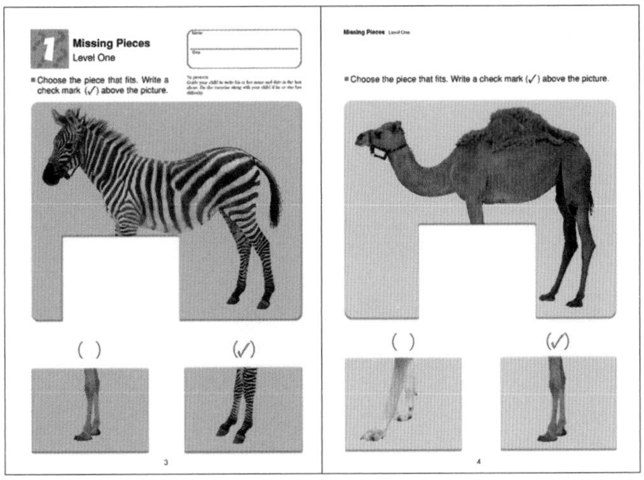

pages 3 and 4

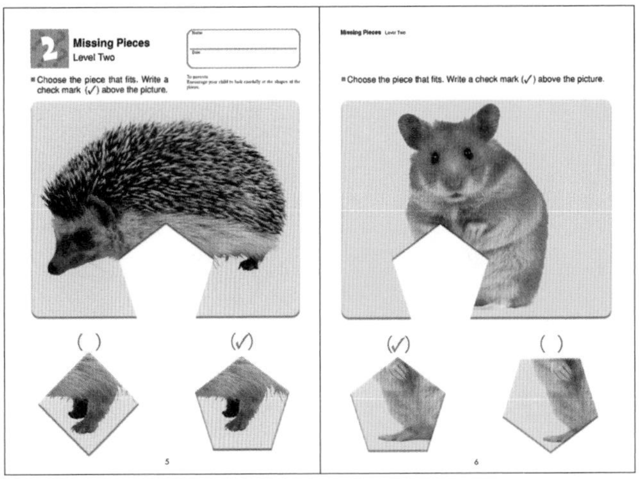

pages 5 and 6

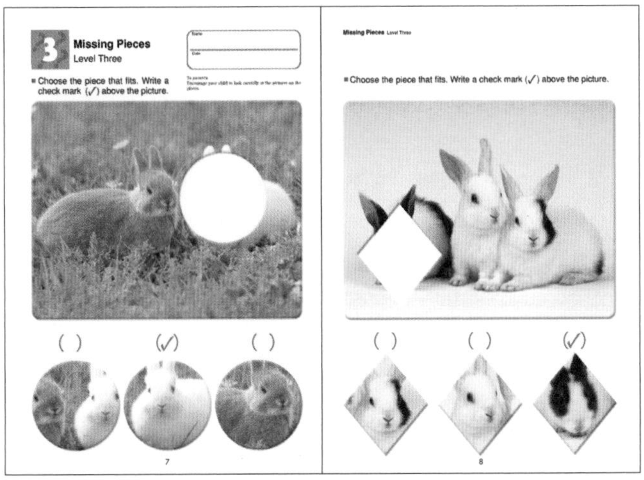

pages 7 and 8

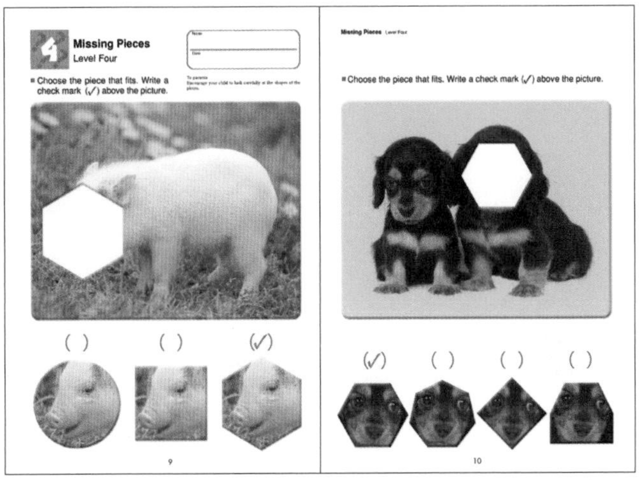

pages 9 and 10

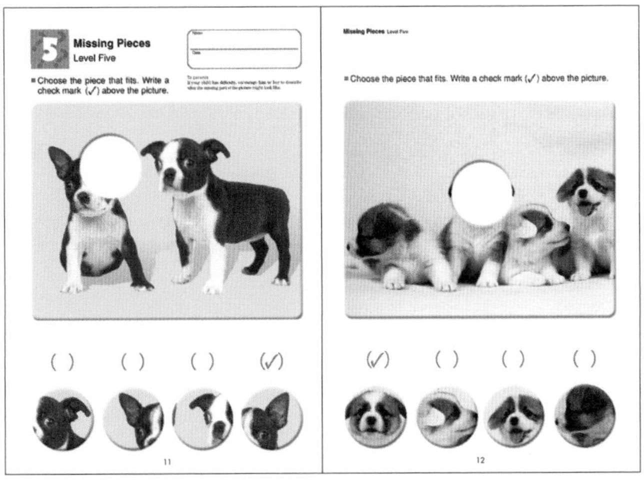

pages 11 and 12

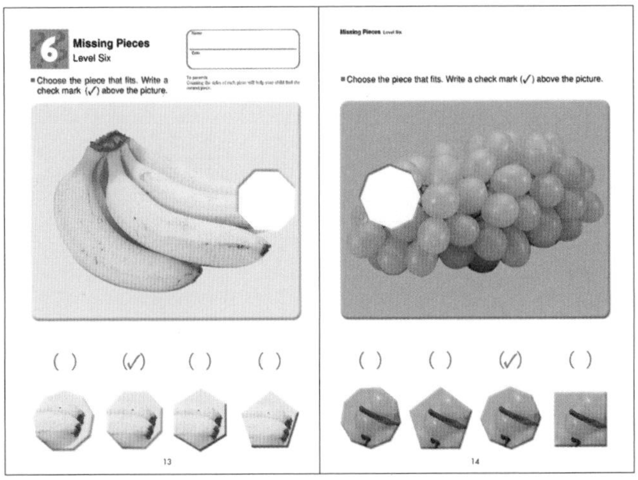

pages 13 and 14

pages 15 and 16

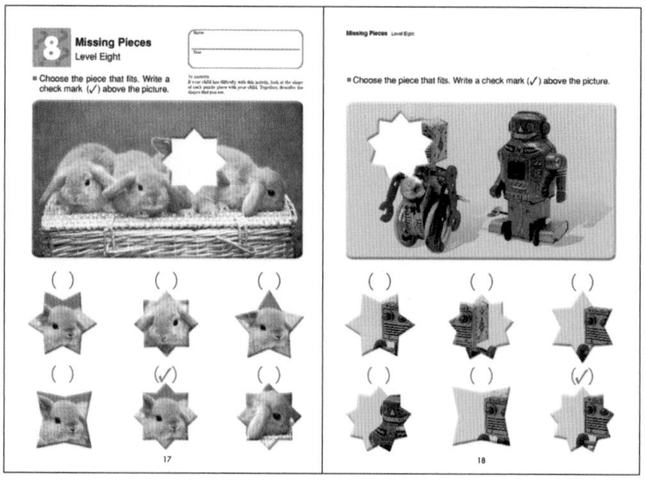

pages 17 and 18

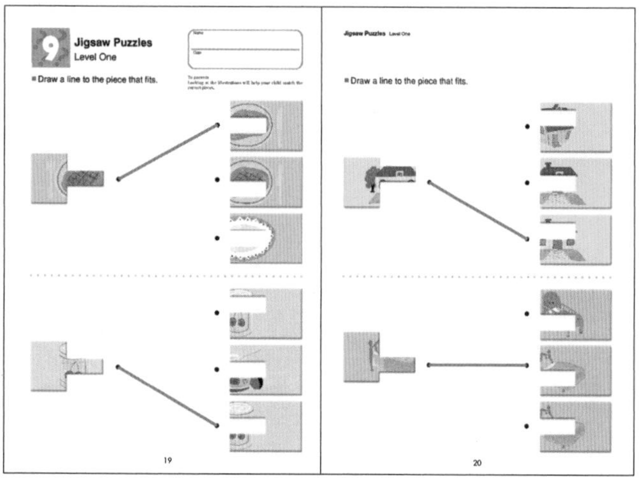

pages 19 and 20

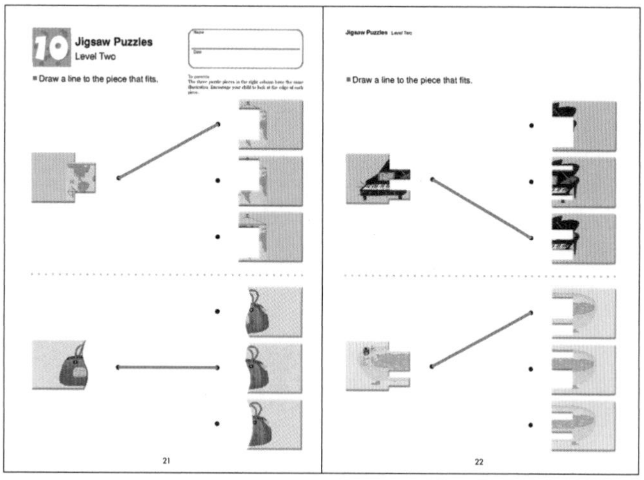

pages 21 and 22

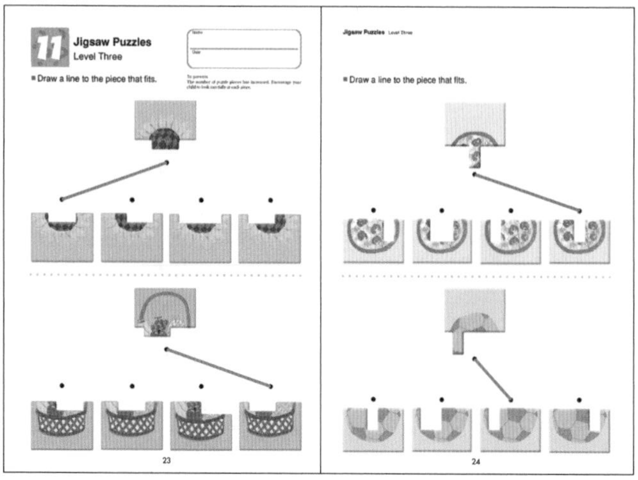

pages 23 and 24

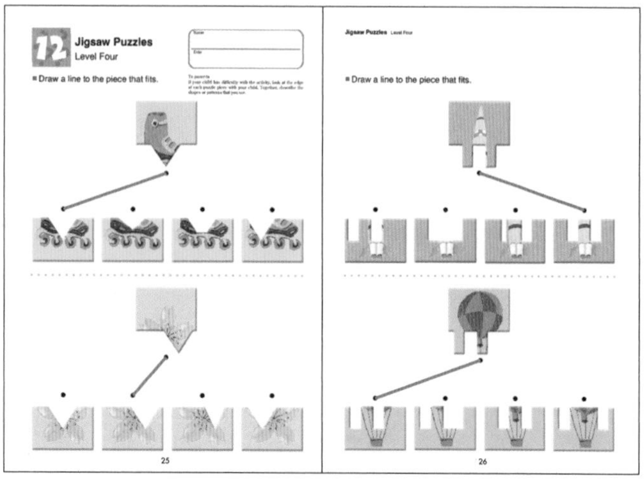

pages 25 and 26

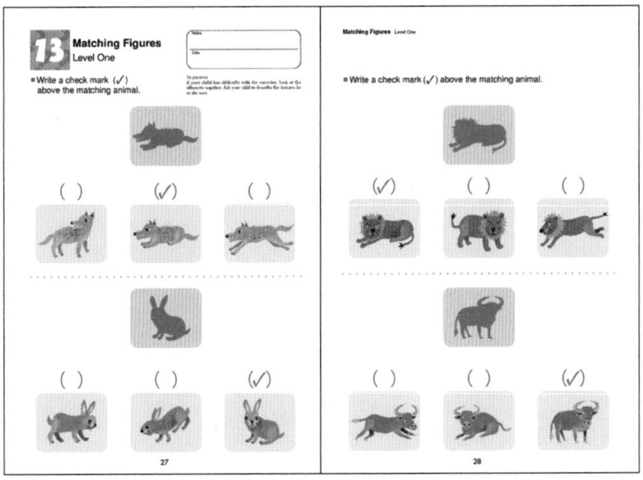

pages 27 and 28

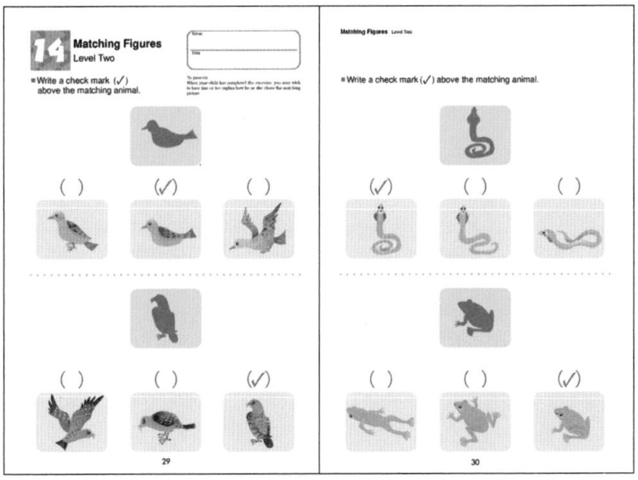

pages 29 and 30

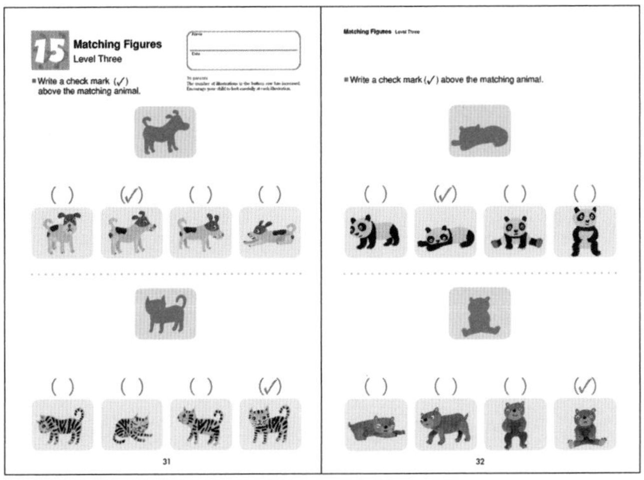

pages 31 and 32

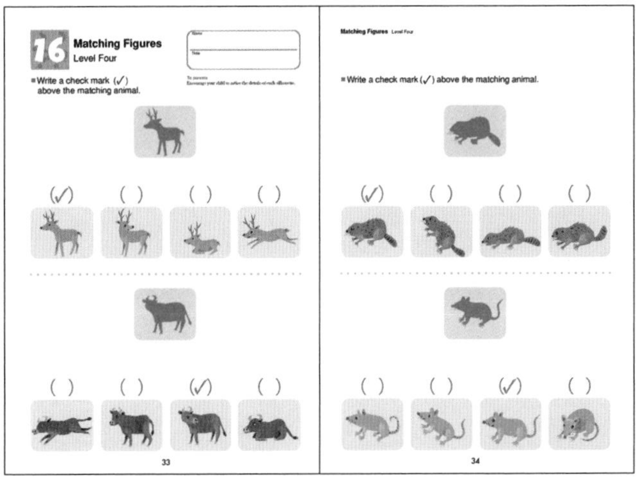

pages 33 and 34

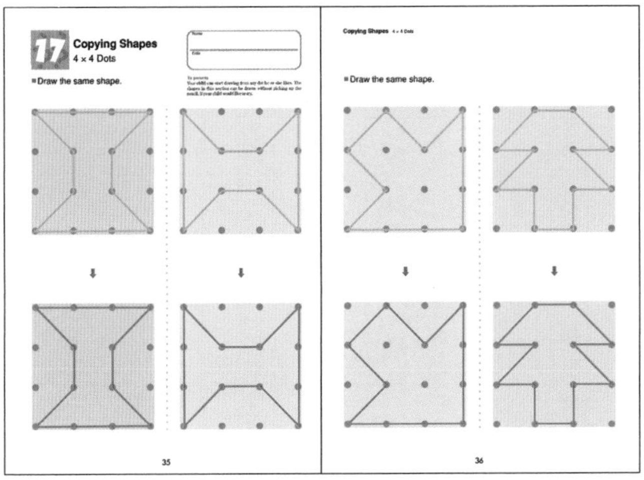

pages 35 and 36

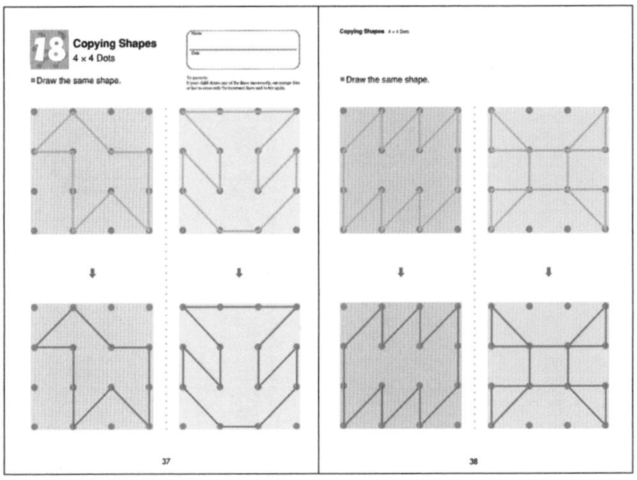

pages 37 and 38

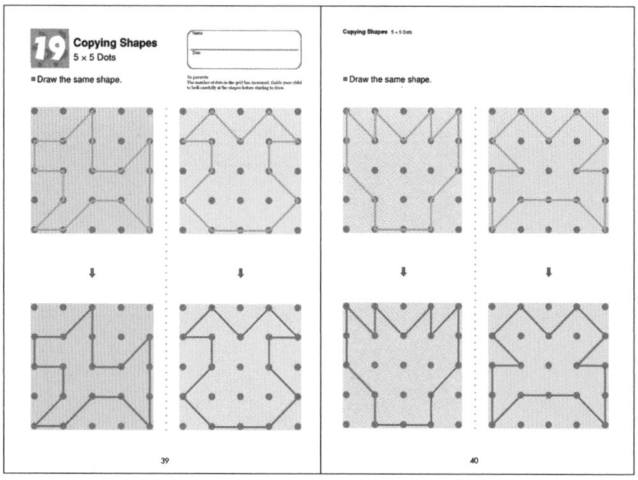
19
Copying Shapes
5 x 5 Dots
Draw the same shape.
Copying Shapes
Draw the same shape.
39
40
pages 39 and 40

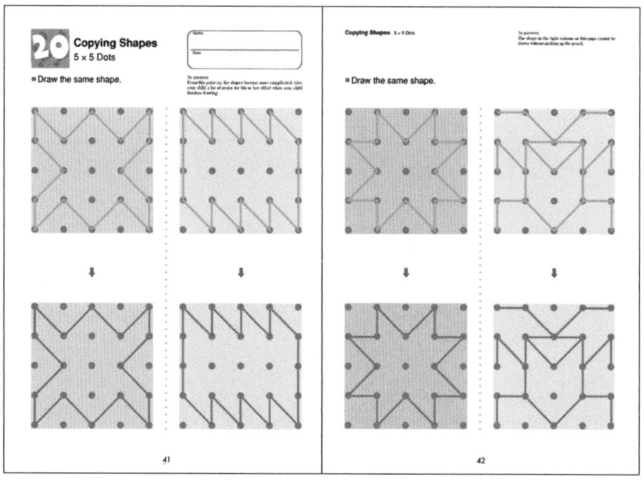
20
Copying Shapes
5 x 5 Dots
Draw the same shape.
Copying Shapes
Draw the same shape.
41
42
pages 41 and 42

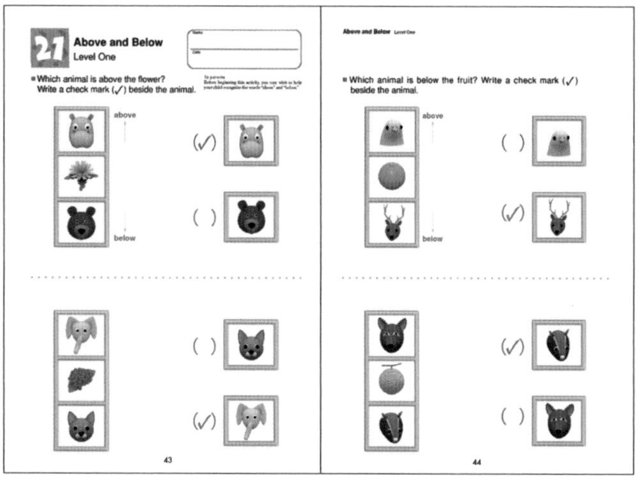
21
Above and Below
Level One
Which animal is above the flower?
Write a check mark (✓) beside the animal.
above
below
Above and Below
Which animal is below the fruit? Write a check mark (✓) beside the animal.
43
44
pages 43 and 44

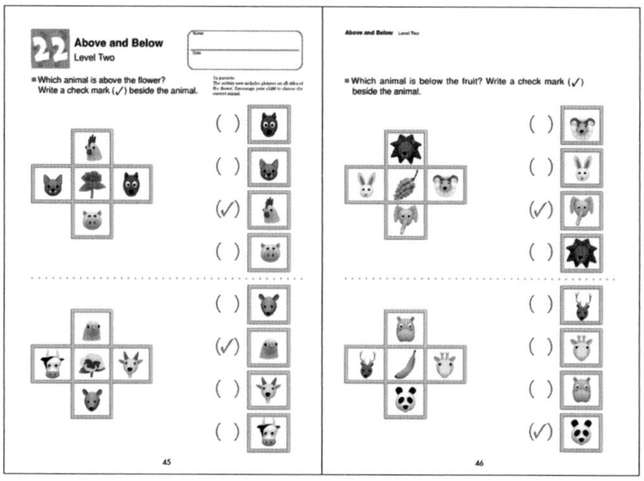
22
Above and Below
Level Two
Which animal is above the flower?
Write a check mark (✓) beside the animal.
Above and Below
Which animal is below the fruit? Write a check mark (✓) beside the animal.
45
46
pages 45 and 46

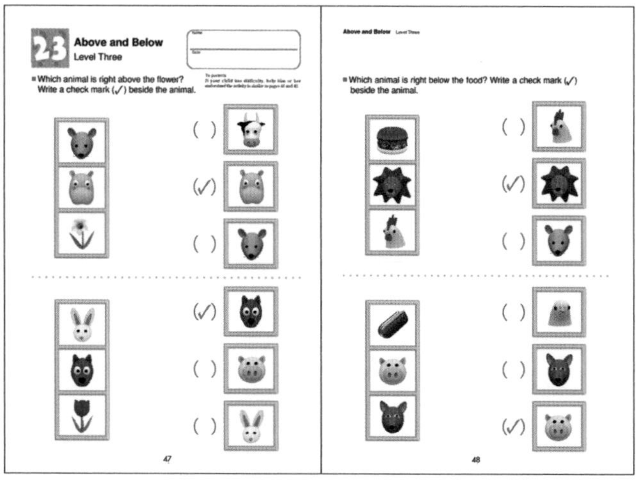
23
Above and Below
Level Three
Which animal is right above the flower?
Write a check mark (✓) beside the animal.
Above and Below
Which animal is right below the food? Write a check mark (✓) beside the animal.
47
48
pages 47 and 48

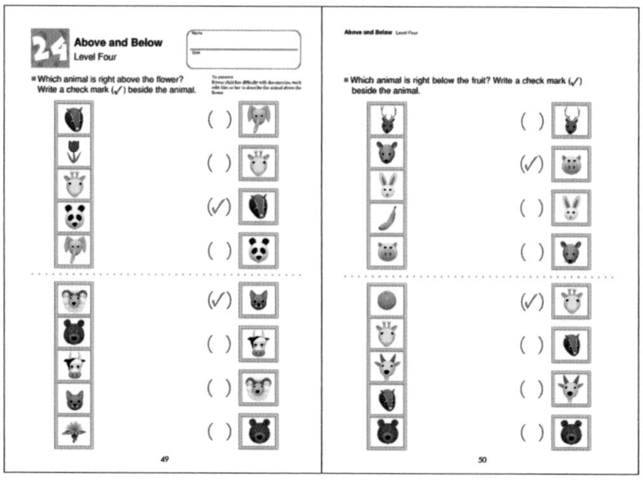
24
Above and Below
Level Four
Which animal is right above the flower?
Write a check mark (✓) beside the animal.
Above and Below
Which animal is right below the fruit? Write a check mark (✓) beside the animal.
49
50
pages 49 and 50

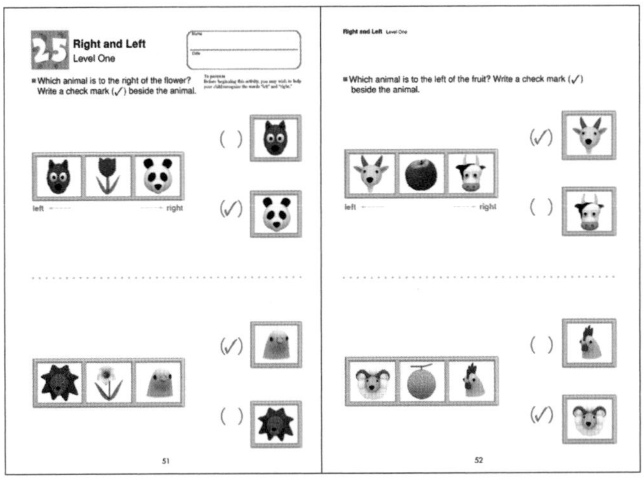
25 Right and Left
Level One
■ Which animal is to the right of the flower? Write a check mark (✓) beside the animal.
( )
(✓)
left — right
(✓)
( )
51
Right and Left Level One
■ Which animal is to the left of the fruit? Write a check mark (✓) beside the animal.
(✓)
( )
left — right
( )
(✓)
52

pages 51 and 52

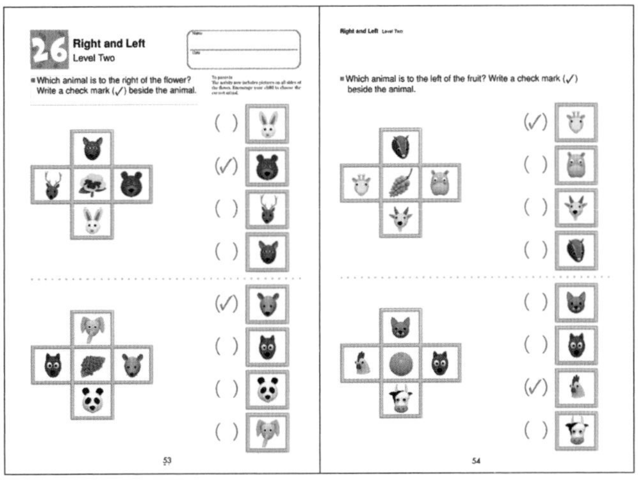
26 Right and Left
Level Two
■ Which animal is to the right of the flower? Write a check mark (✓) beside the animal.
( ) (✓) ( ) ( )
(✓) ( ) ( ) ( )
53
Right and Left Level Two
■ Which animal is to the left of the fruit? Write a check mark (✓) beside the animal.
(✓) ( ) ( ) ( )
( ) ( ) (✓) ( )
54

pages 53 and 54

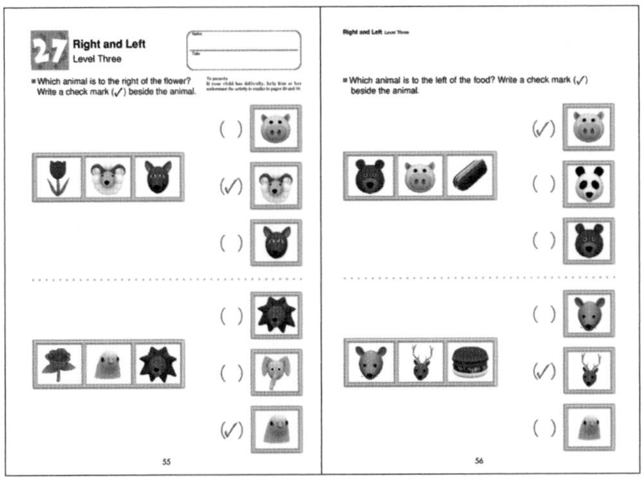
27 Right and Left
Level Three
■ Which animal is to the right of the flower? Write a check mark (✓) beside the animal.
( ) (✓) ( )
( ) ( ) (✓)
55
Right and Left Level Three
■ Which animal is to the left of the food? Write a check mark (✓) beside the animal.
(✓) ( ) ( )
( ) (✓) ( )
56

pages 55 and 56

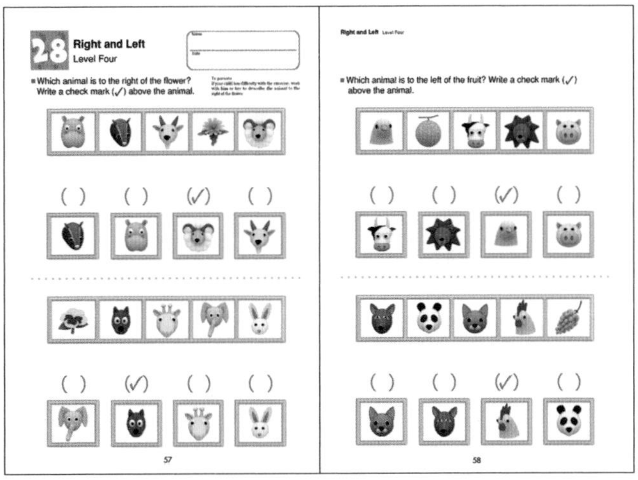
28 Right and Left
Level Four
■ Which animal is to the right of the flower? Write a check mark (✓) above the animal.
( ) ( ) (✓) ( )
( ) (✓) ( ) ( )
57
Right and Left Level Four
■ Which animal is to the left of the fruit? Write a check mark (✓) above the animal.
( ) ( ) (✓) ( )
( ) ( ) (✓) ( )
58

pages 57 and 58

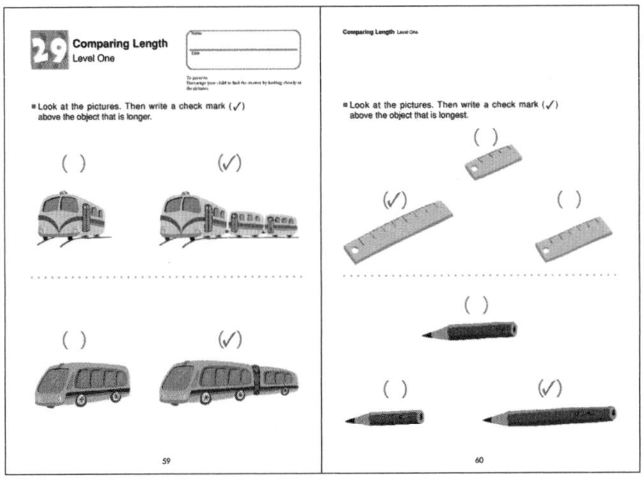
29 Comparing Length
Level One
■ Look at the pictures. Then write a check mark (✓) above the object that is longer.
( ) (✓)
( ) (✓)
59
Comparing Length Level One
■ Look at the pictures. Then write a check mark (✓) above the object that is longest.
( ) (✓) ( )
( ) ( ) (✓)
60

pages 59 and 60

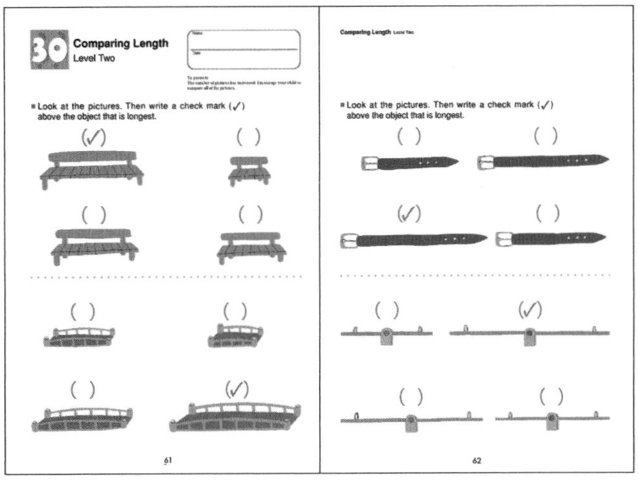
30 Comparing Length
Level Two
■ Look at the pictures. Then write a check mark (✓) above the object that is longest.
(✓) ( ) ( ) ( )
( ) ( ) ( ) (✓)
61
Comparing Length Level Two
■ Look at the pictures. Then write a check mark (✓) above the object that is longest.
( ) ( ) (✓) ( )
( ) (✓) ( ) ( )
62

pages 61 and 62

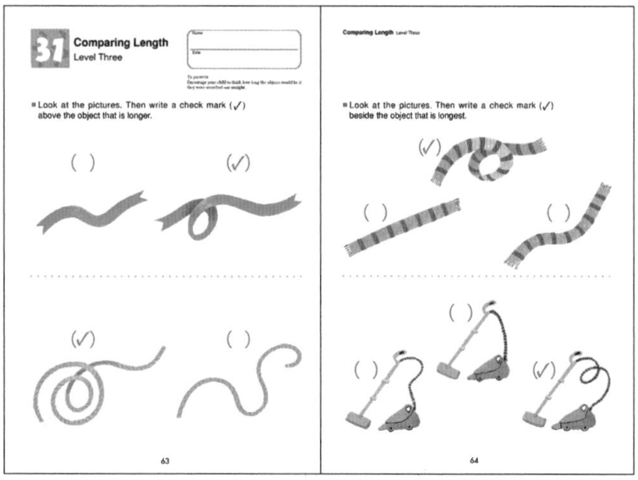
31
Comparing Length
Level Three
Look at the pictures. Then write a check mark (✓) above the object that is longer.
Look at the pictures. Then write a check mark (✓) beside the object that is longest.
63
64
pages 63 and 64

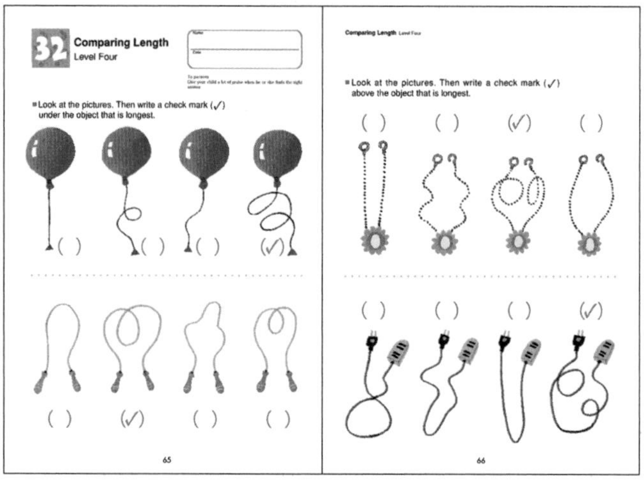
32
Comparing Length
Level Four
Look at the pictures. Then write a check mark (✓) under the object that is longest.
Look at the pictures. Then write a check mark (✓) above the object that is longest.
65
66
pages 65 and 66

33
Coloring Patterns
Four Colors
Color each pattern with the correct color.
67
68
pages 67 and 68

34
Coloring Patterns
Five Colors
Color each pattern with the correct color.
69
70
pages 69 and 70

35
Coloring Patterns
Five and Six Colors
Color each pattern with the correct color.
71
72
pages 71 and 72

36
Coloring Patterns
Six and Seven Colors
Color each pattern with the correct color.
73
74
pages 73 and 74

Logic

Table of Contents

To parents:

Logic

In this section, your child will complete activities to develop his or her logical thinking skills. This section contains activities such as making comparisons, distinguishing real from pretend, and analyzing patterns. By completing this section your child will strengthen his or her ability to think logically about problems and questions.

Each skill is introduced in a step-by-step manner that allows your child to master it without frustration. Over the course of the section, the difficulty level of these activities increases as your child gains confidence in his or her ability to think logically.

1 Picture Patterns

Two Pictures

Name

Date

To parents
Guide your child to write his or her name and date in the box above. Do the exercise along with your child if he or she has difficulty.

■ Write a check mark (✓) above the picture that comes next in the pattern.

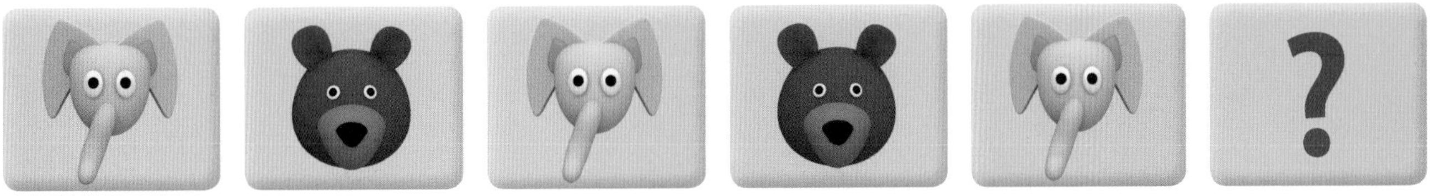

( )　　(✓)

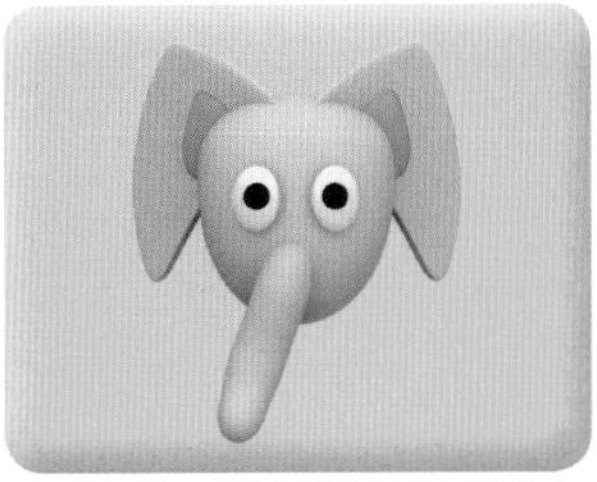

( )　　( )

■ Write a check mark (✓) above the picture that comes next in the pattern.

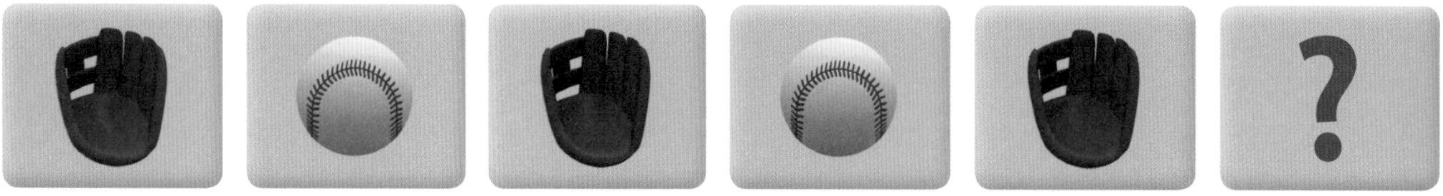

( ) ( )

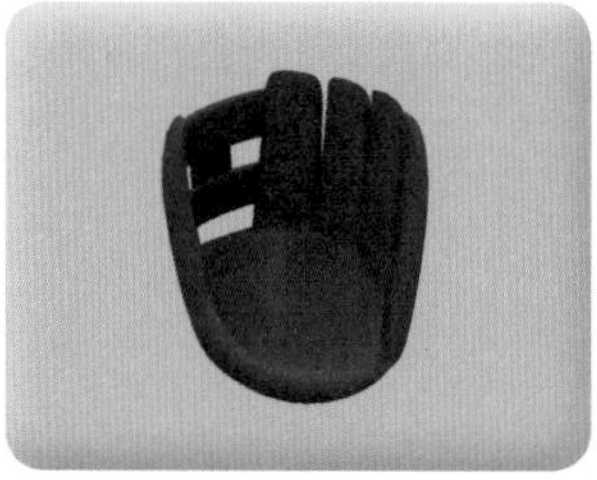

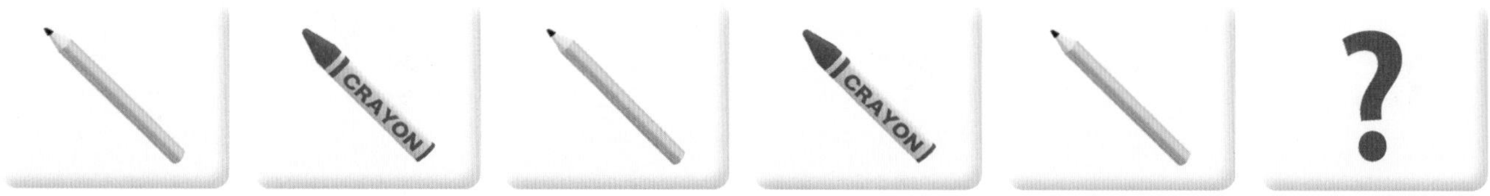

( ) ( )

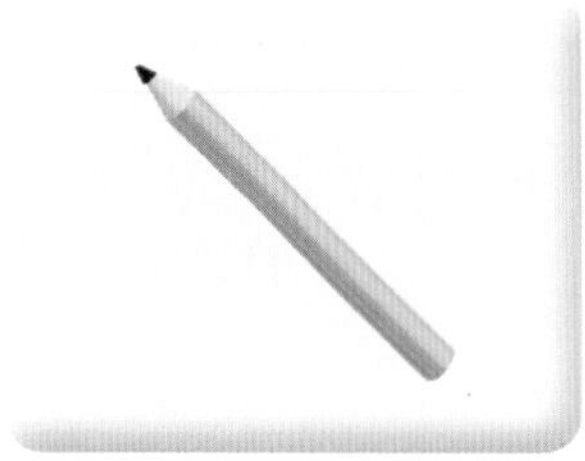

2 Picture Patterns

Two Pictures

Name

Date

To parents
The patterns are now arranged vertically. Guide your child to start with the top picture.

■ Write a check mark (✓) above the picture that comes next in the pattern.

■ Write a check mark (✓) above the picture that comes next in the pattern.

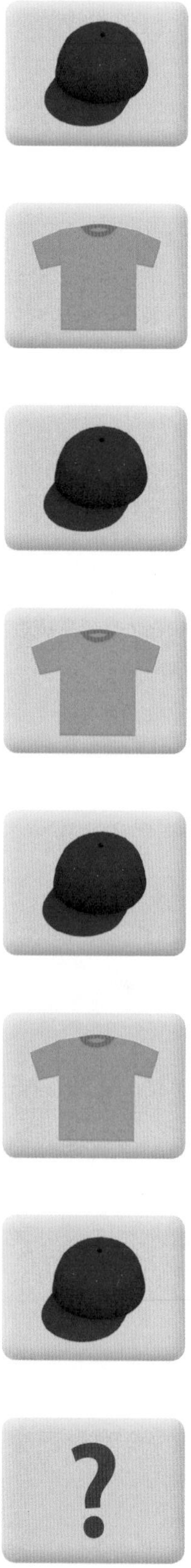

( )

( )

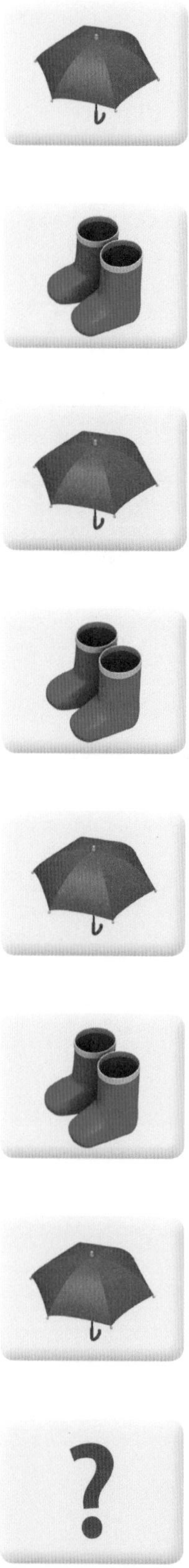

( )

( )

3 Picture Patterns

Three Pictures

Name

Date

To parents
Encourage your child to differentiate between the pictures.

■ Write a check mark (✓) above the picture that comes next in the pattern.

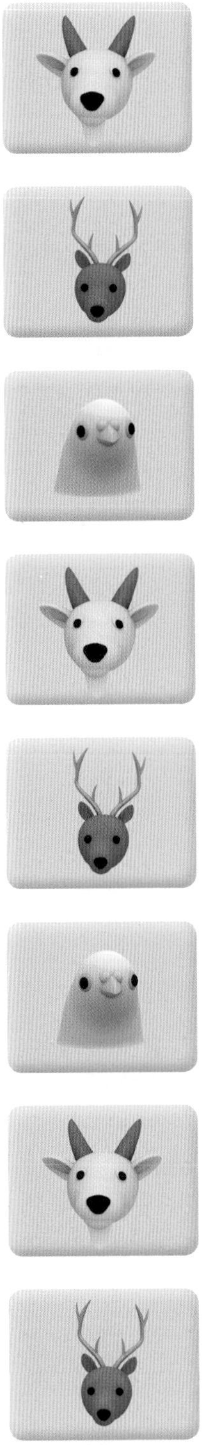

?

( )

( )

( )

?

( )

( )

( )

■ Write a check mark (✓) above the picture that comes next in the pattern.

Picture Patterns

Three Pictures

Name

Date

To parents
If your child has difficulty, encourage him or her to say the sequence of pictures out loud.

- Write a check mark (✓) above the picture that comes next in the pattern.

■ Write a check mark (✓) above the picture that comes next in the pattern.

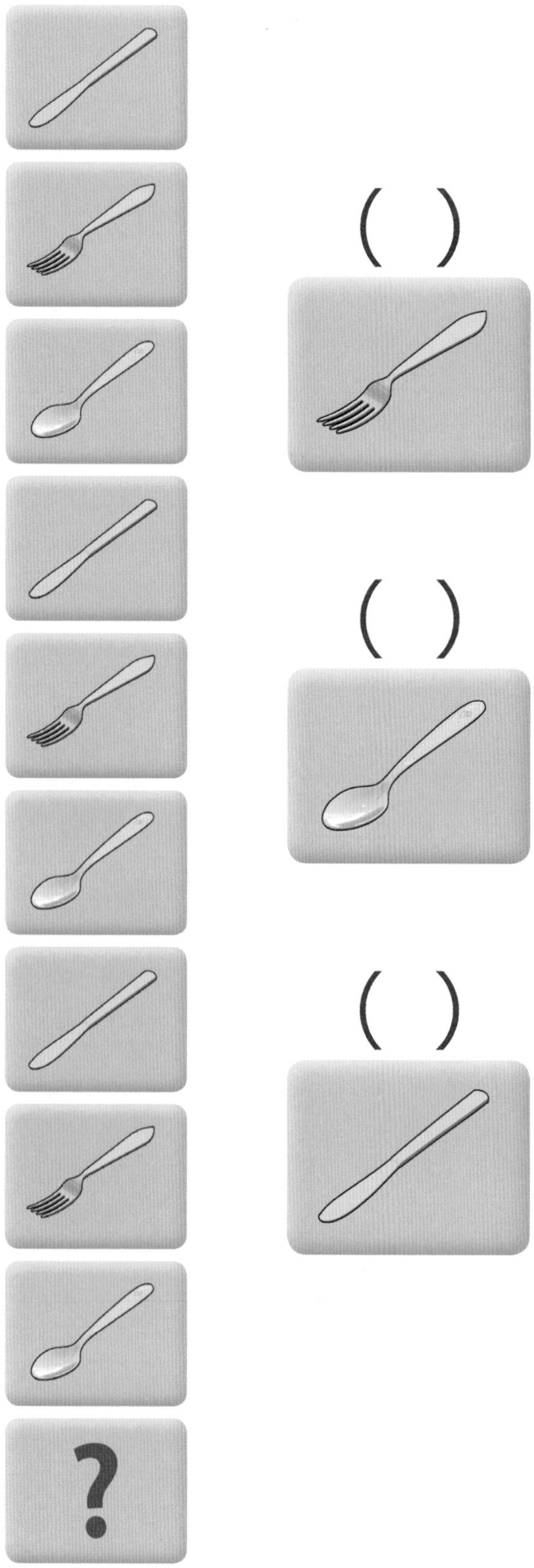

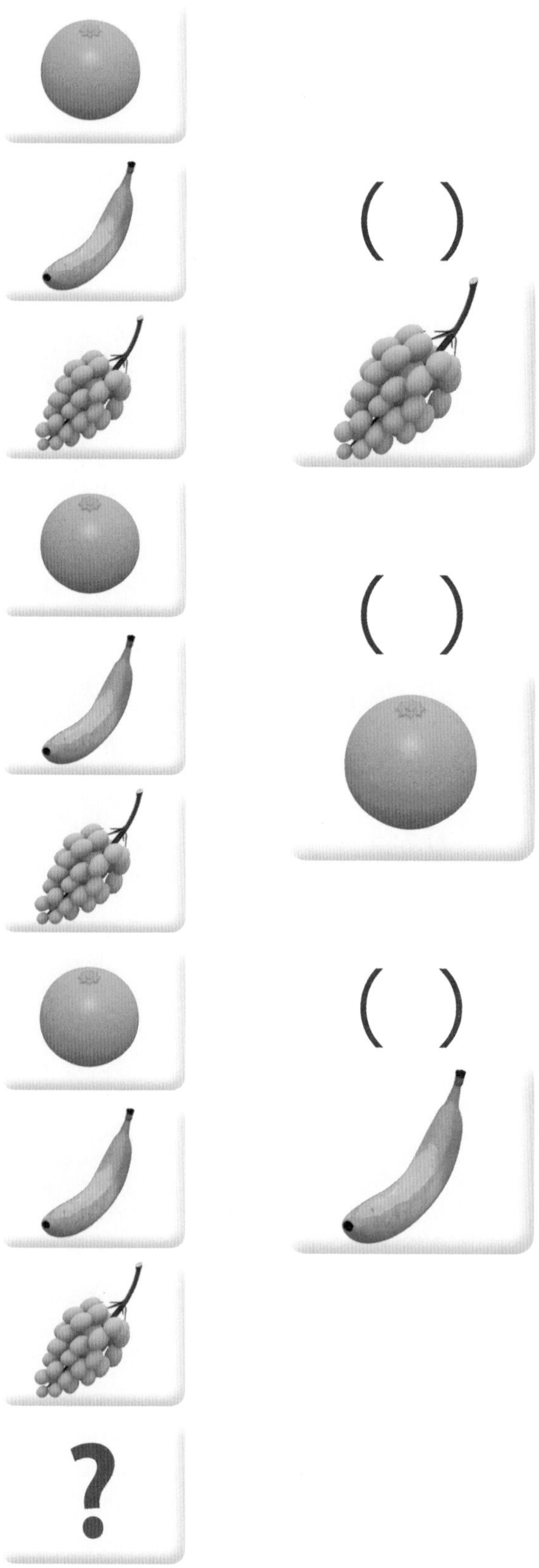

5 Picture Patterns

Two Shapes

Name

Date

To parents
The patterns are now made up of geometric shapes. Encourage your child to differentiate between the shapes.

■ Write a check mark (✓) above the picture that comes next in the pattern.

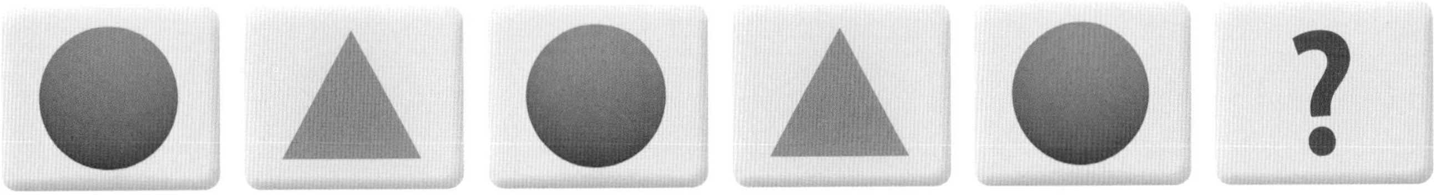

( )　　( )

( )　　( )

■ Write a check mark (✓) above the picture that comes next in the pattern.

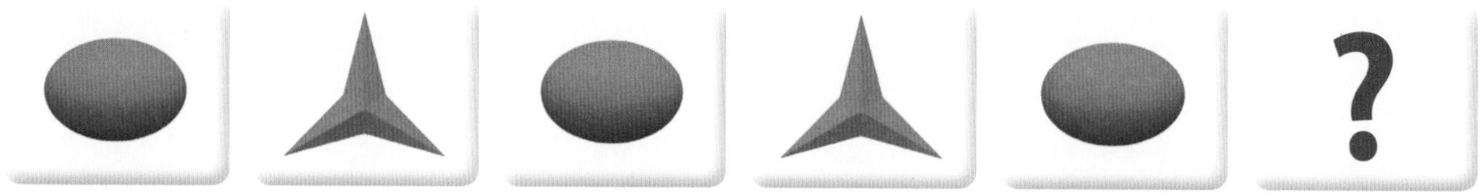

( )

( )

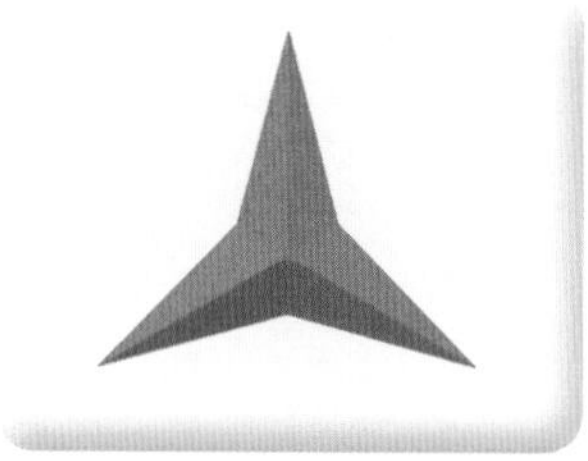

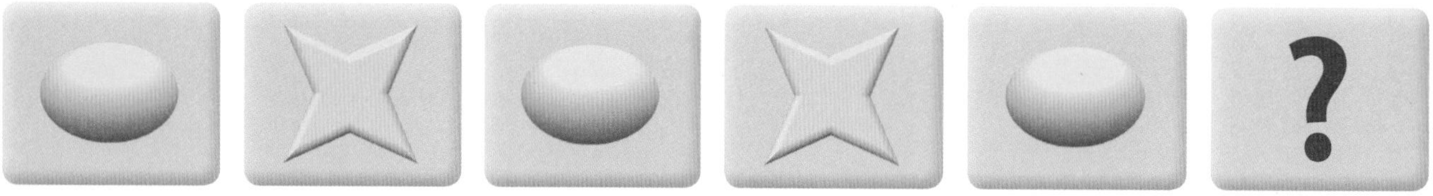

( )

( )

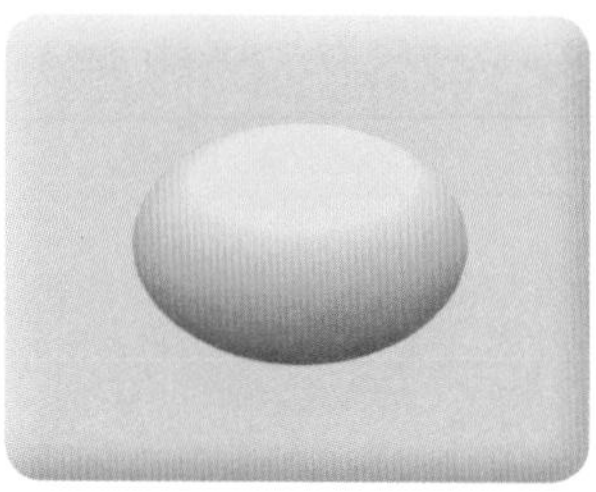

6

Picture Patterns

Two Shapes

Name

Date

To parents
If your child has difficulty, ask him or her to describe the two different shapes in the sequence.

■ Write a check mark (✓) above the picture that comes next in the pattern.

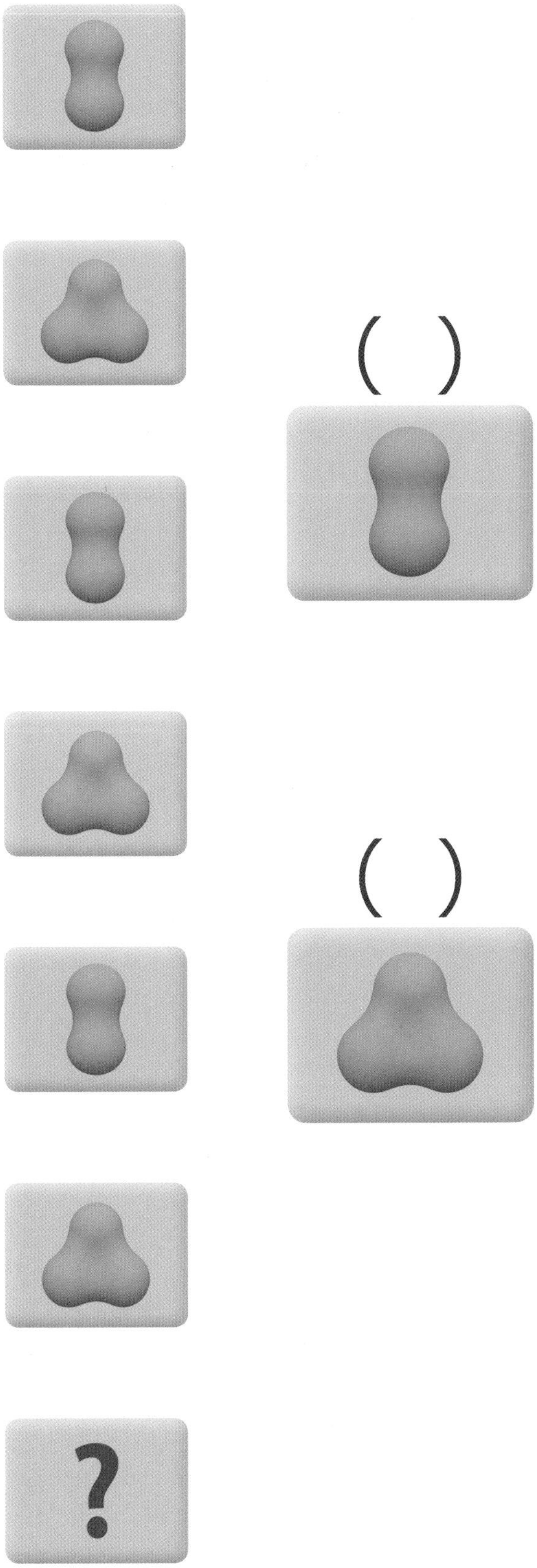

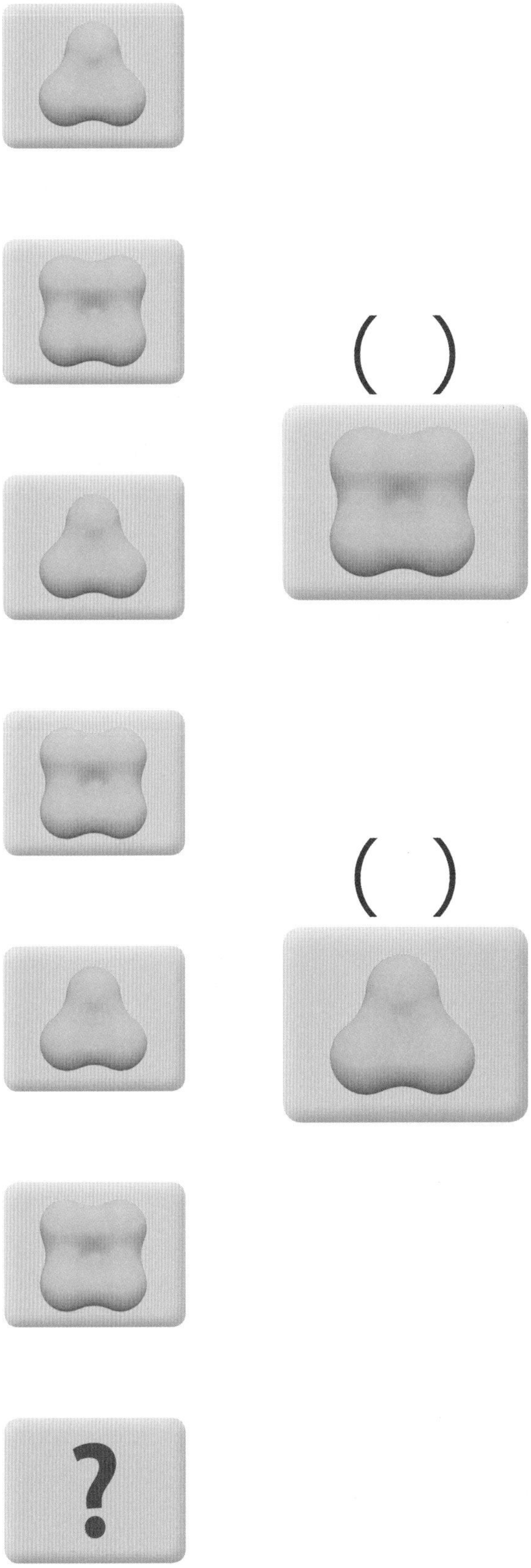

■ Write a check mark (✓) above the picture that comes next in the pattern.

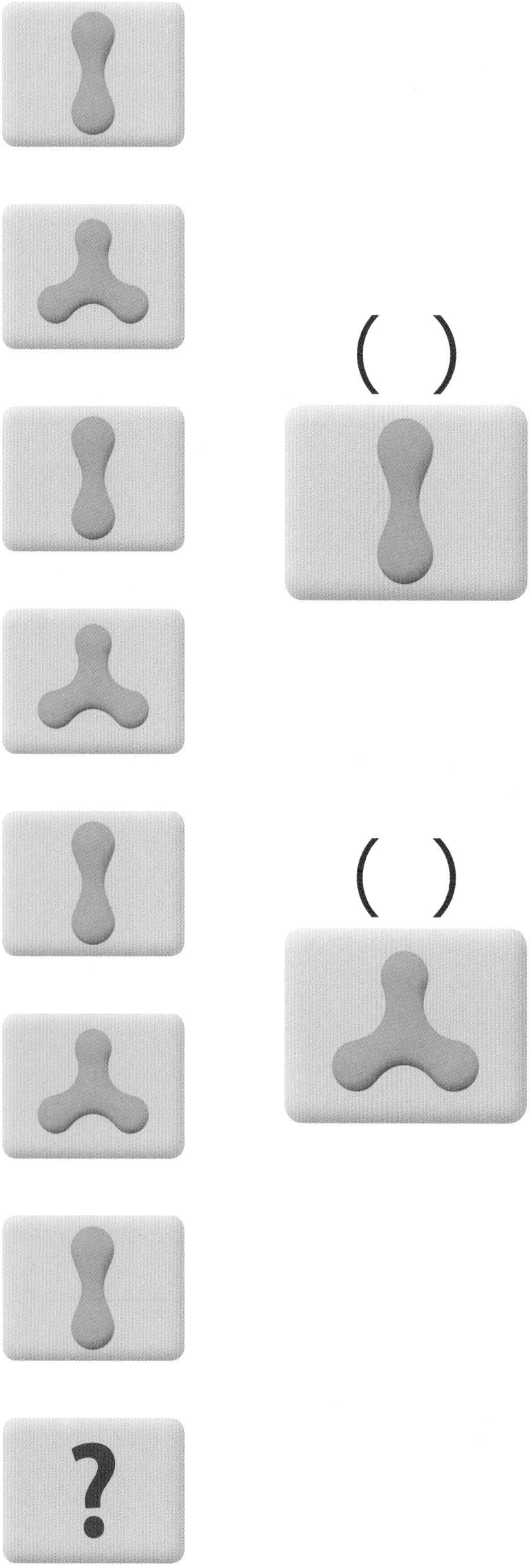

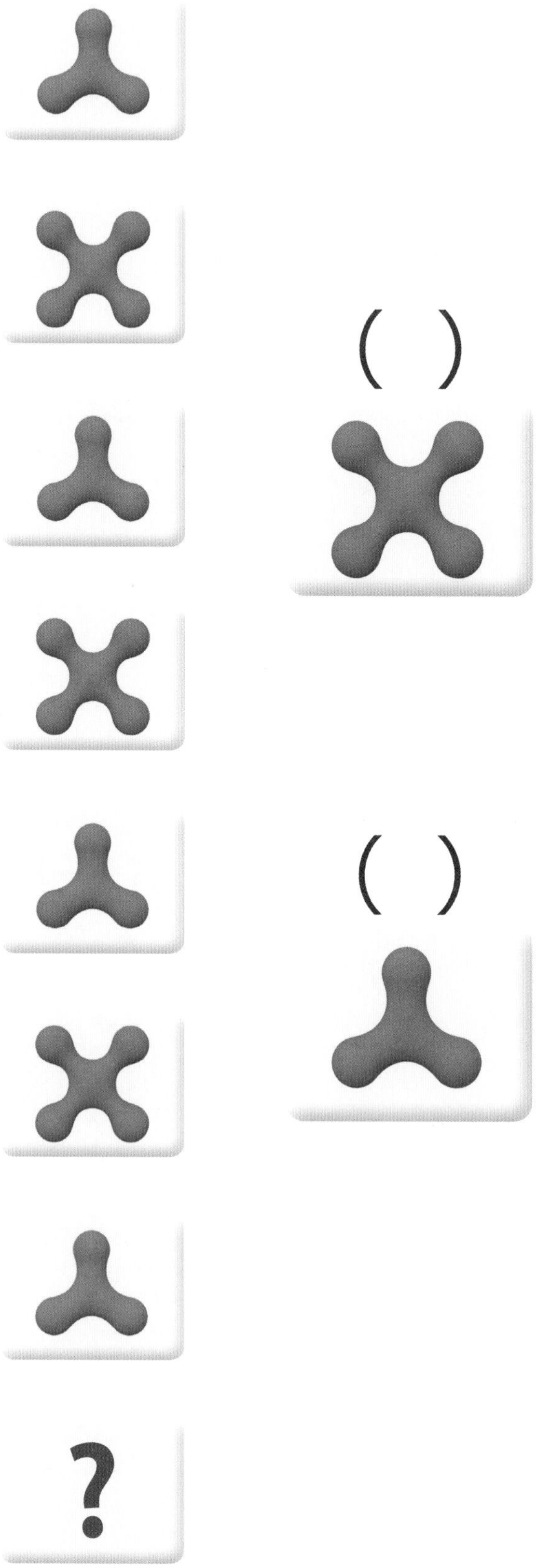

7 Picture Patterns

Three Shapes

Name

Date

To parents
The patterns are now made up of three shapes. Encourage your child to differentiate between the shapes.

■ Write a check mark (✓) above the picture that comes next in the pattern.

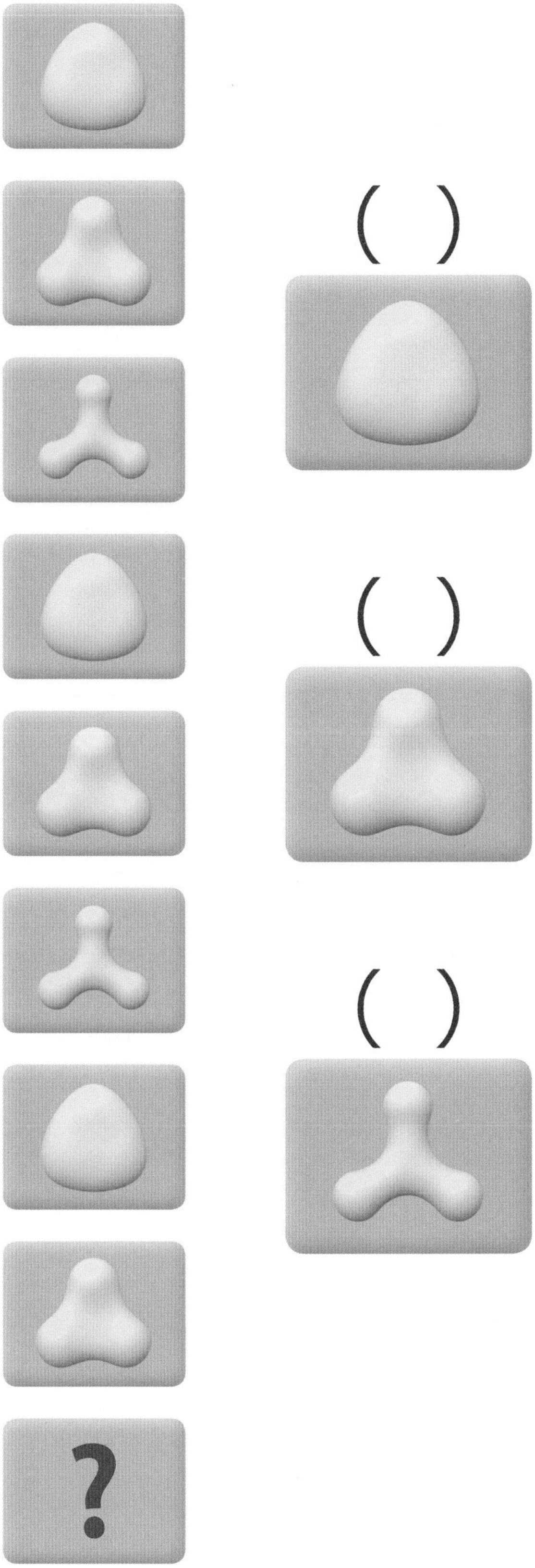

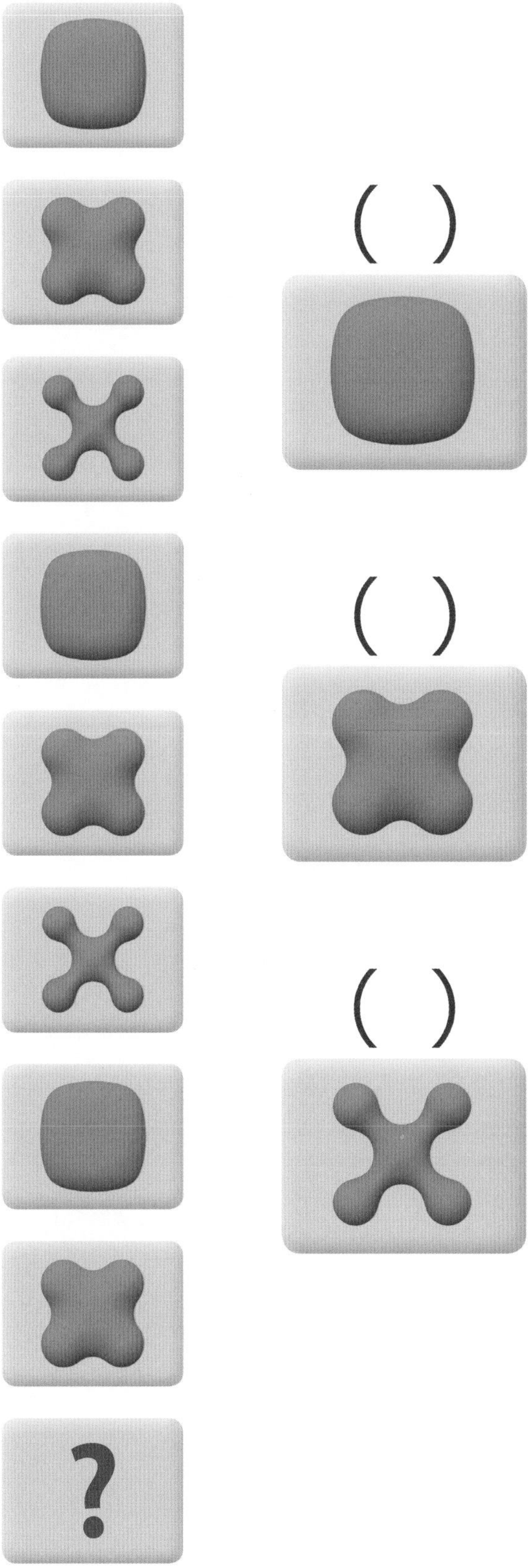

■ Write a check mark (✓) above the picture that comes next in the pattern.

( )

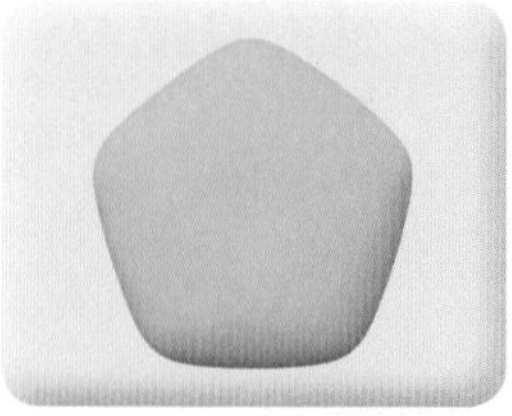

( )

( )

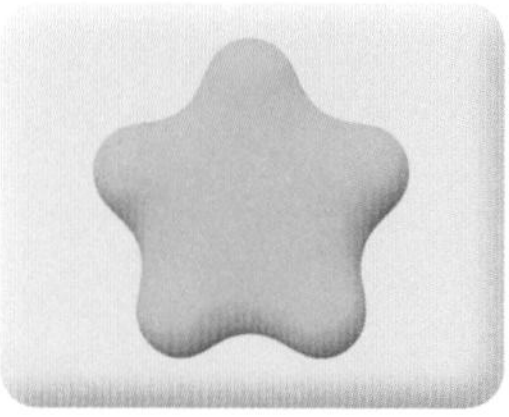

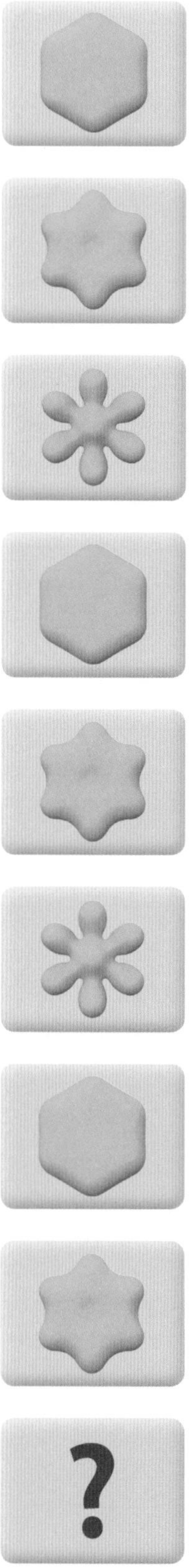

( )

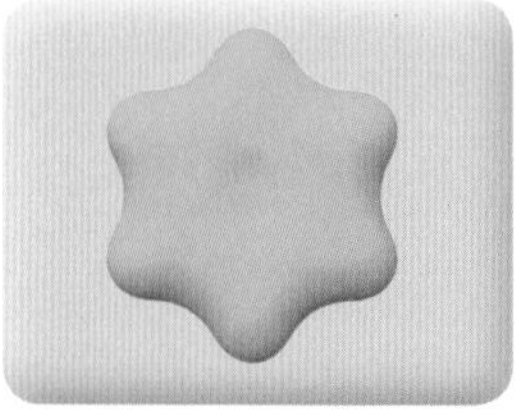

( )

( )

8 Picture Patterns
Three Shapes

Name

Date

To parents
If your child has difficulty, encourage him or her to compare the center parts of the shapes.

■ Write a check mark (✓) above the picture that comes next in the pattern.

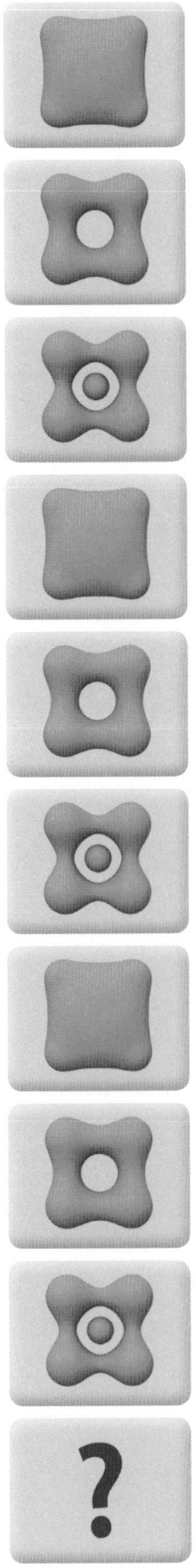

( )

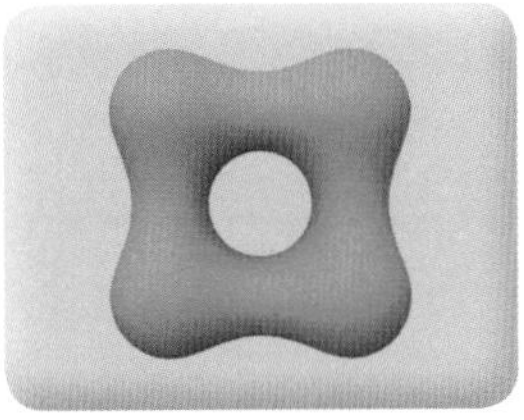

( )

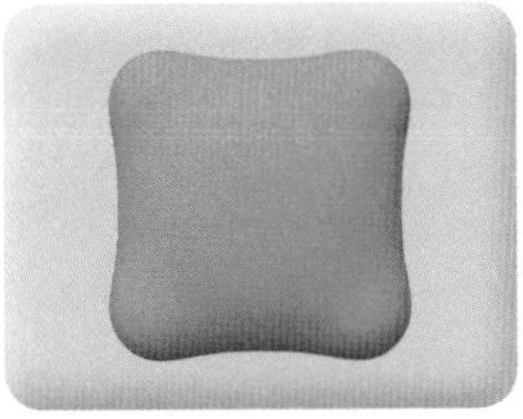

( )

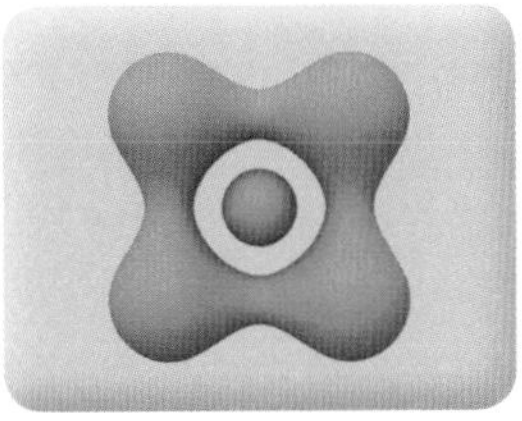

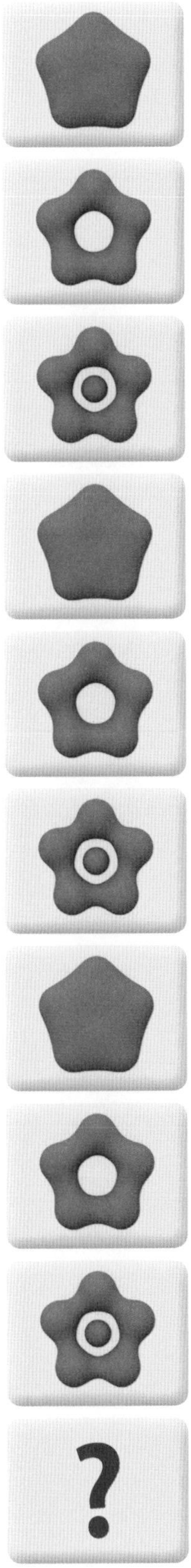

( )

( )

( )

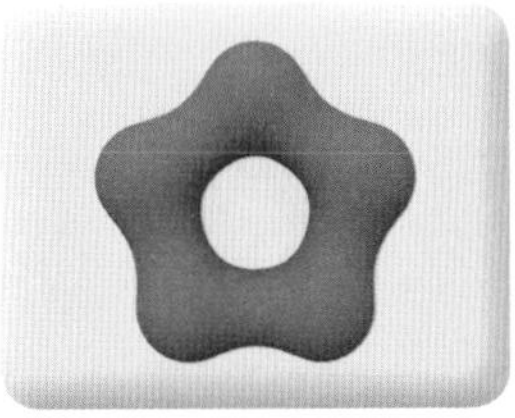

■ Write a check mark (✓) above the picture that comes next in the pattern.

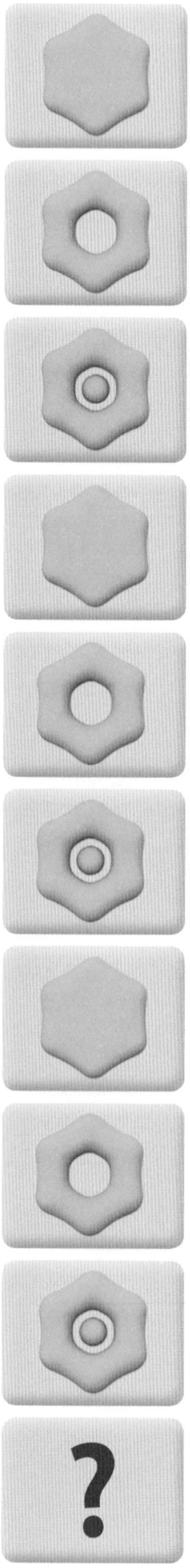

( )

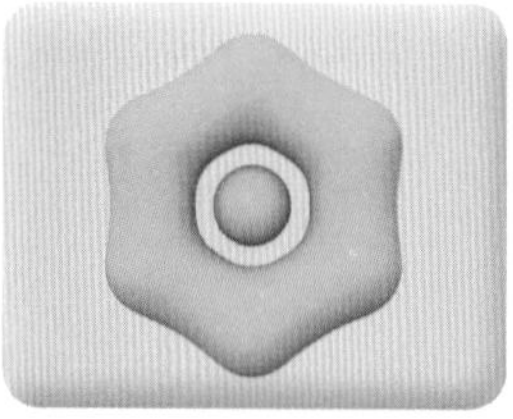

( )

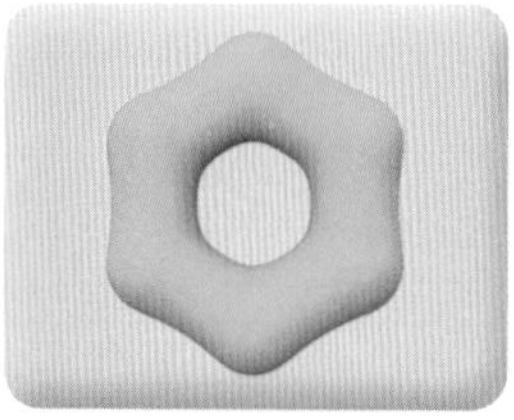

( )

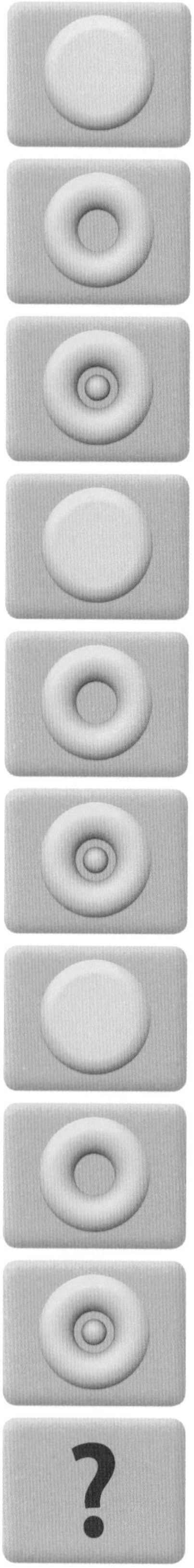

( )

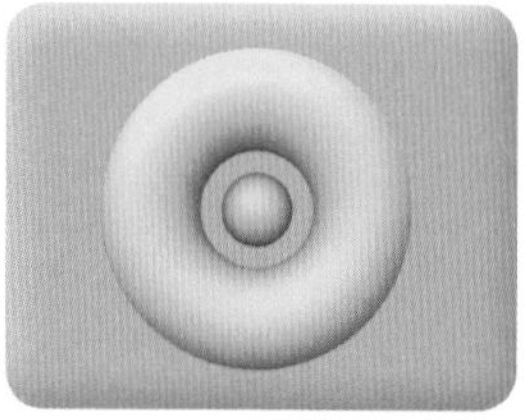

( )

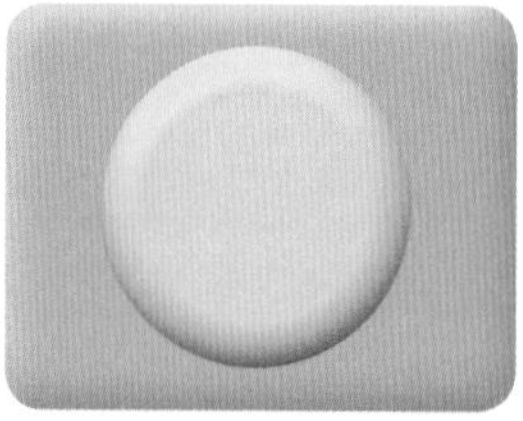

( )

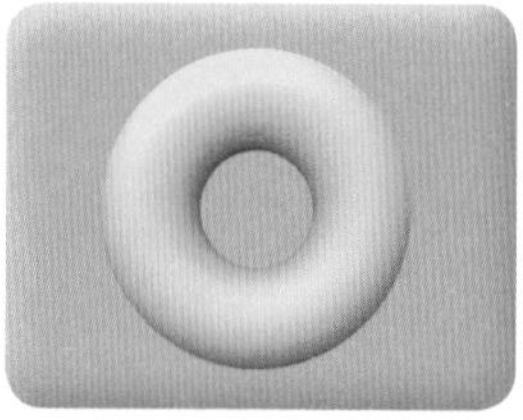

9

Picture Patterns

Three Pictures

Name

Date

To parents
The patterns are now more complicated. Encourage your child to look carefully to find the end of each sequence.

■ Write a check mark (✓) above the picture that comes next in the pattern.

■ Write a check mark (✓) above the picture that comes next in the pattern.

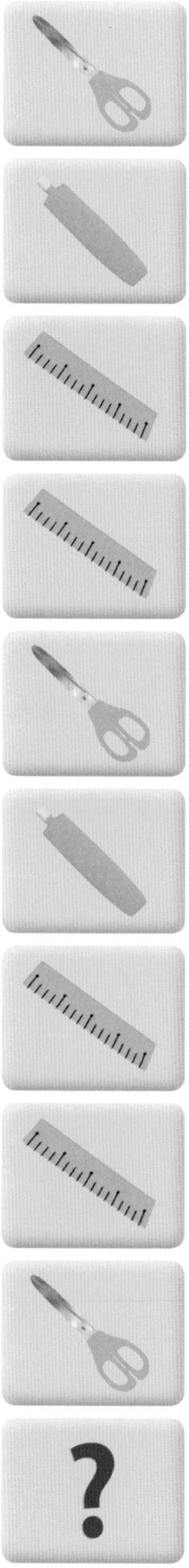

( )

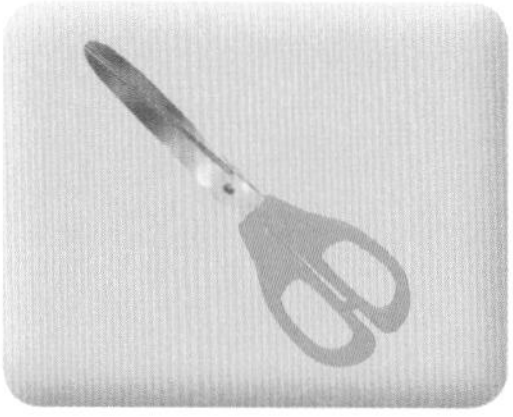

( )

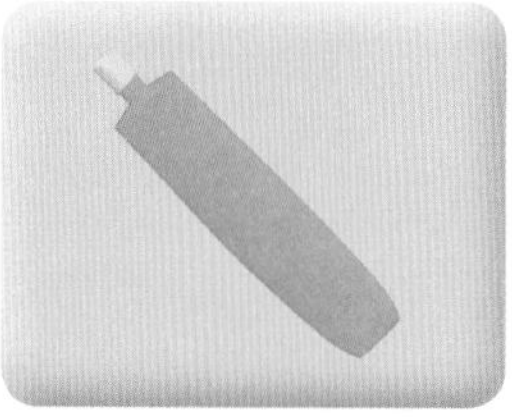

( )

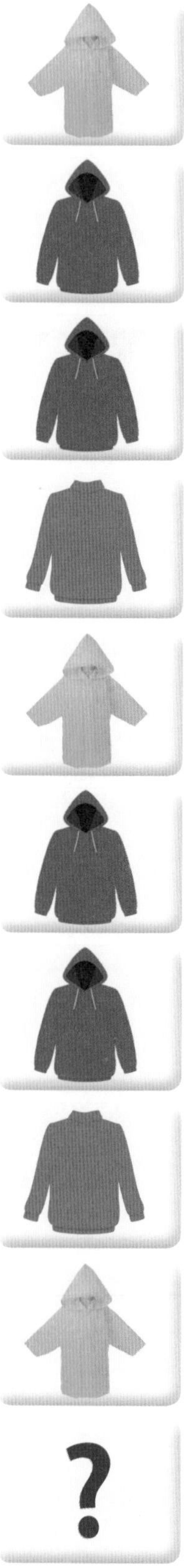

( )

( )

( )

10 Picture Patterns

Three Pictures

Name

Date

To parents
If your child has difficulty, encourage him or her to say the sequence of pictures out loud.

■ Write a check mark (✓) above the picture that comes next in the pattern.

■ Write a check mark (✓) above the picture that comes next in the pattern.

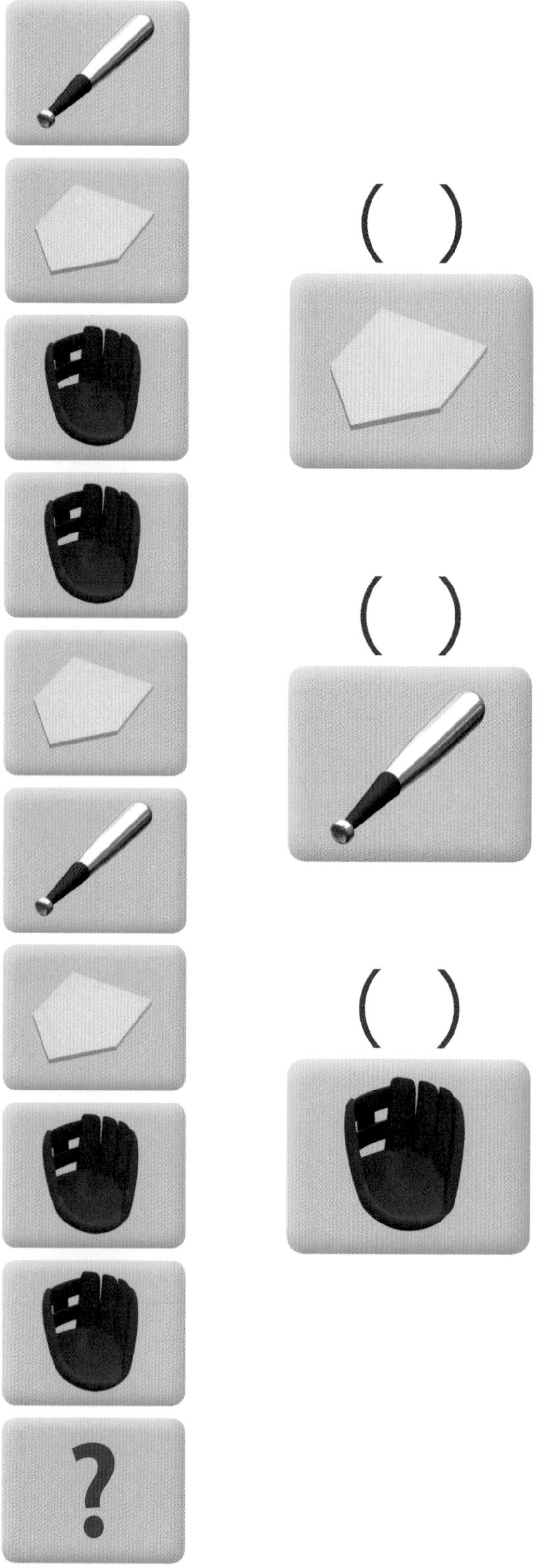

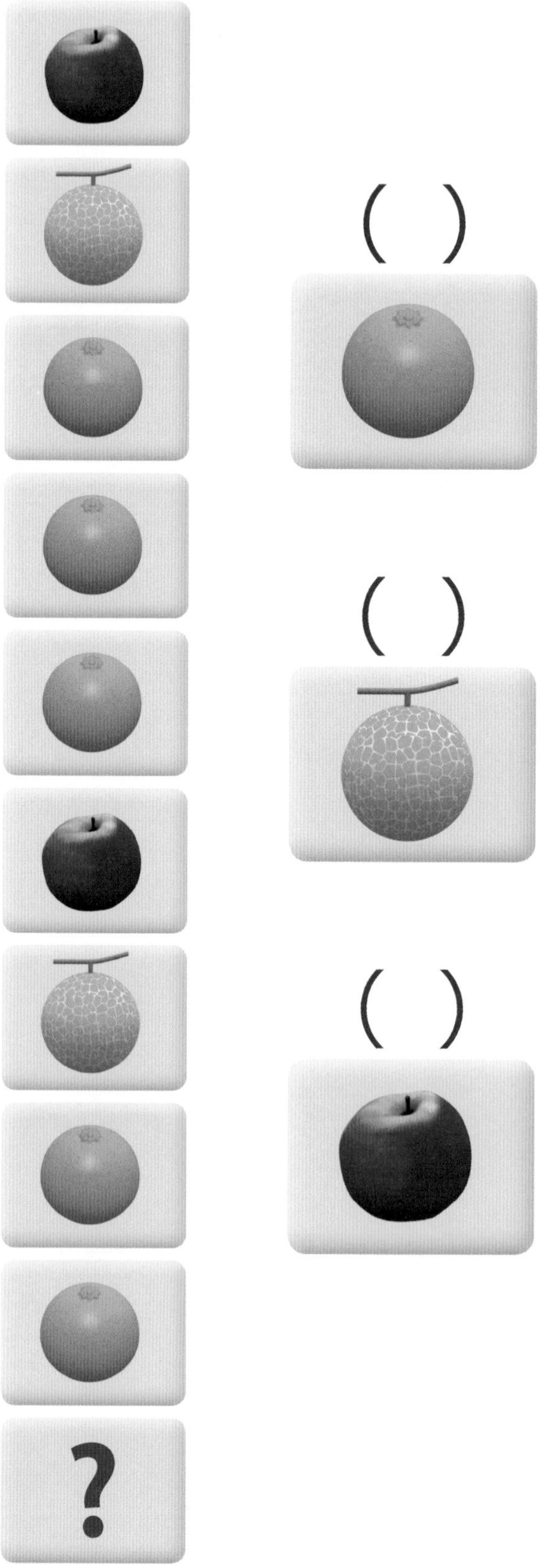

11 Picture Patterns

Three Shapes

Name

Date

To parents
The patterns are now made up of geometric shapes. Encourage your child to differentiate between the shapes.

■ Write a check mark (✓) above the picture that comes next in the pattern.

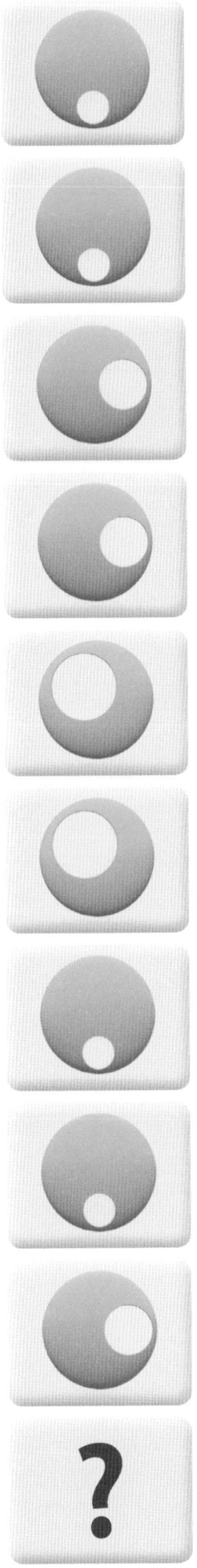

( )

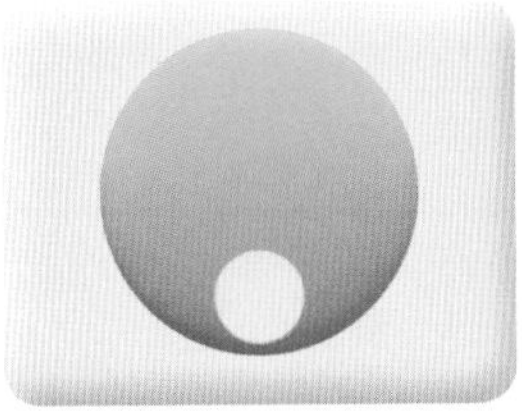

( )

( )

( )

( )

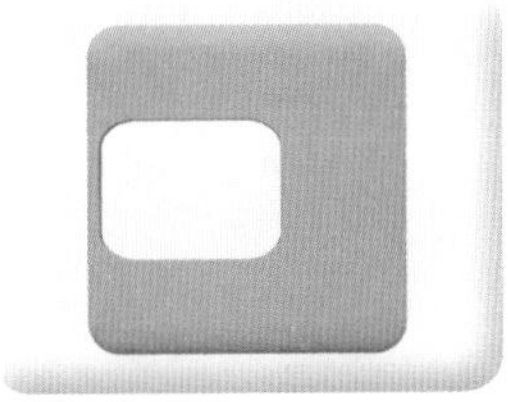

( )

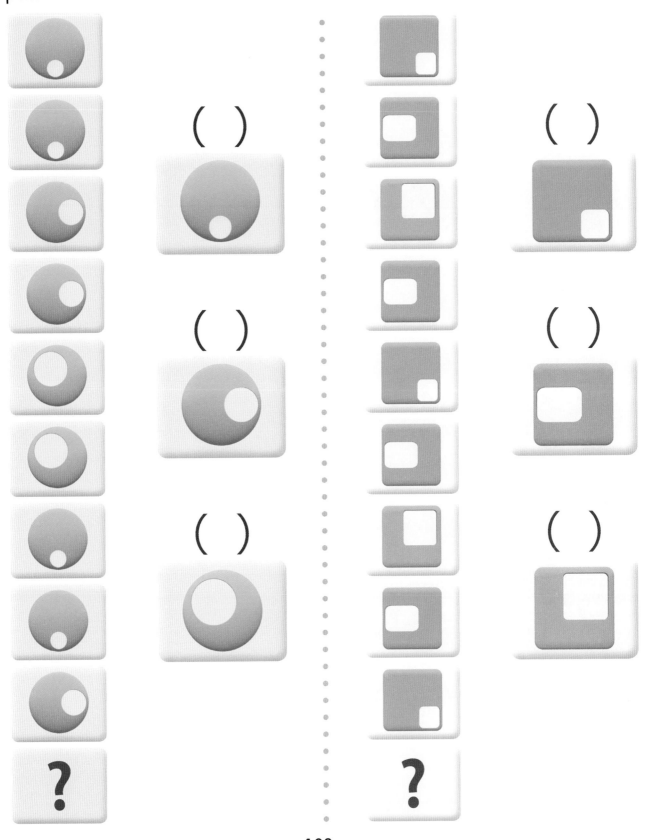

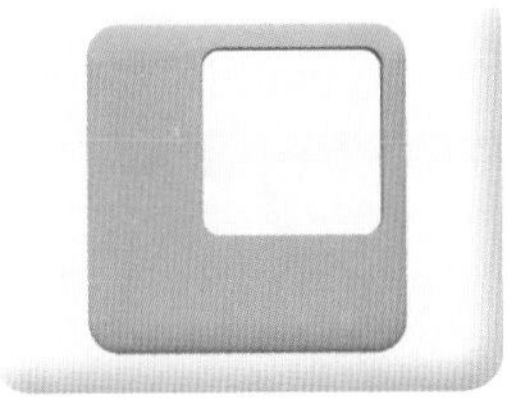

■ Write a check mark (✓) above the picture that comes next in the pattern.

( )

( )

( )

( )

( )

( )

12 Picture Patterns

Three Shapes

Name

Date

To parents
It is okay for your child to take his or her time when working on these exercises.

■ Write a check mark (✓) above the picture that comes next in the pattern.

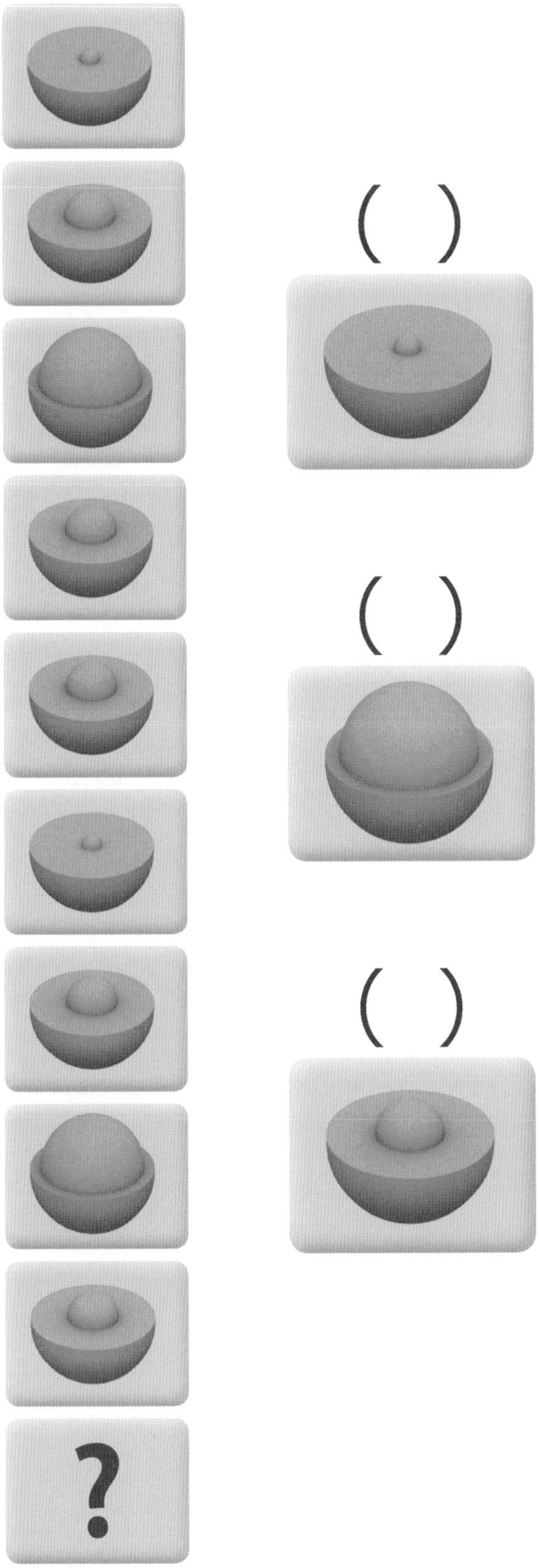

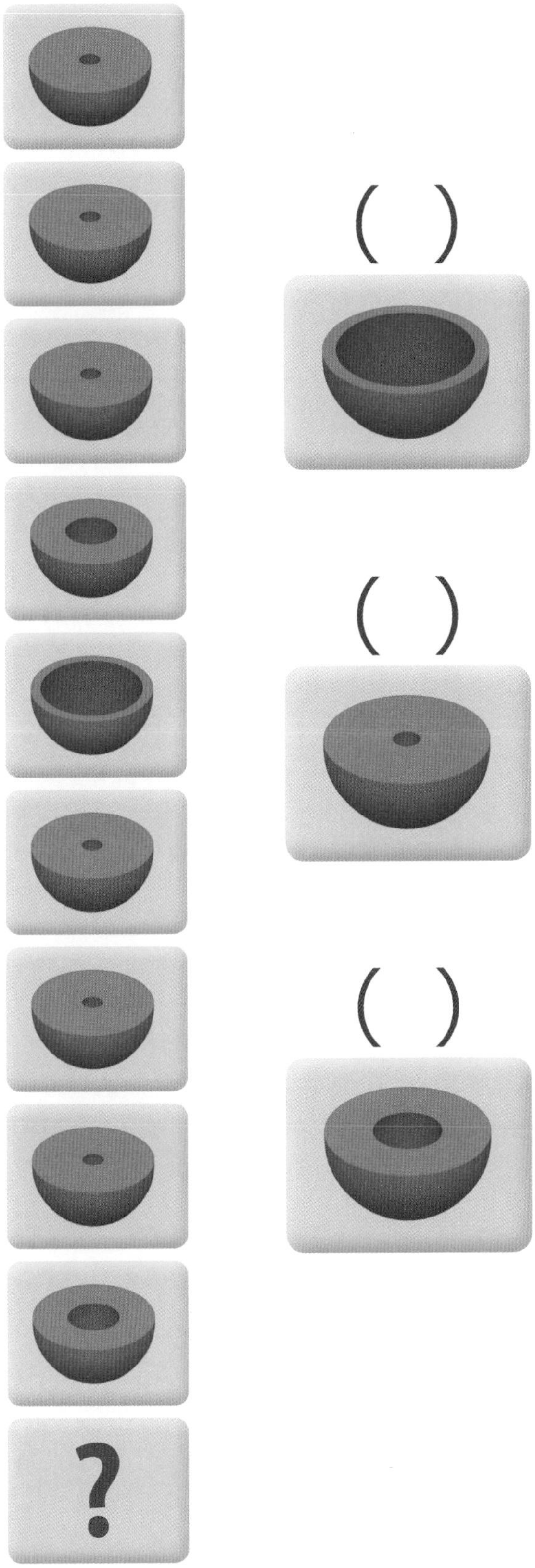

■ Write a check mark (✓) above the picture that comes next in the pattern.

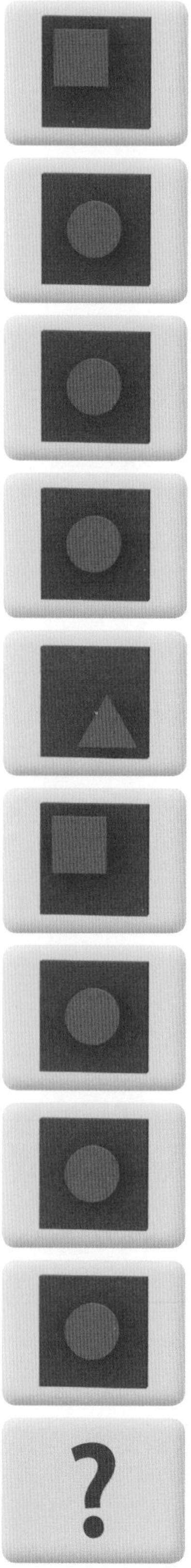

( )

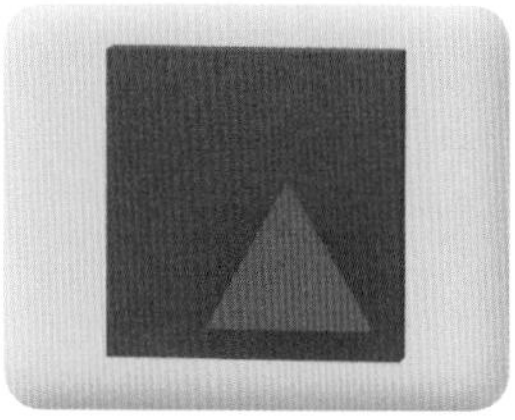

( )

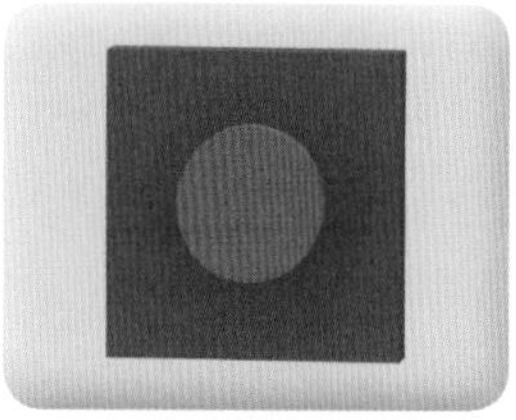

( )

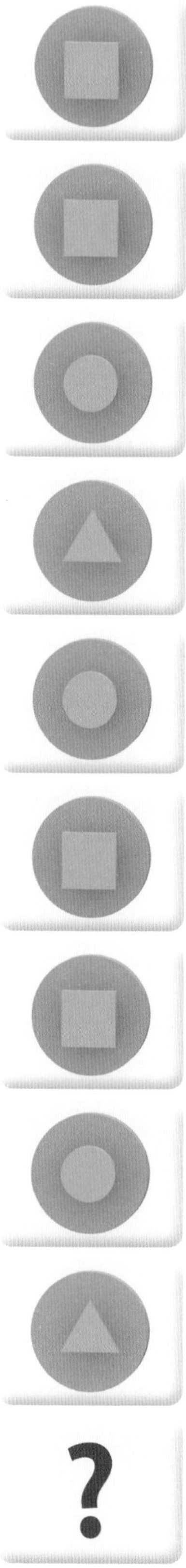

( )

( )

( )

13 Mazes
Level One

Name

Date

To parents
Do the activities along with your child if he or she has difficulty. Make sure that your child draws only vertical and horizontal lines, not diagonal lines, to connect the pictures.

■ Draw a line from the arrow (➔) to the star (★), connecting only pansies ( ).

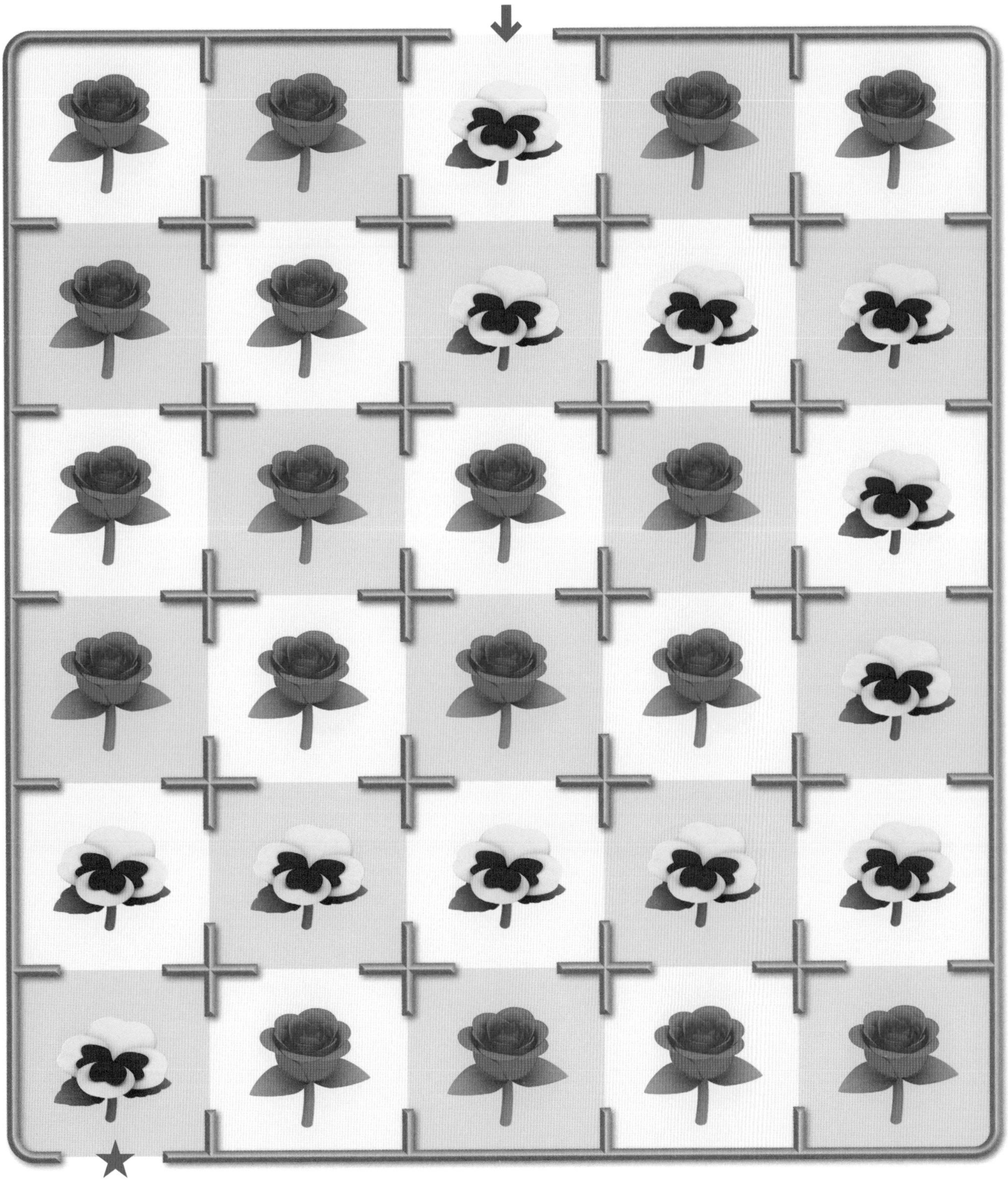

■ Draw a line from the arrow (➔) to the star (★), connecting only hamburgers ().

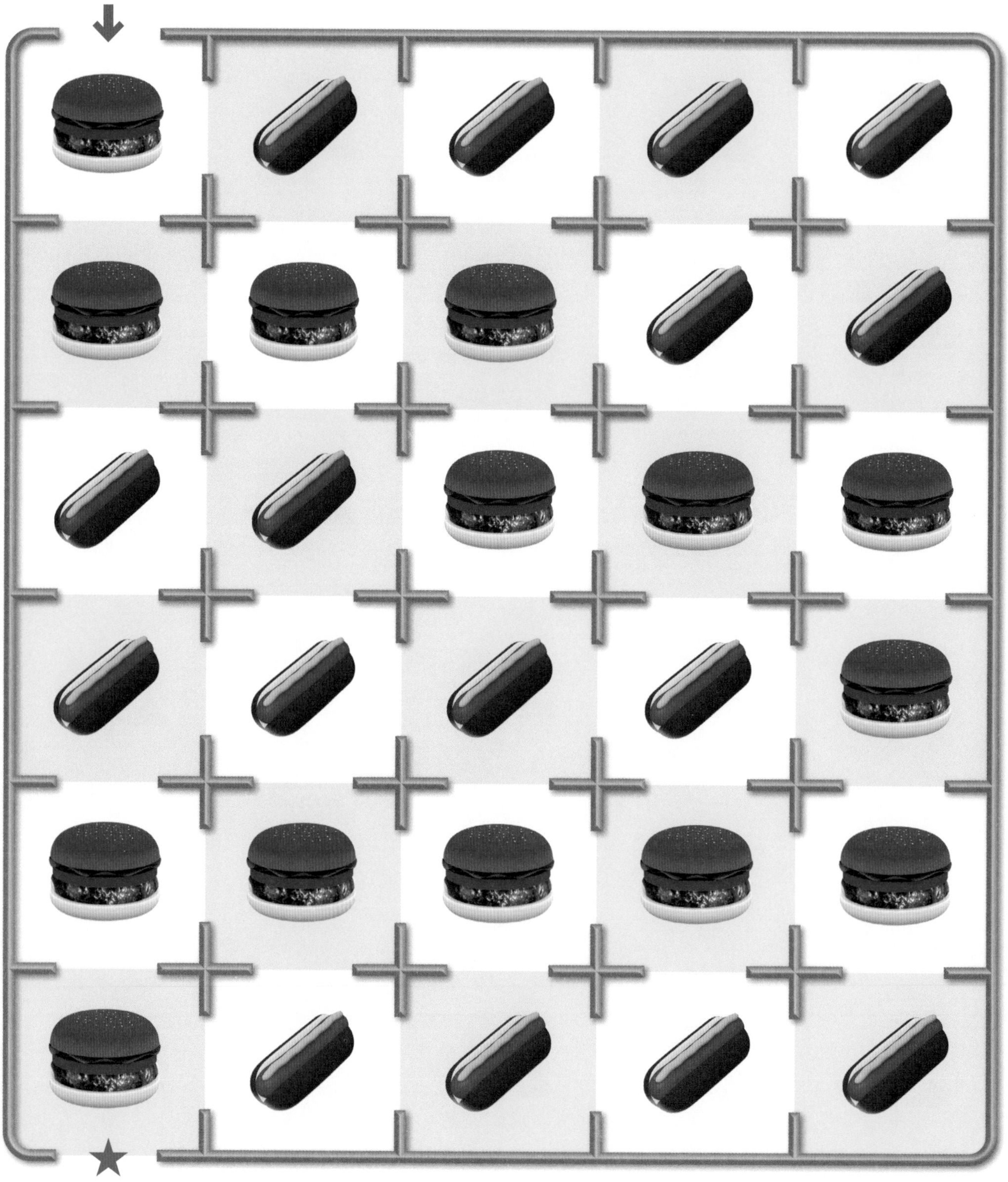

14 Mazes
Level Two

Name

Date

To parents
If your child has difficulty, encourage him or her to identify the objects out loud as he or she finds the path through the maze.

- Draw a line from the arrow (➔) to the star (★), connecting only boots ().

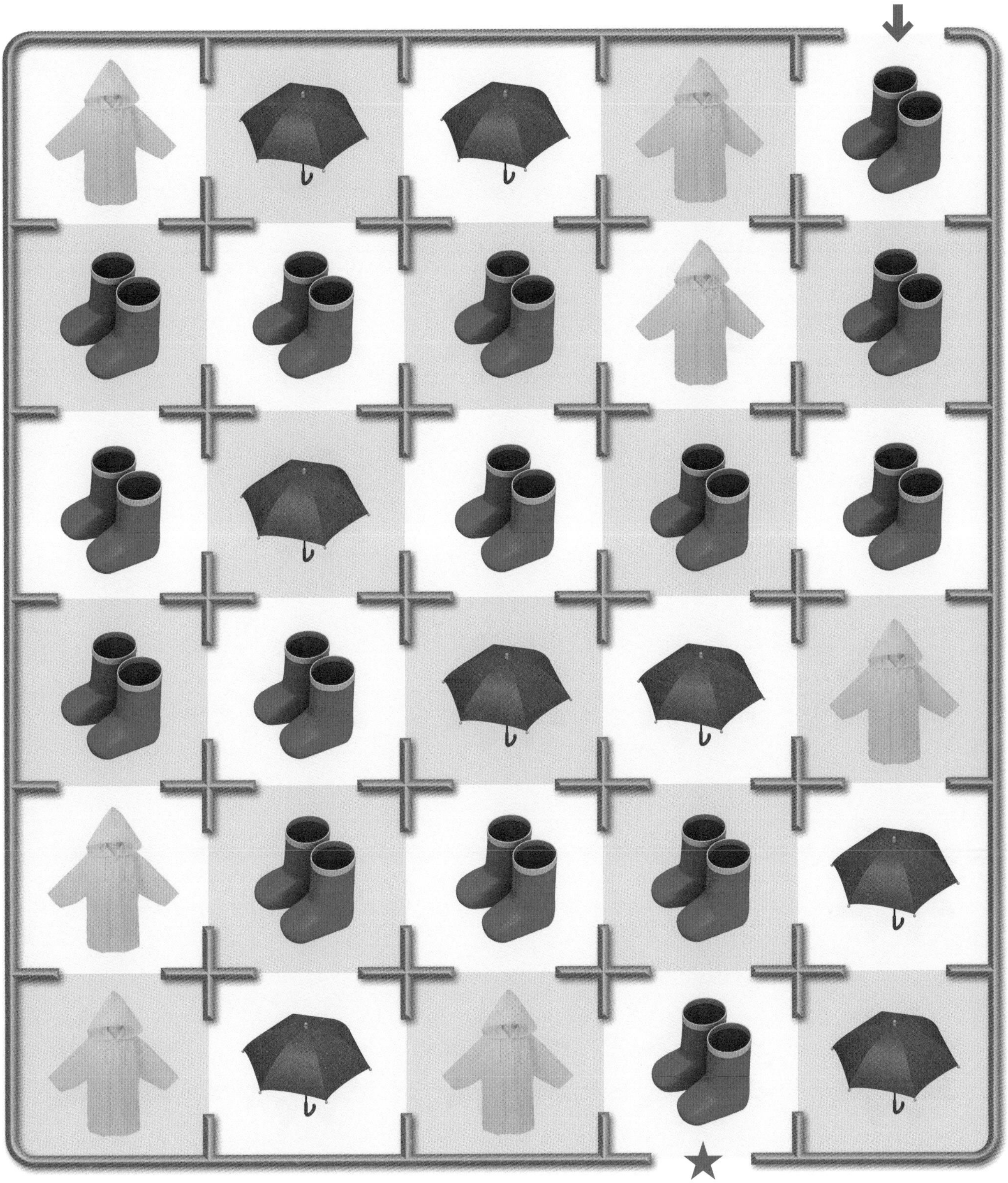

■ Draw a line from the arrow (➔) to the star (★), connecting only lions ().

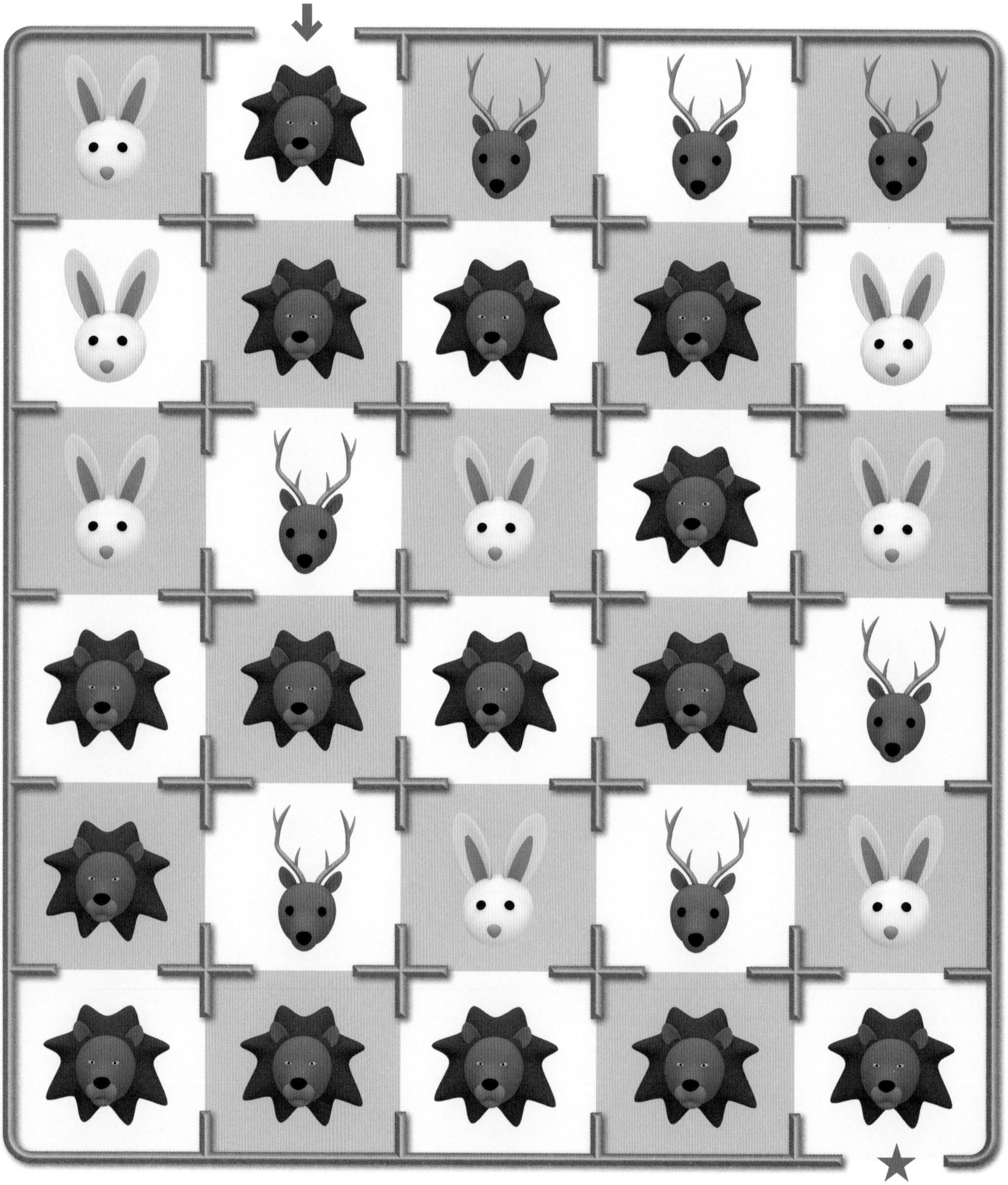

15 Mazes
Level Three

Name

Date

To parents
If your child has difficulty, help him or her understand that the path through the maze now includes two kinds of pictures.

■ Draw a line from the arrow (→) to the star (★), connecting only dandelions (dandelion) and tulips (tulip).

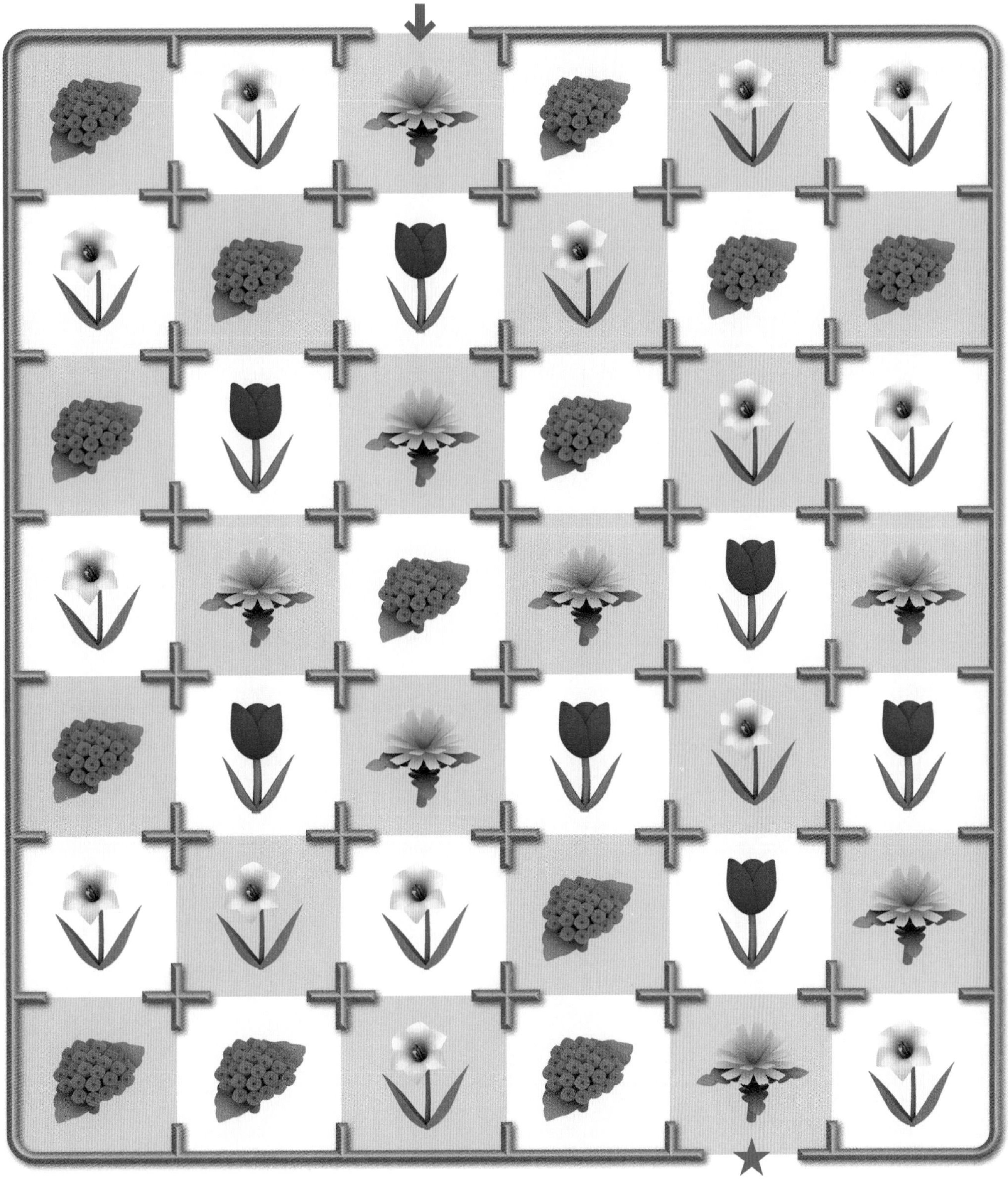

■ Draw a line from the arrow (➔) to the star (★), connecting only suns (☀) and moons (☽).

16 Mazes
Level Four

Name

Date

To parents
Five kinds of pictures are now in the maze. Encourage your child to differentiate between the pictures.

■ Draw a line from the arrow (➔) to the star (★), connecting only balls ( ) and bats ( ).

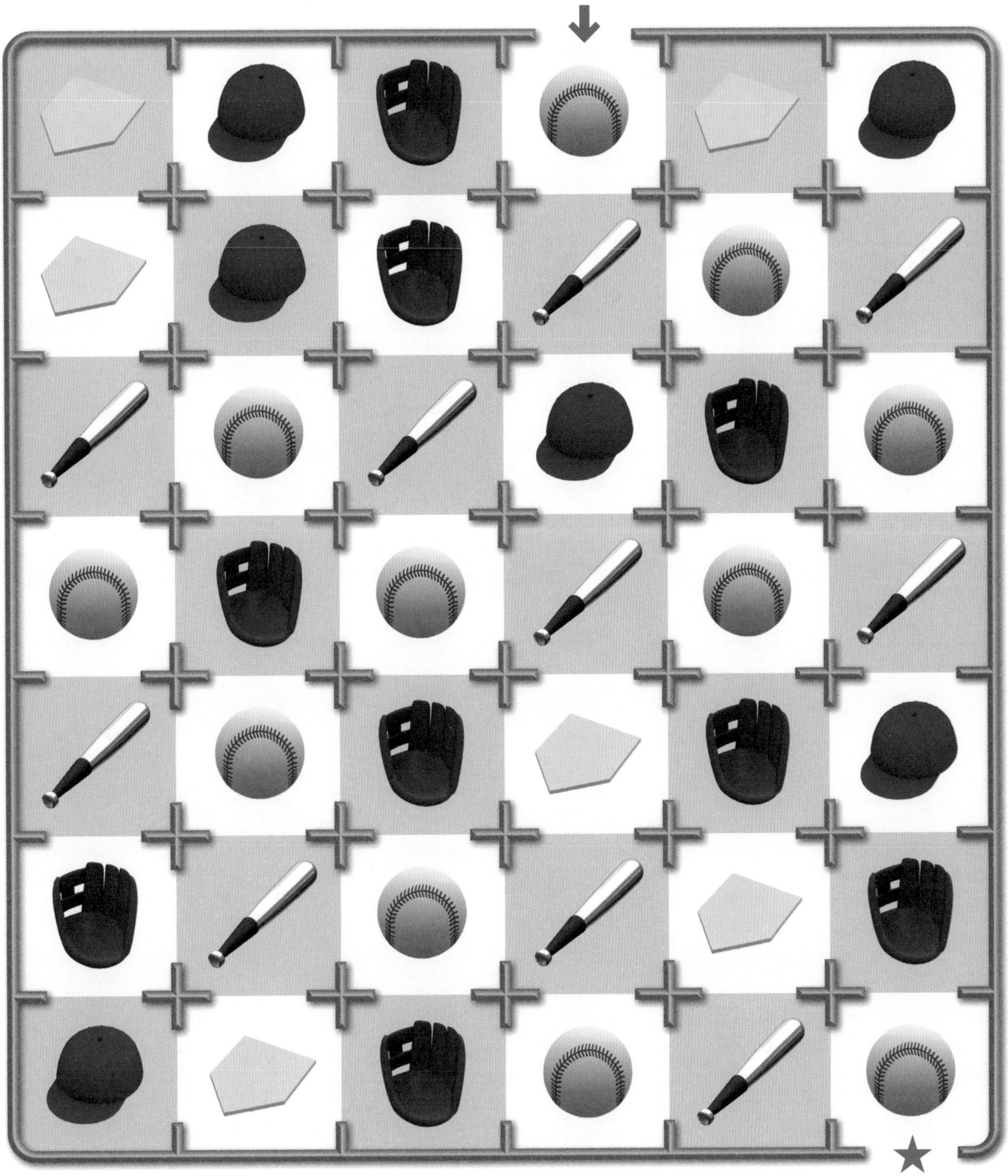

■ Draw a line from the arrow (→) to the star (★), connecting only cows ( ) and sheep ( ).

17 Mazes

Level Five

Name

Date

To parents
If your child has difficulty, help him or her understand that the path through the maze now includes three kinds of pictures.

■ Draw a line from the arrow (→) to the star (★), connecting only melons ( ), grapes ( ), and apples ( ).

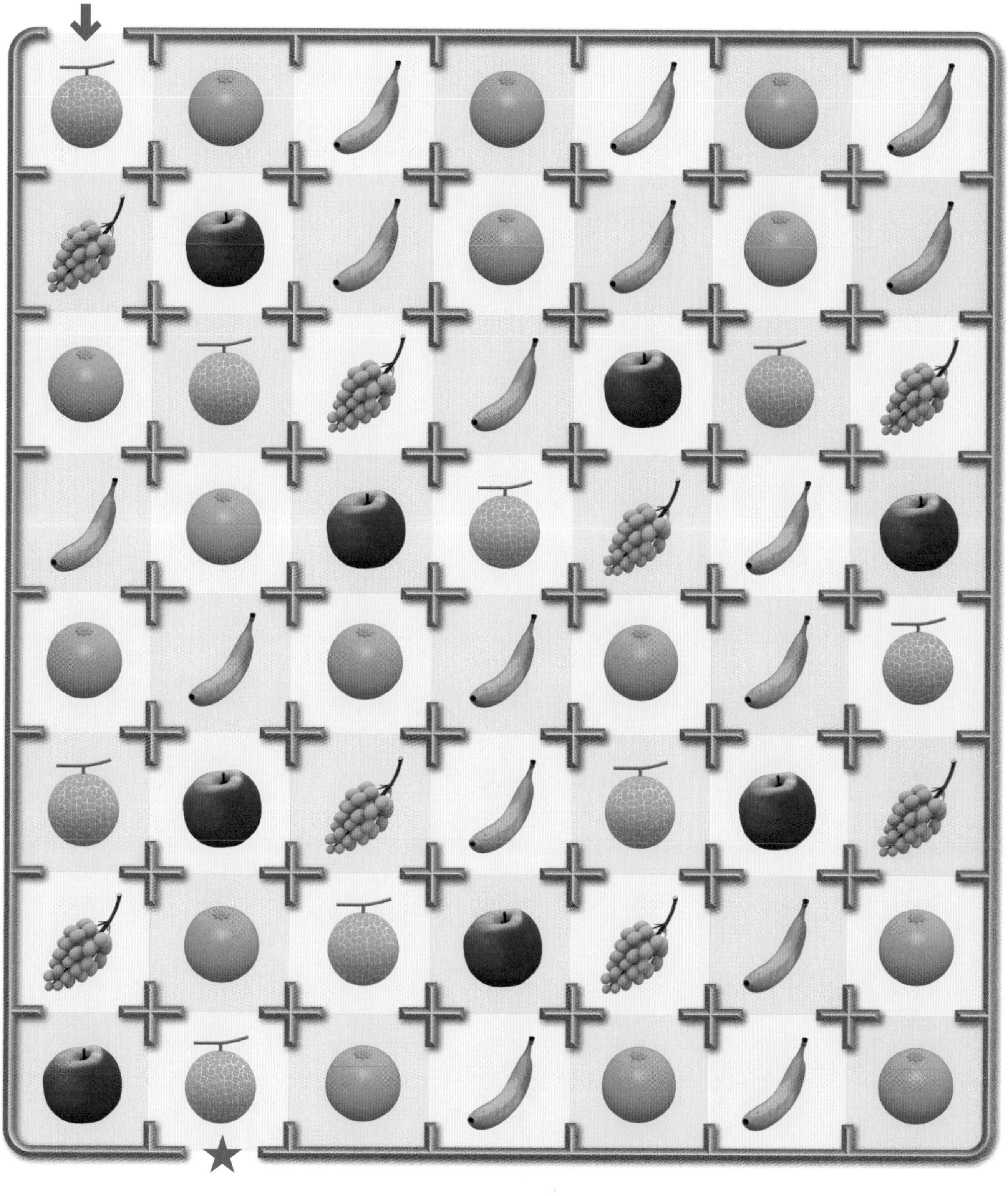

■ Draw a line from the arrow (➔) to the star (★), connecting only vests ( ), sweatshirts ( ), and T-shirts ( ).

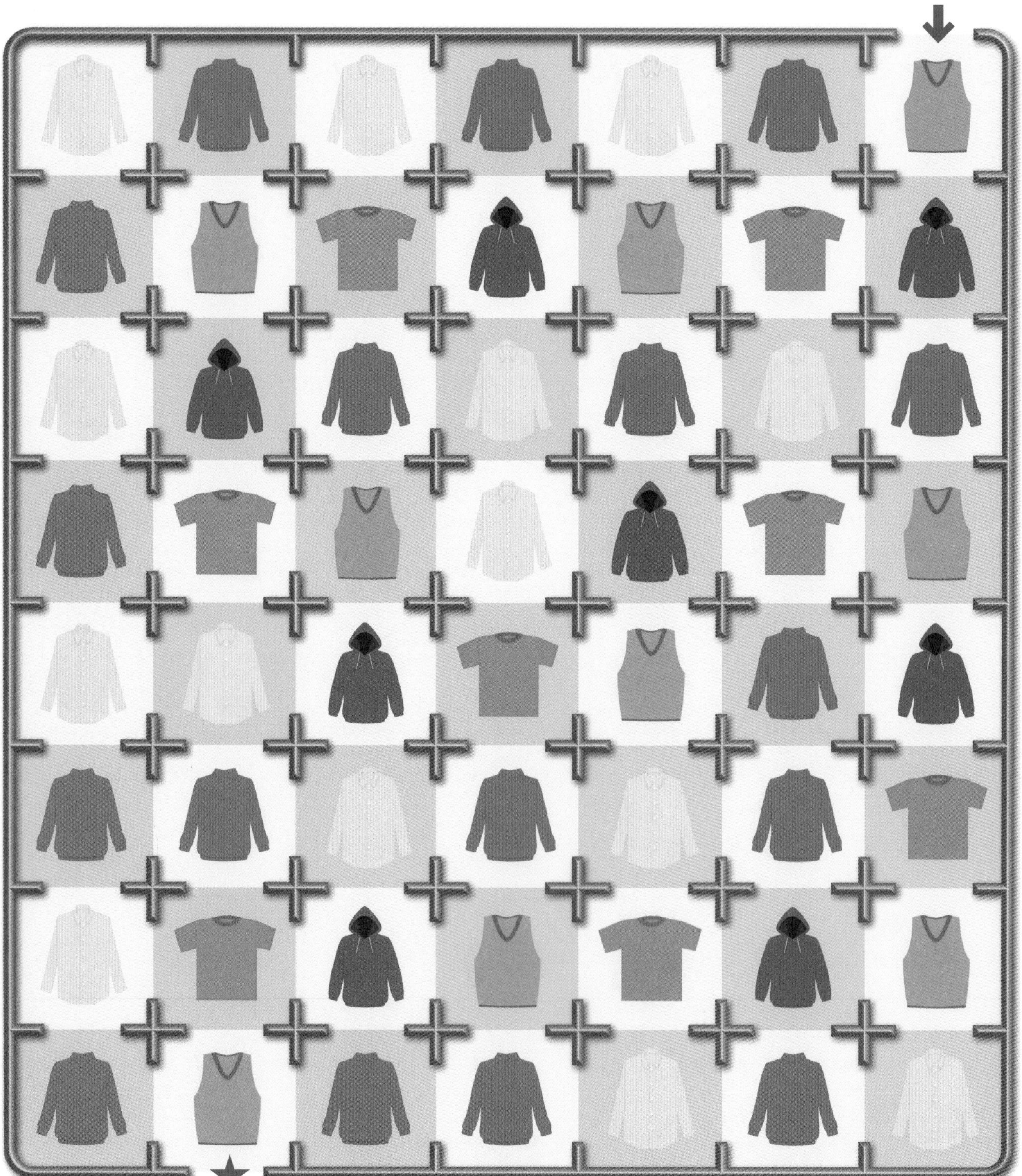

18 Mazes

Level Six

Name

Date

To parents
Six kinds of pictures are now in the maze. Encourage your child to differentiate between the pictures.

■ Draw a line from the arrow (➔) to the star (★), connecting only scissors ( ), highlighters ( ), and pencils ( ).

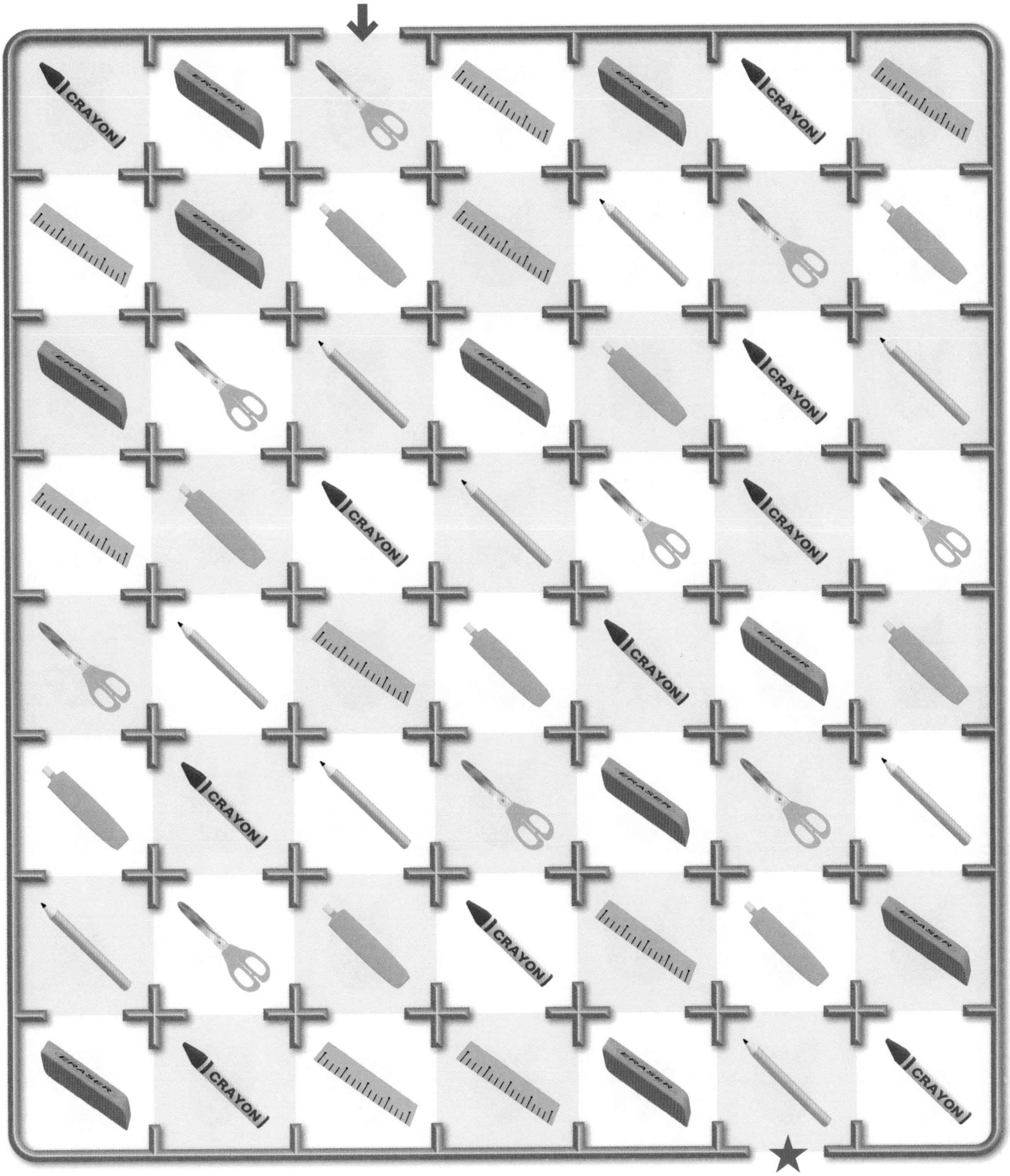

■ Draw a line from the arrow (→) to the star (★), connecting only dogs ( ), cats ( ), and pigeons ( ).

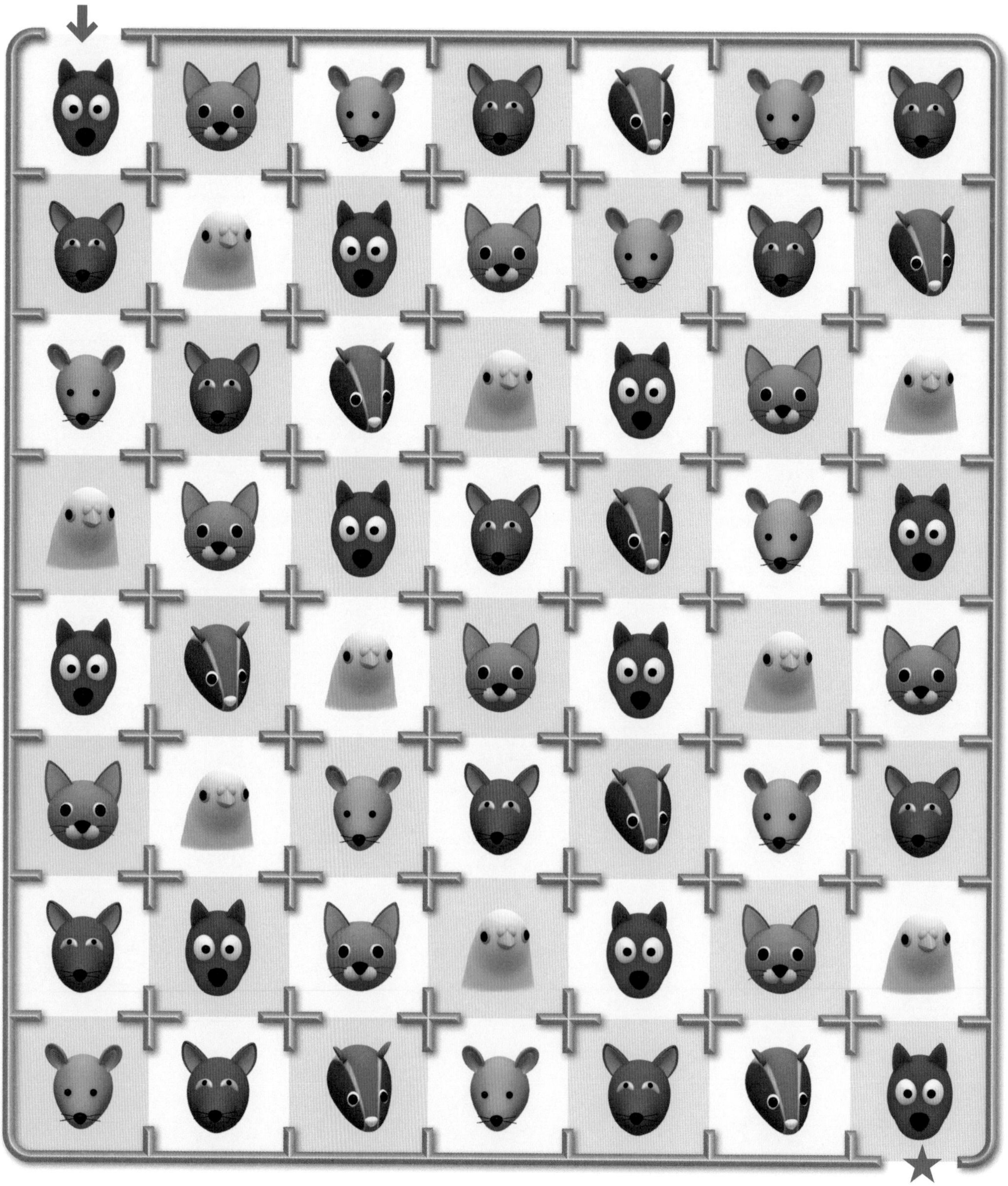

19 Real or Pretend

Level One

Name

Date

To parents
Guide your child to find the parts of each picture that do not happen in real life.

■ Circle the three parts of the picture that are pretend.

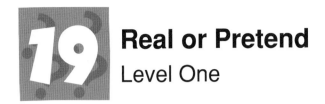

■ Circle the three parts of the picture that are pretend.

20 Real or Pretend
Level Two

Name

Date

To parents
If your child has difficulty, ask him or her to describe the picture.

■ Circle the four parts of the picture that are pretend.

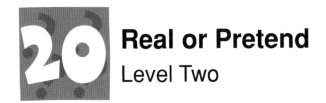

■ Circle the four parts of the picture that are pretend.

21 Real or Pretend
Level Three

Name

Date

To parents
If your child has difficulty, ask him or her to find something in the picture that does not happen in real life.

■ Circle the five parts of the picture that are pretend.

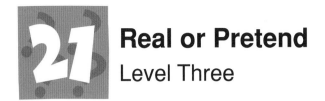

■ Circle the five parts of the picture that are pretend.

22

Real or Pretend

Level Four

Name

Date

To parents
The number of pretend events has increased. Encourage your child to find all of them.

■ Circle the six parts of the picture that are pretend.

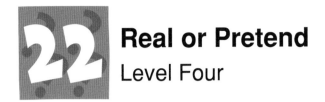

■ Circle the six parts of the picture that are pretend.

23 Patterns with Rotating Blocks

One Quarter Turn

Name

Date

To parents
The cube has been rotated one quarter turn. If your child has difficulty, it may help to rotate this workbook a quarter turn.

■ Write a check mark (✓) above the picture that comes next in the pattern.

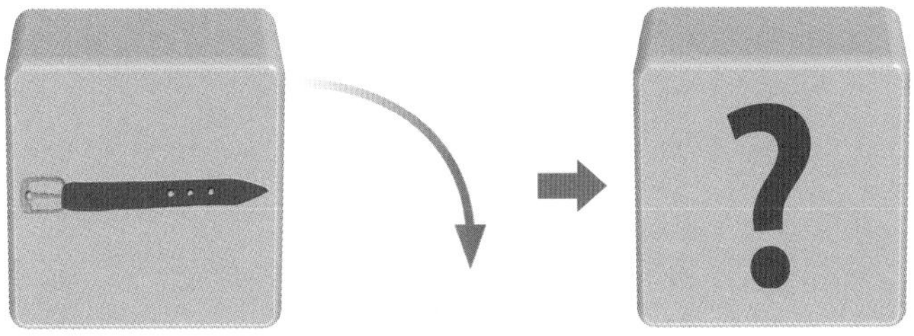

(✓)

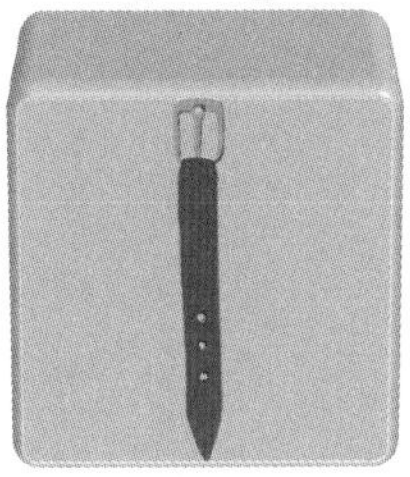

( )

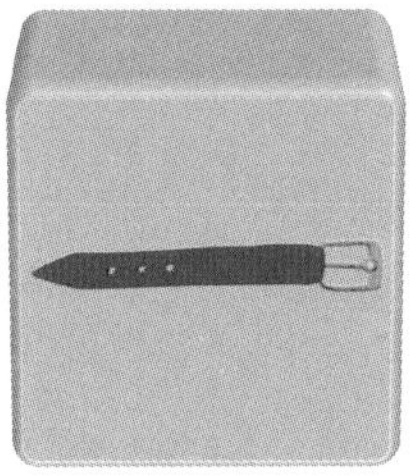

( )

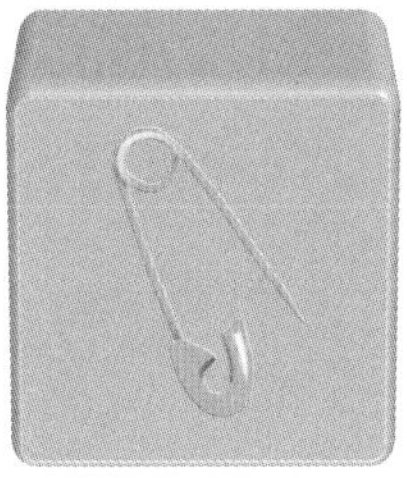

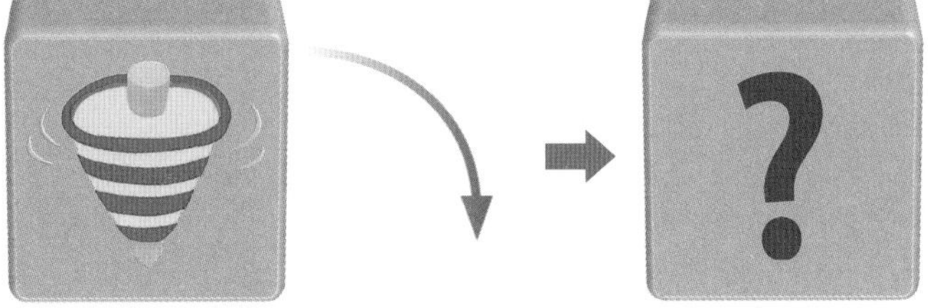

( )

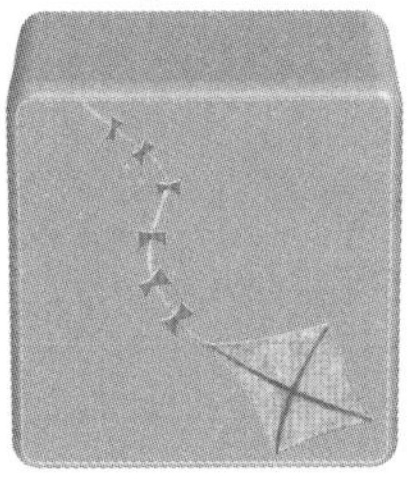

( )

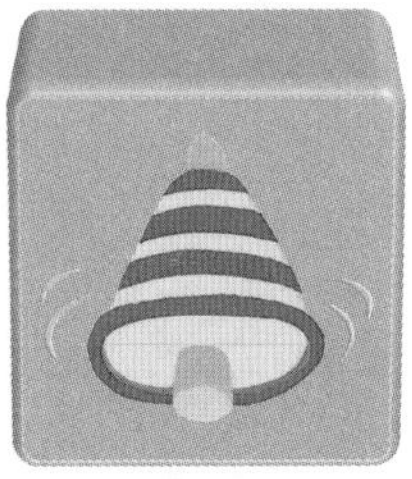

( )

■ Write a check mark (✓) above the picture that comes next in the pattern.

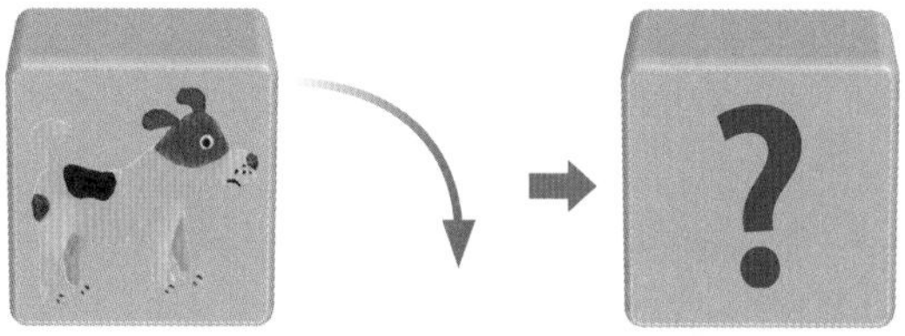

( )

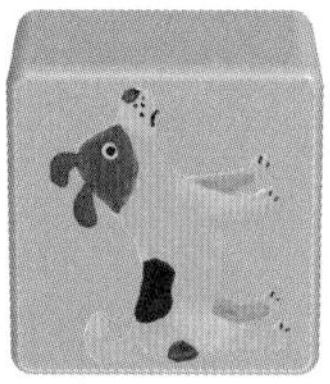

( )

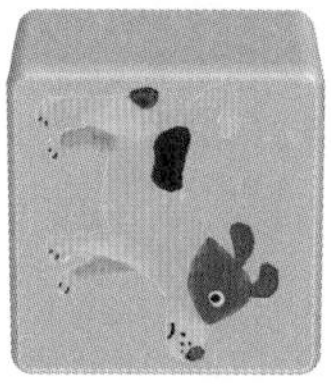

( )

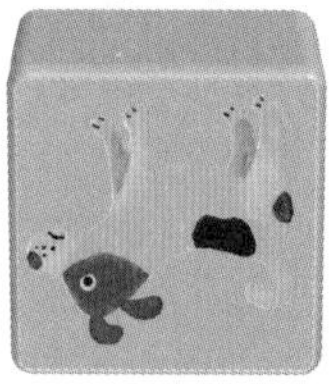

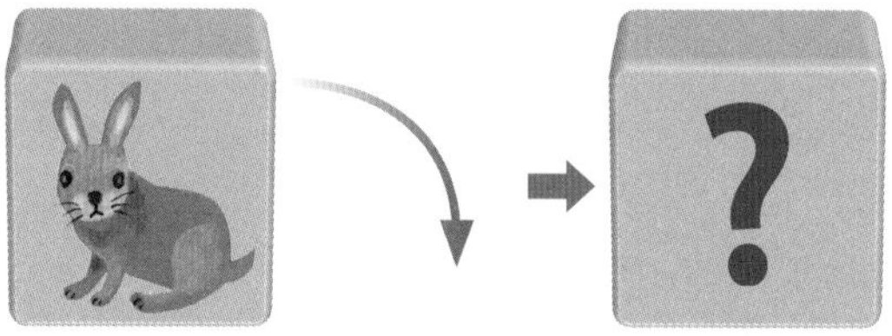

( )

( )

( )

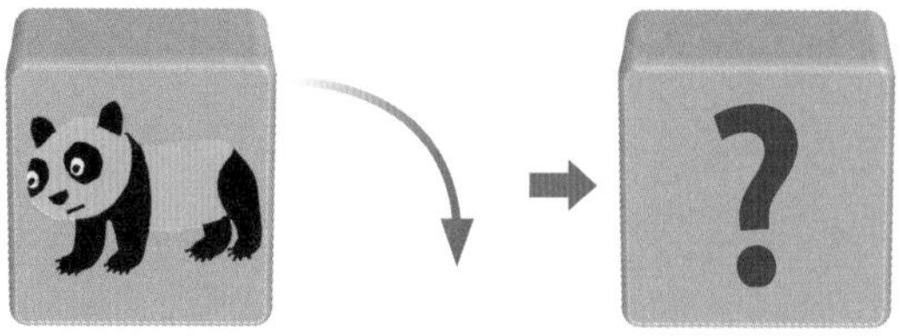

( )

( )

( )

24 Patterns with Rotating Blocks

Two Quarter Turns

Name

Date

To parents
Help your child understand that the cube is upside down after two quarter turns.

■ Write a check mark (✓) above the picture that comes next in the pattern.

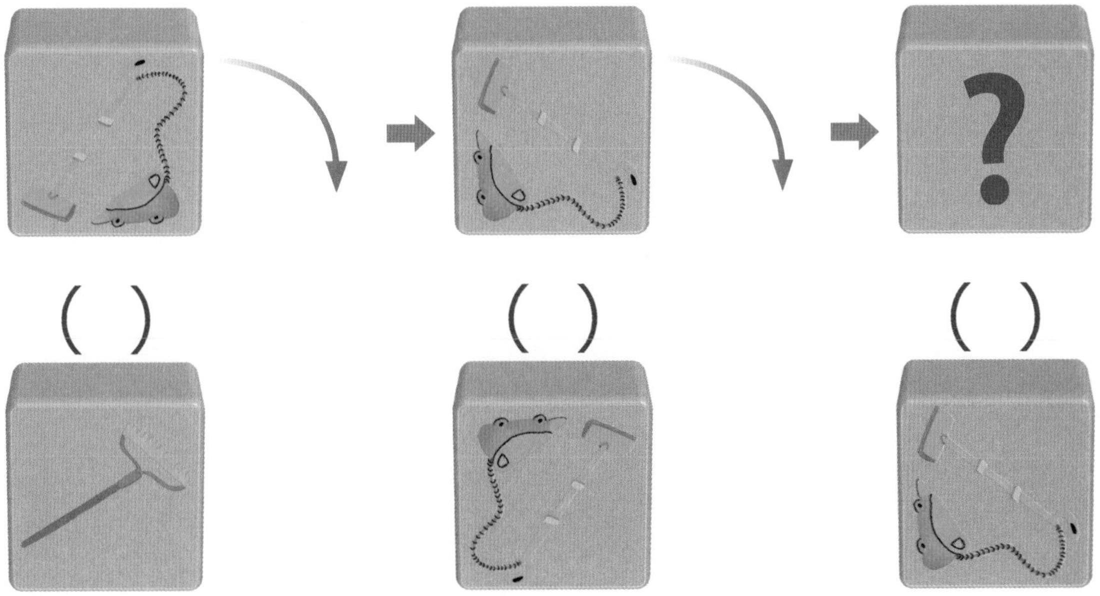

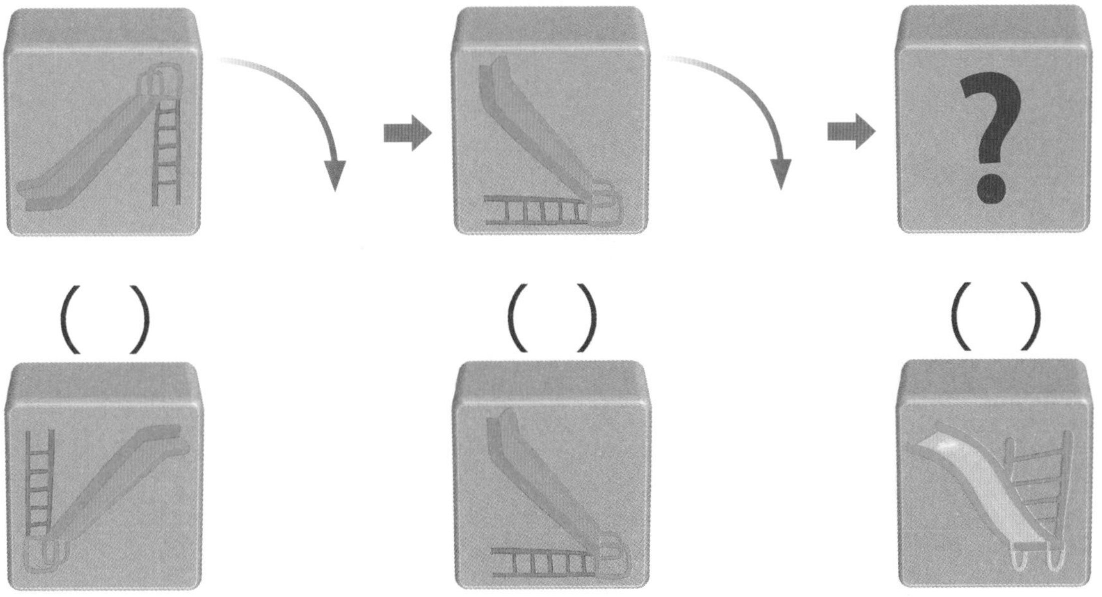

■ Write a check mark (✓) above the picture that comes next in the pattern.

( ) ( ) ( )

( ) ( ) ( )

( ) ( ) ( )

25 Patterns with Rotating Blocks

Three Quarter Turns

Name

Date

To parents
The cube has been rotated three quarter turns. If your child has difficulty, it may help to rotate this workbook three quarter turns.

■ Write a check mark (✓) above the picture that comes next in the pattern.

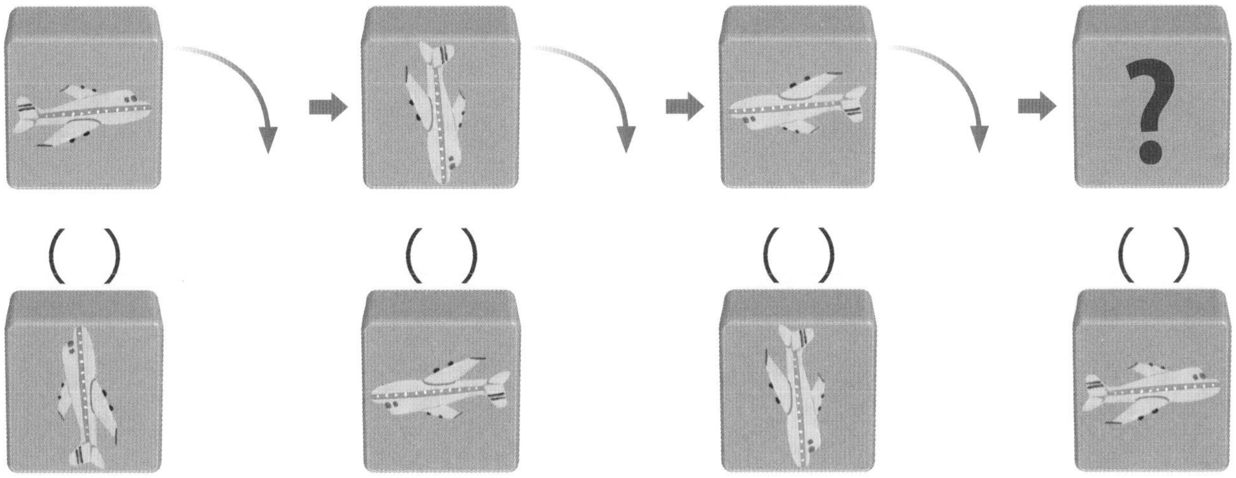

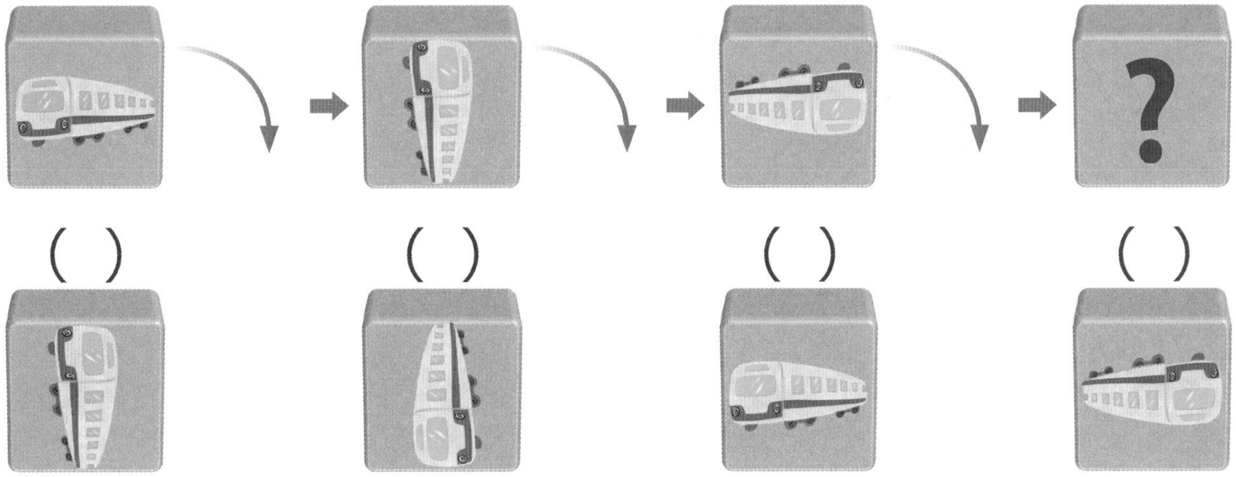

■ Write a check mark (✓) above the picture that comes next in the pattern.

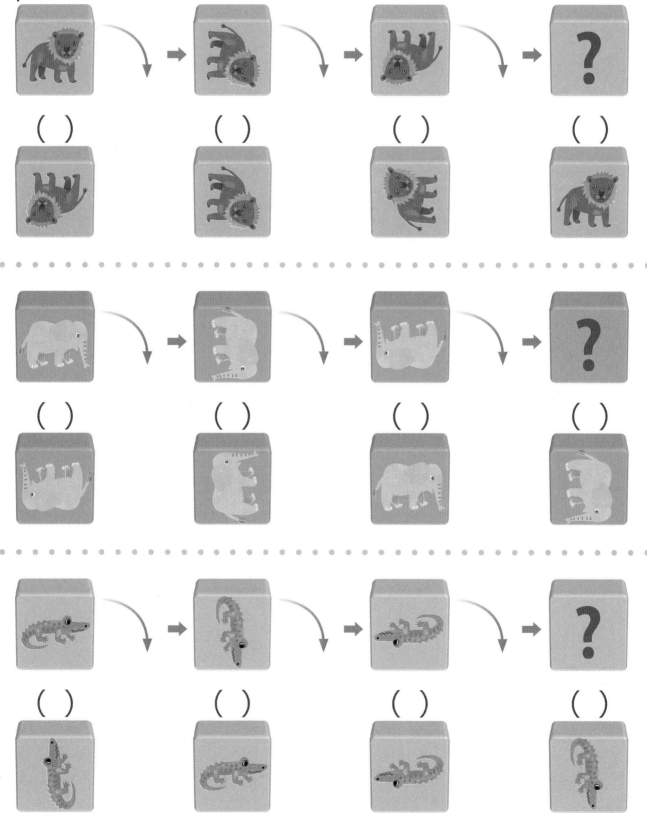

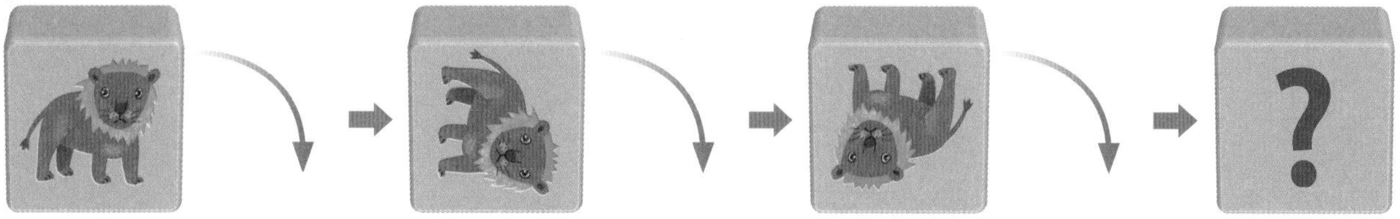

( ) ( ) ( ) ( )

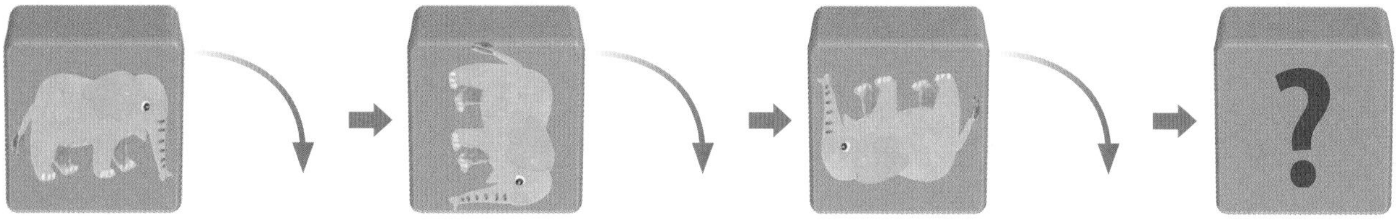

( ) ( ) ( ) ( )

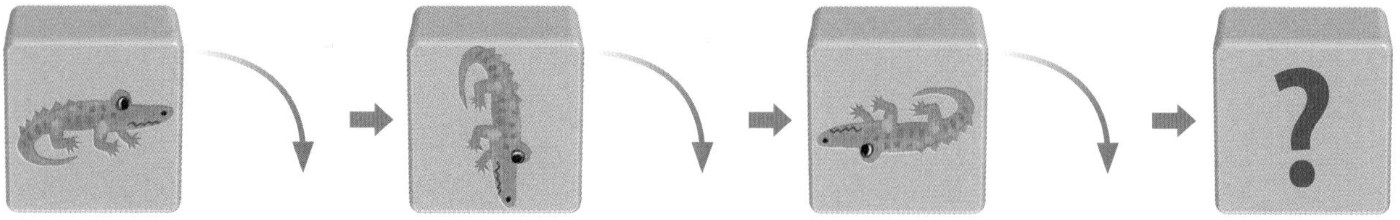

( ) ( ) ( ) ( )

26 Patterns with Rotating Blocks

One to Three Quarter Turns

Name

Date

To parents
After this activity, you may wish to ask your child what the picture on a cube would look like after four quarter turns.

■ Write a check mark (✓) above the picture that comes next in the pattern.

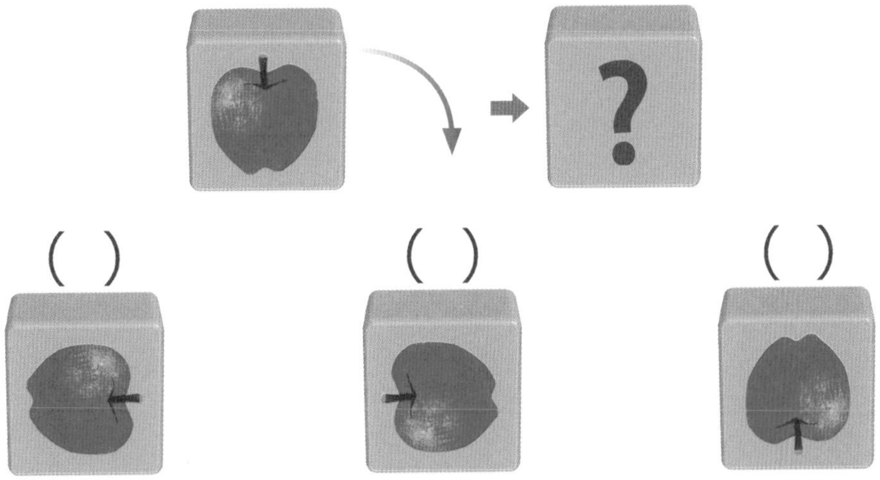

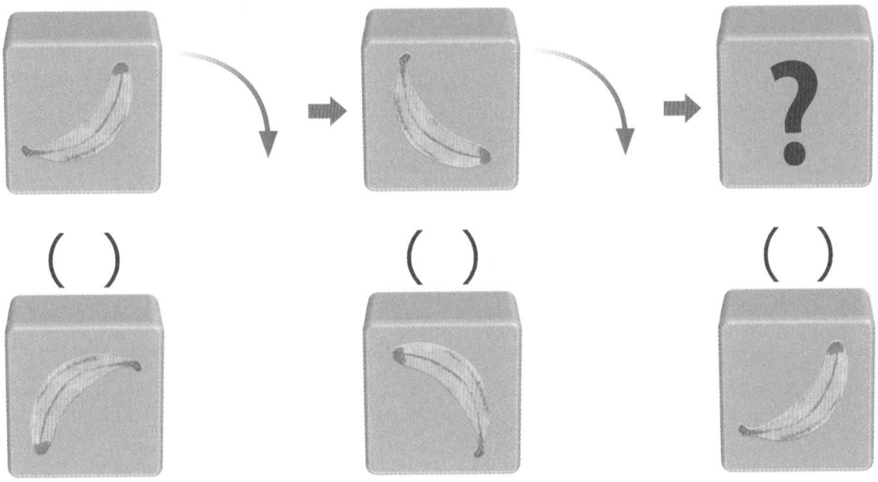

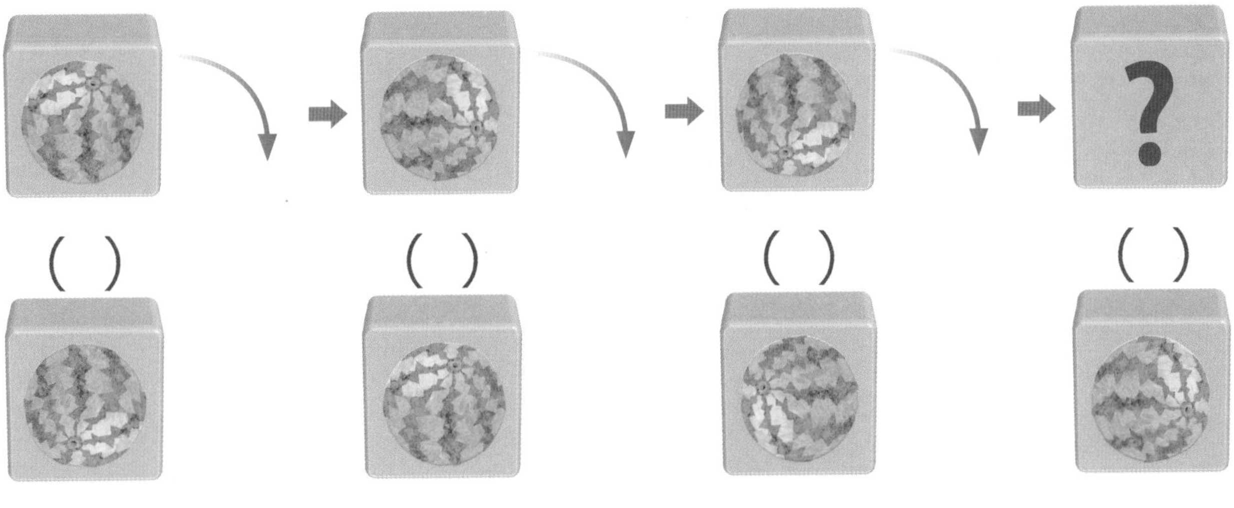

■ Write a check mark (✓) above the picture that comes next in the pattern.

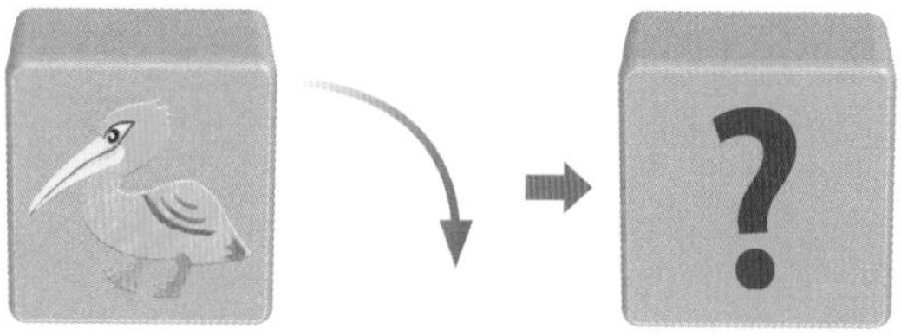

( ) ( ) ( )

( ) ( ) ( )

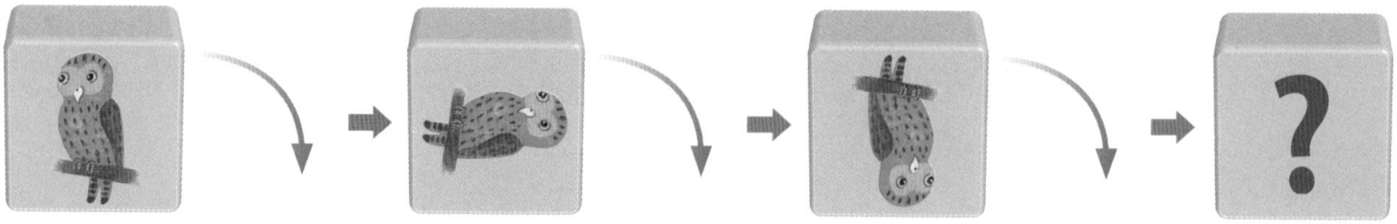

( ) ( ) ( ) ( )

27 Pattern Puzzles
Level One

Name

Date

To parents
Guide your child to use the complete sequence shown in the top picture to choose the correct answer.

■ Write a check mark (✓) above the picture that shows the missing ball.

( ) ( ) ( ) ( ) ( )

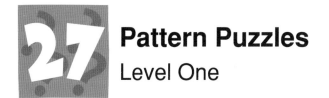

■ Write a check mark (✓) above the picture that shows the missing animal.

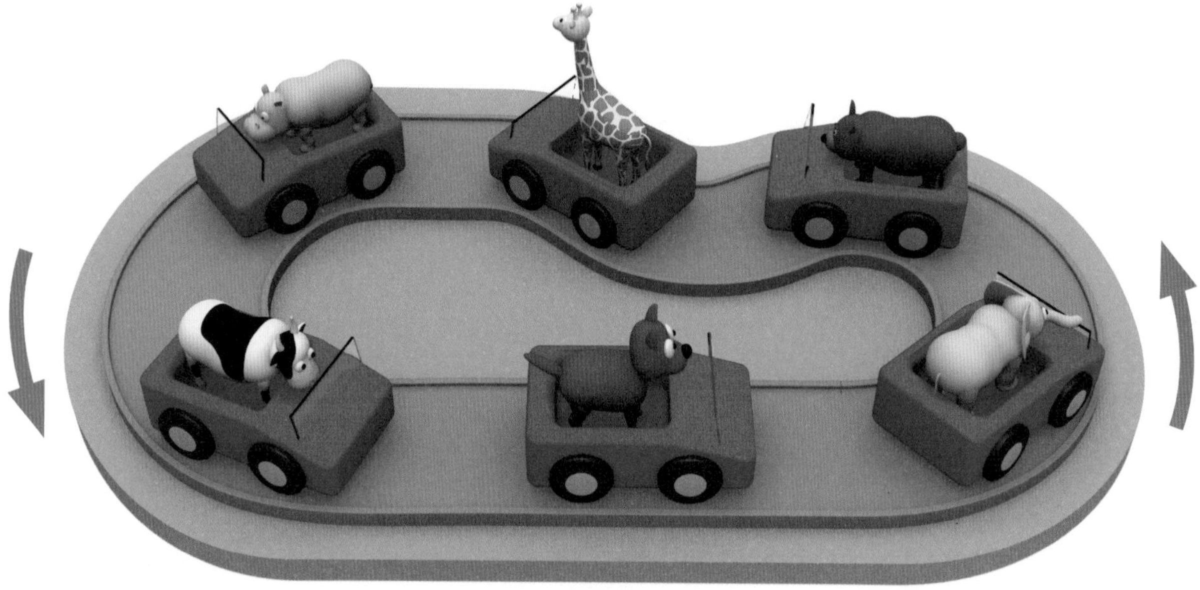

( ) ( ) ( ) ( ) ( ) ( )

28 Pattern Puzzles
Level Two

Name

Date

To parents
If your child has difficulty, ask him or her how many positions an animal has moved.

■ Write a check mark (✓) above the picture that shows the missing animal.

( ) ( ) ( ) ( ) ( ) ( ) ( )

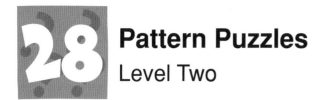

■ Write a check mark (✓) above the picture that shows the missing animal.

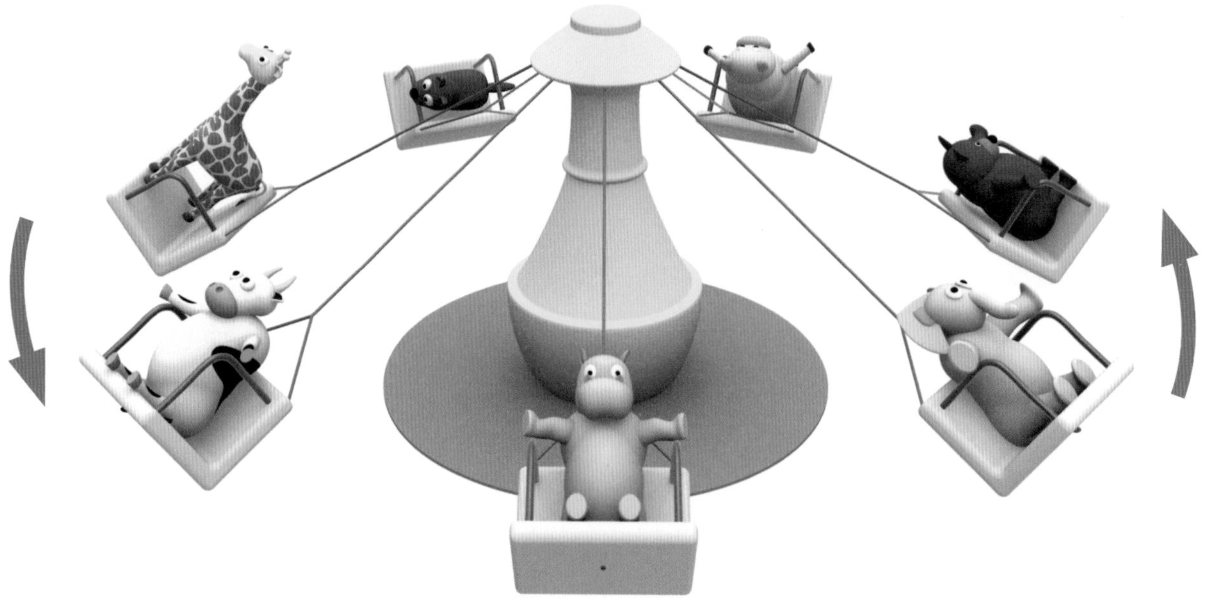

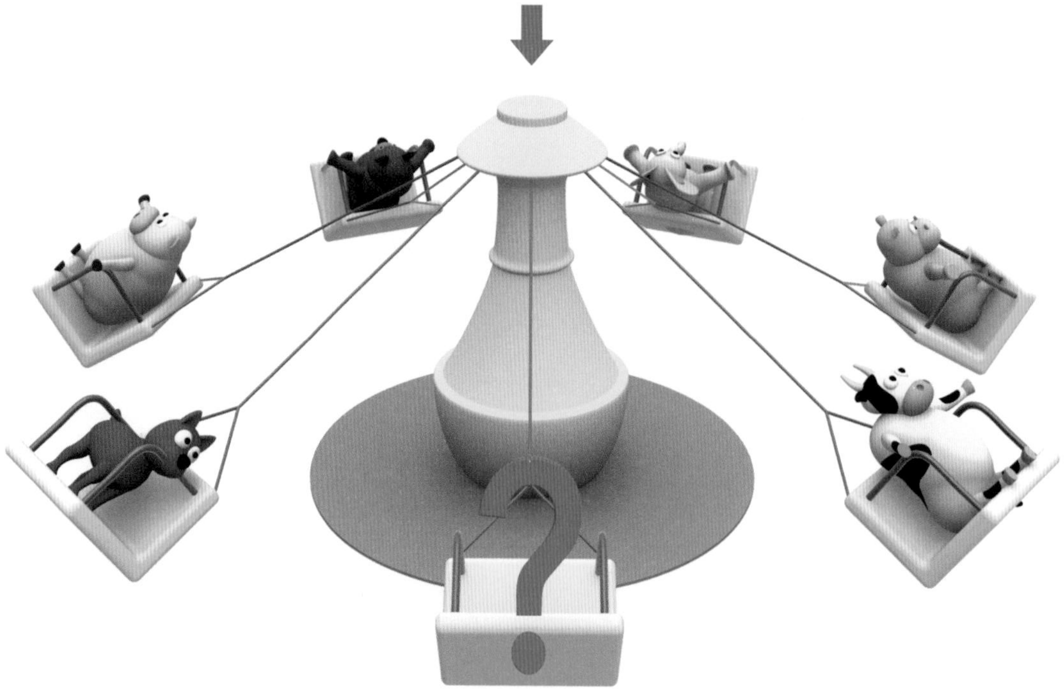

(　)　(　)　(　)　(　)　(　)　(　)　(　)

29 Pattern Puzzles

Level Three

Name

Date

To parents
The activities are now more difficult because part of the sequence is hidden. Encourage your child to find a pattern.

■ Write a check mark (✓) above the picture that shows the missing ball.

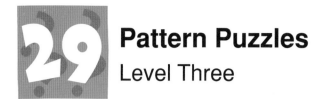

■ Write a check mark (✓) above the picture that shows the missing animal.

( ) ( ) ( ) ( ) ( )

30 Pattern Puzzles
Level Four

Name

Date

To parents
To identify the missing animal, it may help to identify which animals are hidden.

■ Write a check mark (✓) above the picture that shows the missing animal.

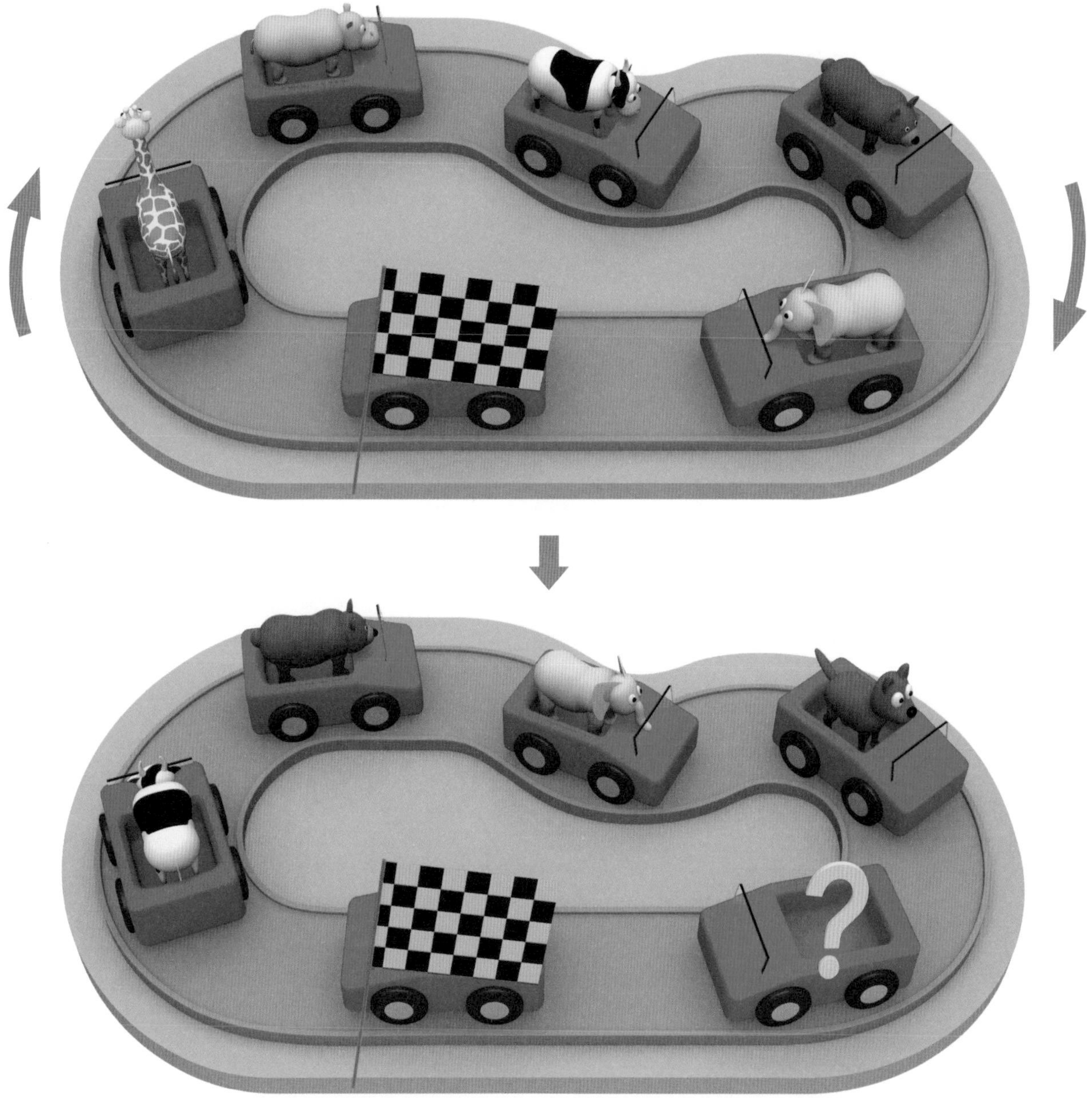

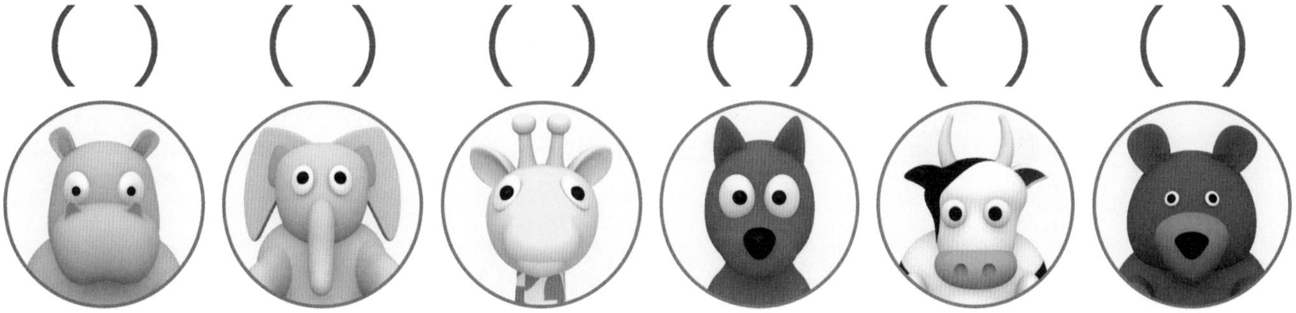

■ Write a check mark (✓) above the picture that shows the missing animal.

( ) ( ) ( ) ( ) ( ) ( )

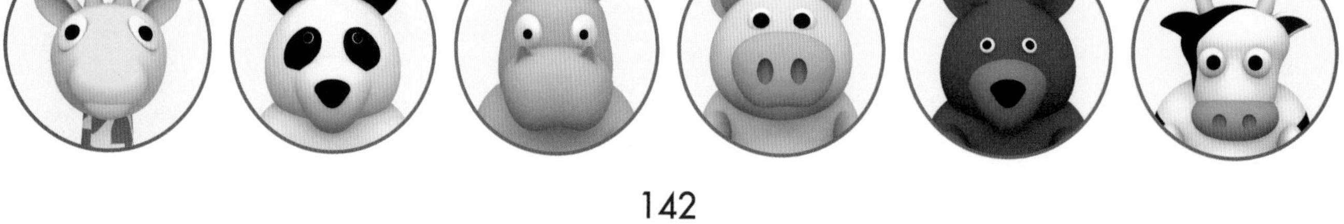

31 Pattern Puzzles

Level Five

Name

Date

To parents
If your child has difficulty, it may help for your child to trace the direction of rotation with his or her finger.

■ Write a check mark (✓) above the picture that shows the missing animal.

( ) ( ) ( ) ( ) ( ) ( ) ( )

■ Write a check mark (✓) above the picture that shows the missing animal.

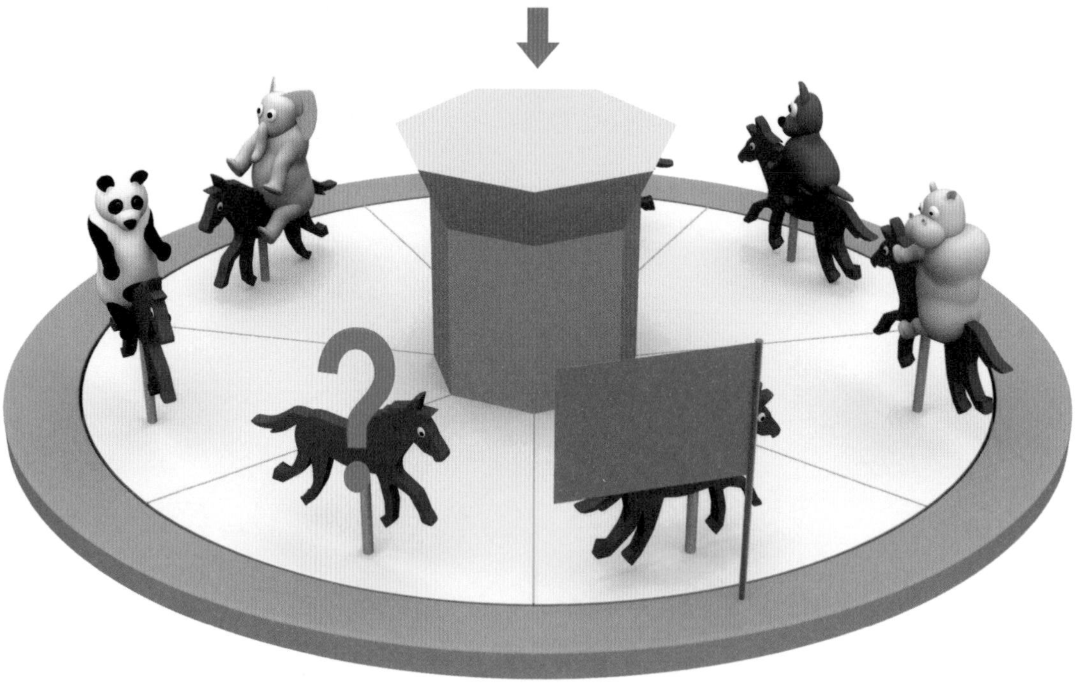

( ) ( ) ( ) ( ) ( ) ( ) ( )

32 Pattern Puzzles
Level Six

Name

Date

To parents
The number of animals has increased. If your child has difficulty, it may help for your child to count how many positions an animal has moved.

■ Write a check mark (✓) above the picture that shows the missing animal.

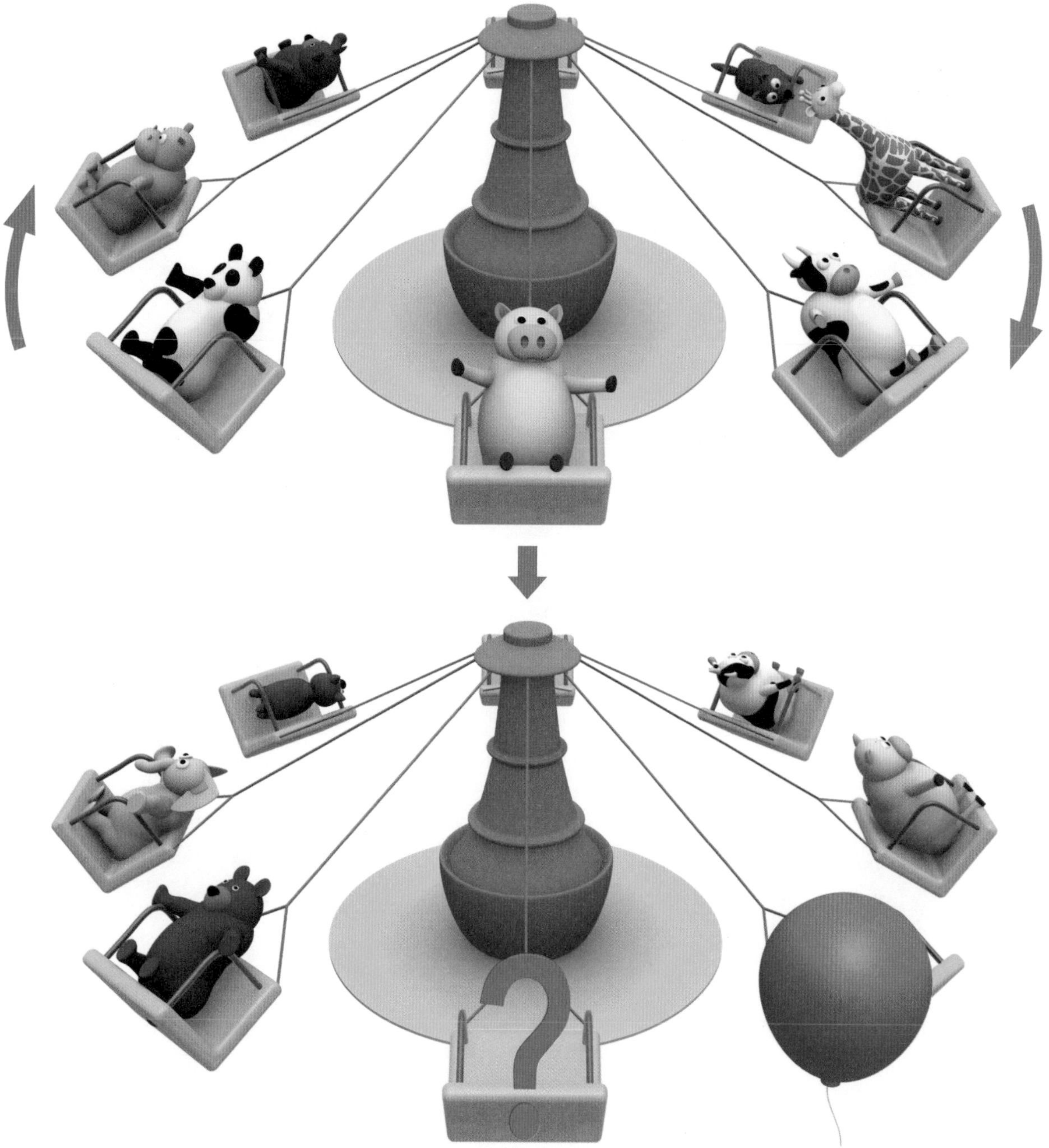

■ Write a check mark (✓) above the picture that shows the missing animal.

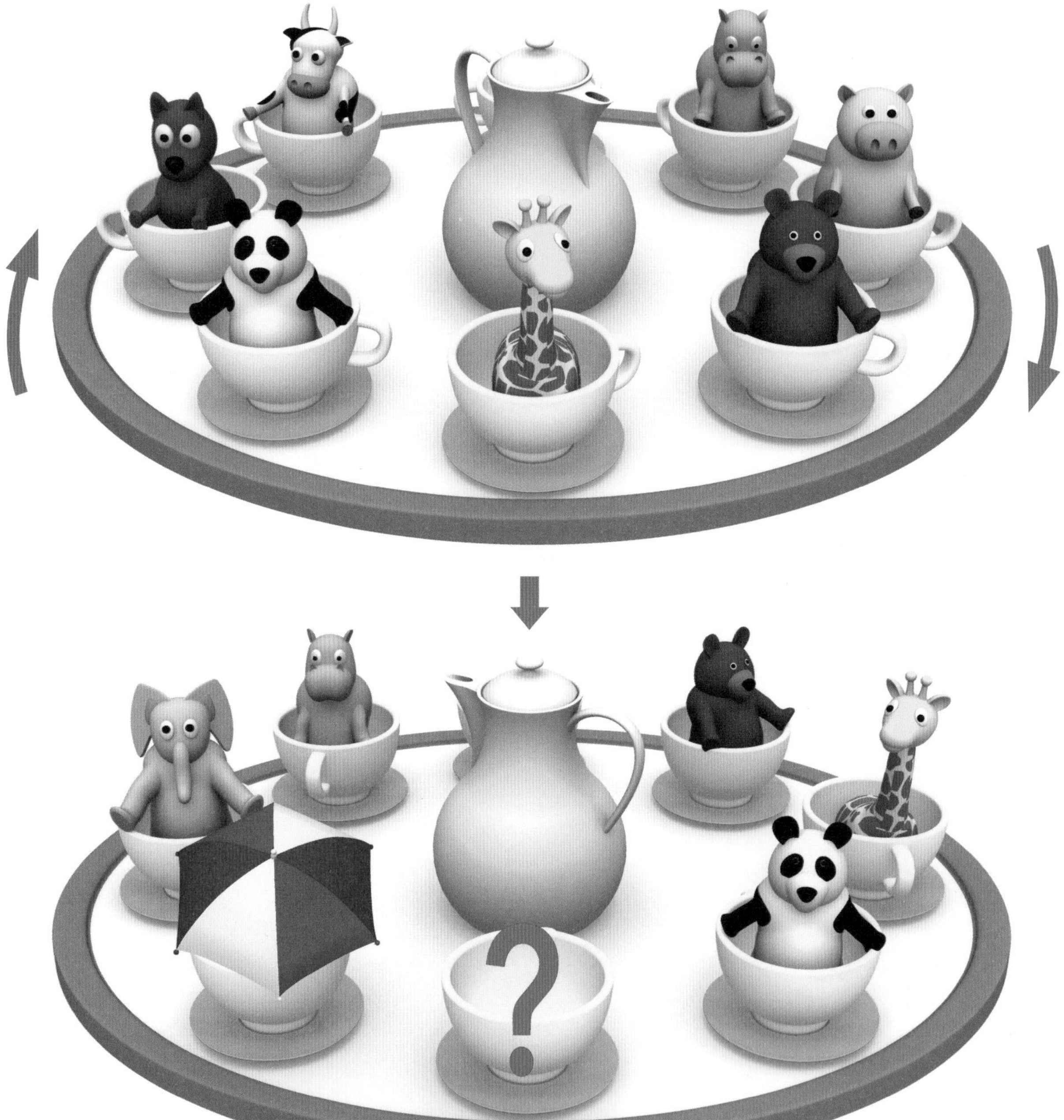

( ) ( ) ( ) ( ) ( ) ( ) ( ) ( )

33 Color and Shape Patterns
Level One

Name

Date

To parents
Colored pencils work best for these activities because the shape will remain visible after coloring.

■ Follow the pattern to color the picture in the margin.

■ Follow the pattern to color the correct picture in the margin.

34 Color and Shape Patterns

Level Two

Name

Date

To parents
If your child has difficulty with this exercise, guide him or her to select the shape first and then the color.

■ Follow the pattern to color the correct picture in the margin.

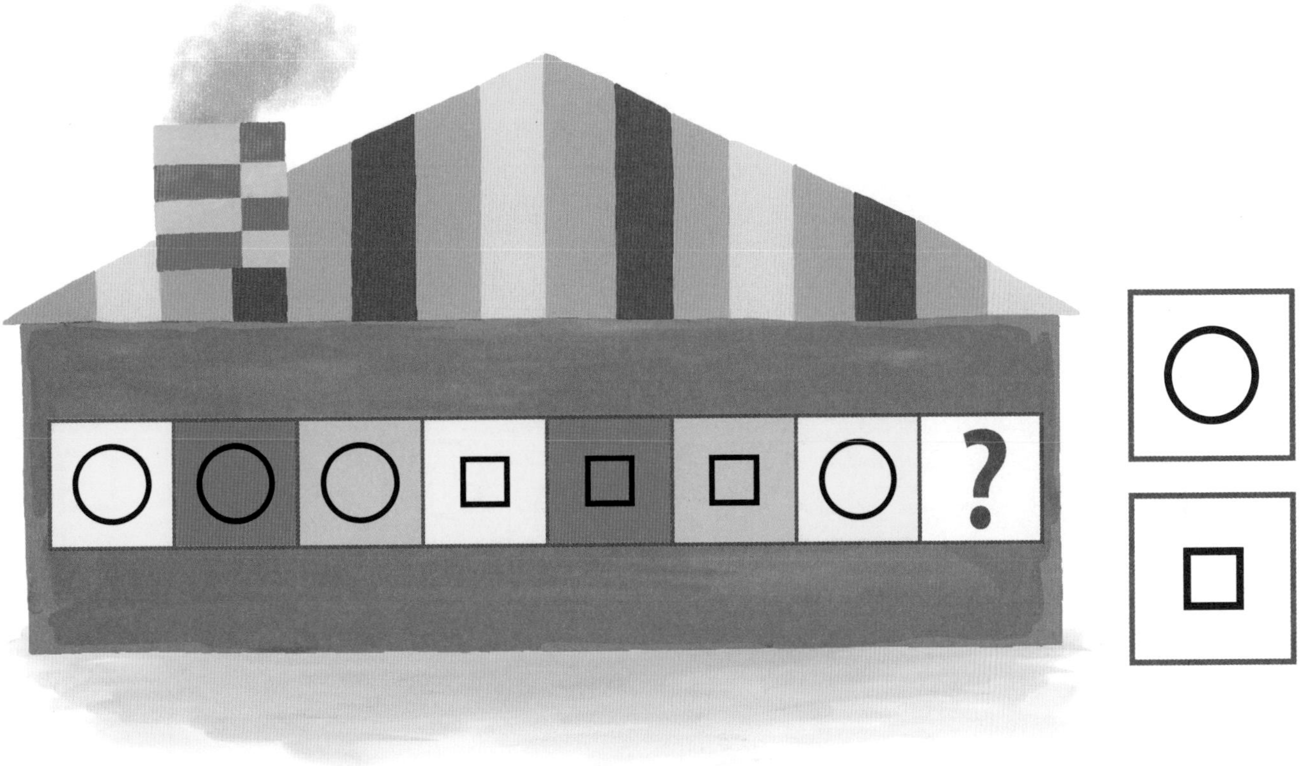

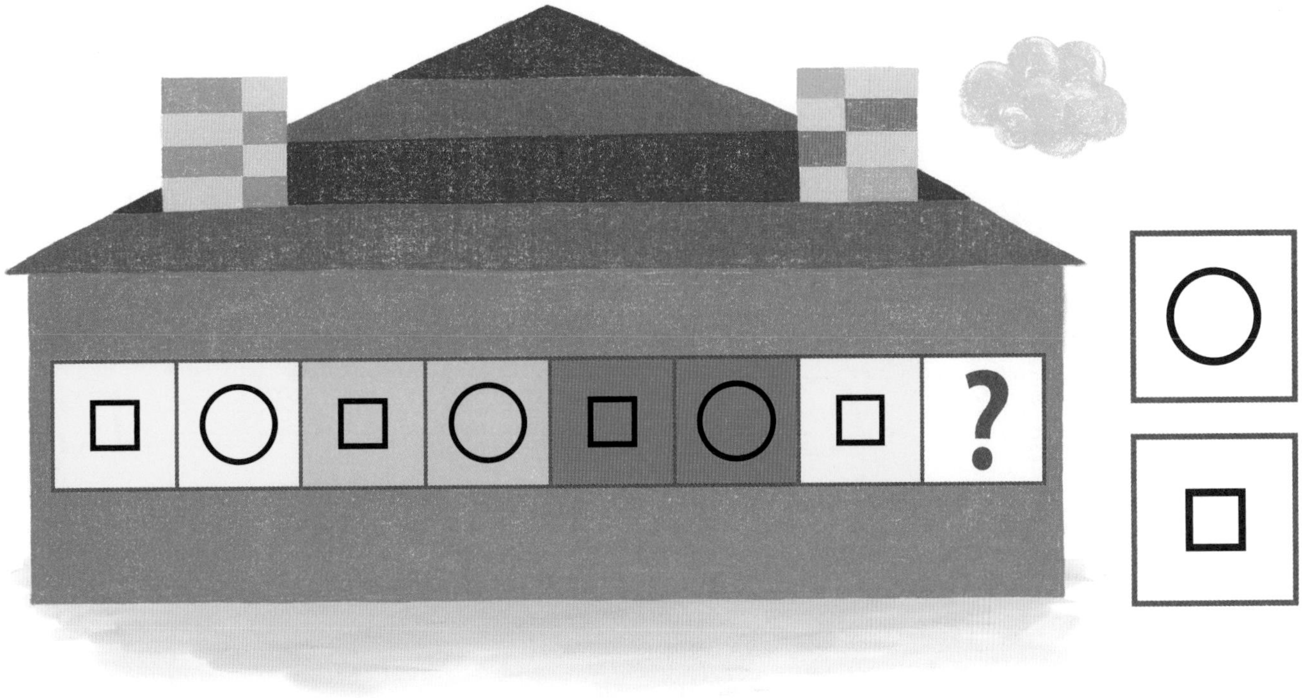

■ Follow the pattern to color the correct picture in the margin.

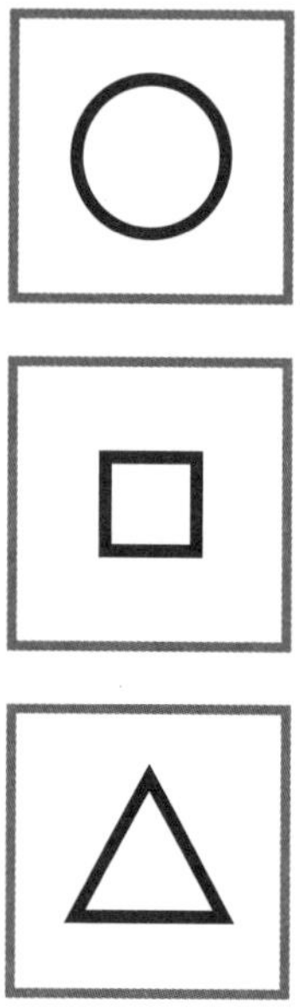

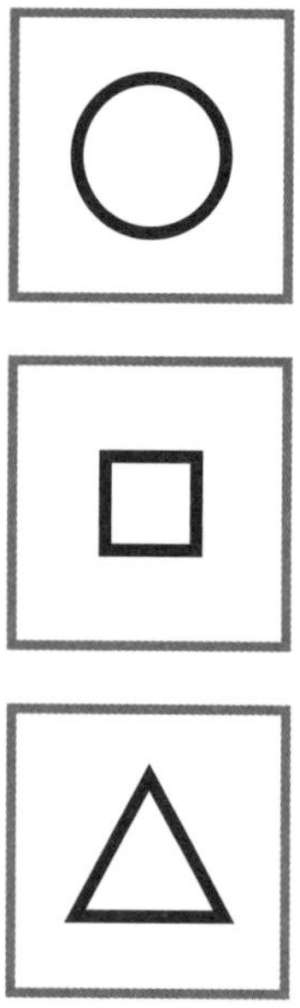

35 Color and Shape Patterns

Level Three

Name

Date

To parents
The activities are now more difficult because part of the sequence is hidden. Encourage your child to find a pattern.

■ Follow the pattern to color the picture in the margin.

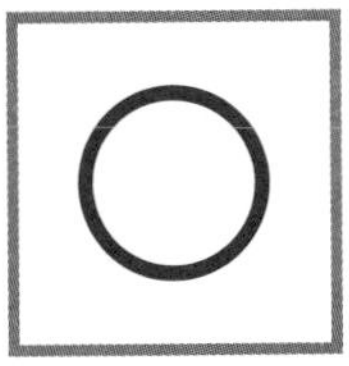

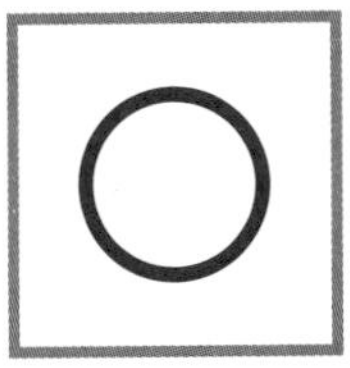

■ Follow the pattern to color the correct picture in the margin.

36 Color and Shape Patterns

Level Four

Name

Date

To parents
For each pattern, the complete sequence is shown at least once.

■ Follow the pattern to color the correct picture in the margin.

To parents
This is the last exercise of this section. Please praise your child for the effort it took to complete this workbook.

■ Follow the pattern to color the correct picture in the margin.

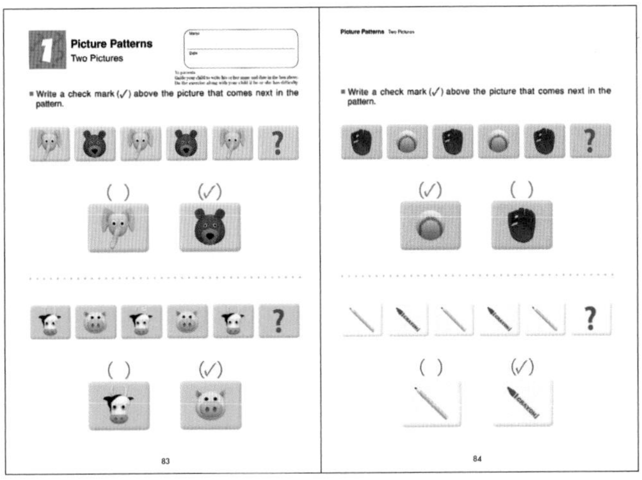

pages 83 and 84

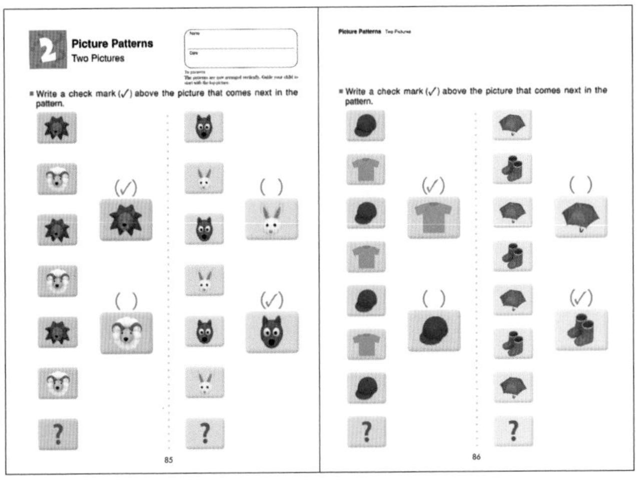

pages 85 and 86

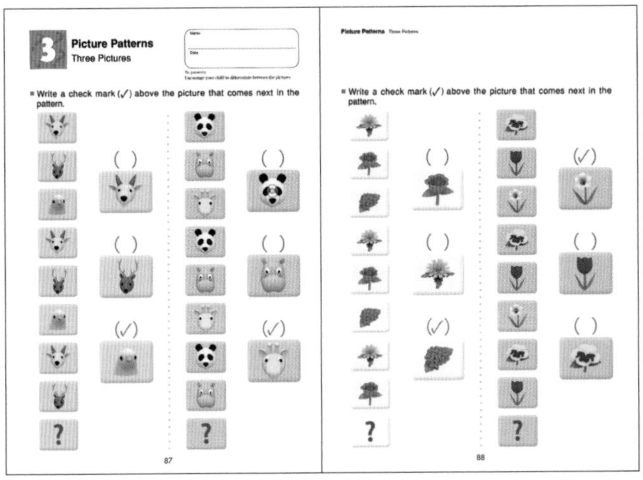

pages 87 and 88

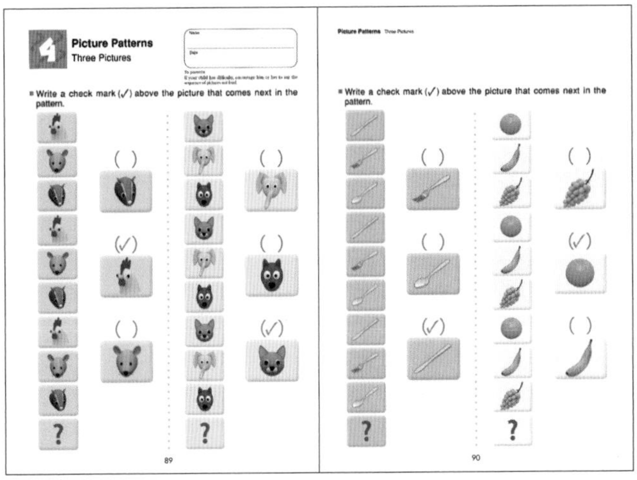

pages 89 and 90

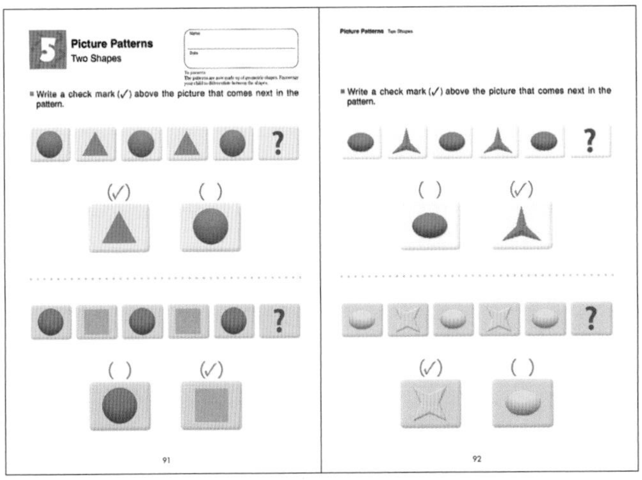

pages 91 and 92

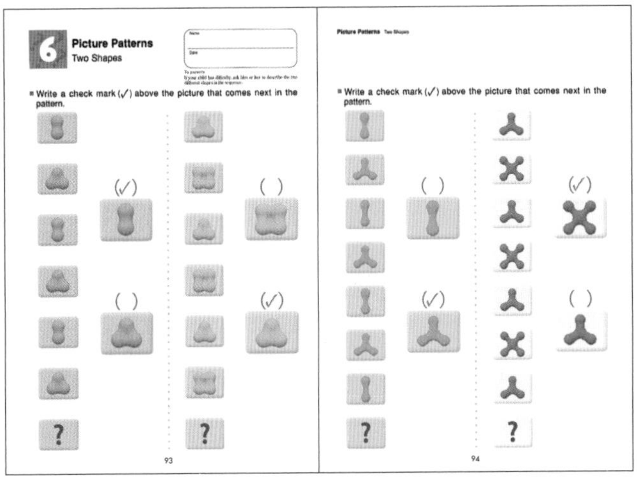

pages 93 and 94

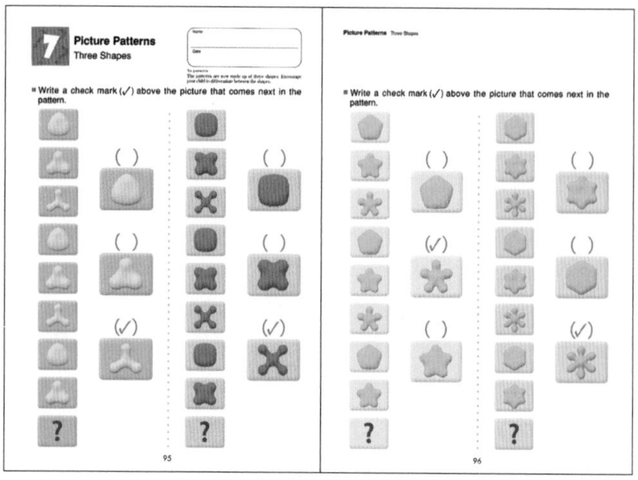
7
Picture Patterns
Three Shapes
Write a check mark (✓) above the picture that comes next in the pattern.

pages 95 and 96

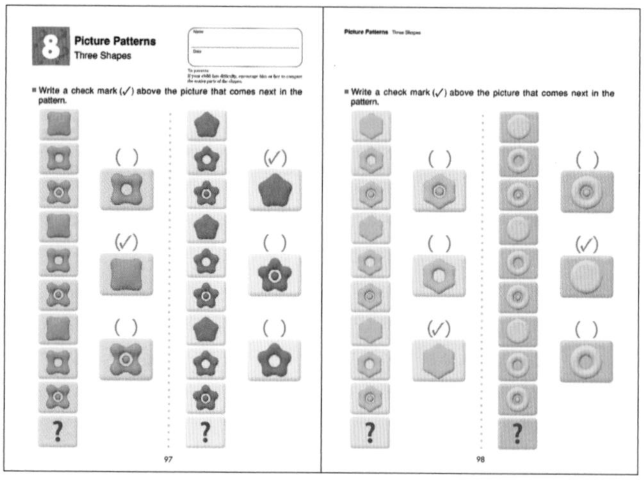
8
Picture Patterns
Three Shapes
Write a check mark (✓) above the picture that comes next in the pattern.

pages 97 and 98

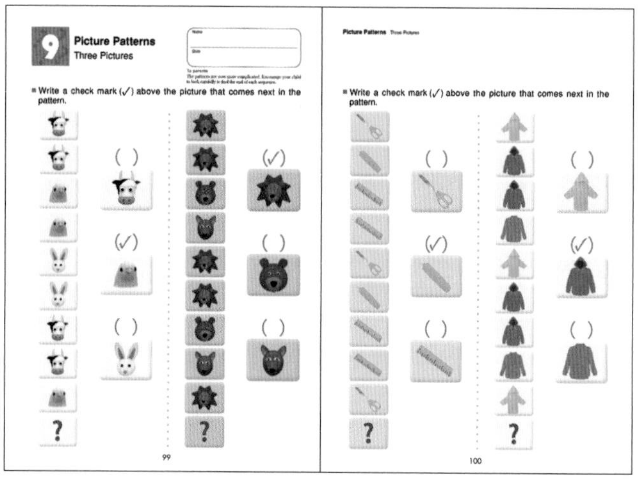
9
Picture Patterns
Three Pictures
Write a check mark (✓) above the picture that comes next in the pattern.

pages 99 and 100

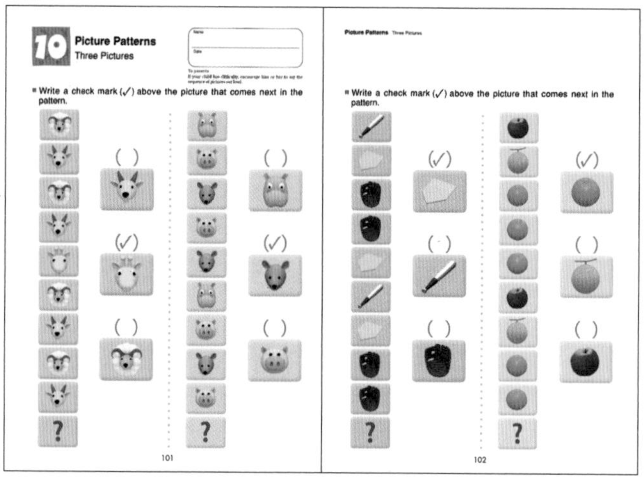
10
Picture Patterns
Three Pictures
Write a check mark (✓) above the picture that comes next in the pattern.

pages 101 and 102

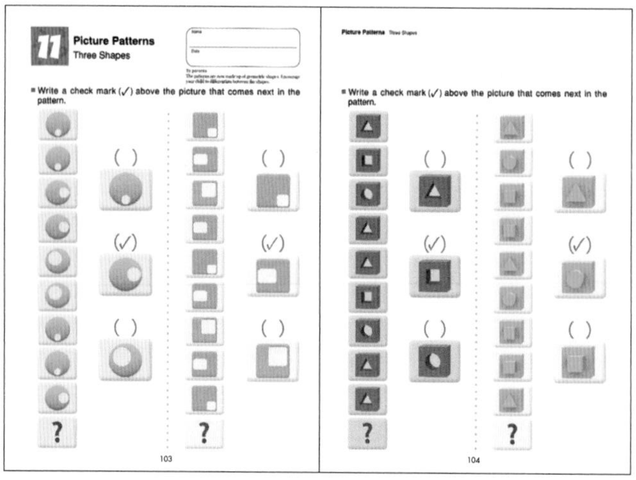
11
Picture Patterns
Three Shapes
Write a check mark (✓) above the picture that comes next in the pattern.

pages 103 and 104

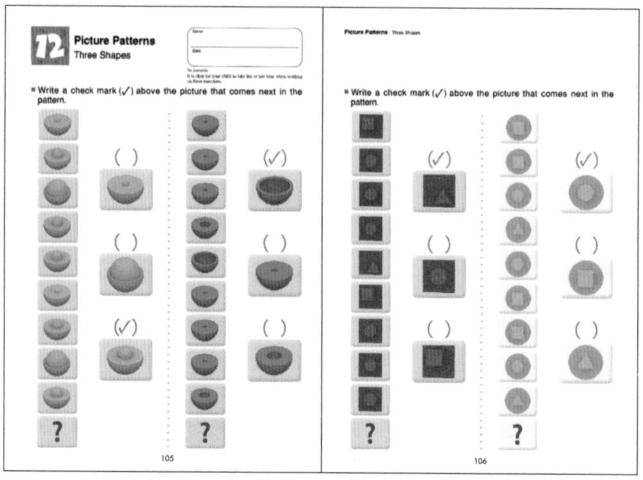
12
Picture Patterns
Three Shapes
Write a check mark (✓) above the picture that comes next in the pattern.

pages 105 and 106

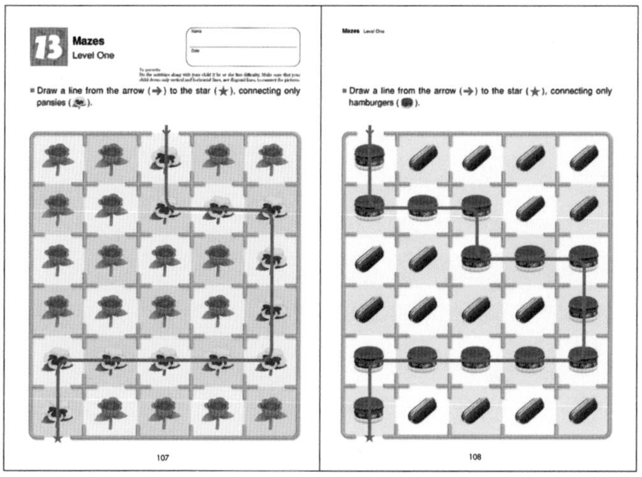
13 Mazes
Level One
Draw a line from the arrow (→) to the star (★), connecting only pansies.
Draw a line from the arrow (→) to the star (★), connecting only hamburgers.
107
108

pages 107 and 108

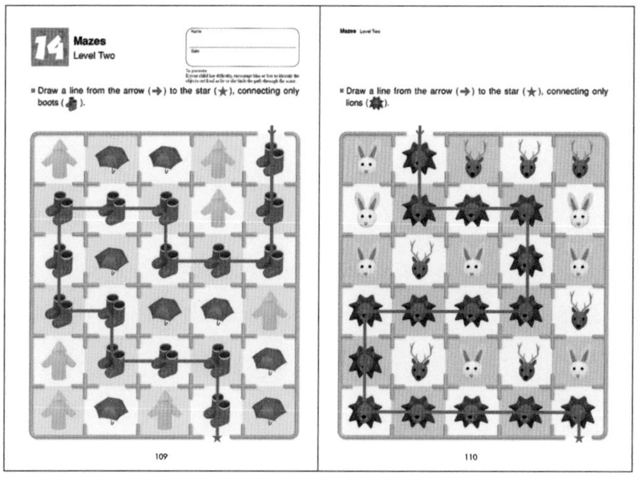
14 Mazes
Level Two
Draw a line from the arrow (→) to the star (★), connecting only boots.
Draw a line from the arrow (→) to the star (★), connecting only lions.
109
110

pages 109 and 110

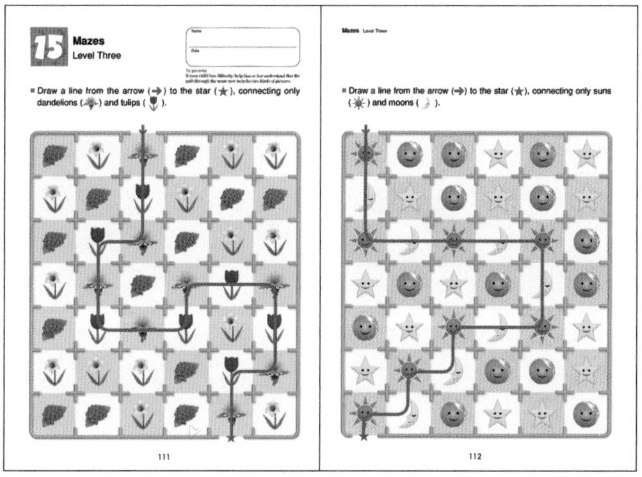
15 Mazes
Level Three
Draw a line from the arrow (→) to the star (★), connecting only dandelions and tulips.
Draw a line from the arrow (→) to the star (★), connecting only suns and moons.
111
112

pages 111 and 112

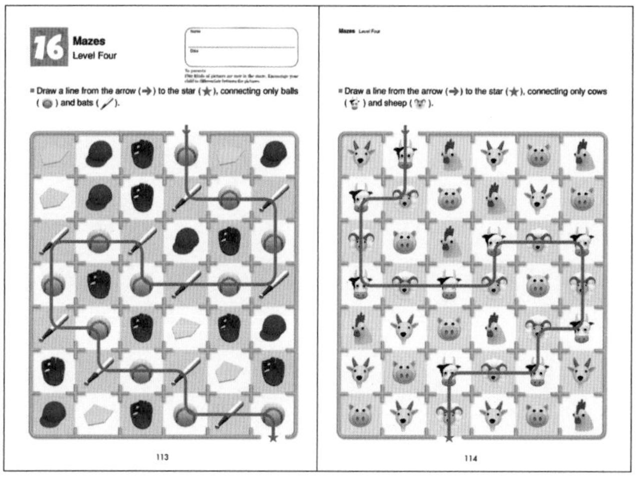
16 Mazes
Level Four
Draw a line from the arrow (→) to the star (★), connecting only balls and bats.
Draw a line from the arrow (→) to the star (★), connecting only cows and sheep.
113
114

pages 113 and 114

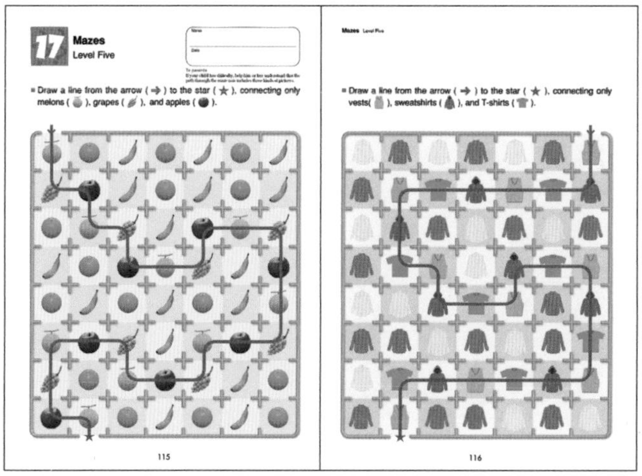
17 Mazes
Level Five
Draw a line from the arrow (→) to the star (★), connecting only melons, grapes, and apples.
Draw a line from the arrow (→) to the star (★), connecting only vests, sweatshirts, and T-shirts.
115
116

pages 115 and 116

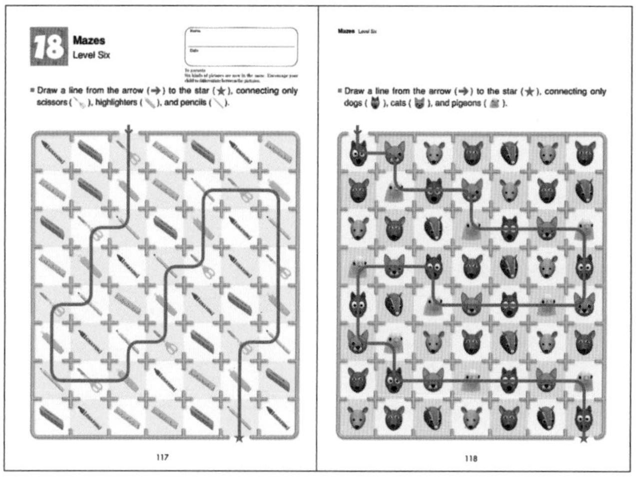
18 Mazes
Level Six
Draw a line from the arrow (→) to the star (★), connecting only scissors, highlighters, and pencils.
Draw a line from the arrow (→) to the star (★), connecting only dogs, cats, and pigeons.
117
118

pages 117 and 118

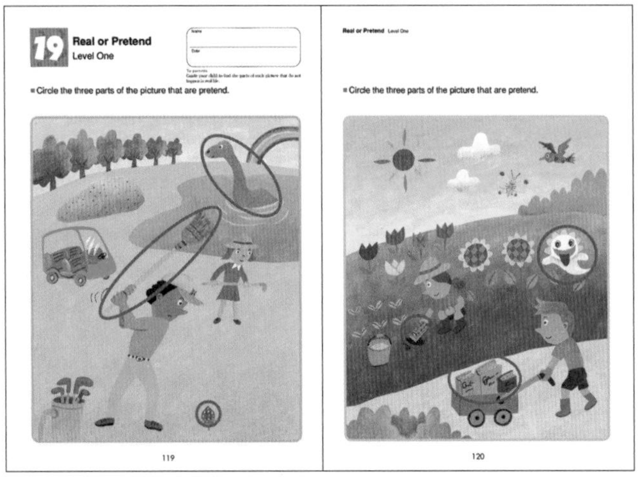
19
Real or Pretend
Level One
Circle the three parts of the picture that are pretend.
Circle the three parts of the picture that are pretend.
119
120
pages 119 and 120

20
Real or Pretend
Level Two
Circle the four parts of the picture that are pretend.
Circle the four parts of the picture that are pretend.
121
122
pages 121 and 122

21
Real or Pretend
Level Three
Circle the five parts of the picture that are pretend.
Circle the five parts of the picture that are pretend.
123
124
pages 123 and 124

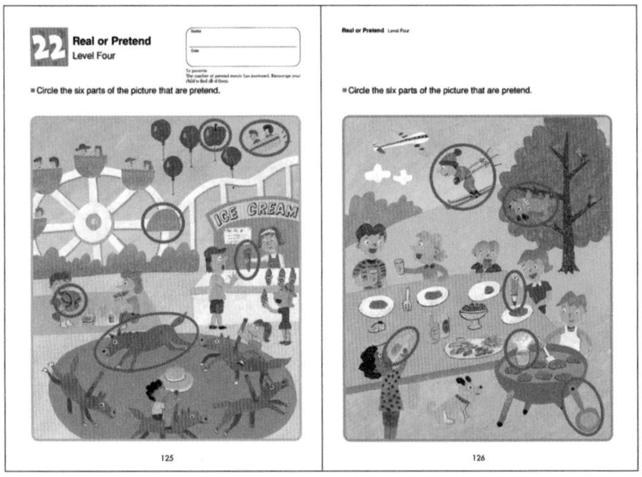
22
Real or Pretend
Level Four
Circle the six parts of the picture that are pretend.
ICE CREAM
Circle the six parts of the picture that are pretend.
125
126
pages 125 and 126

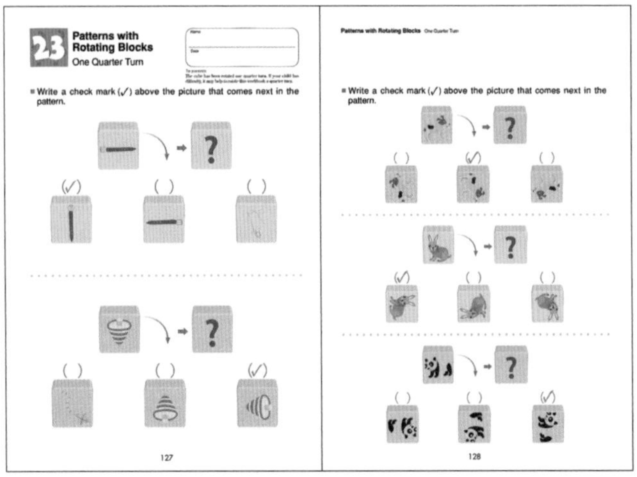
23
Patterns with Rotating Blocks
One Quarter Turn
Write a check mark (✓) above the picture that comes next in the pattern.
Write a check mark (✓) above the picture that comes next in the pattern.
127
128
pages 127 and 128

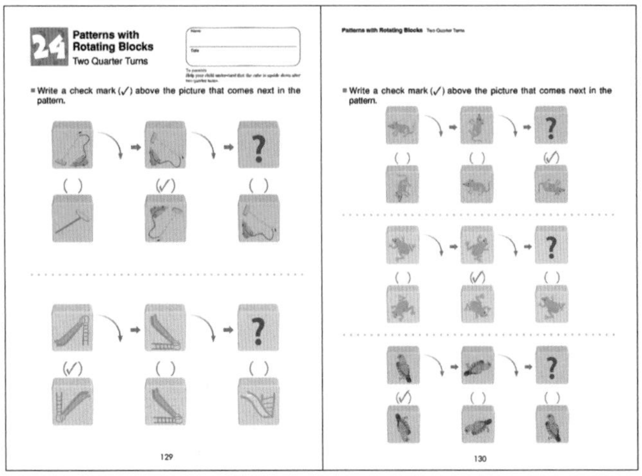
24
Patterns with Rotating Blocks
Two Quarter Turns
Write a check mark (✓) above the picture that comes next in the pattern.
Write a check mark (✓) above the picture that comes next in the pattern.
129
130
pages 129 and 130

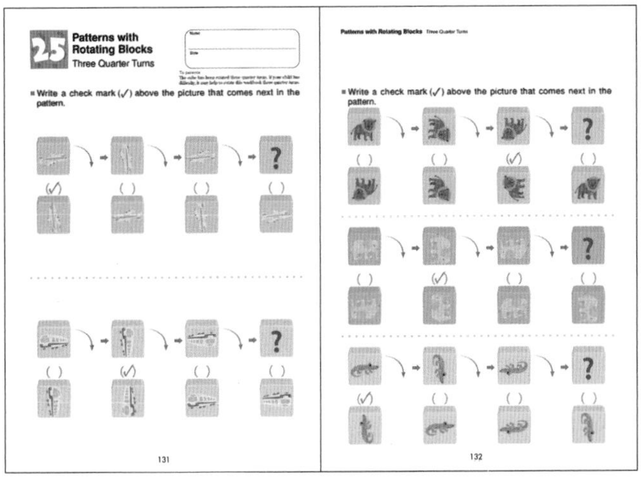
25 Patterns with Rotating Blocks
Three Quarter Turns
Write a check mark (✓) above the picture that comes next in the pattern.

pages 131 and 132

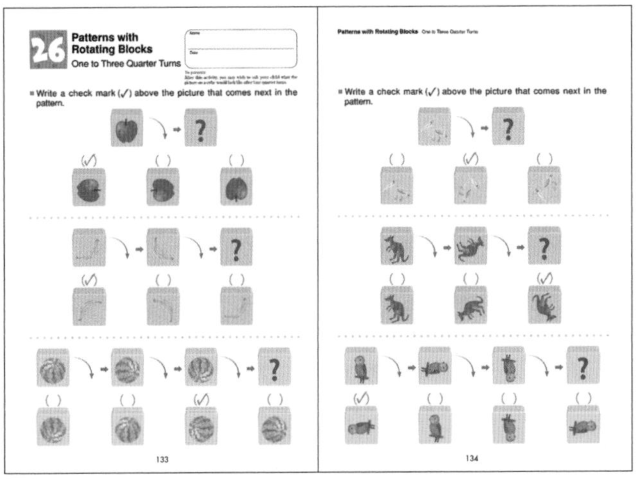
26 Patterns with Rotating Blocks
One to Three Quarter Turns
Write a check mark (✓) above the picture that comes next in the pattern.

pages 133 and 134

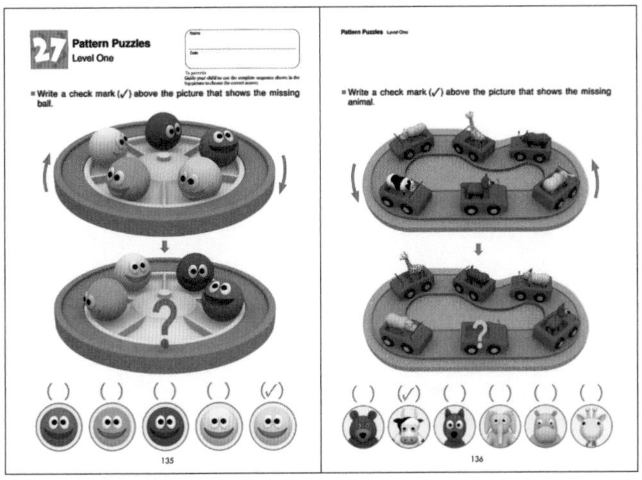
27 Pattern Puzzles
Level One
Write a check mark (✓) above the picture that shows the missing ball.
Write a check mark (✓) above the picture that shows the missing animal.

pages 135 and 136

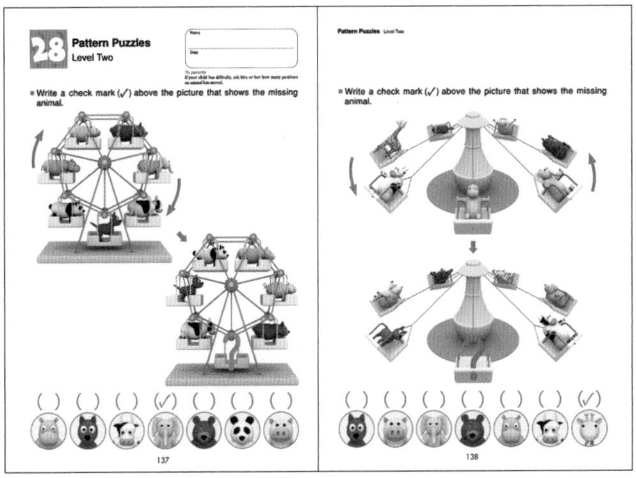
28 Pattern Puzzles
Level Two
Write a check mark (✓) above the picture that shows the missing animal.

pages 137 and 138

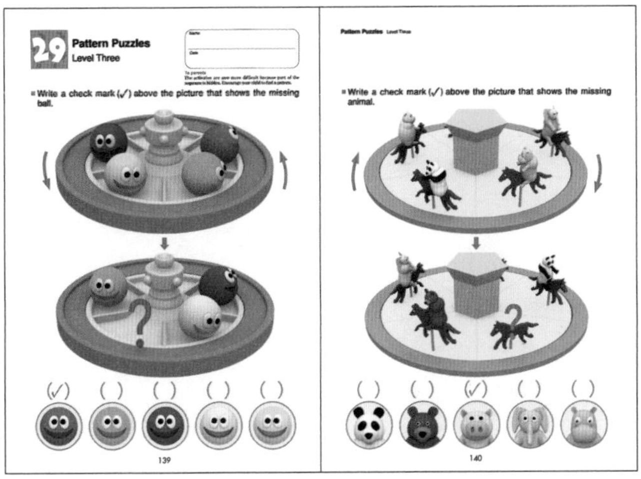
29 Pattern Puzzles
Level Three
Write a check mark (✓) above the picture that shows the missing ball.
Write a check mark (✓) above the picture that shows the missing animal.

pages 139 and 140

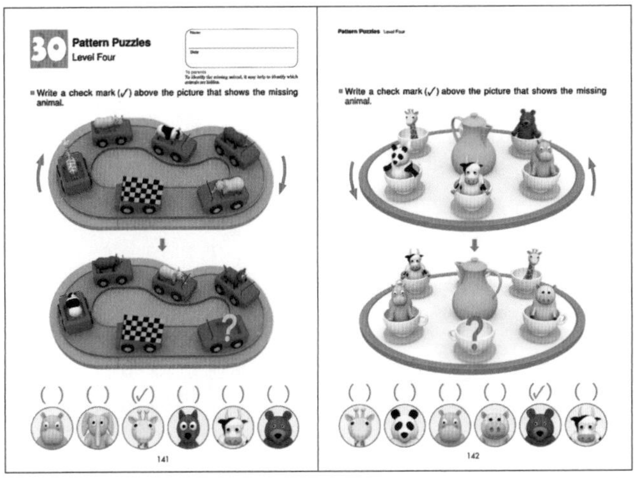
30 Pattern Puzzles
Level Four
Write a check mark (✓) above the picture that shows the missing animal.

pages 141 and 142

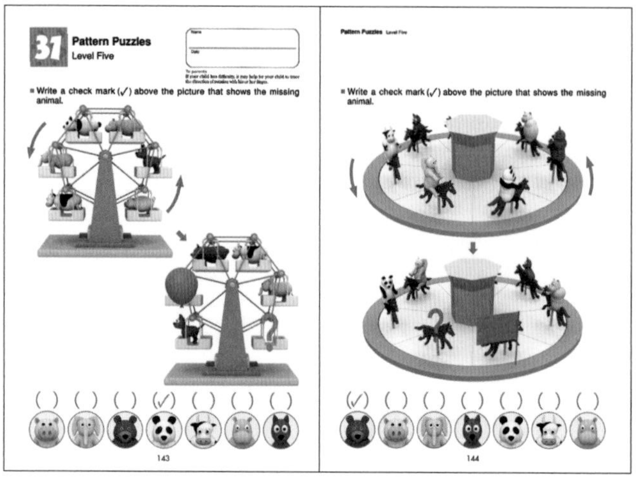

37 Pattern Puzzles
Level Five

Name
Date

■ Write a check mark (✓) above the picture that shows the missing animal.

143

Pattern Puzzles Level Five

■ Write a check mark (✓) above the picture that shows the missing animal.

144

pages 143 and 144

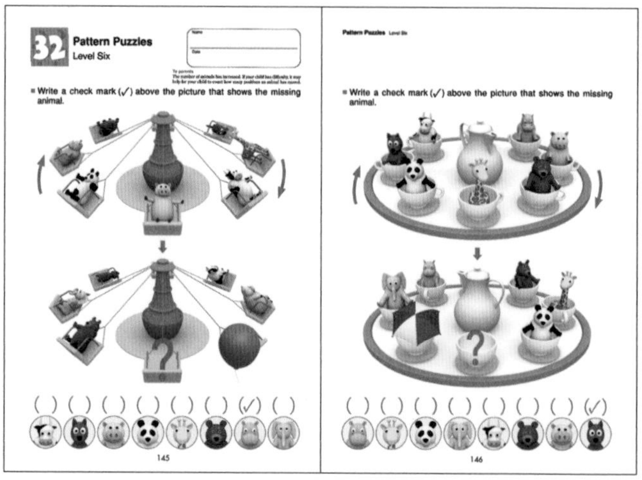

32 Pattern Puzzles
Level Six

Name
Date

■ Write a check mark (✓) above the picture that shows the missing animal.

145

Pattern Puzzles Level Six

■ Write a check mark (✓) above the picture that shows the missing animal.

146

pages 145 and 146

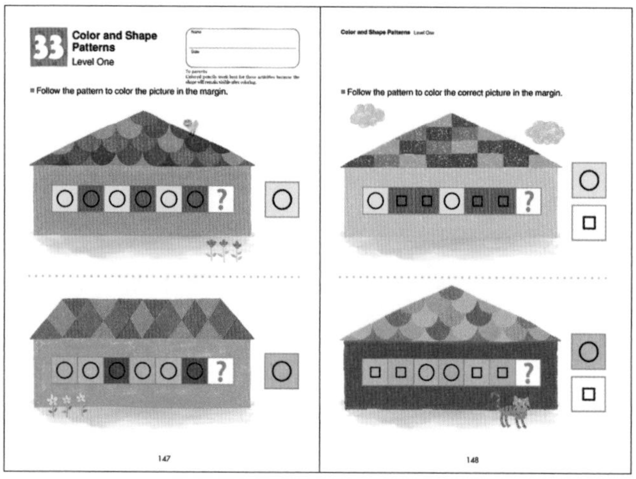

33 Color and Shape Patterns
Level One

Name
Date

■ Follow the pattern to color the picture in the margin.

147

Color and Shape Patterns Level One

■ Follow the pattern to color the correct picture in the margin.

148

pages 147 and 148

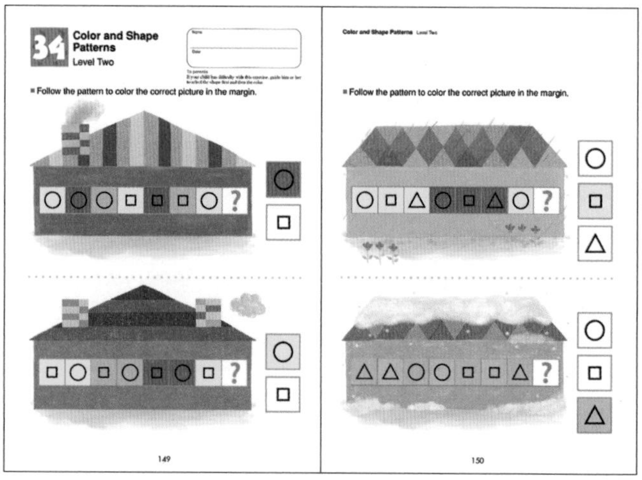

34 Color and Shape Patterns
Level Two

Name
Date

■ Follow the pattern to color the correct picture in the margin.

149

Color and Shape Patterns Level Two

■ Follow the pattern to color the correct picture in the margin.

150

pages 149 and 150

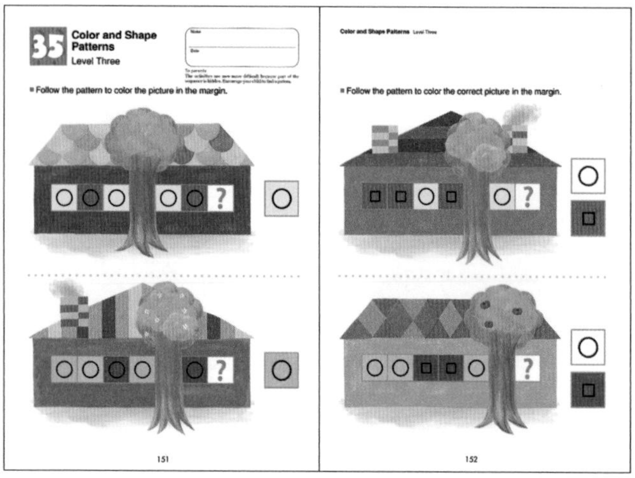

35 Color and Shape Patterns
Level Three

Name
Date

■ Follow the pattern to color the picture in the margin.

151

Color and Shape Patterns Level Three

■ Follow the pattern to color the correct picture in the margin.

152

pages 151 and 152

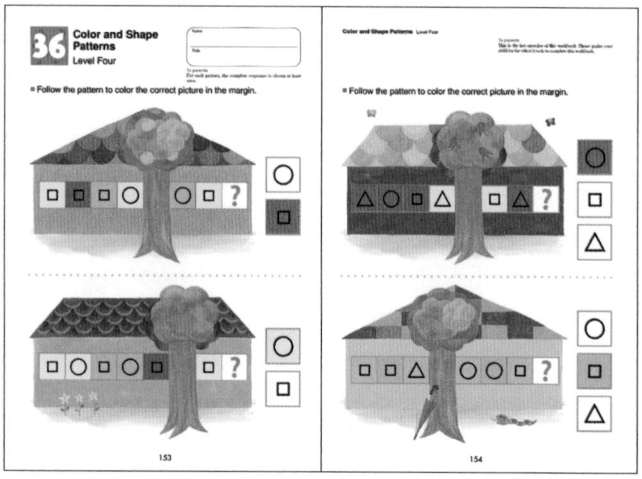

36 Color and Shape Patterns
Level Four

Name
Date

■ Follow the pattern to color the correct picture in the margin.

153

Color and Shape Patterns Level Four

■ Follow the pattern to color the correct picture in the margin.

154

pages 153 and 154

Same and Different

Table of Contents

To parents:

Same and Different

In this section, your child will complete activities that will develop his or her differentiation skills. This section contains activities such as categorization and recognizing similarities and differences. By completing this section your child will strengthen his or her ability to find the similarities or differences between objects. Development of this skill will strengthen your child's critical thinking ability.

Each skill is introduced in a step-by-step manner that allows your child to master it without frustration. Over the course of the section, the difficulty level of these activities increases as your child gains confidence in his or her differentiation abilities.

1 Matching
Level One

Name

Date

To parents

Guide your child to write his or her name and date in the box above. Do the exercise along with your child if he or she has difficulty.

■ Draw a line to the matching animal.

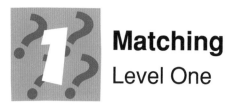

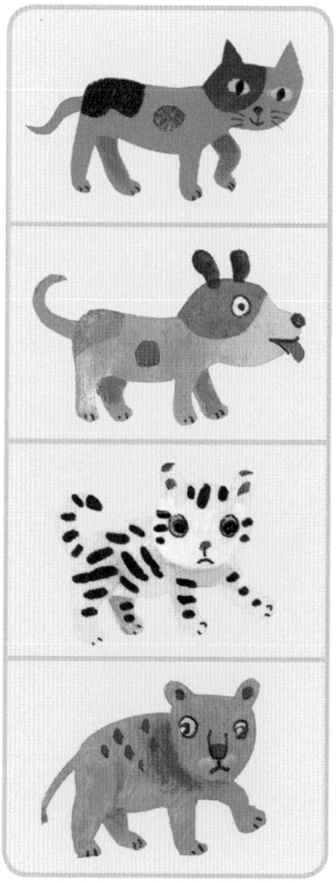

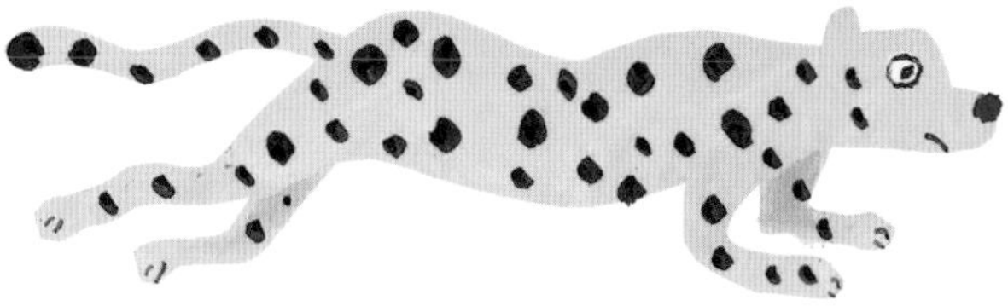

■ Draw a line to the matching animal.

2 Matching
Level Two

Name

Date

To parents
Now the pictures on the right show the same animal in a different pose. Encourage your child to find the same animal.

■ Draw a line to the matching animal.

■ Draw a line to the matching animal.

3 Matching
Level Three

Name

Date

■ Draw a line to the matching animal.

To parents
This exercise has many answer choices. Guide your child to look carefully for the matching animal.

■ Draw a line to the matching animal.

Matching
Level Four

Name

Date

To parents

The activity is now more difficult because the animal is partly hidden. Guide your child to look at the features that are visible.

■ Draw a line to the matching animal.

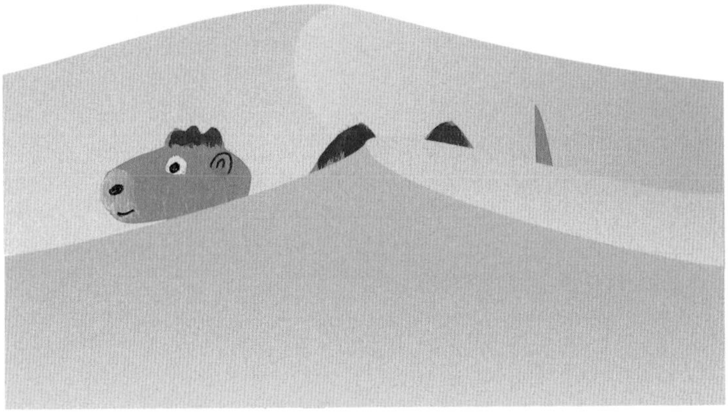

■ Draw a line to the matching animal.

Matching

Level Five

Name

Date

To parents

If your child has difficulty, ask him or her to try to identify the animal hidden behind the plant.

■ Draw a line to the matching animal.

■ Draw a line to the matching animal.

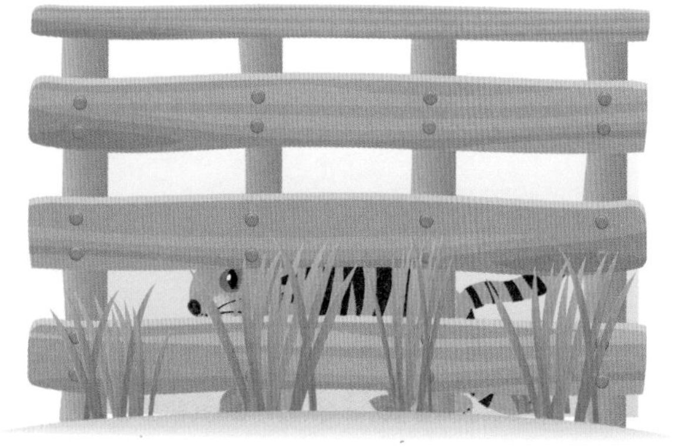

Name

Date

6 Matching
Level Six

To parents

The number of answer choices has increased. If your child has difficulty, help him or her eliminate answer choices one by one.

■ Draw a line to the matching animal.

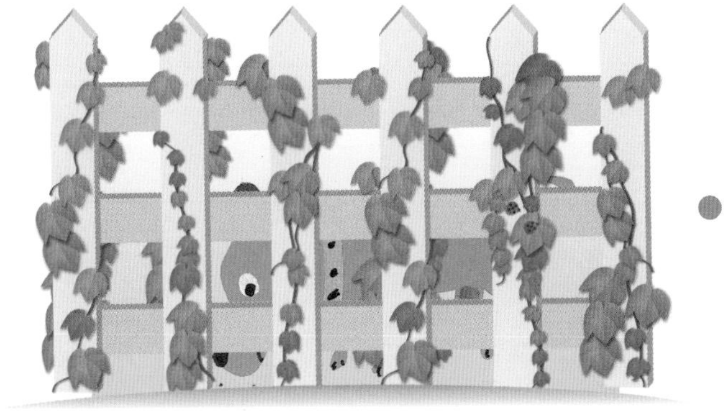

■ Draw a line to the matching animal.

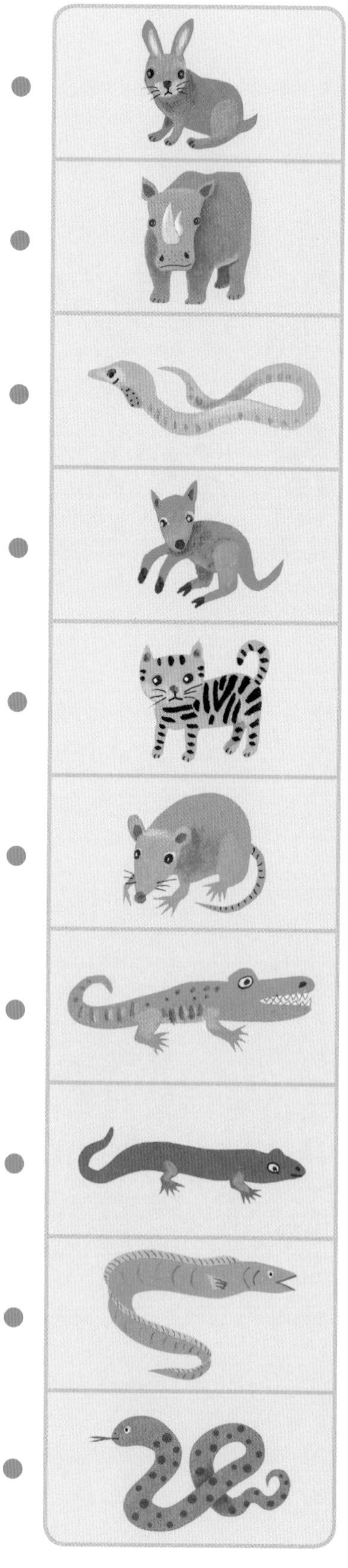

7 Matching
Level Seven

Name

Date

To parents
It is okay if your child does not recognize all of the animals. Encourage your child to look carefully at the pictures.

■ Draw a line to the matching animal.

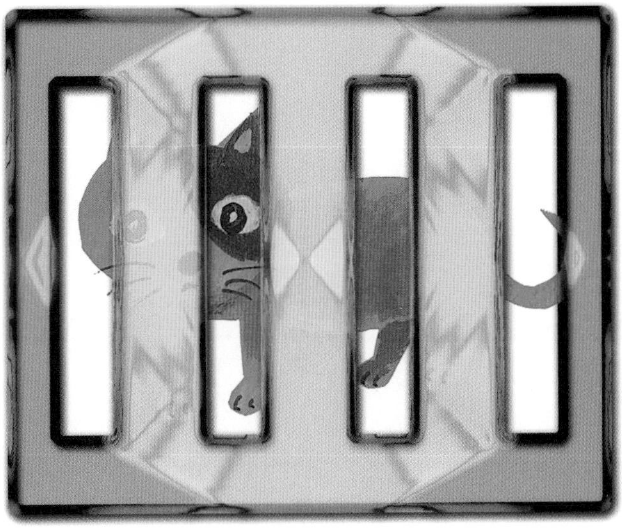

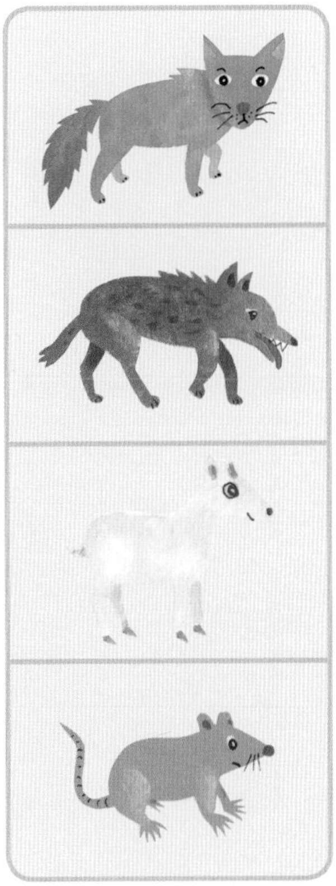

■ Draw a line to the matching animal.

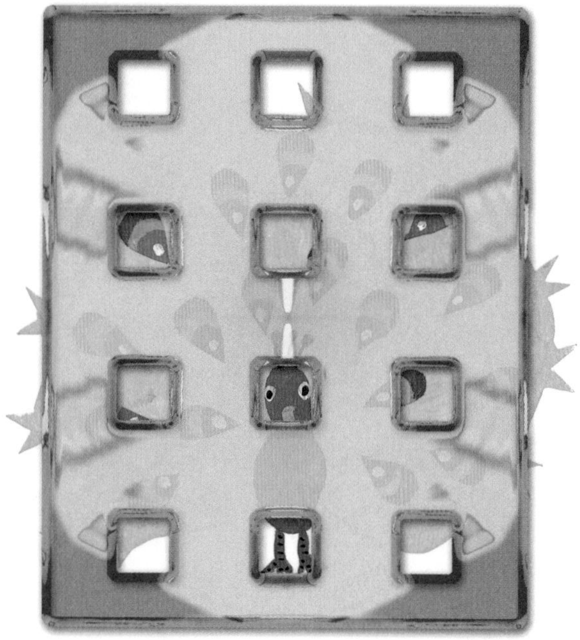

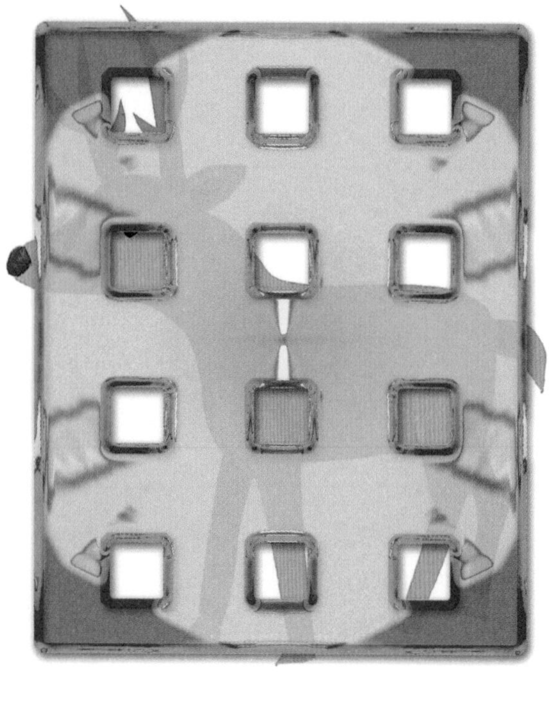

8 Matching
Level Eight

Name

Date

To parents
If your child has difficulty, ask him or her to identify the animal shown on the left first, before looking for the matching picture.

■ Draw a line to the matching animal.

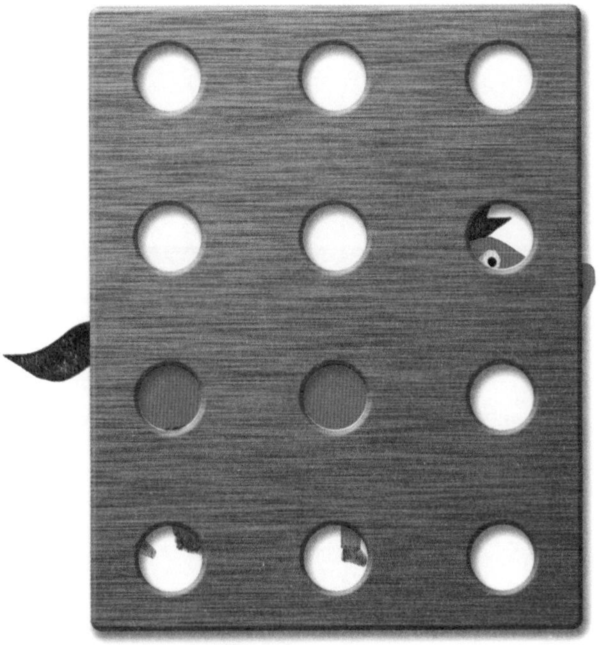

■ Draw a line to the matching animal.

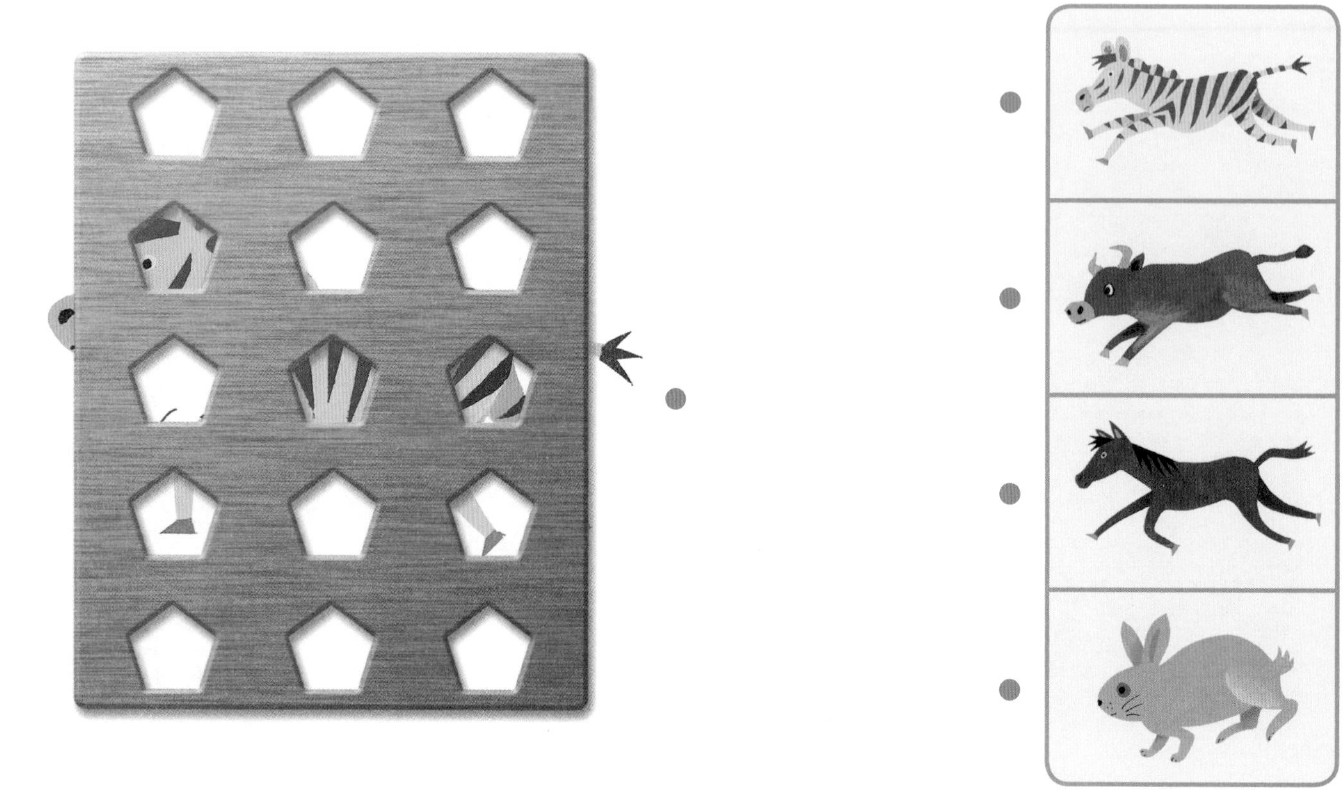

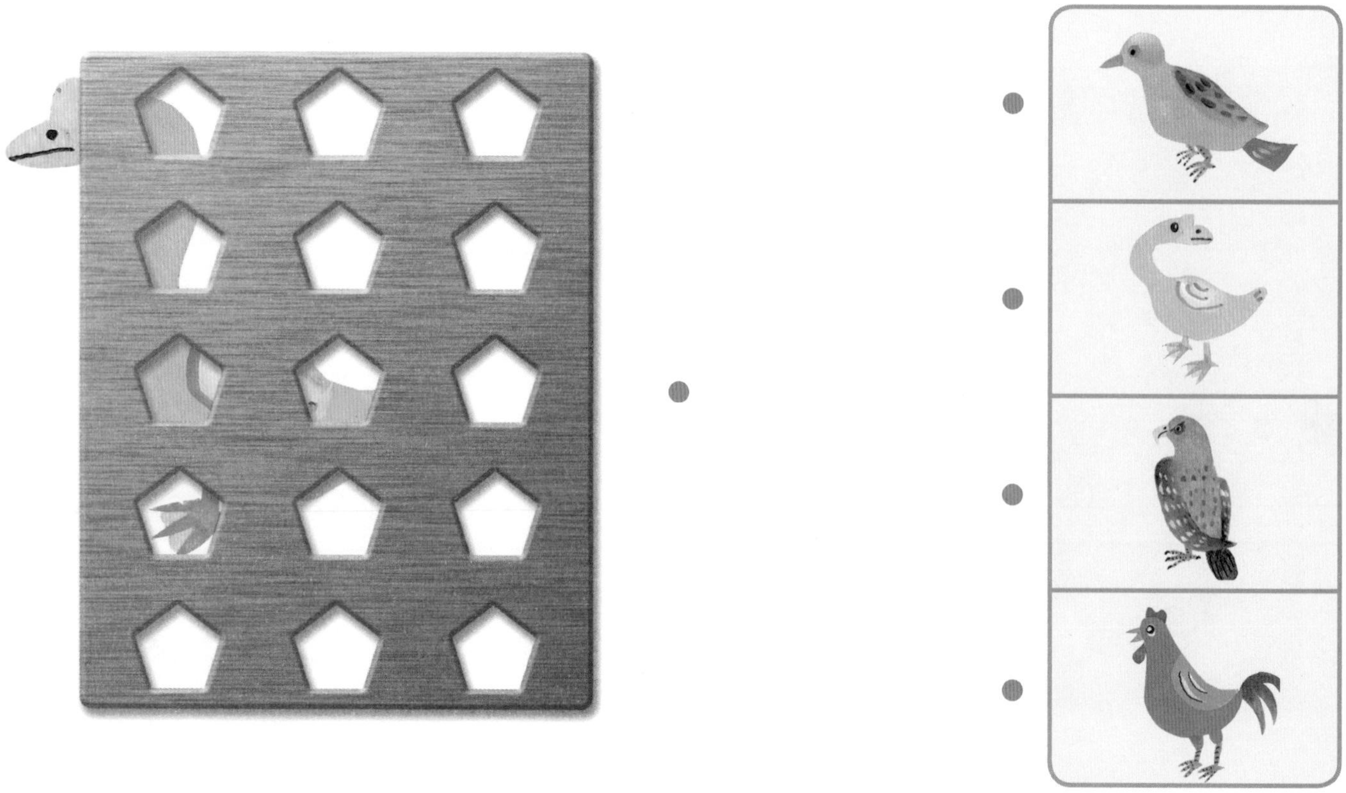

Matching
Level Nine

Name

Date

To parents
The number of answer choices has increased. Encourage your child to look carefully at each one.

■ Draw a line to the matching animal.

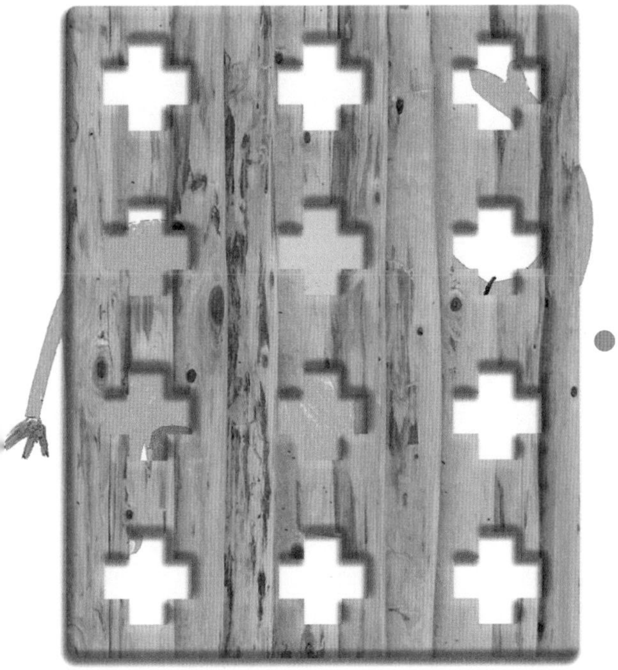

■ Draw a line to the matching animal.

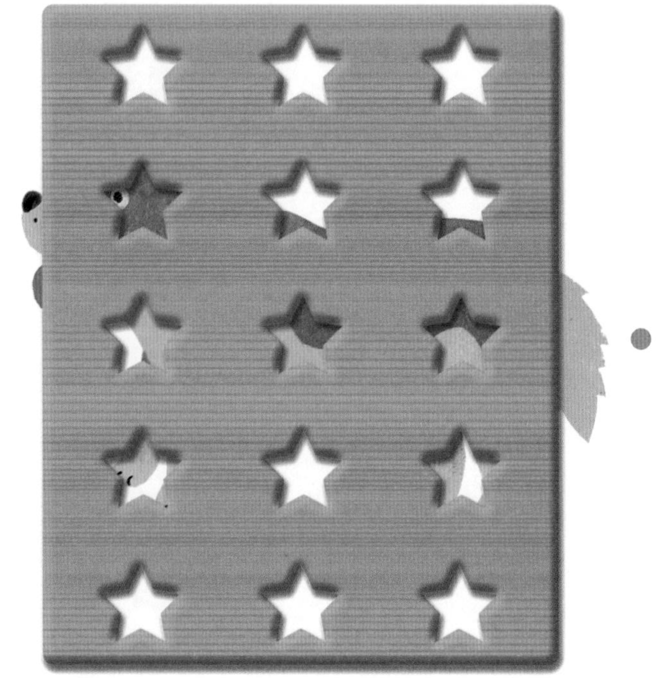

10 Matching
Level One

Name

Date

To parents
Help your child look carefully at the position or pose shown in each picture.

■ Draw a line to the matching picture.

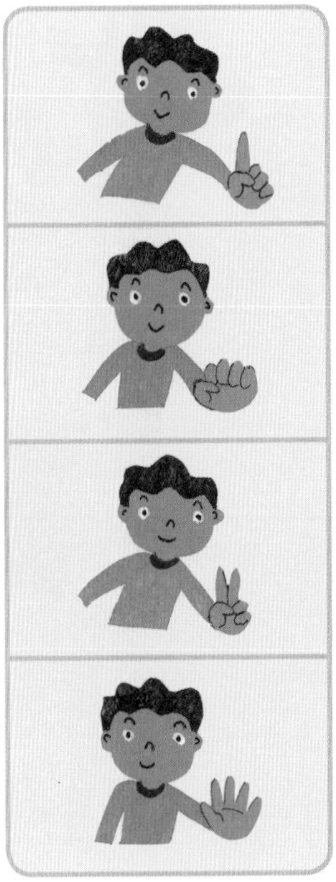

■ Draw a line to the matching picture.

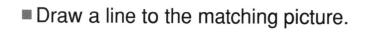

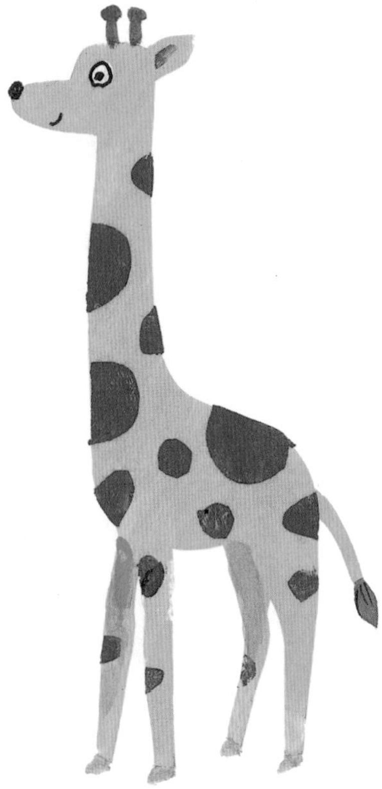

11 Matching
Level Two

Name

Date

To parents
Now the pictures on the right show a different person. Encourage your child to match the same position or pose.

■ Draw a line to the picture that shows the same position.

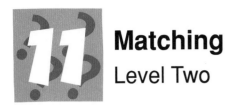

■ Draw a line to the picture that shows the same position.

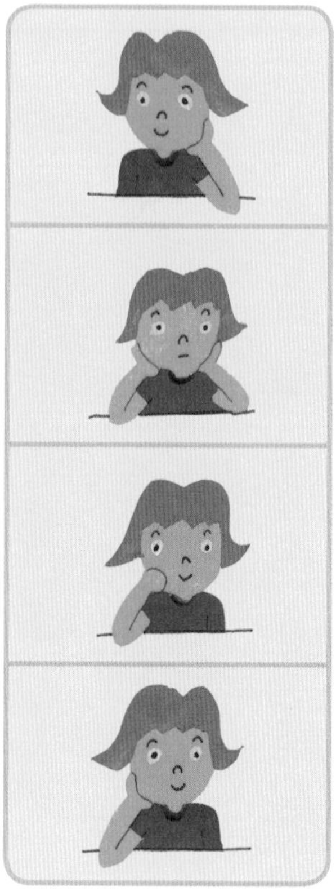

12 Matching
Level Three

Name

Date

To parents
If your child has difficulty, work together to point out small details in the pictures such as whether an animal's mouth is open or closed.

■ Draw a line to the picture that shows the same position.

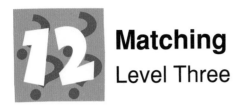

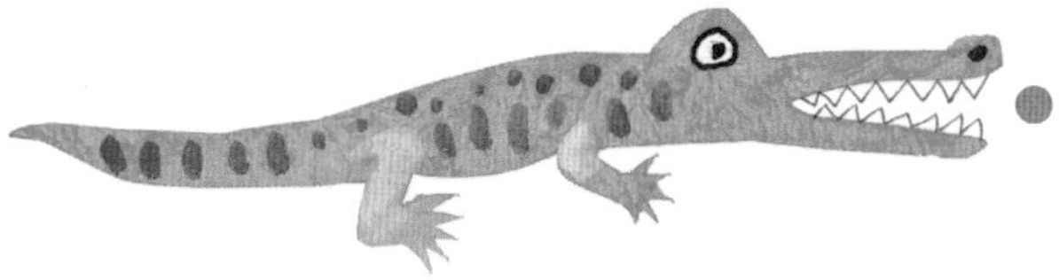

■ Draw a line to the picture that shows the same position.

13 Matching Mirror Images

Level One

Name

Date

To parents

For a hands-on example, place a small mirror at a right angle with one of the pictures on this page. Have your child compare the picture with the mirror image.

■ Draw a line to the mirror image.

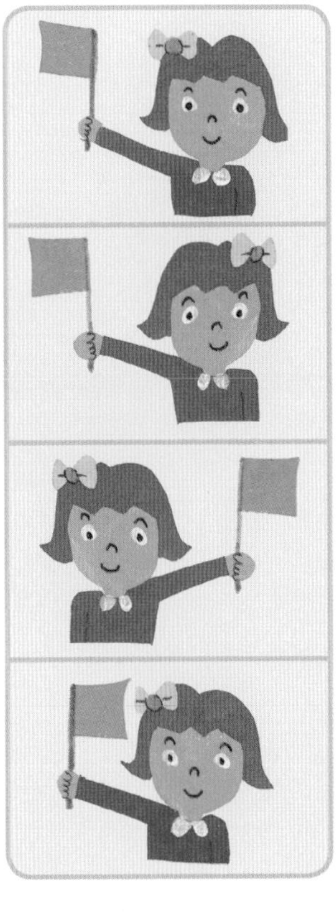

■ Draw a line to the mirror image.

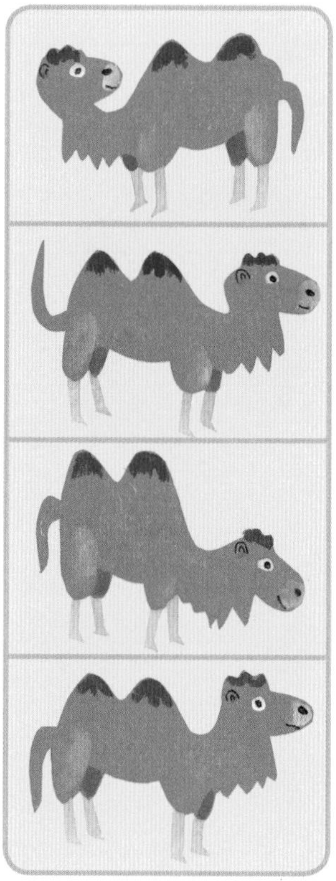

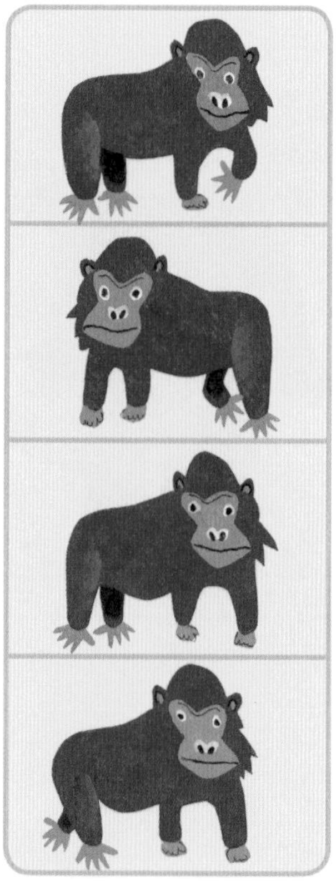

14 Matching Mirror Images

Level Two

Name

Date

To parents

Now the pictures on the right show a different person. Encourage your child to match the mirror image of the position or pose.

■ Draw a line to the mirror image of the position.

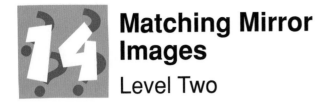

■ Draw a line to the mirror image of the position.

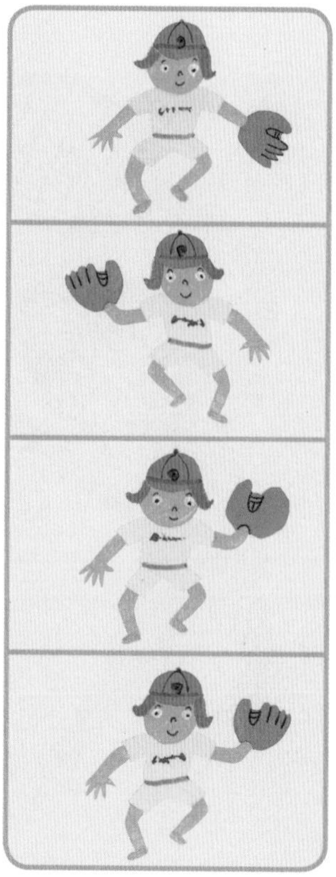

15 Matching Mirror Images

Level Three

Name

Date

To parents

The number of answer choices has increased. Encourage your child to look carefully at each one.

■ Draw a line to the mirror image of the position.

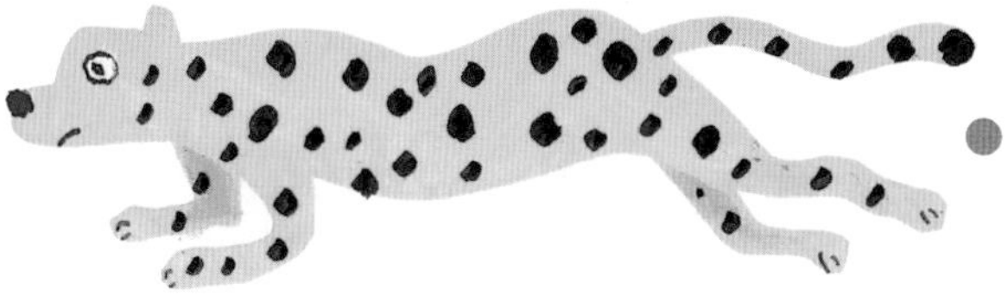

■ Draw a line to the mirror image of the position.

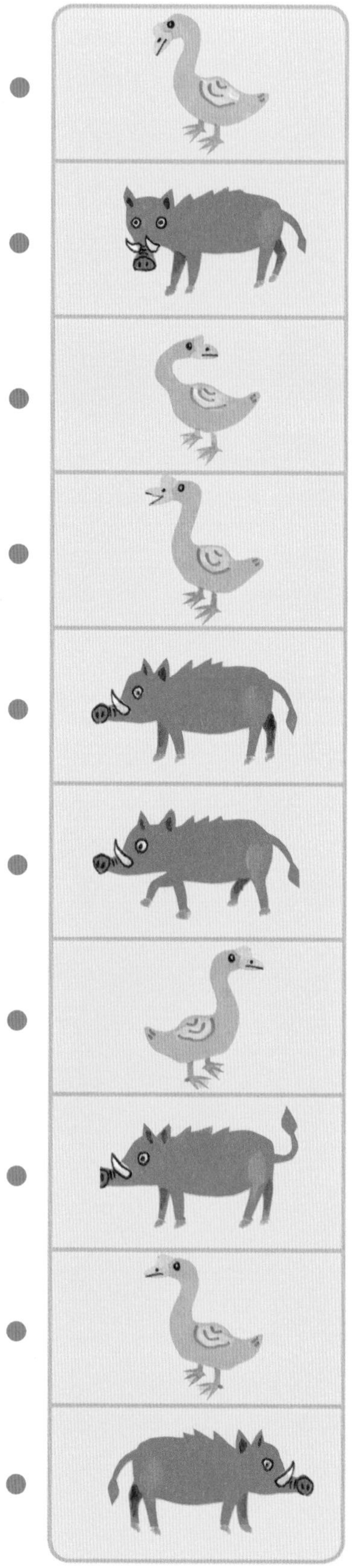

16 Matching Quantity
Level One

Name

Date

To parents

If your child has difficulty, count the objects in the pictures together.

- Draw a line to the picture that has same number of objects.

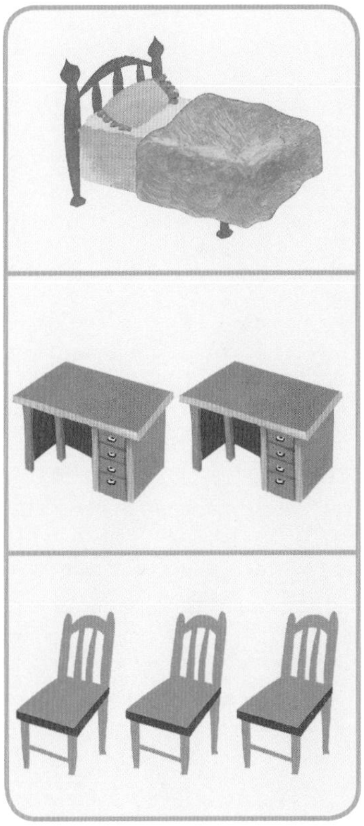

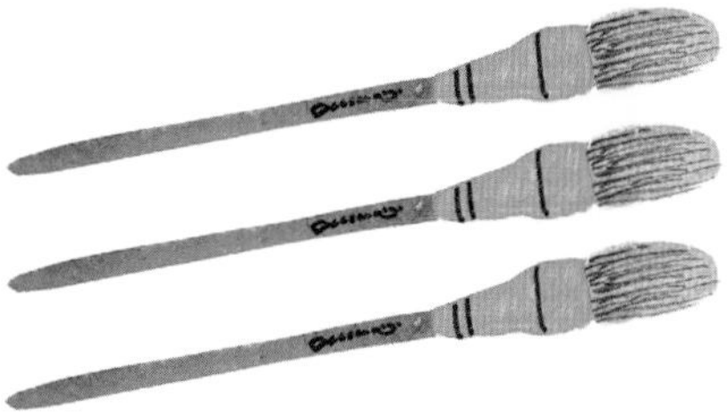

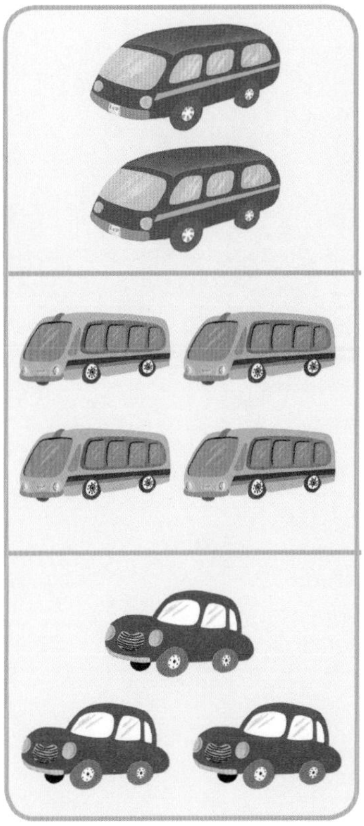

■ Draw a line to the picture that has same number of objects.

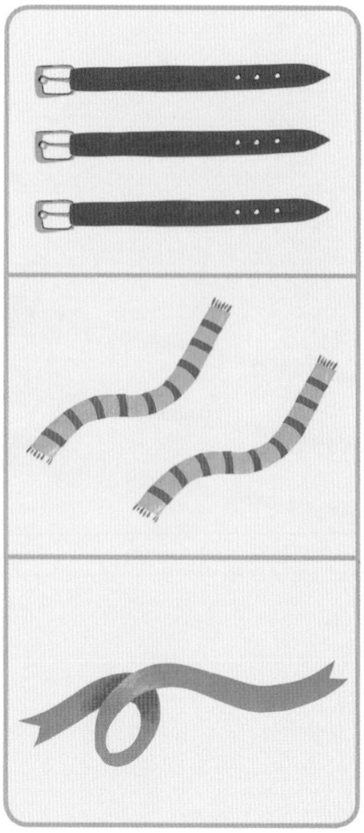

17 Matching Quantity
Level Two

Name

Date

To parents

The number of answer choices in the right column has increased. Encourage your child to look carefully at each one.

■ Draw a line to the picture that has same number of objects.

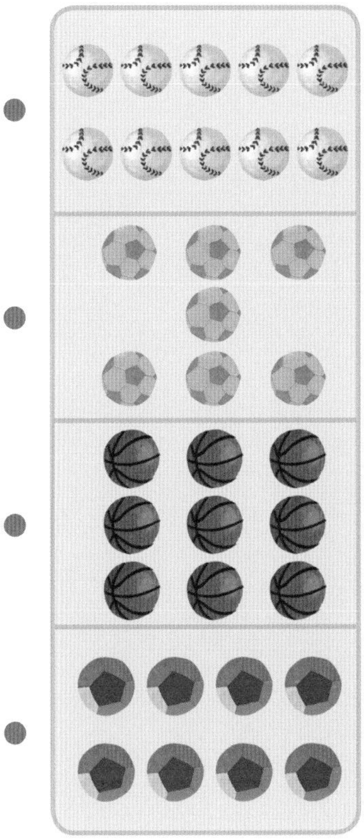

■ Draw a line to the picture that has same number of objects.

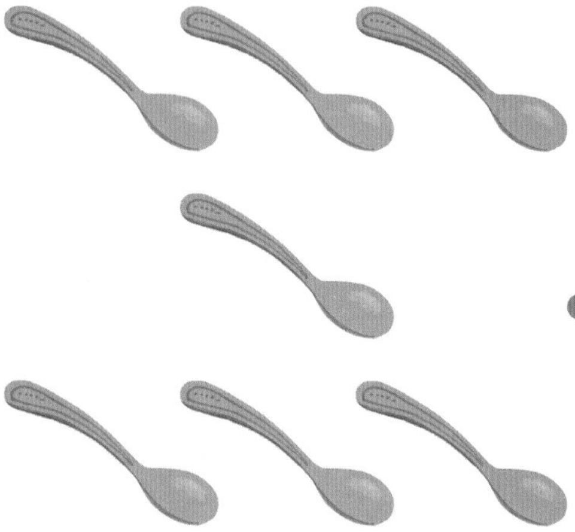

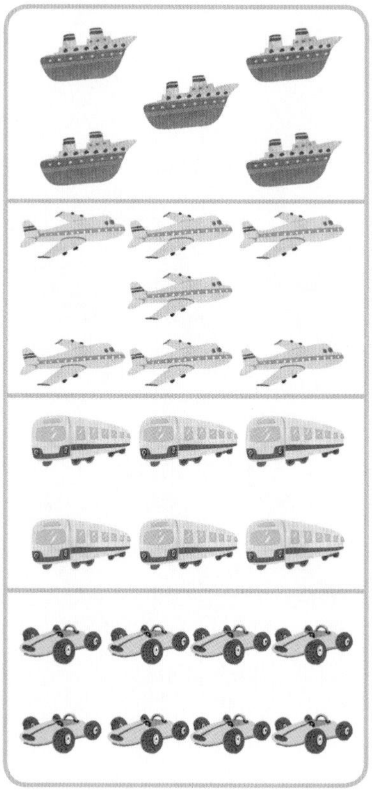

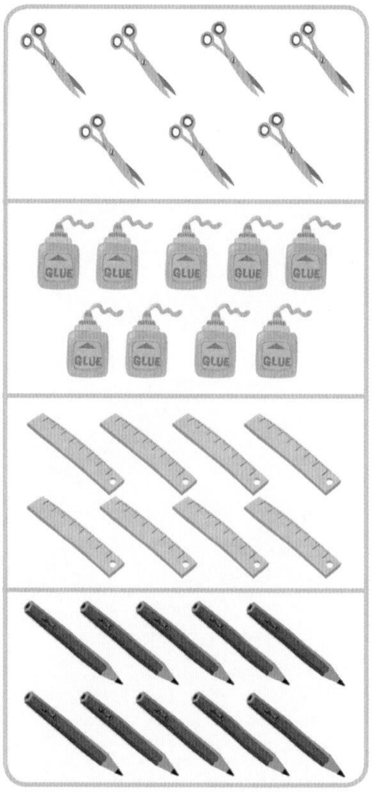

18 Matching Quantity
Level Three

Name

Date

■ Draw a line between the pictures that have the same number of objects.

To parents
If your child has difficulty, guide him or her to match each picture on the left with one on the right.

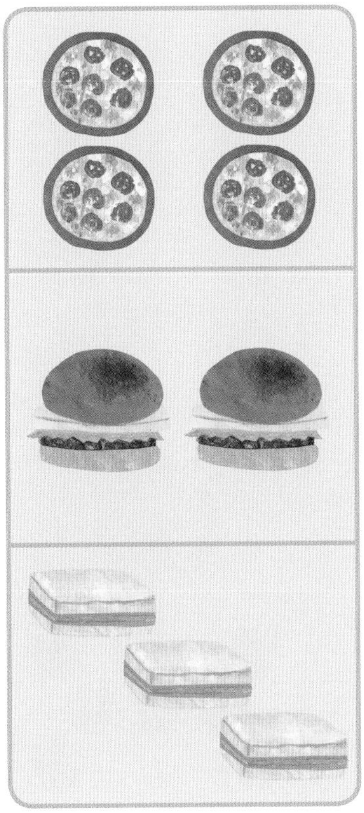

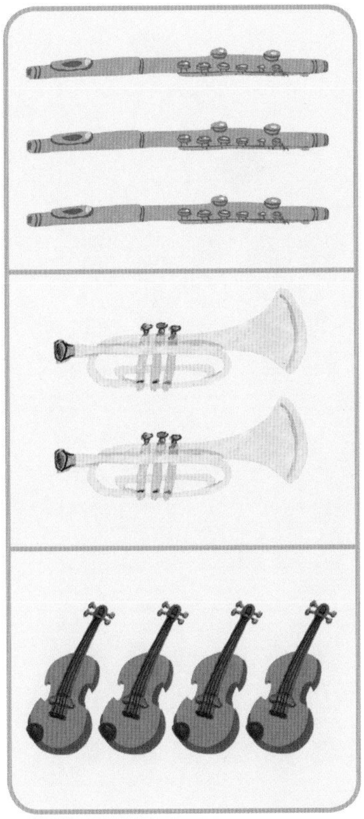

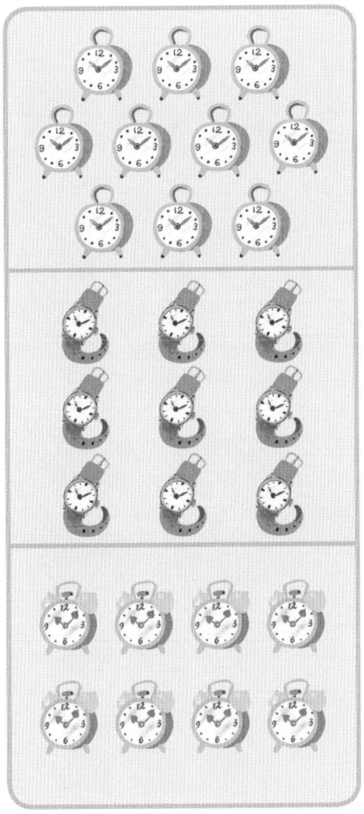

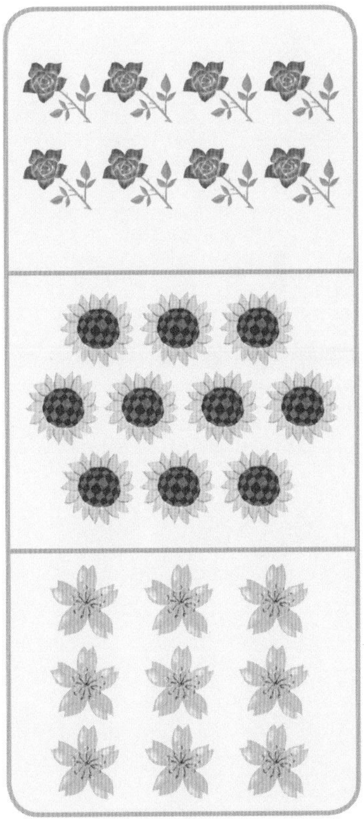

■ Draw a line between the pictures that have the same number of objects.

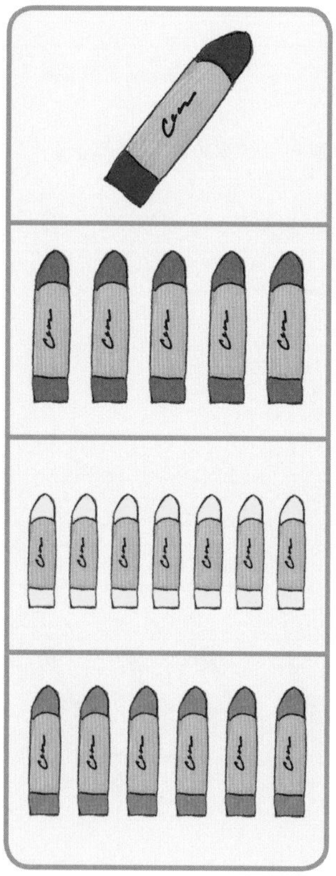

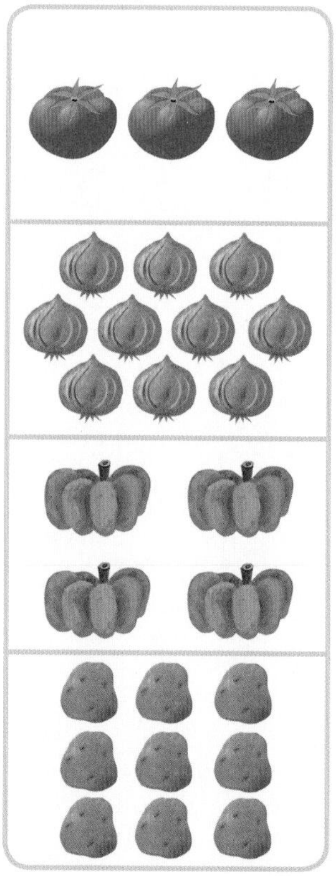

19 Matching Quantity
Level Four

Name

Date

To parents
If your child has difficulty, ask him or her to describe how much water is in each glass.

■ Draw a line to the matching picture.

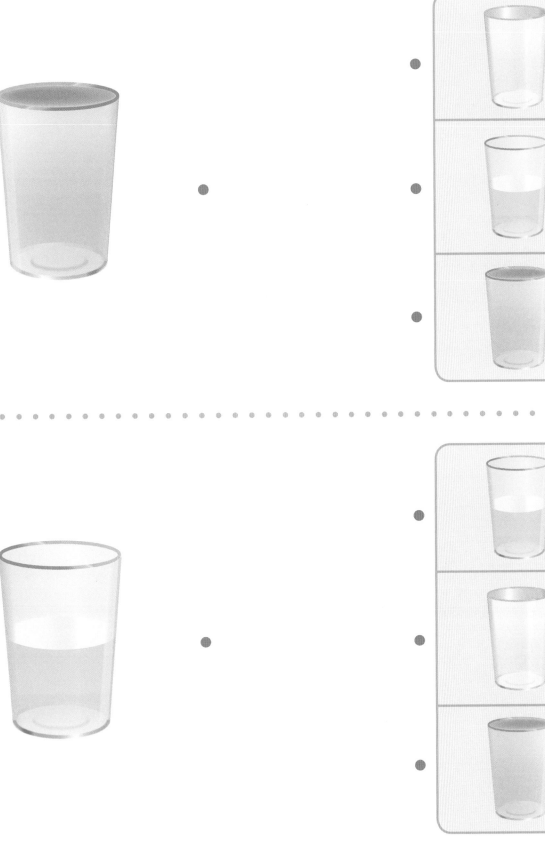

■ Draw a line to the matching picture.

20 Matching Quantity
Level Five

Name

Date

To parents
There are now four answer choices. If your child has difficulty, encourage him or her to look at each glass carefully.

■ Draw a line to the matching picture.

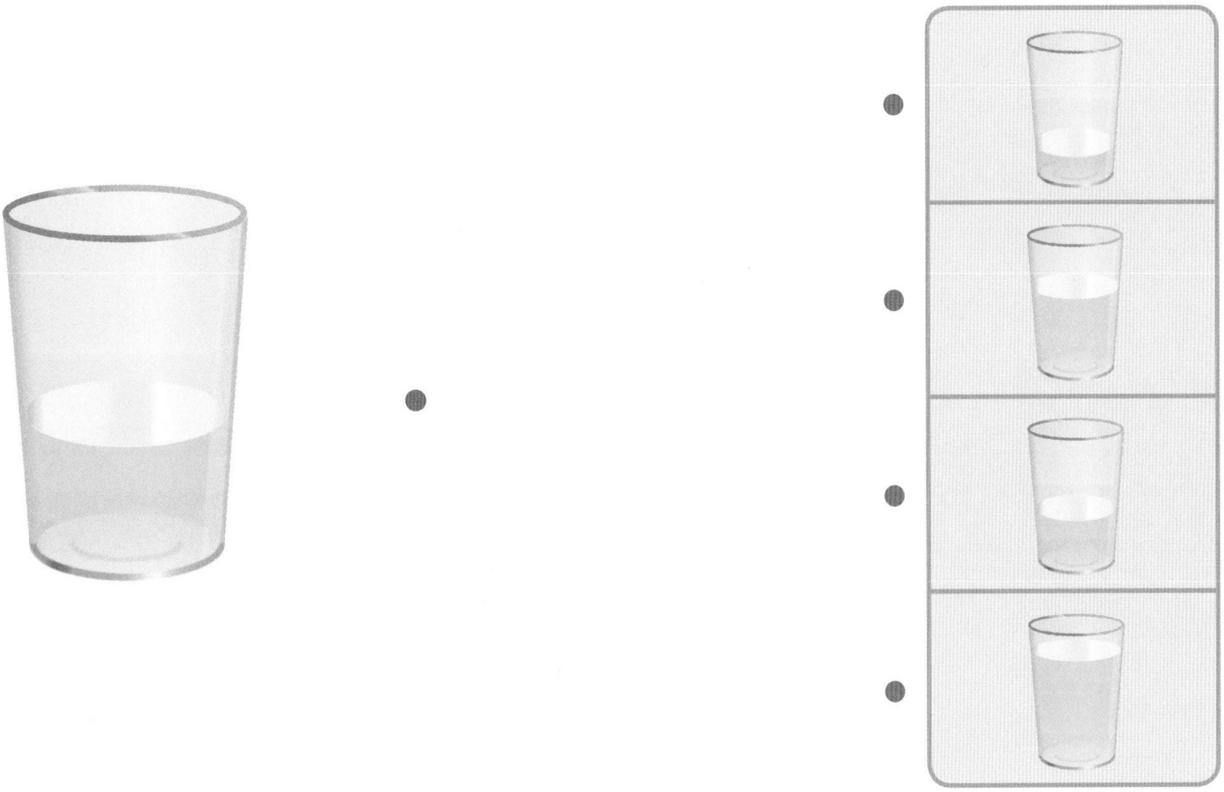

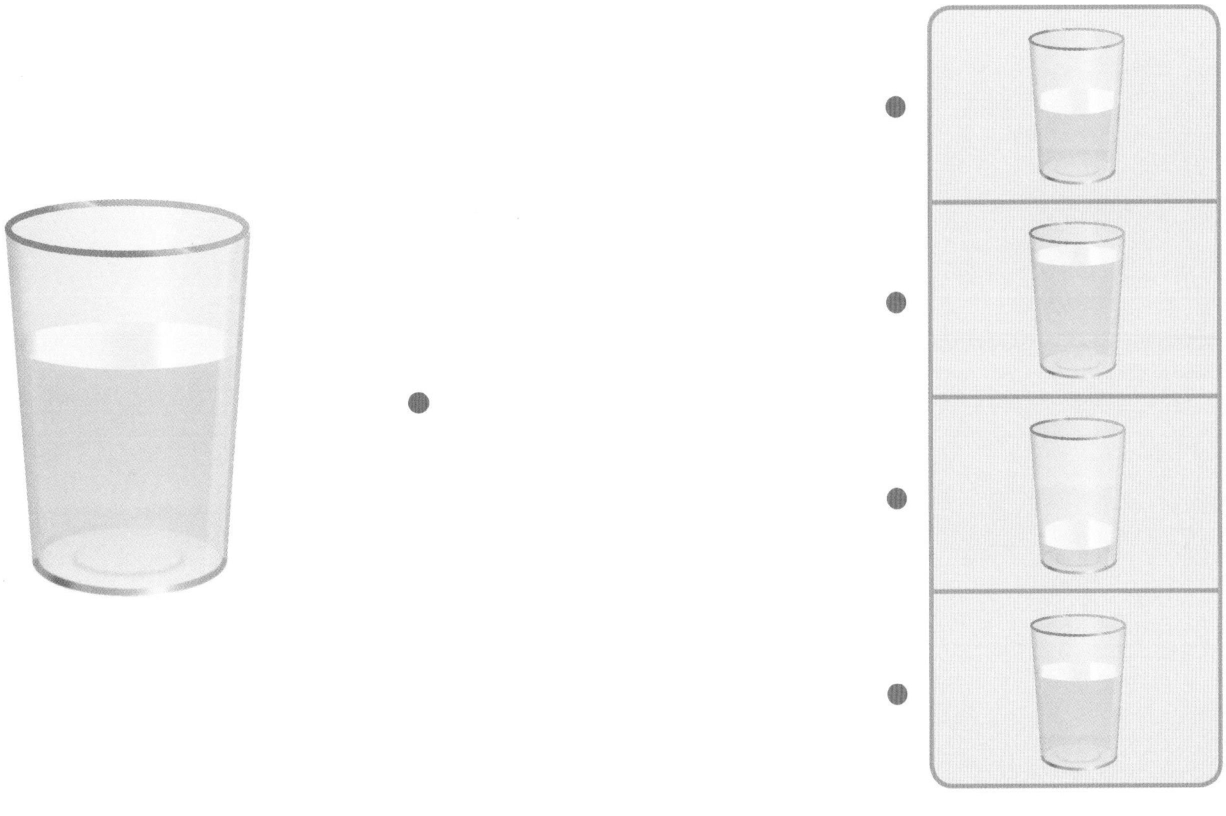

■ Draw a line to the matching picture.

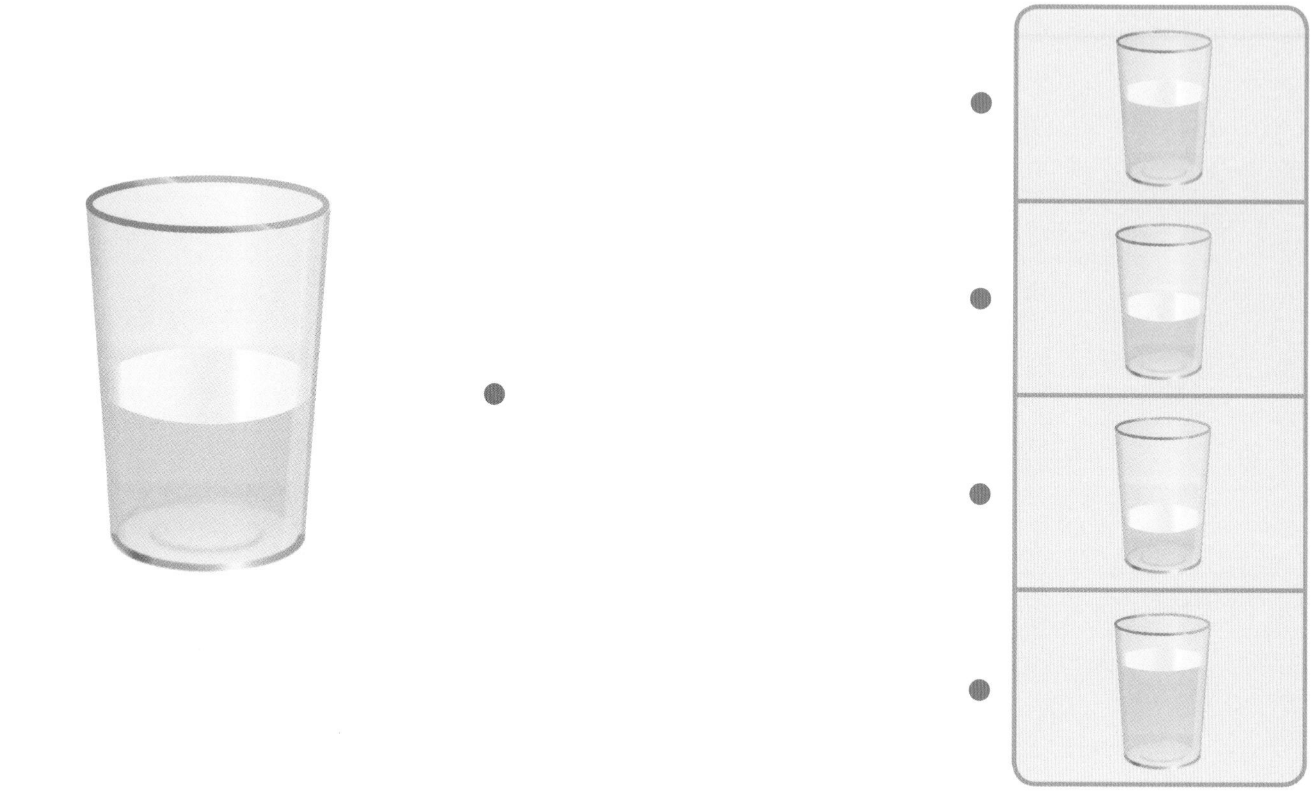

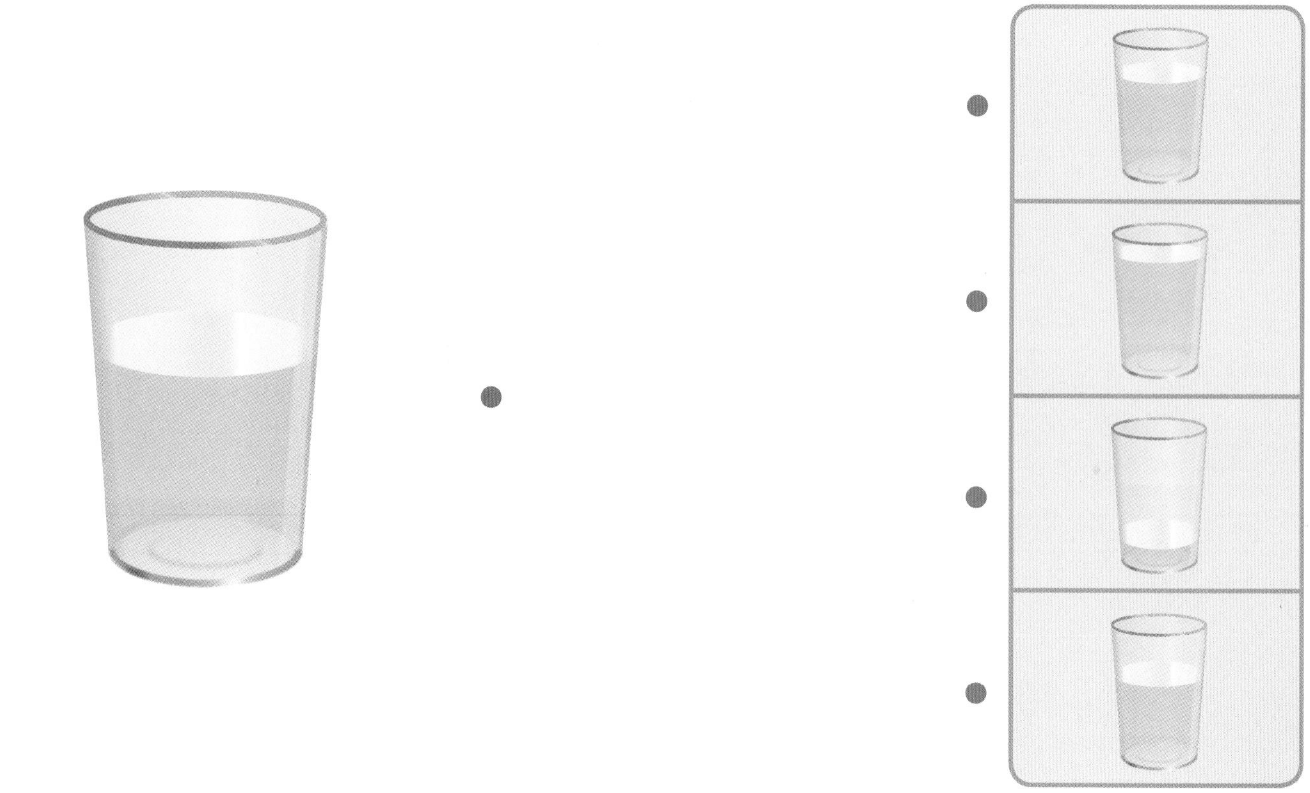

21 Matching Quantity
Level Six

Name

Date

■ Draw a line between the matching pictures.

To parents
If your child has difficulty, guide him or her to match each picture on the left with one on the right.

■ Draw a line between the matching pictures.

22 Finding the Missing Object

Level One

Name

Date

To parents

If your child has difficulty, ask him or her to identify each person's job.

■ Draw a line to the object that goes best with the picture.

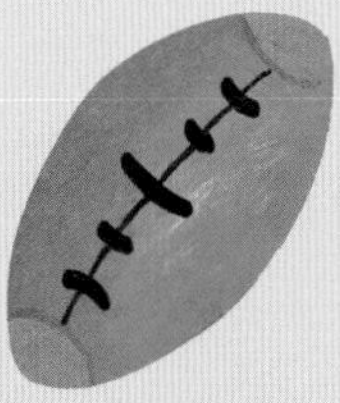

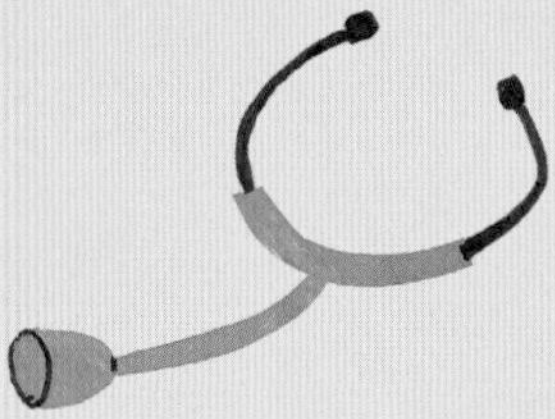

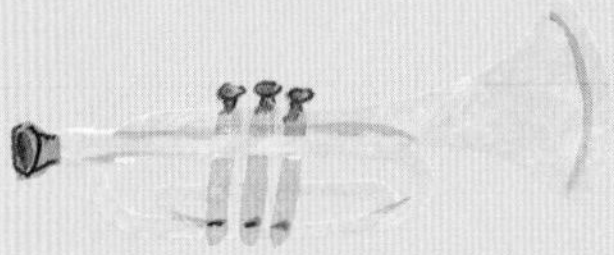

■ Draw a line to the object that goes best with the picture.

23 Finding the Missing Object

Level Two

Name

Date

To parents

If your child has difficulty, ask him or her what object each person is holding.

■ Draw a line to the object that goes best with the picture.

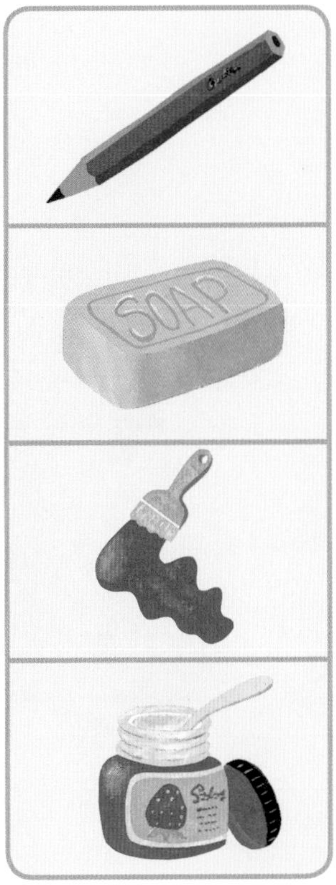

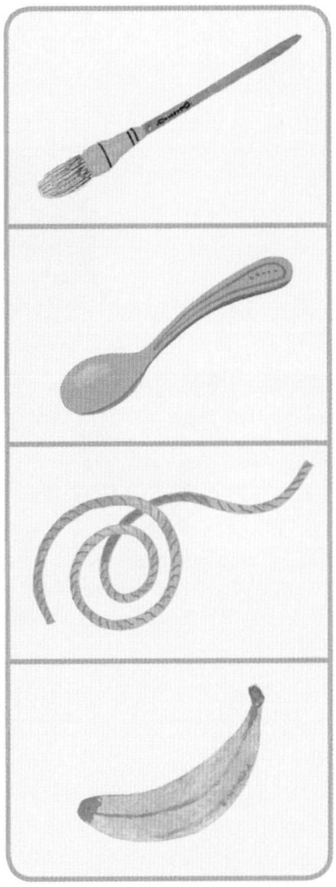

■ Draw a line to the object that goes best with the picture.

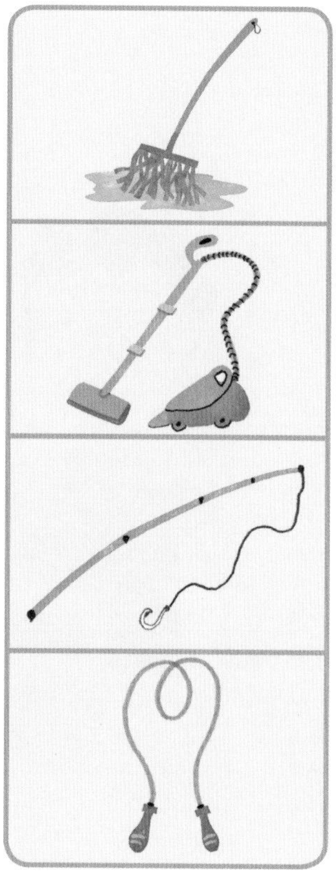

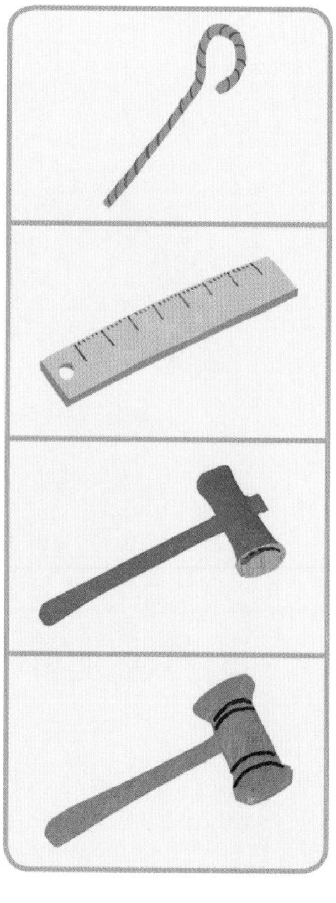

24 Finding the Missing Object
Level Three

Name

Date

To parents
Encourage your child to look carefully at all the colors in the box to find the missing color.

■ Draw a line to the missing object.

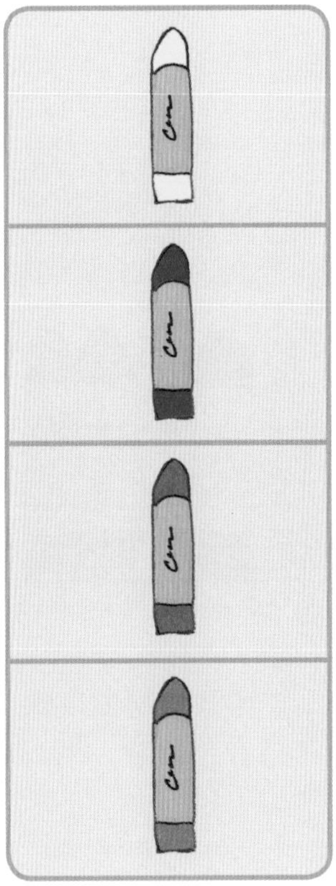

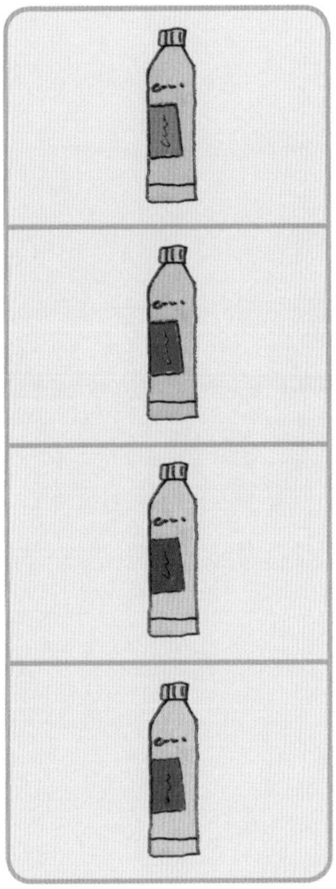

■ Draw a line to the missing object.

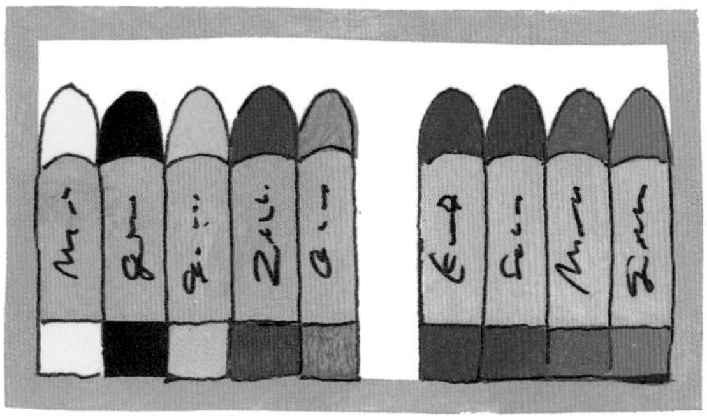

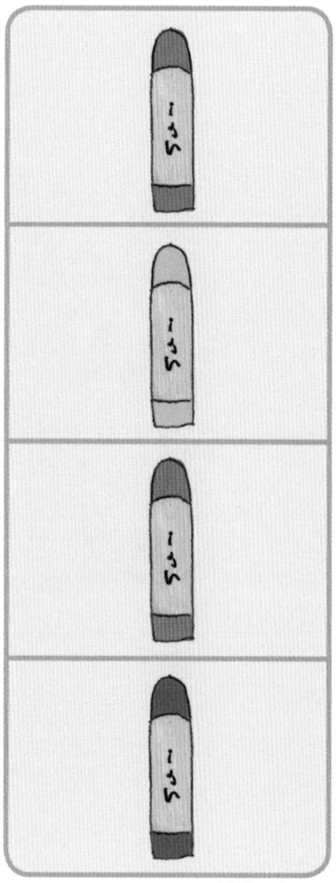

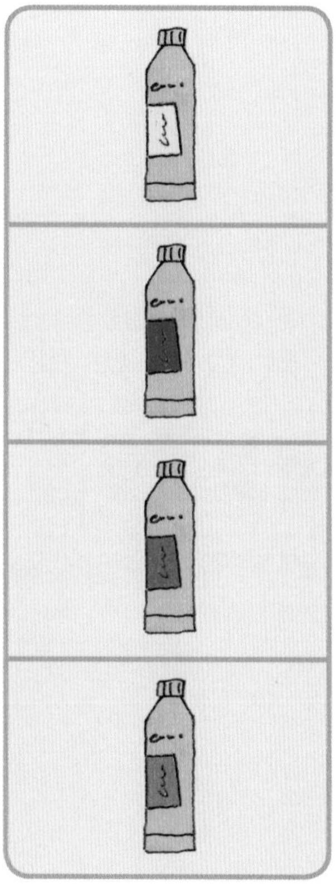

25 Differentiation
Level One

Name

Date

To parents
All five objects are in the same general category. Help your child find the two that are the most similar.

■ Write a check mark (✓) above the two pictures that are the most similar.

( )

( )

( )

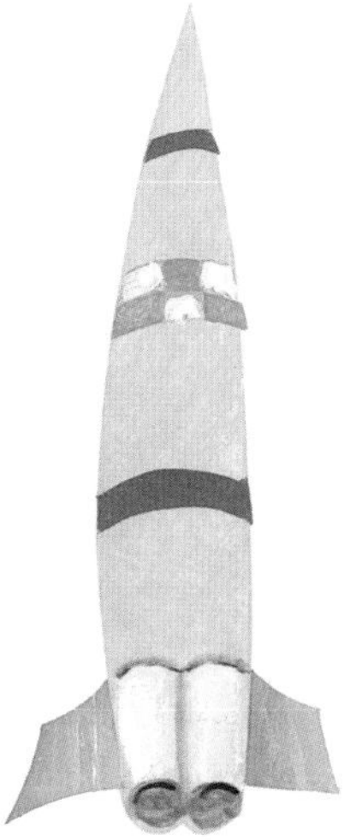

( )

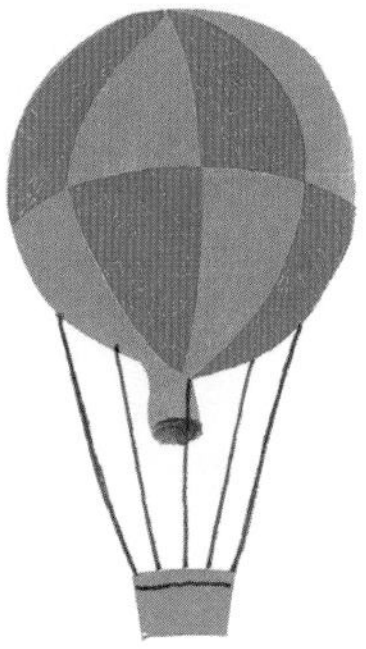

( )

( )

( )

( )

( )

( )

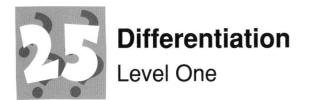

■ Write a check mark (✓) above the two pictures that are the most similar.

( )

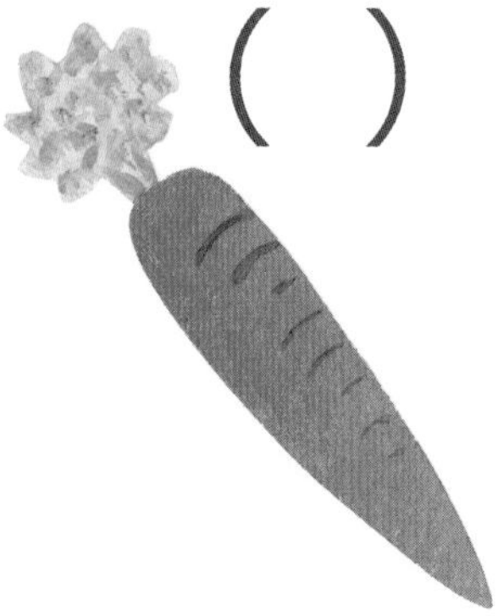

( )

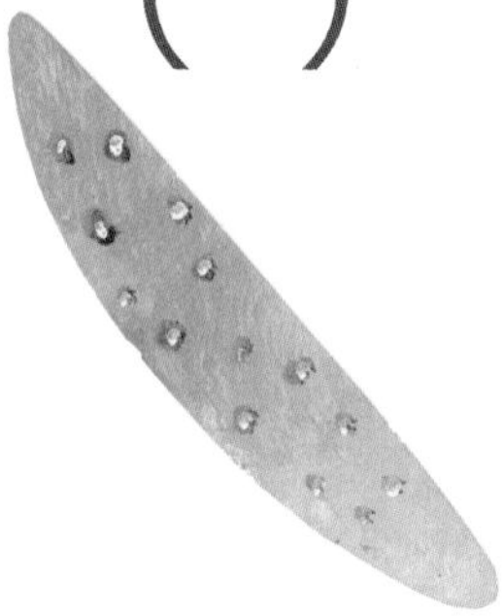

( )

( )

( )

( )

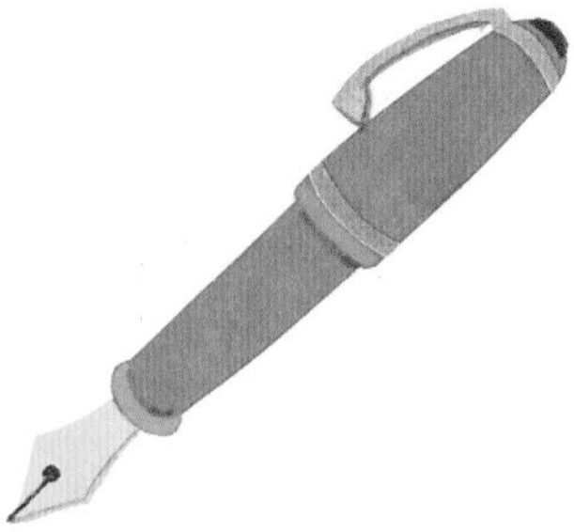

( )

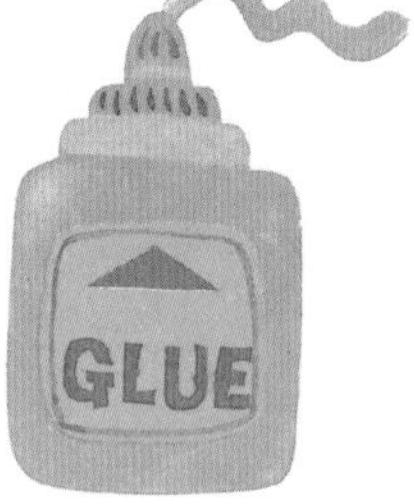

( )

( )

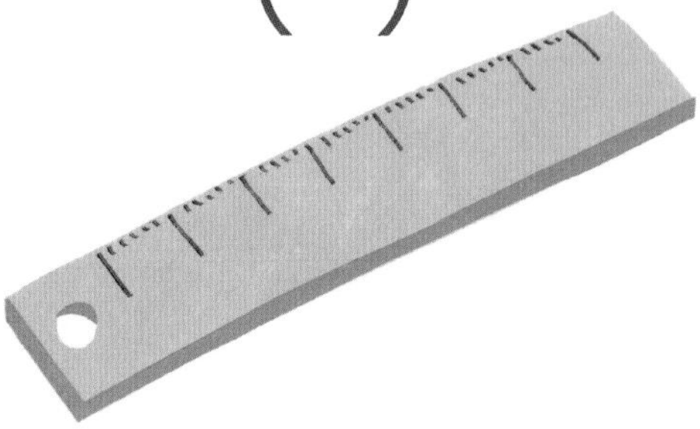

( )

26 Differentiation

Level Two

Name

Date

To parents
If your child has difficulty, help him or her look for a group of exactly three animals that do something similar.

■ Write a check mark (✓) above the three animals that are the most similar.

( )

( )

( )

( )

( )

( )
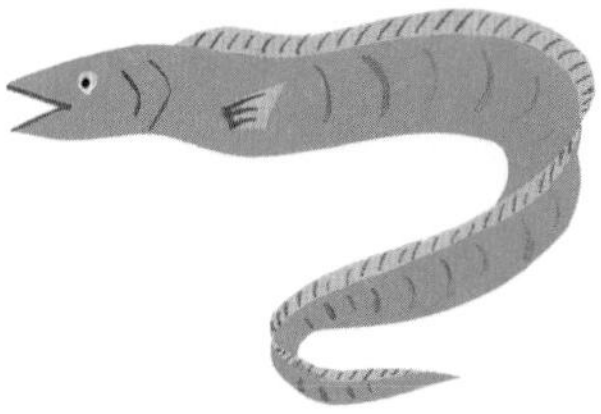

( )

( )

( )

( )

■ Write a check mark (✓) above the three animals that are the most similar.

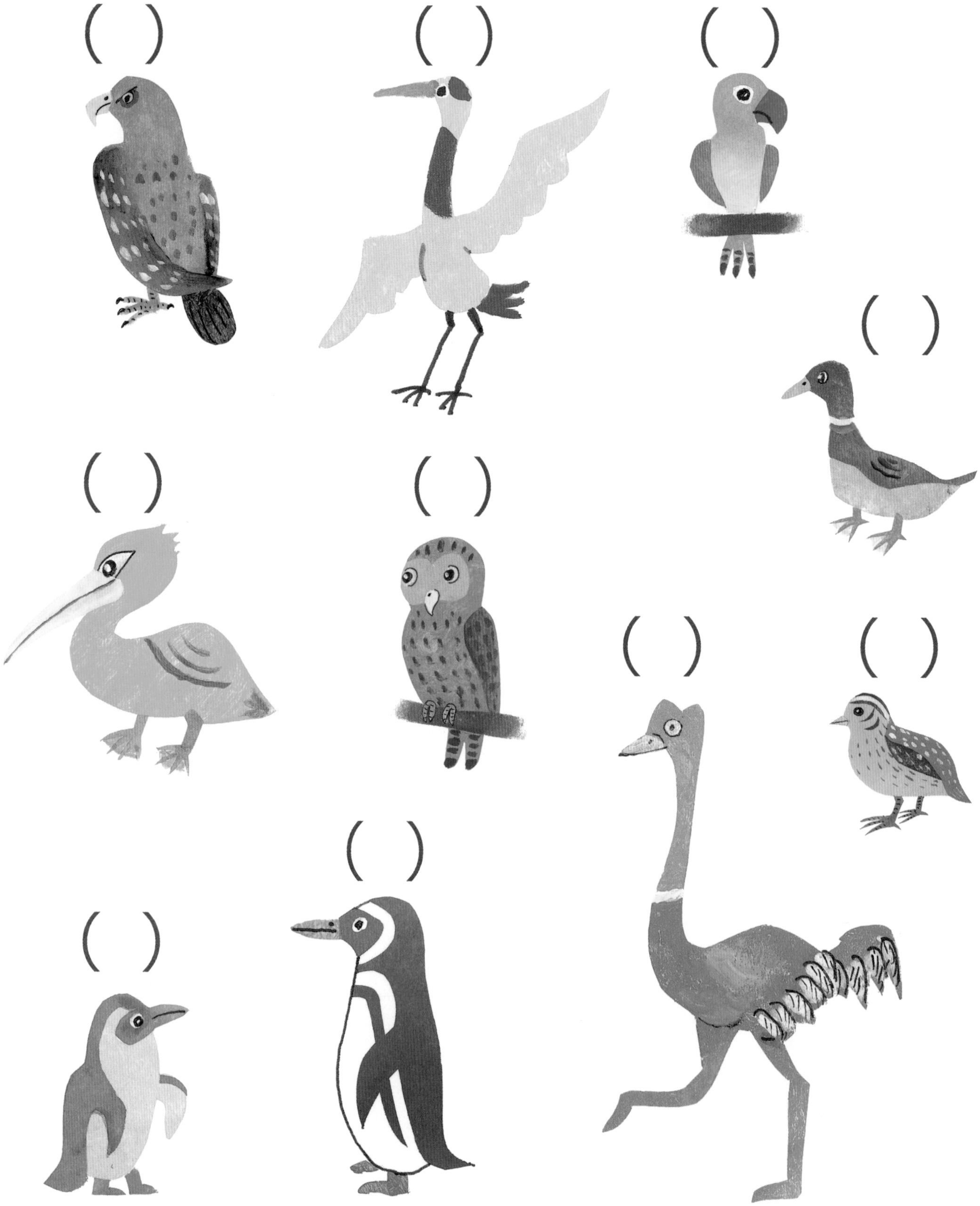

27 Differentiation
Level Three

Name

Date

To parents
If your child has difficulty, ask him or her to briefly describe each object to find similar characteristics.

■ Write a check mark (✓) above the three pictures that are the most similar.

( )
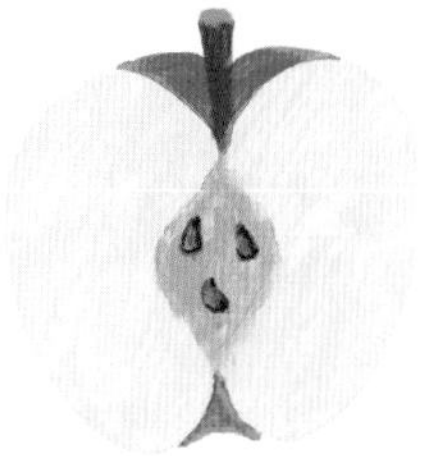

( )
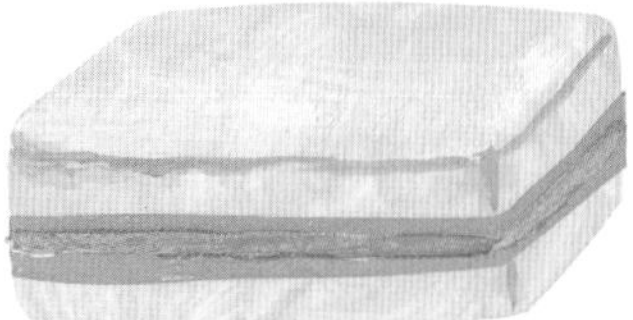

( )
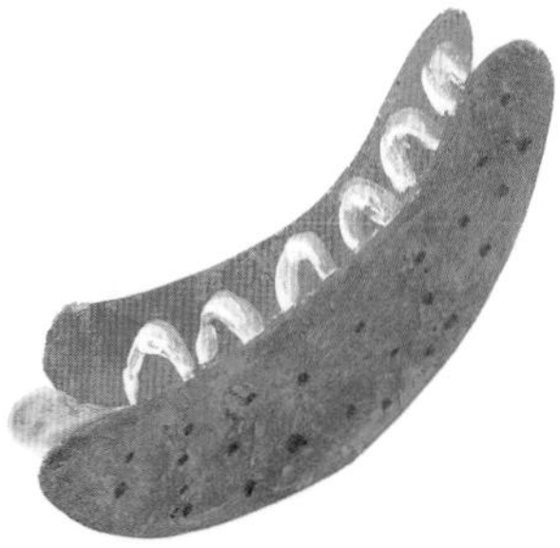

( )
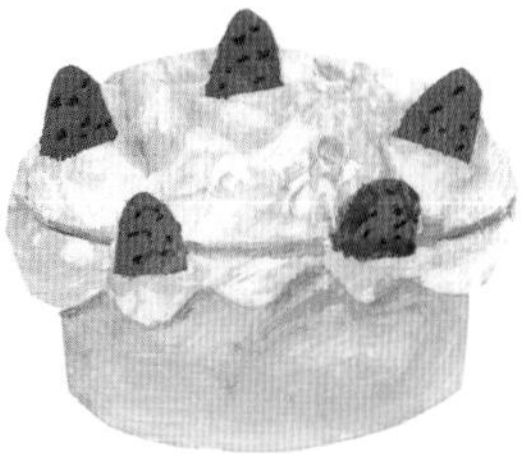

( )
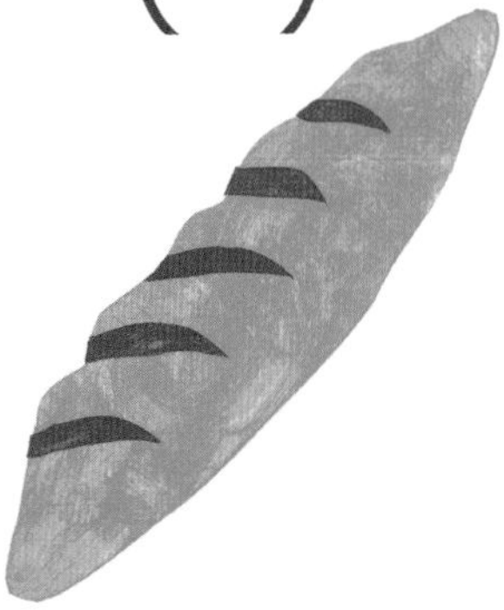

( )
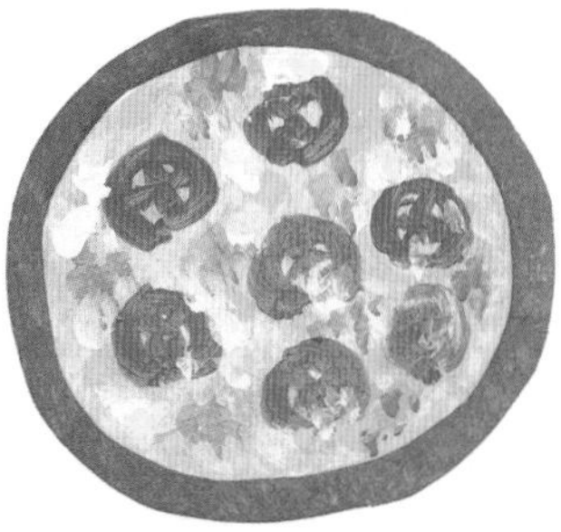

( )

( )

( )

( )

( )
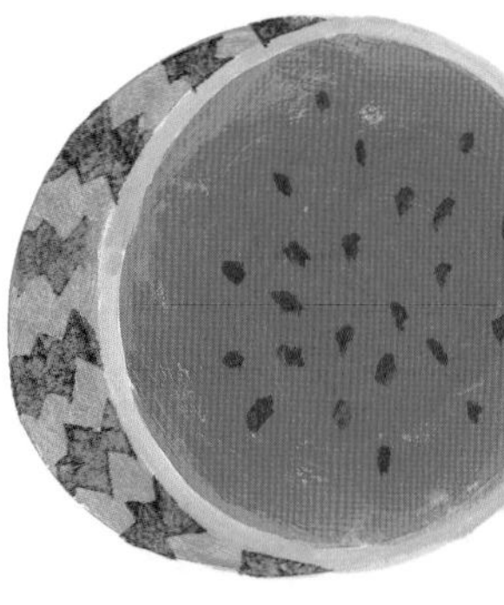

( )
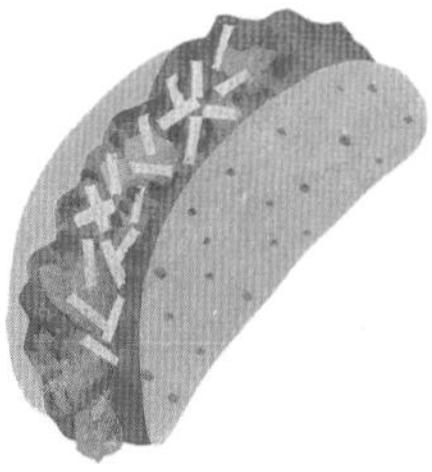

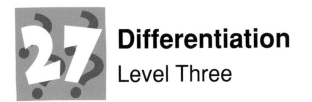

■ Write a check mark (✓) above the three animals that are doing something similar.

( ) ( ) ( )

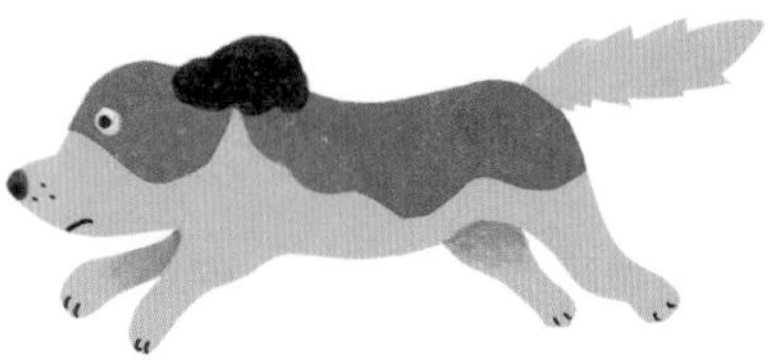  

( ) ( ) ( )

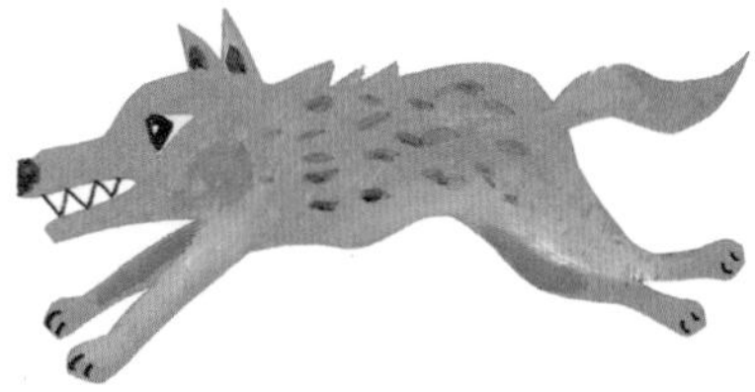  

( ) ( ) ( )

( ) ( ) ( )

28 Matching Pairs
Level One

Name

Date

To parents
If your child has difficulty, show him or her how to eliminate answer choices by crossing off matching pairs.

■ Write a check mark (✓) under the picture without a match.

( )

( )

( )

( )

( )

( )

( )

( )

( )

( )

( )

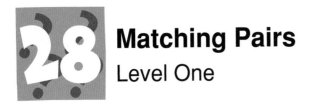

■ Write a check mark (✓) under the picture without a match.

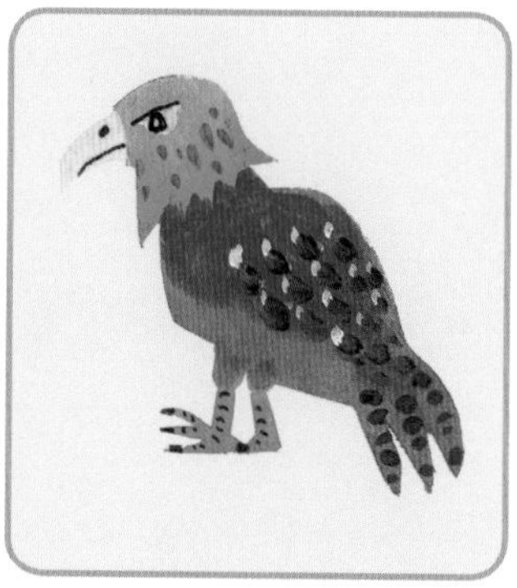
( )

( )

( )

( )

( )

( )

( )

( )

( )

( )

( )

29 Matching Pairs
Level Two

Name

Date

To parents
If your child has difficulty, guide him or her to look at each picture one by one and check if it has a match.

■ Write a check mark (✓) under the picture without a match.

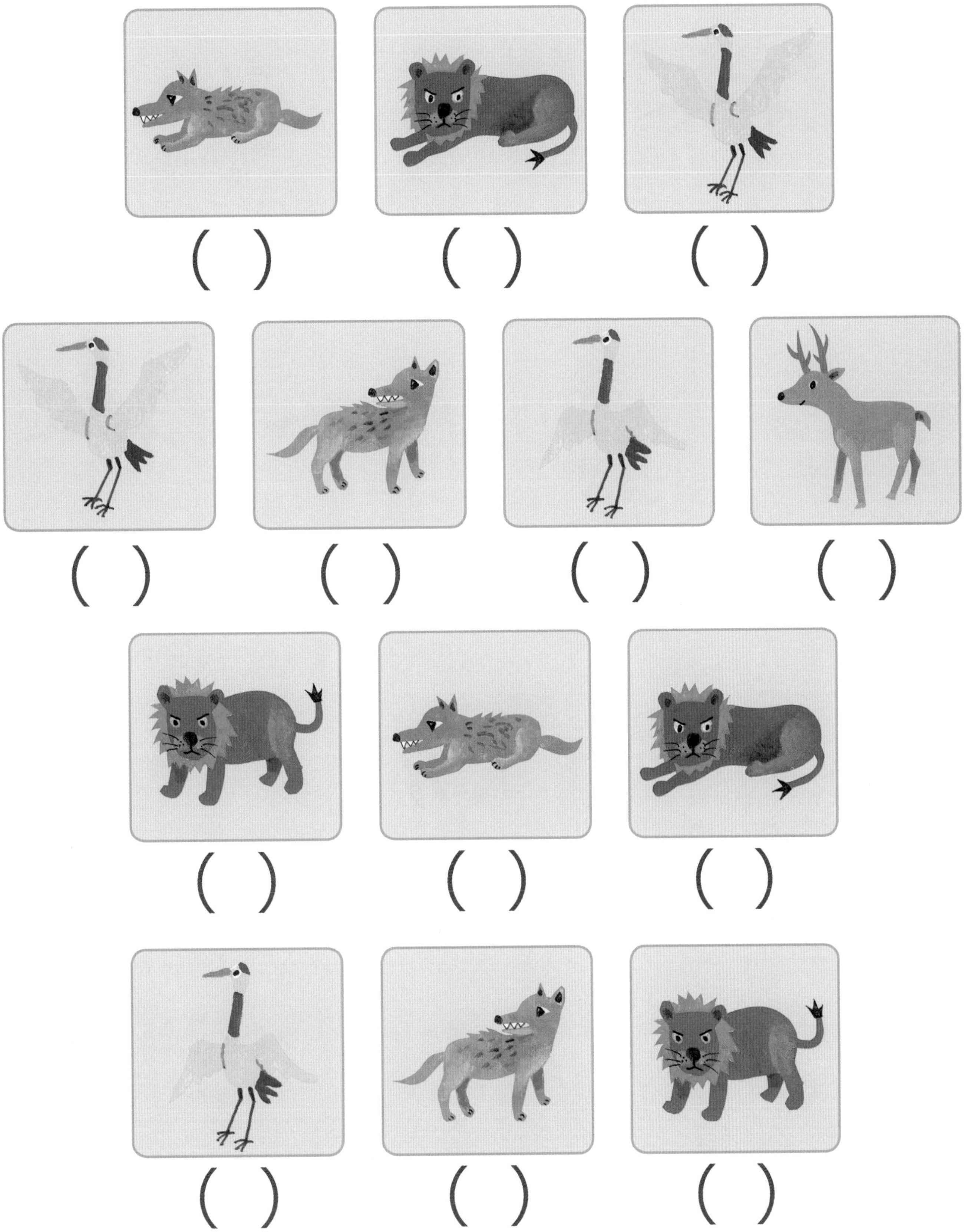

■ Write a check mark (✓) under the picture without a match.

( )

( )

( )

( )

( )

( )

( )

( )

( )

( )

( )

( )

( )

30

Matching Pairs

Level Three

Name

Date

To parents

Encourage your child to look carefully at each animal's pose or position.

■ Write a check mark (✓) under the picture without a match.

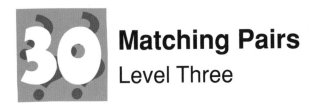

■ Write a check mark (✓) under the picture without a match.

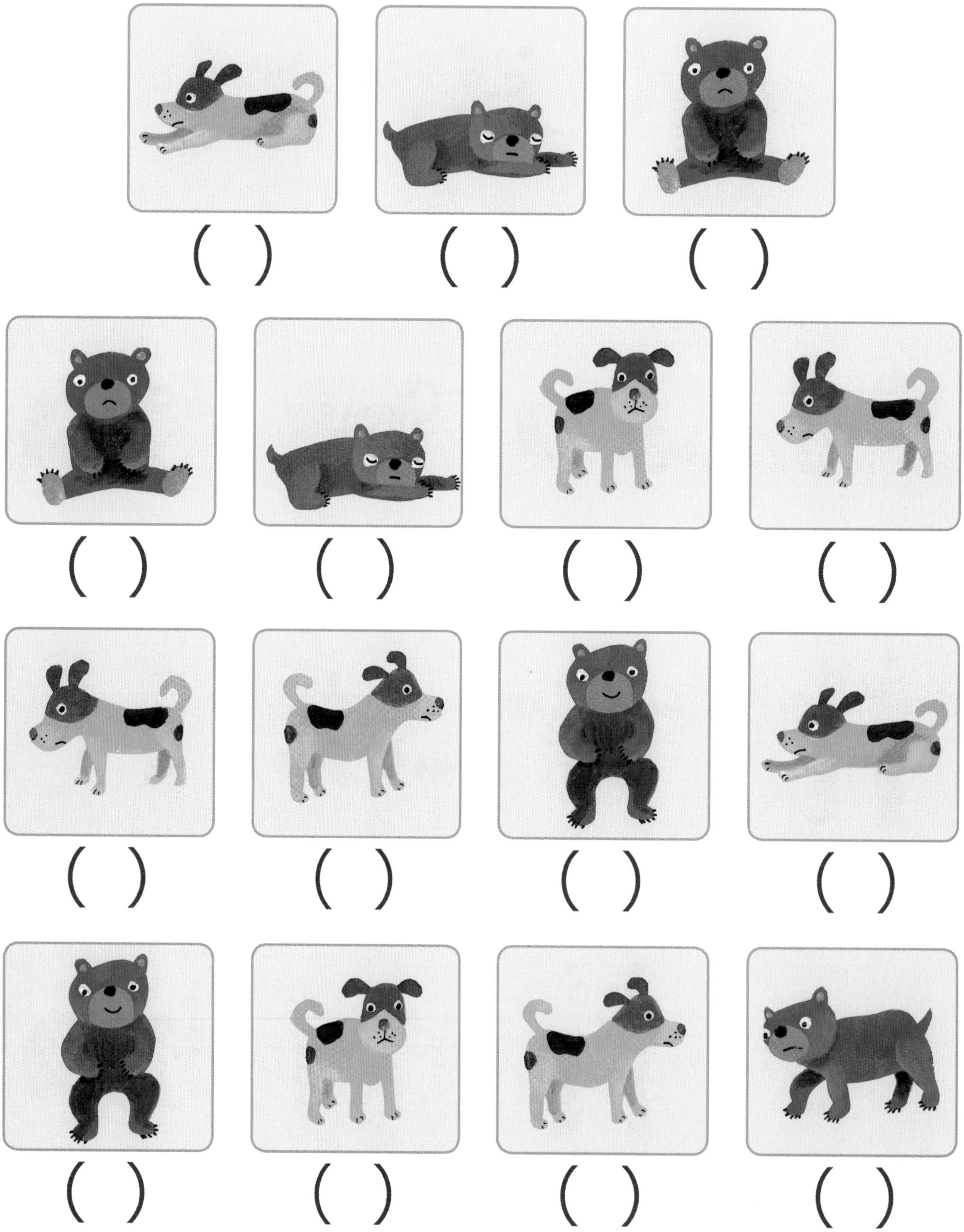

31 Identifying Objects
Level One

Name

Date

To parents
Point to an object shown in the instructions. Guide your child to find the same object in the picture below.

■ Find and circle the following objects in the picture below: () () ()

■ Find and circle the following objects in the picture below:

() () ()

32 Identifying Objects
Level Two

Name

Date

To parents
If your child enjoys looking at the picture, encourage him or her to identify other objects in the scene.

■ Find and circle the following animals in the picture below: () () () ()

■ Find and circle the following fish in the picture below:

() () () ()

33 Identifying Objects
Level Three

Name

Date

To parents

The number of different objects to find and circle has increased. Encourage your child to look for all five objects.

■ Find and circle the following objects in the picture below: () () () () ()

■ Find and circle the following objects in the picture below:

() () () () ()

34 Identifying Objects
Level Four

Name

Date

To parents
Encourage your child to look carefully at the objects in the instructions first.

■ Find and circle the following shells in the picture below: () ()

■ Find and circle the following can and bottle in the picture below:

() ()

35

Identifying Objects

Level Five

Name

Date

To parents

The number of objects in the picture has increased. Guide your child to find the same objects shown in the instructions.

■ Find and circle the following blocks in the picture below: () () ()

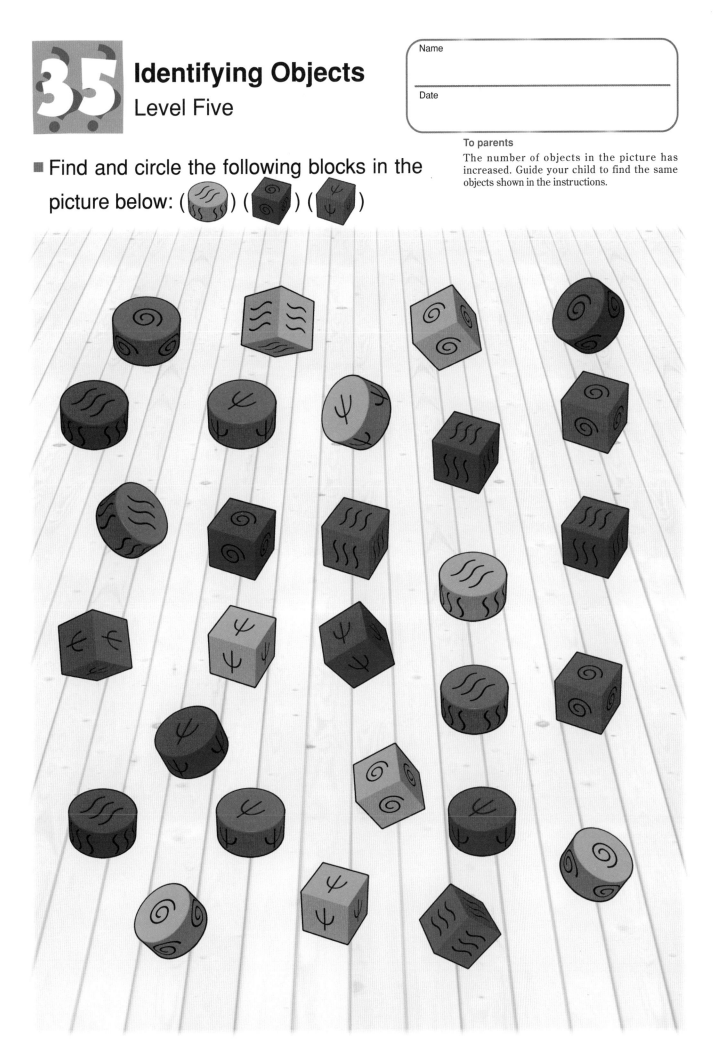

■ Find and circle the following pendants in the picture below:

() (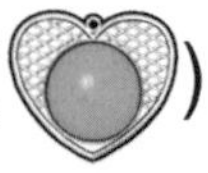) (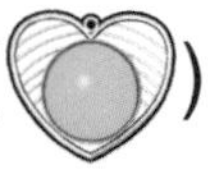)

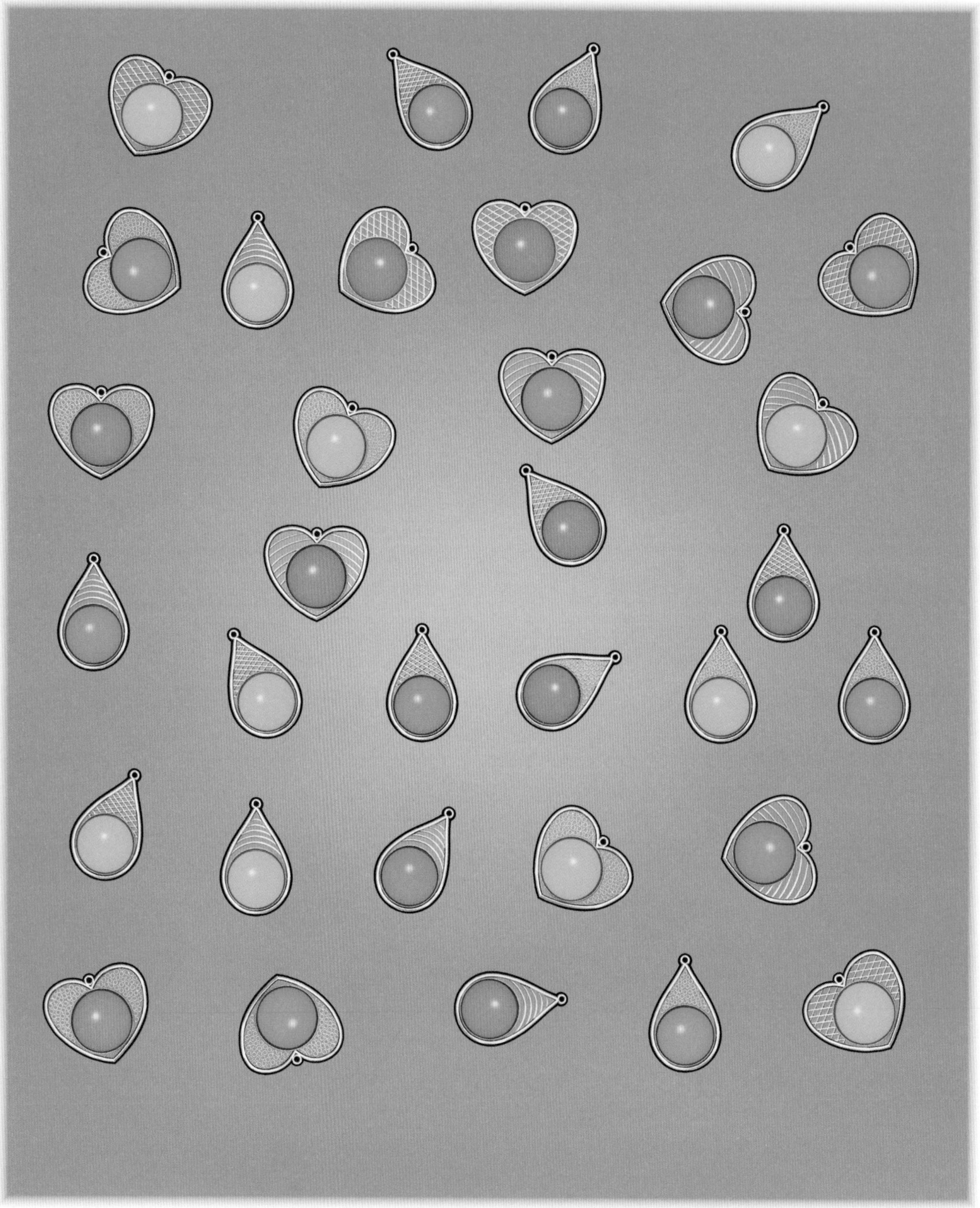

36 Identifying Objects
Level Six

Name

Date

To parents

If your child has difficulty, encourage him or her to look at each object one by one and check if it is one of the objects in the instructions.

■ Find and circle the following cups in the picture below: () () () ()

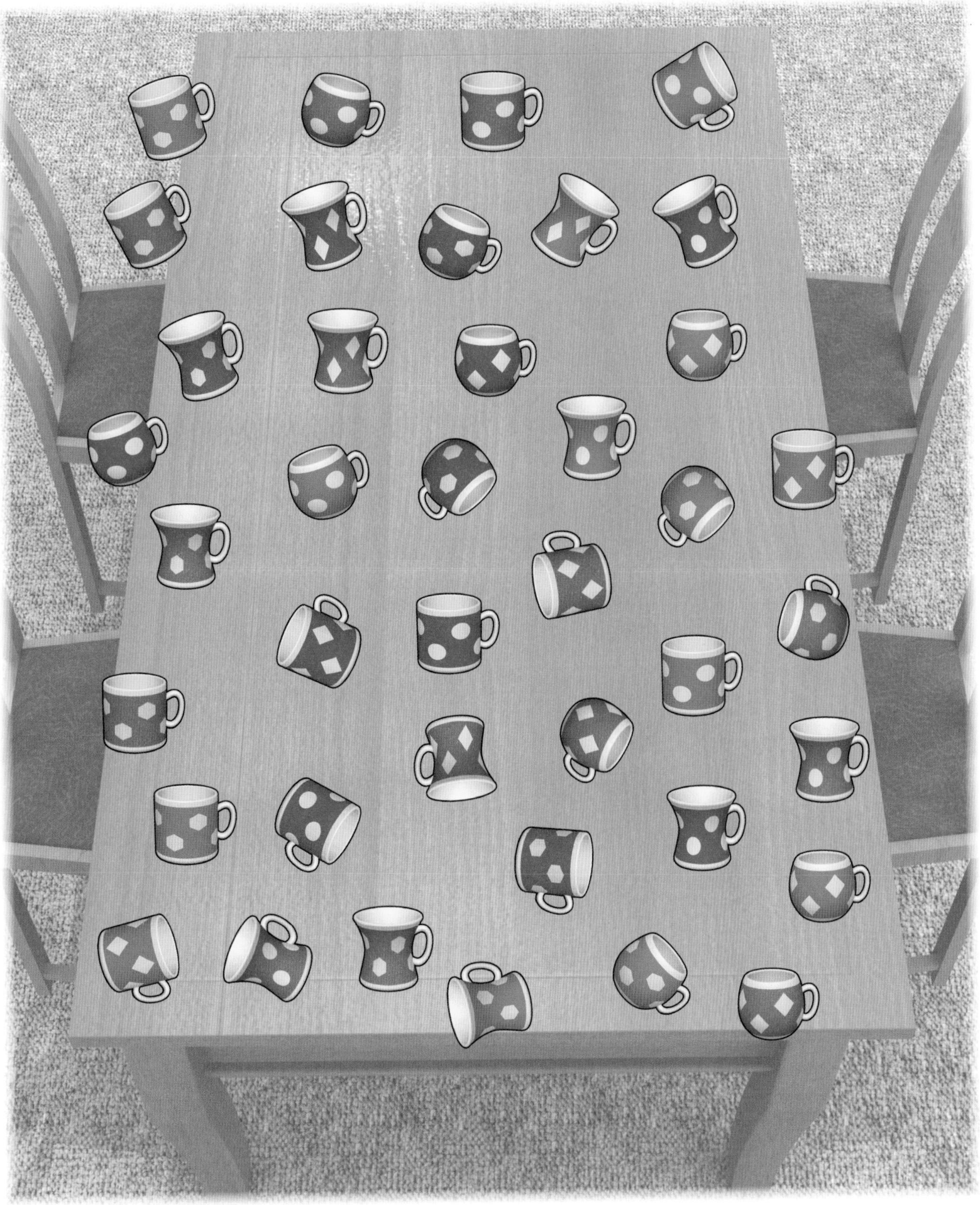

To parents

This is the last exercise of this section. Please praise your child for the effort it took to complete this workbook.

■ Find and circle the following masks in the picture below:

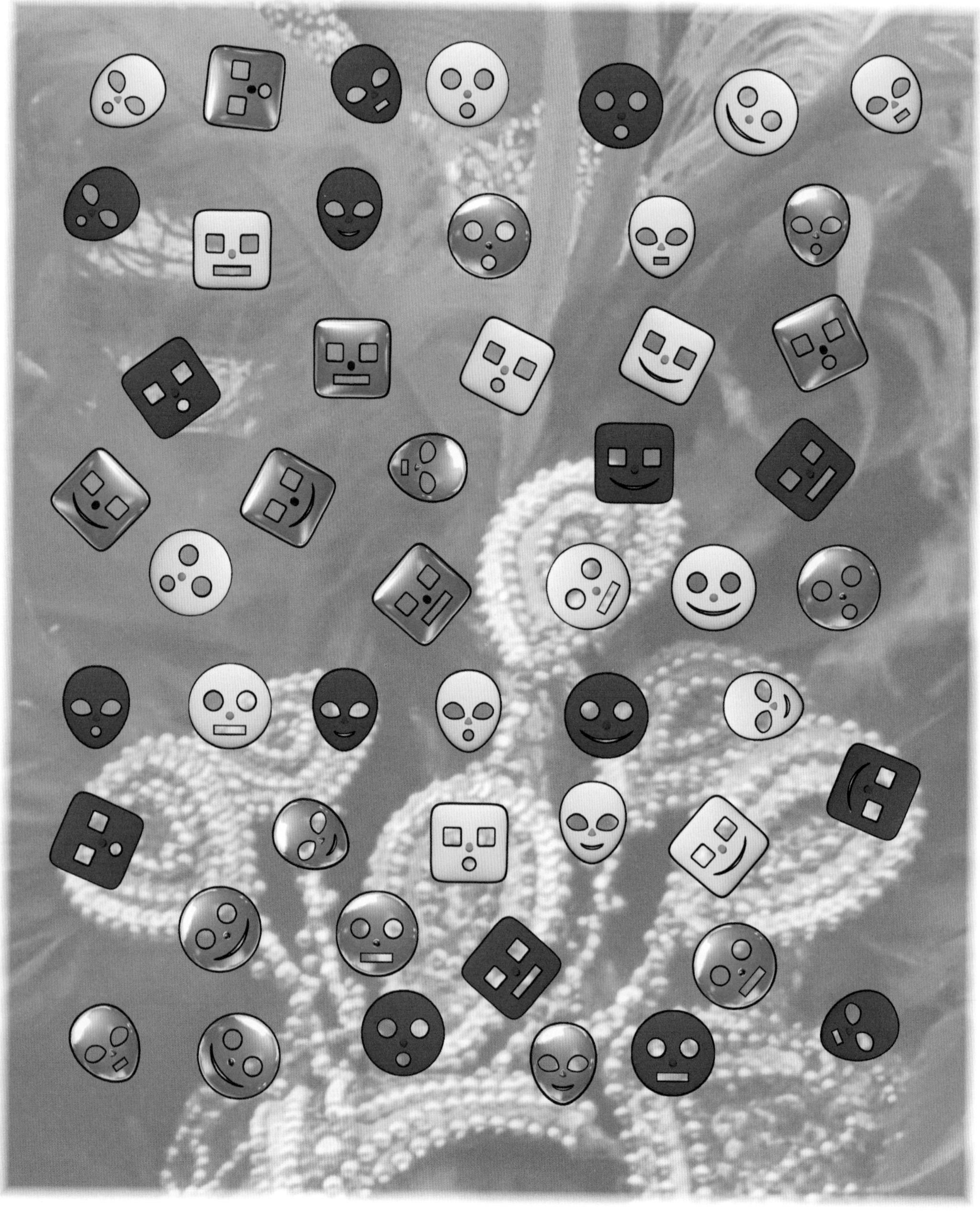

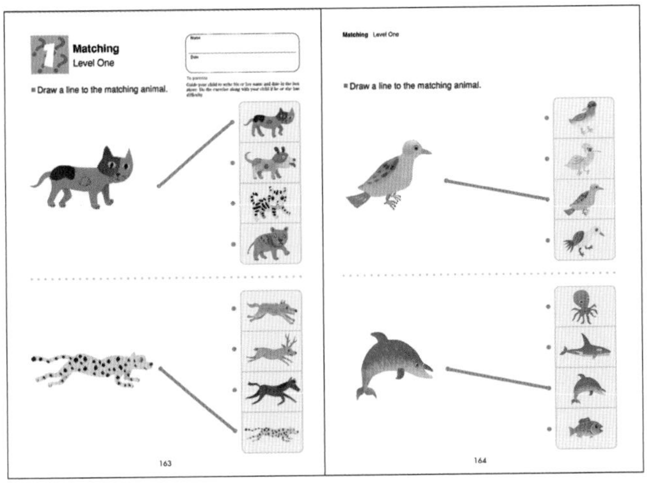

pages 163 and 164

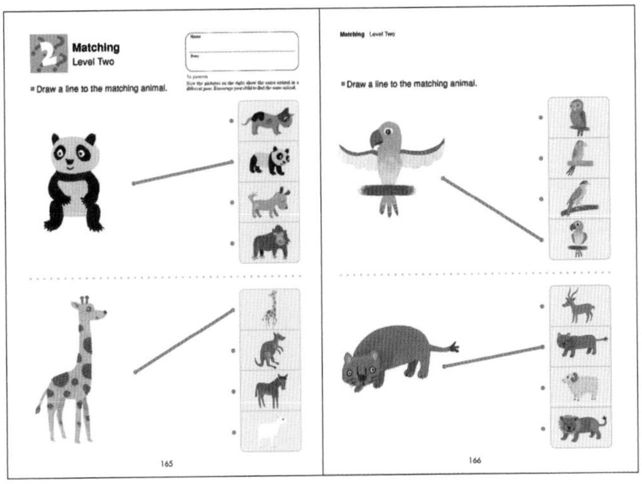

pages 165 and 166

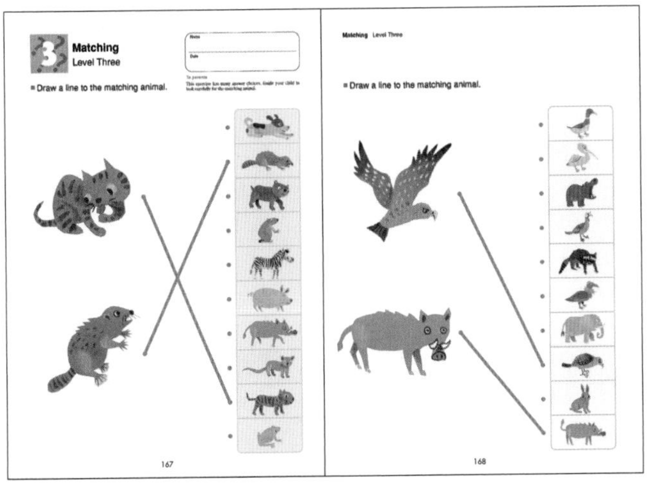

pages 167 and 168

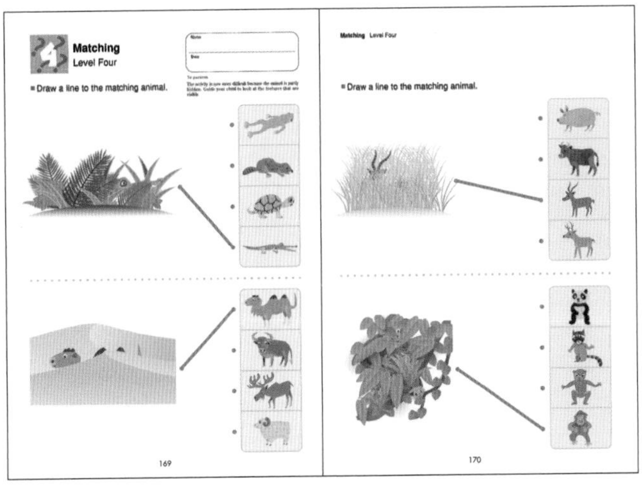

pages 169 and 170

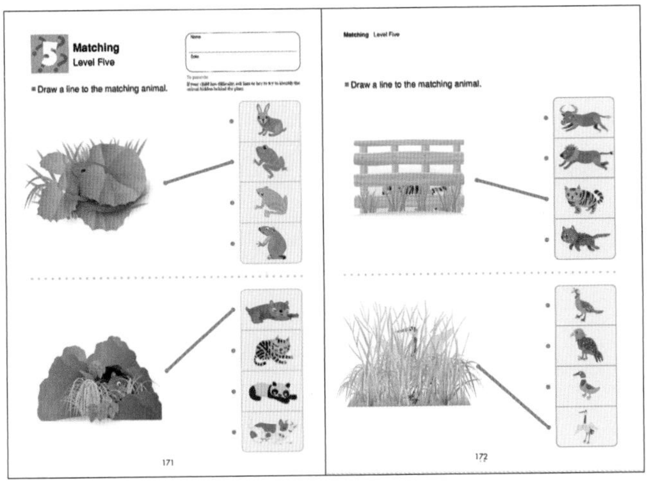

pages 171 and 172

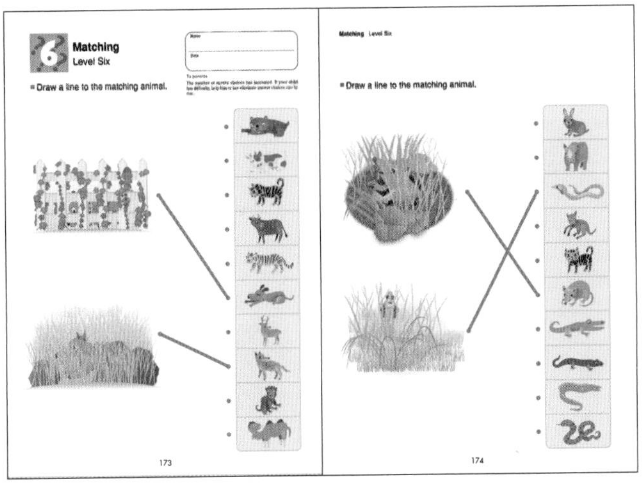

pages 173 and 174

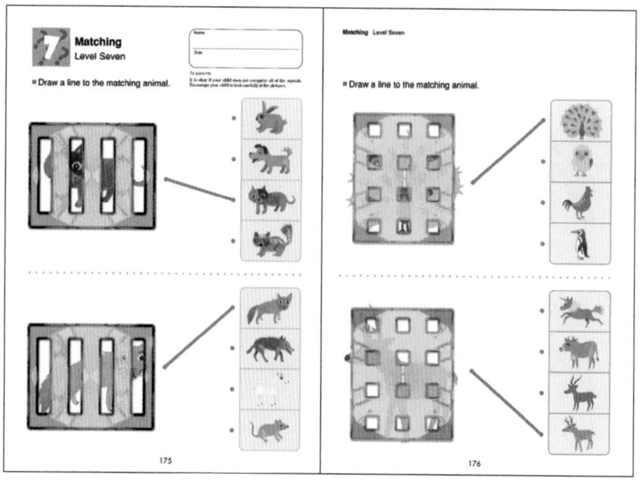
7 Matching Level Seven

Draw a line to the matching animal.

175

Matching Level Seven

Draw a line to the matching animal.

176

pages 175 and 176

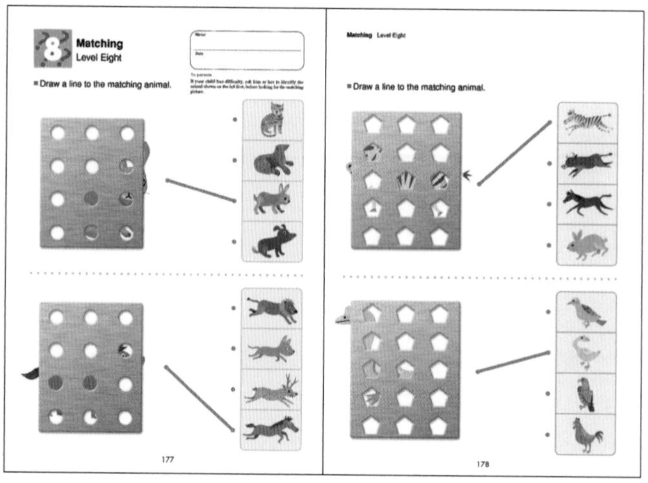
8 Matching Level Eight

Draw a line to the matching animal.

177

Matching Level Eight

Draw a line to the matching animal.

178

pages 177 and 178

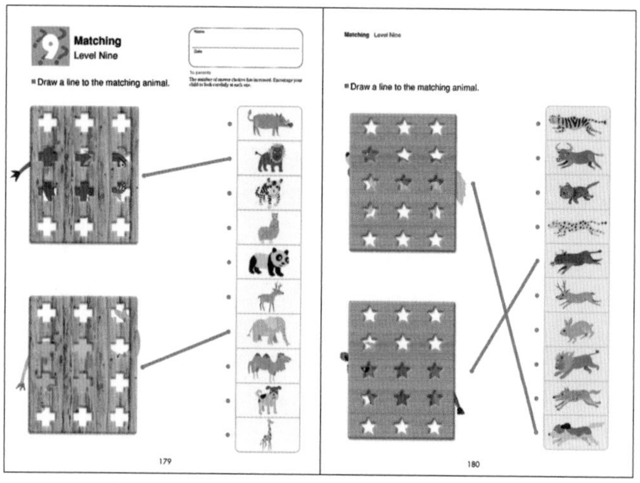
9 Matching Level Nine

Draw a line to the matching animal.

179

Matching Level Nine

Draw a line to the matching animal.

180

pages 179 and 180

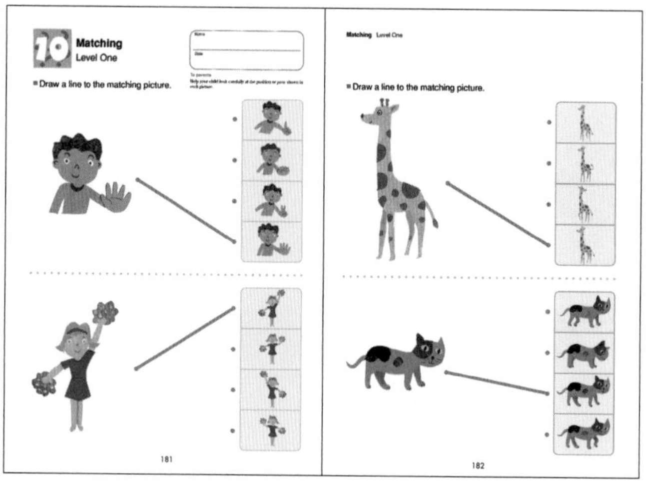
10 Matching Level One

Draw a line to the matching picture.

181

Matching Level One

Draw a line to the matching picture.

182

pages 181 and 182

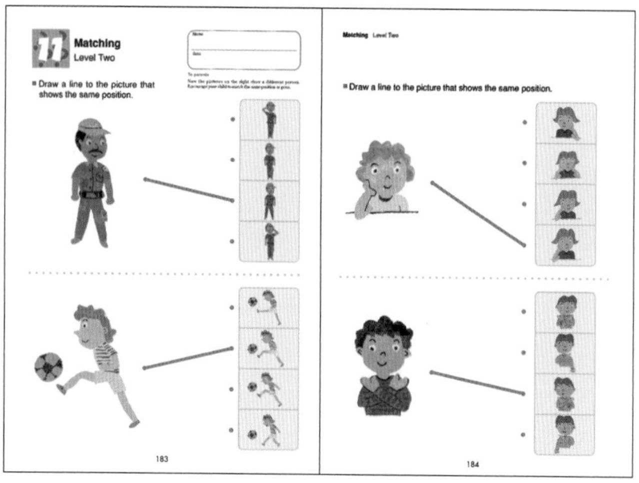
11 Matching Level Two

Draw a line to the picture that shows the same position.

183

Matching Level Two

Draw a line to the picture that shows the same position.

184

pages 183 and 184

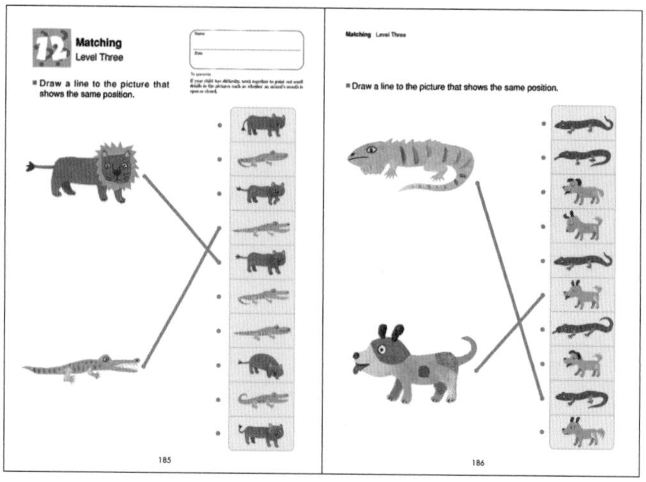
12 Matching Level Three

Draw a line to the picture that shows the same position.

185

Matching Level Three

Draw a line to the picture that shows the same position.

186

pages 185 and 186

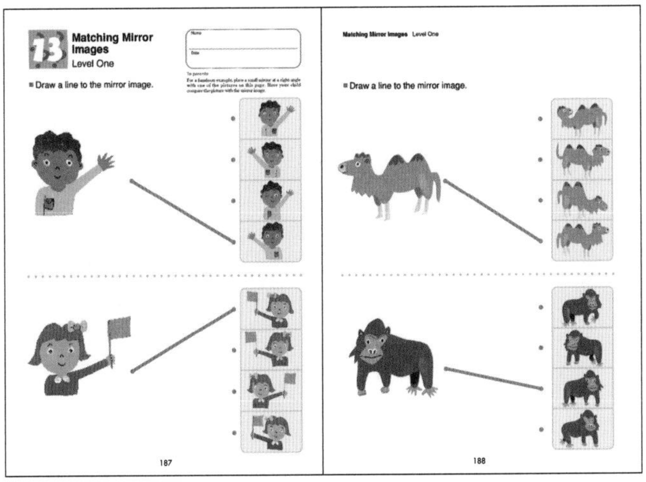

pages 187 and 188

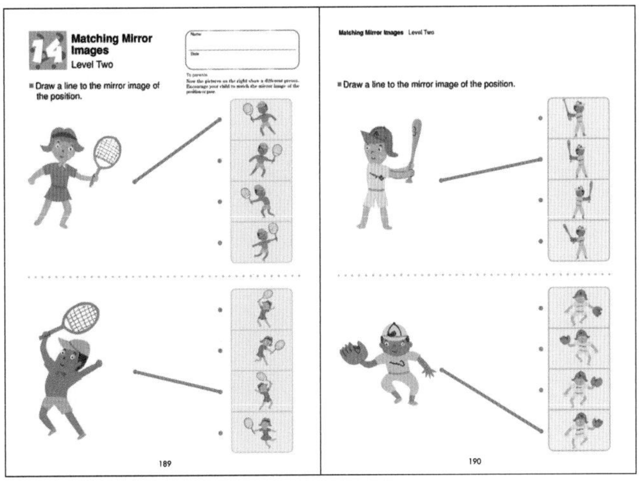

pages 189 and 190

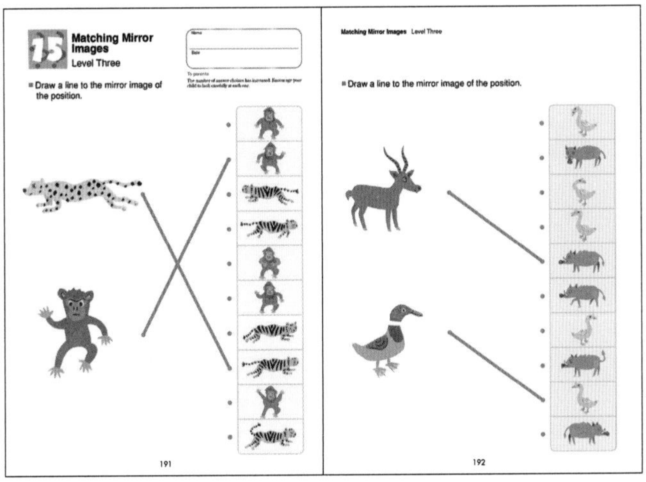

pages 191 and 192

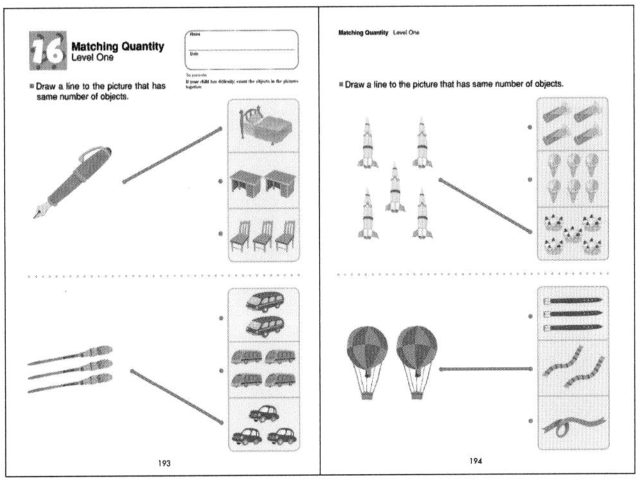

pages 193 and 194

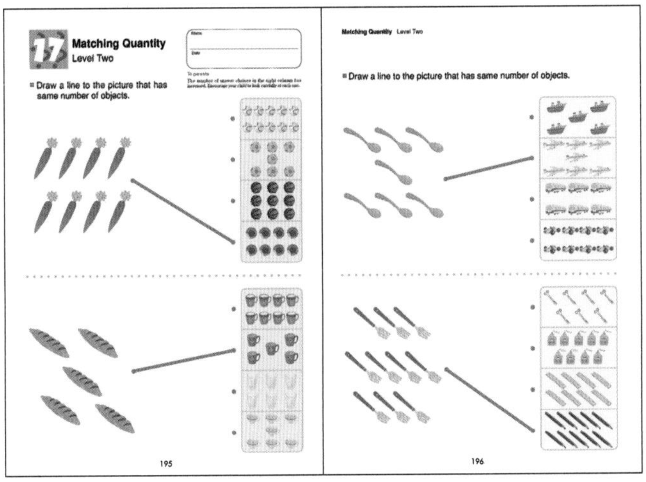

pages 195 and 196

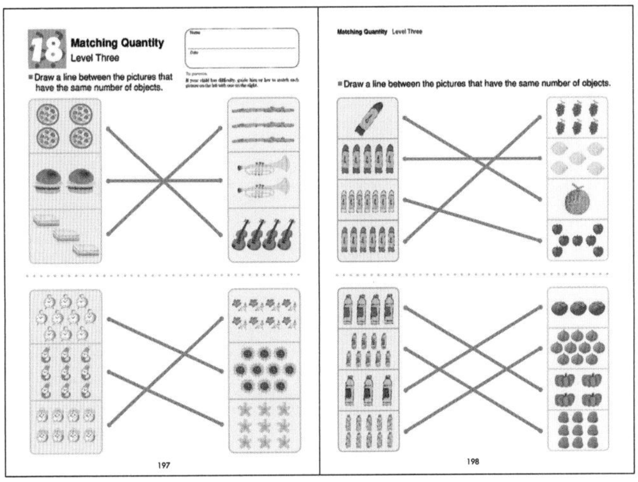

pages 197 and 198

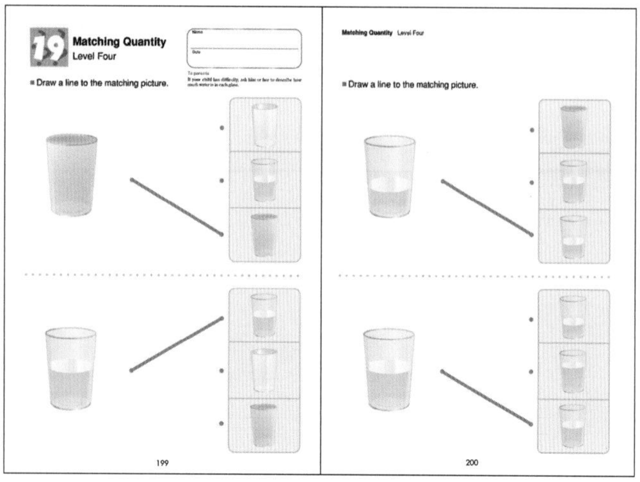

pages 199 and 200

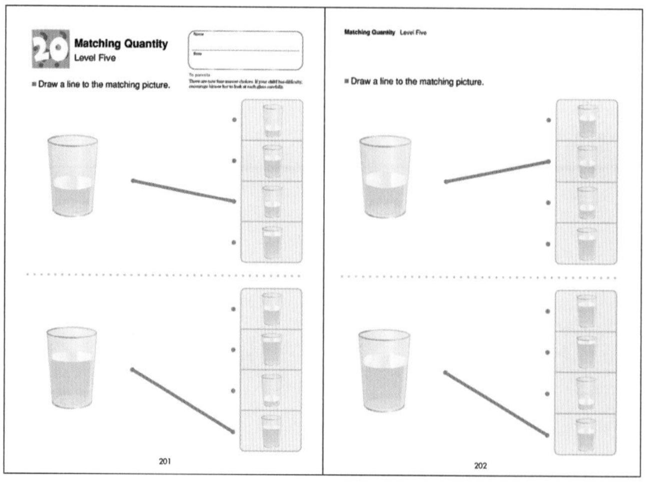

pages 201 and 202

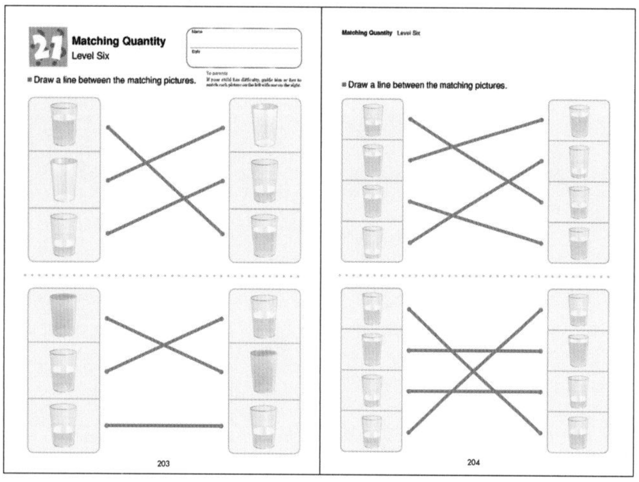

pages 203 and 204

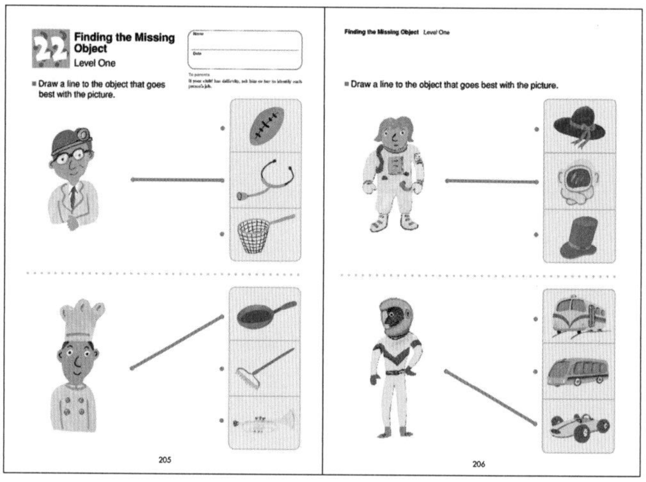

pages 205 and 206

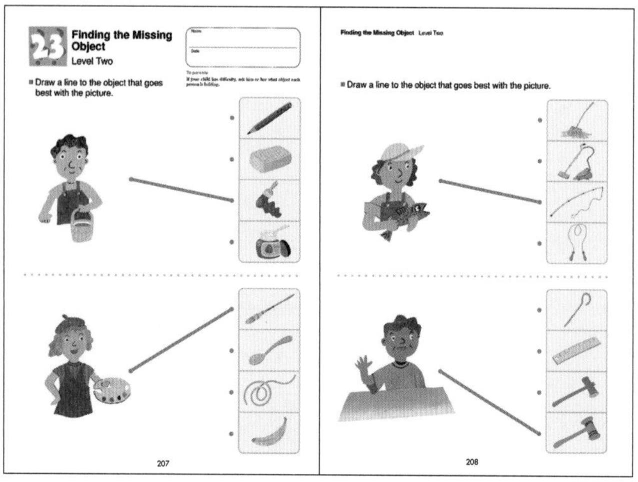

pages 207 and 208

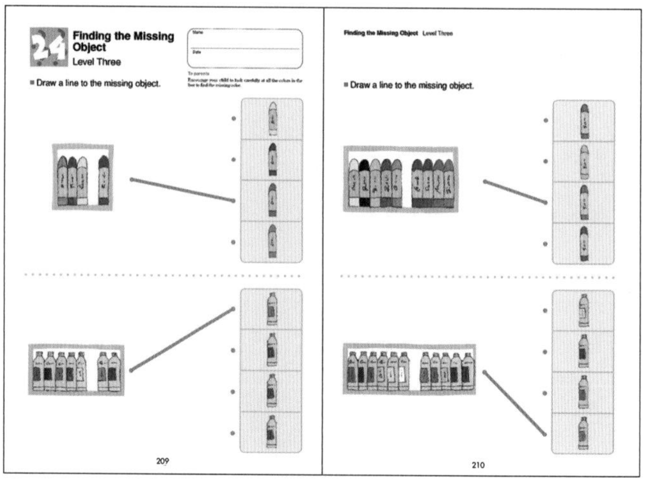

pages 209 and 210

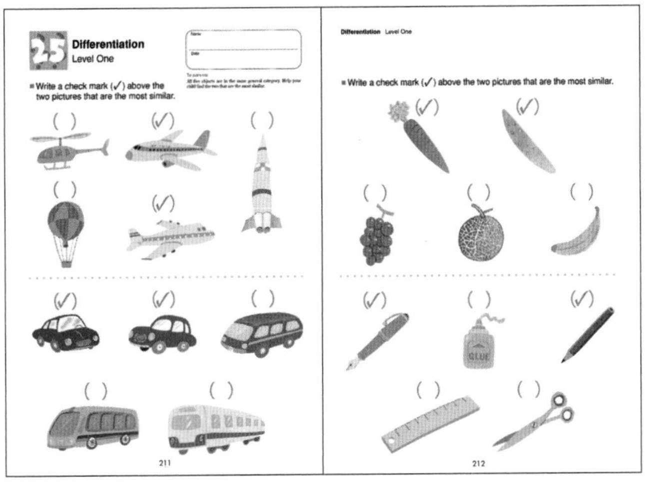

pages 211 and 212

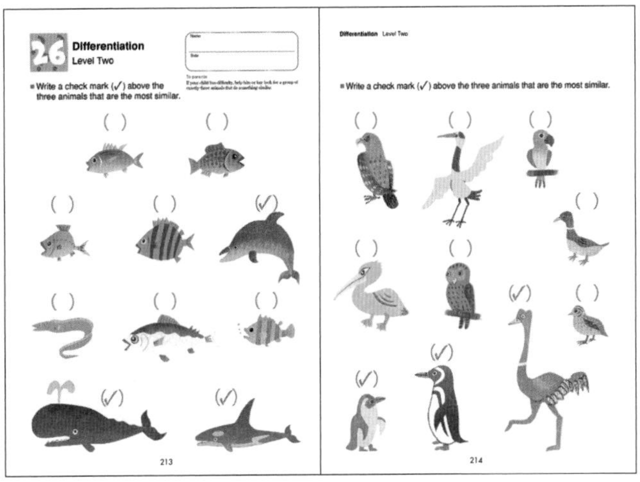

pages 213 and 214

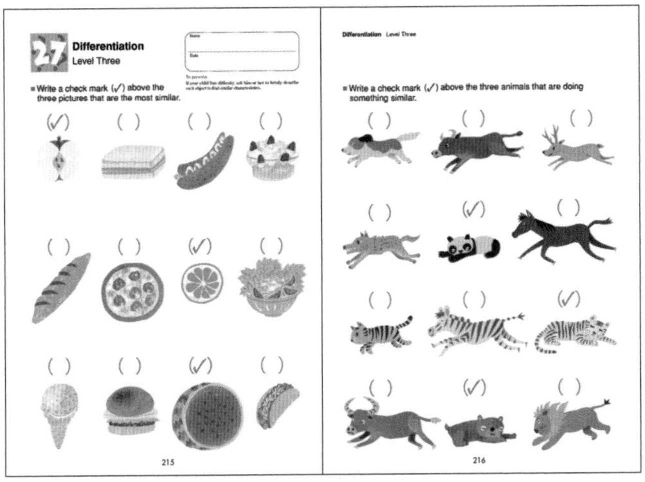

pages 215 and 216

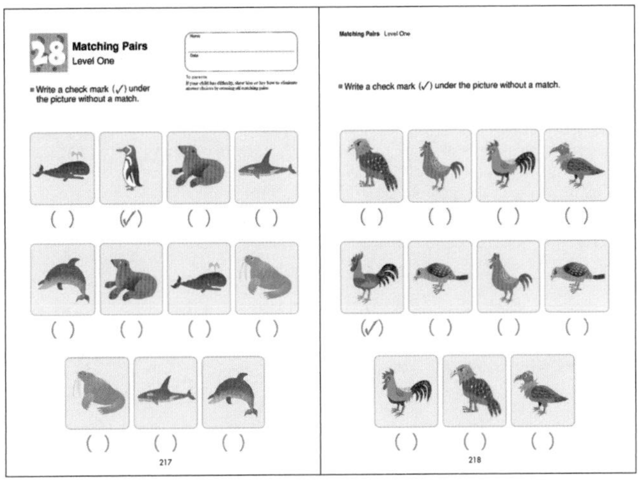

pages 217 and 218

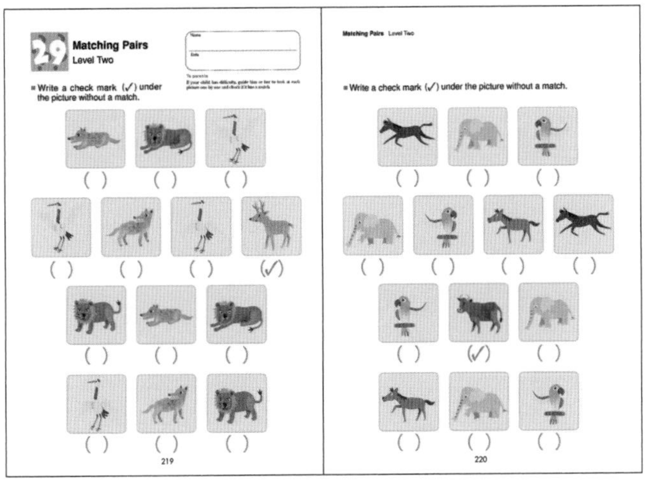

pages 219 and 220

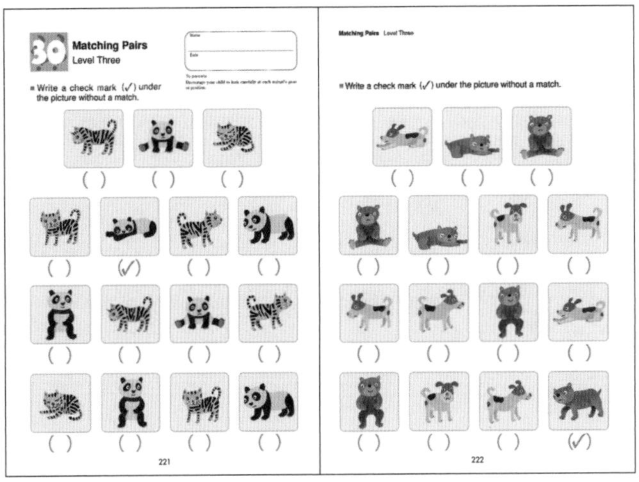

pages 221 and 222

31 Identifying Objects
Level One
Find and circle the following objects in the picture below:
CALENDAR
223
Identifying Objects Level One
Find and circle the following objects in the picture below:
224

pages 223 and 224

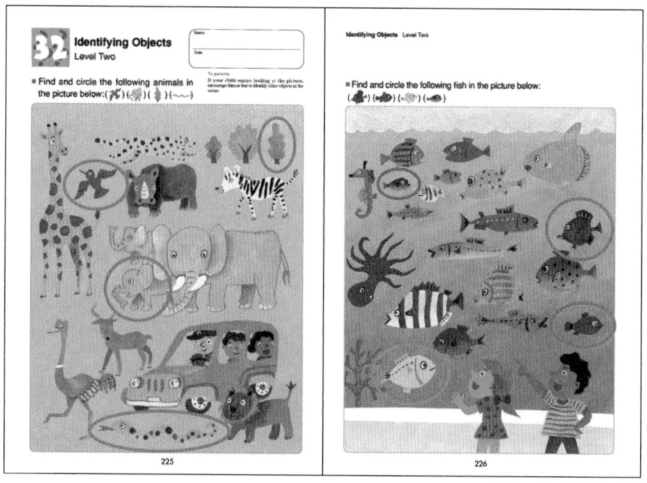
32 Identifying Objects
Level Two
Find and circle the following animals in the picture below:
225
Identifying Objects Level Two
Find and circle the following fish in the picture below:
226

pages 225 and 226

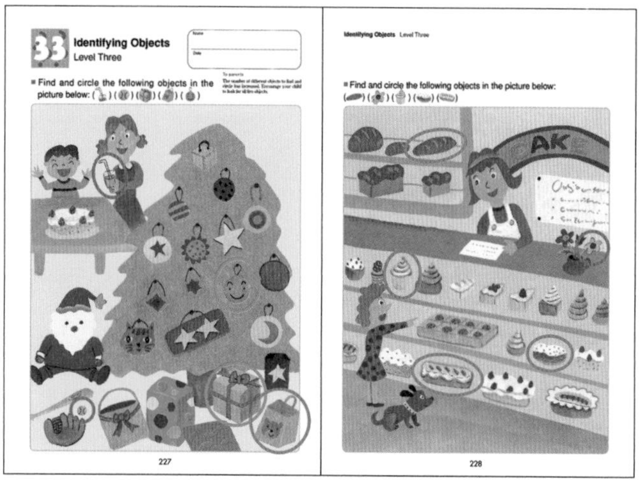
33 Identifying Objects
Level Three
Find and circle the following objects in the picture below:
227
Identifying Objects Level Three
Find and circle the following objects in the picture below:
228

pages 227 and 228

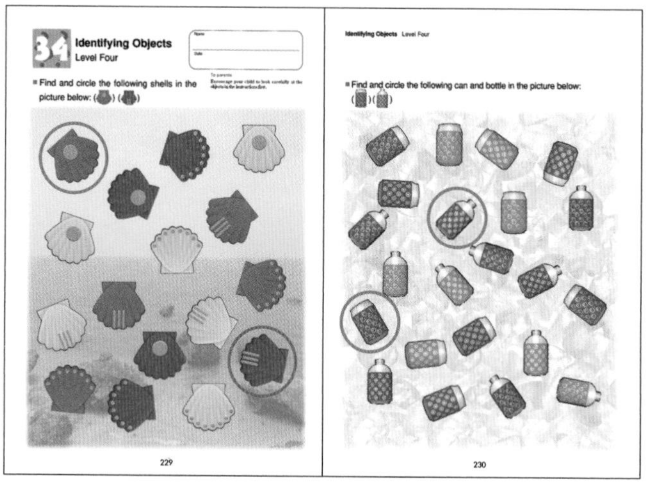
34 Identifying Objects
Level Four
Find and circle the following shells in the picture below:
229
Identifying Objects Level Four
Find and circle the following can and bottle in the picture below:
230

pages 229 and 230

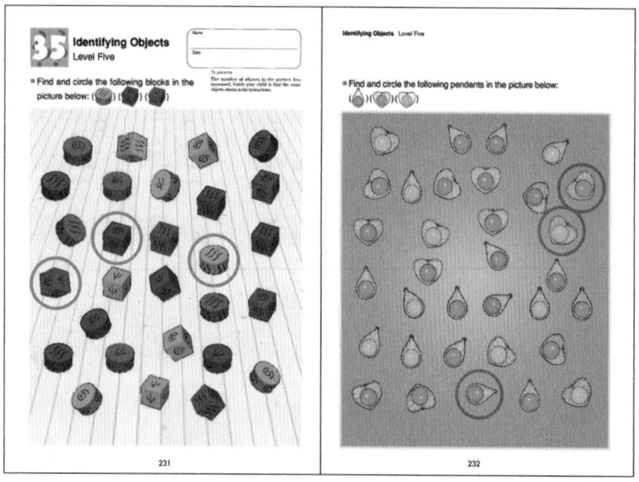
35 Identifying Objects
Level Five
Find and circle the following blocks in the picture below:
231
Identifying Objects Level Five
Find and circle the following pendants in the picture below:
232

pages 231 and 232

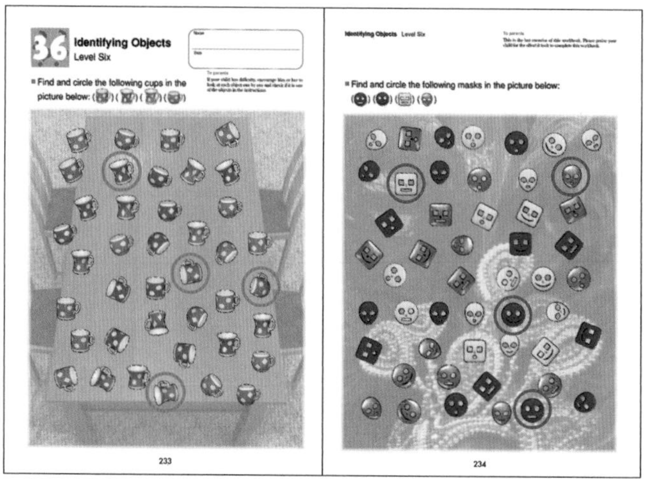
36 Identifying Objects
Level Six
Find and circle the following cups in the picture below:
233
Identifying Objects Level Six
Find and circle the following masks in the picture below:
234

pages 233 and 234

Creativity

Table of Contents

To parents:

Creativity

Many children feel overwhelmed when given a blank page and asked to create something original. Therefore, this section uses a gradual, step-by-step approach that provides more and more opportunities for spontaneous creativity as your child progresses. This approach allows your child to develop creativity without frustration.

In this section, your child will complete activities to develop his or her creative skills. This section contains activities such as tracing, drawing, altering pictures, and completing scenes. Each activity gives your child an opportunity to copy an example or to work more independently, so your child can progress at his or her own pace. By completing this section, your child will strengthen his or her creativity ability.

1 Drawing Imaginary Creatures

Level One

Name

Date

To parents
Guide your child to write his or her name and date in the box above. Do the exercise along with your child if he or she has difficulty. Throughout this book, you may wish to offer your child a choice of markers, crayons, or colored pencils.

■ Look at each sample. Then trace the lines in each picture below.

fairy

elf

■ Trace the lines. Then color each picture.

■ Trace the lines. Draw the eyes, nose, and mouth. Then color.

2 Drawing Imaginary Creatures

Level Two

Name

Date

To parents
Encourage your child to use the sample as a guide if he or she has difficulty.

■ Look at each sample. Then trace the lines in each picture below.

witch

Frankenstein

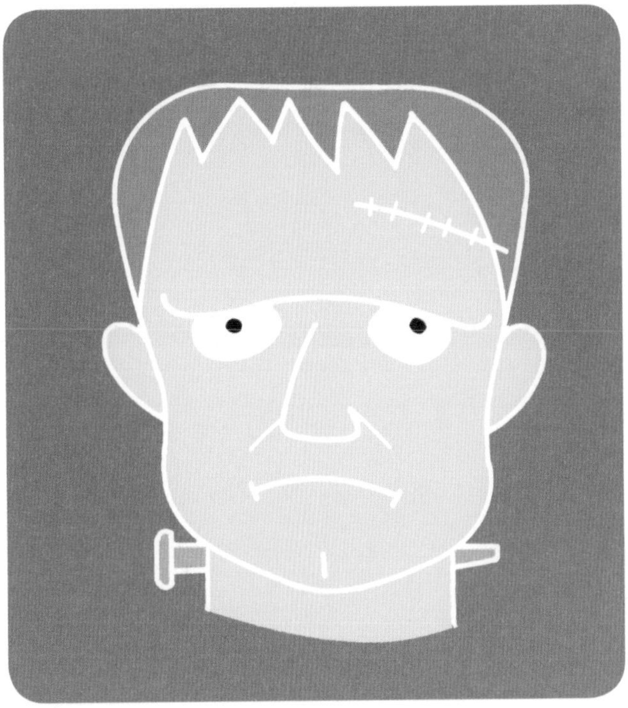

■ Trace the lines. Then color each picture.

■ Trace the lines. Draw the eyes, nose, and mouth. Then color.

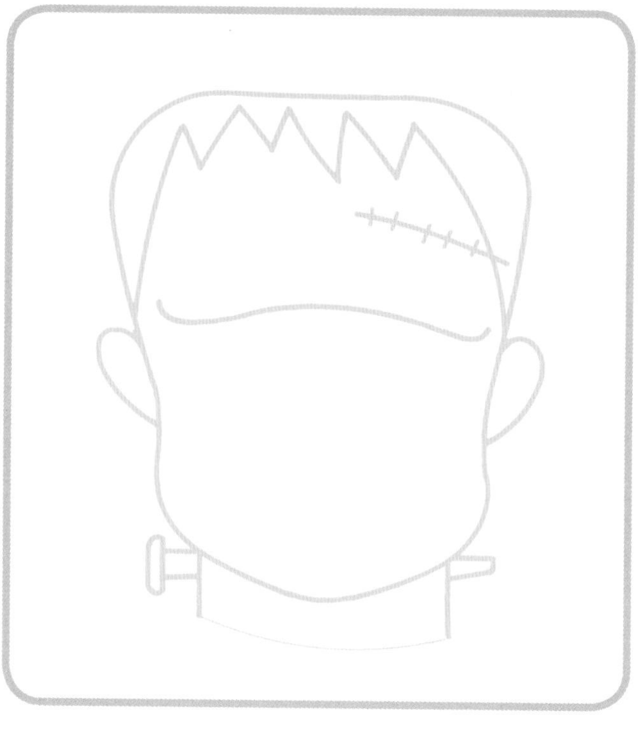

Drawing Scenes
Level One

Name

Date

To parents
Your child may find this activity more difficult because the picture is now more detailed. Encourage him or her to use the sample as a guide. Colored pencils may work best for tracing the lines in these pictures.

■ Look at the sample. Then trace the white lines in the picture below.

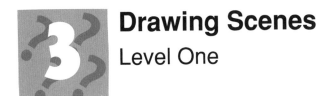

■ Trace the lines. Then color the picture.

■ Draw and color flowers.

4 Drawing Scenes
Level Two

Name

Date

To parents
If your child has difficulty, ask him or her to describe the objects in the picture before drawing. It is okay if your child wishes to use different colors from those shown in the sample.

■ Look at the sample. Then trace the white lines in the picture below.

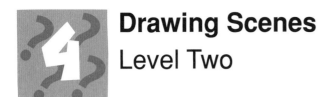

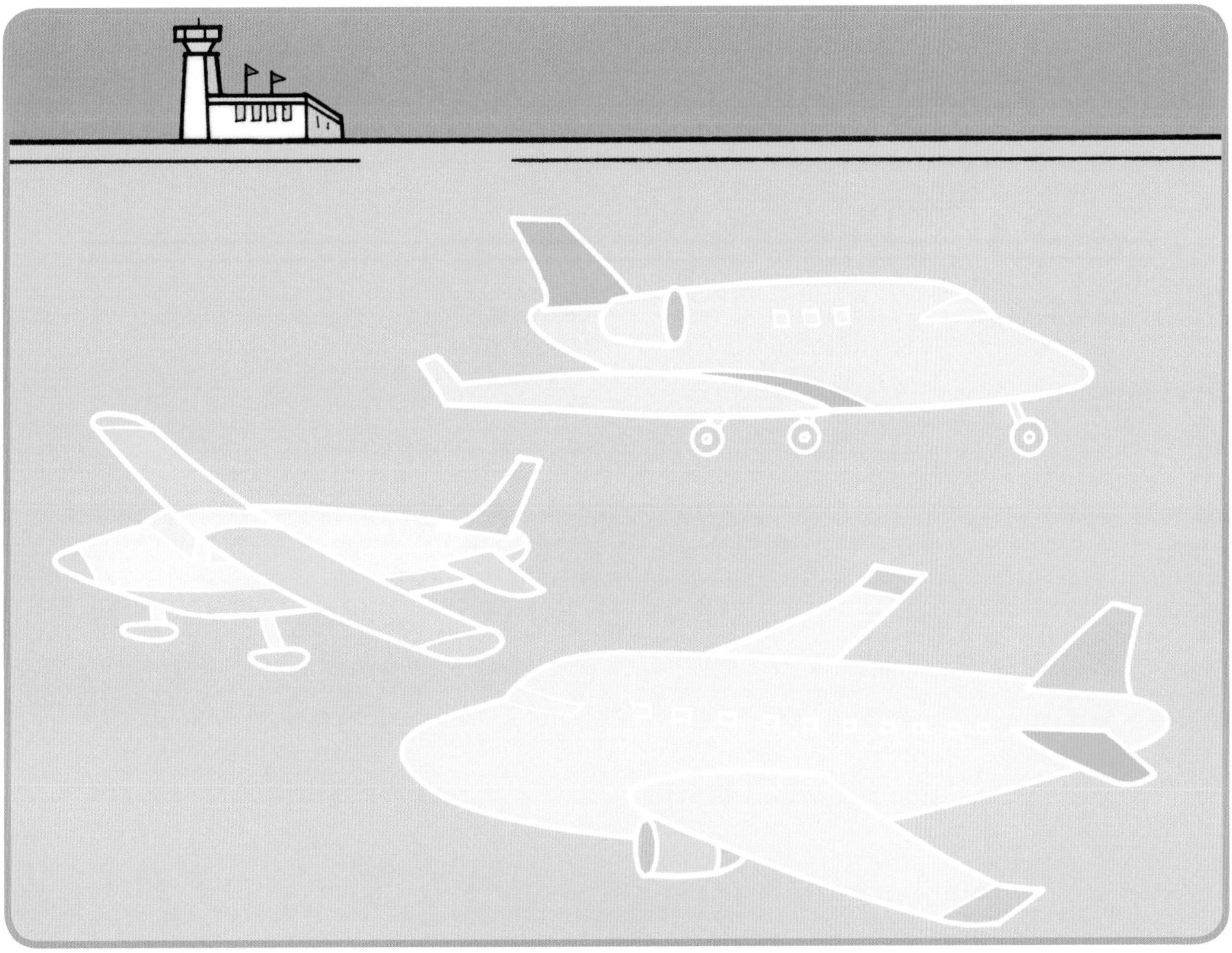

■ Trace the lines. Then color the picture.

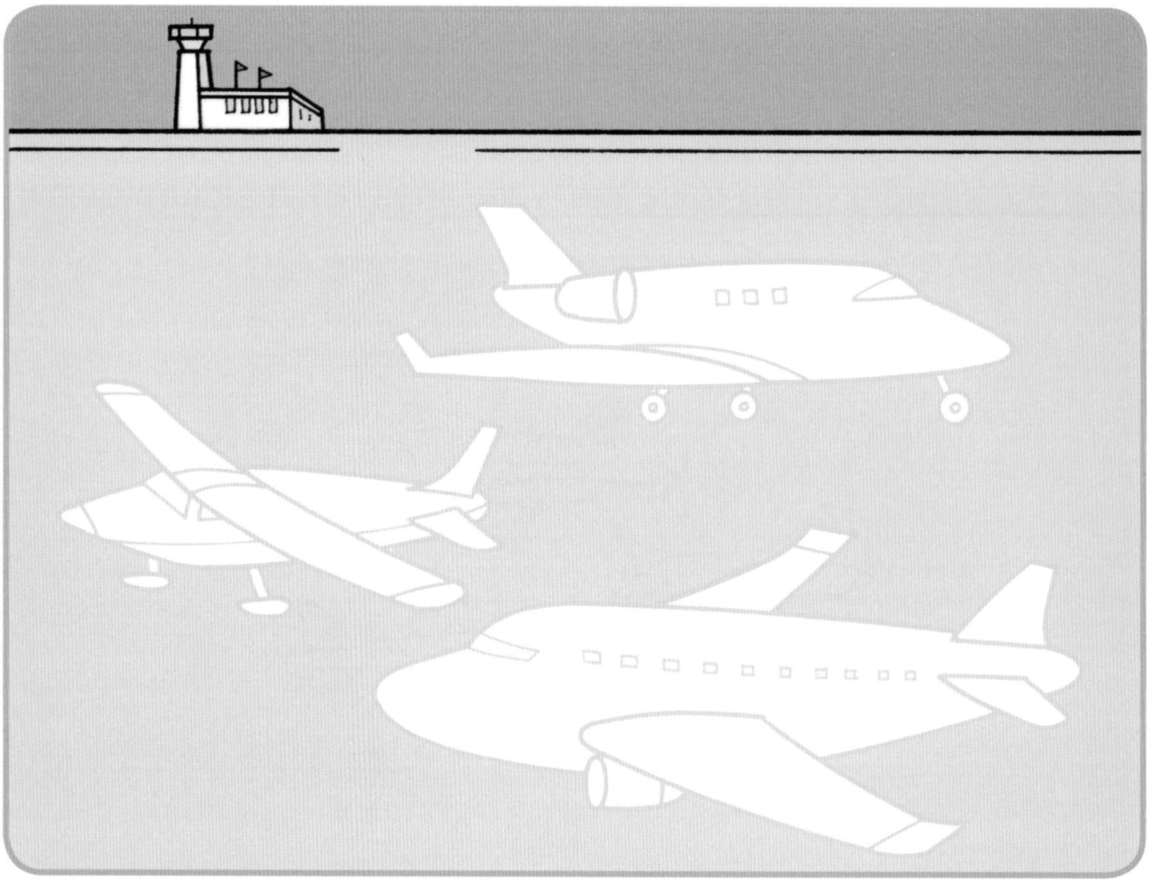

■ Draw and color airplanes.

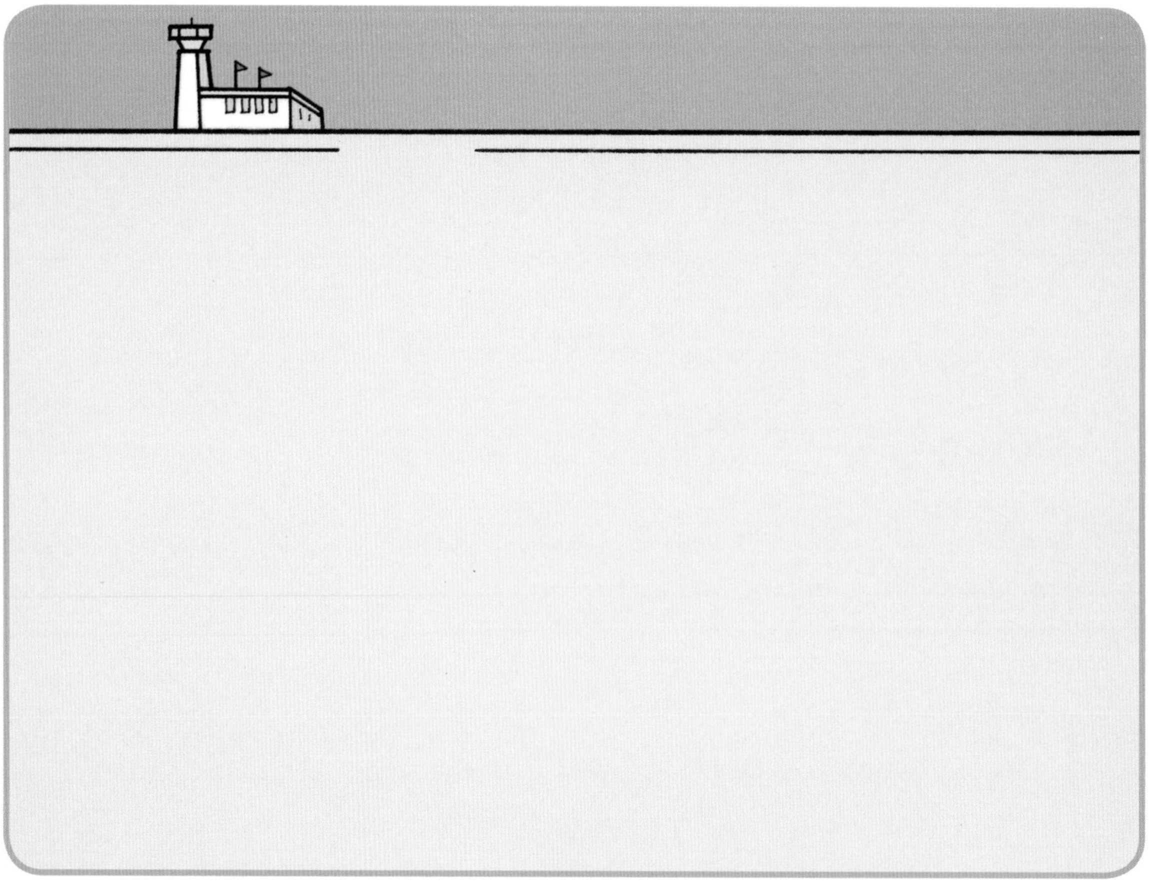

5 Completing Scenes

Level One

Name

Date

To parents
In this activity, your child will start drawing objects that are different from those shown in the sample.

■ Look at the sample. Then trace the white lines in the picture below.

sample

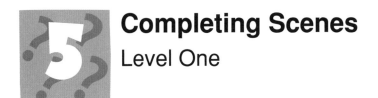

■ Trace the lines. Then color the picture.

■ Draw two butterflies that are different from the sample. Trace the lines. Then color.

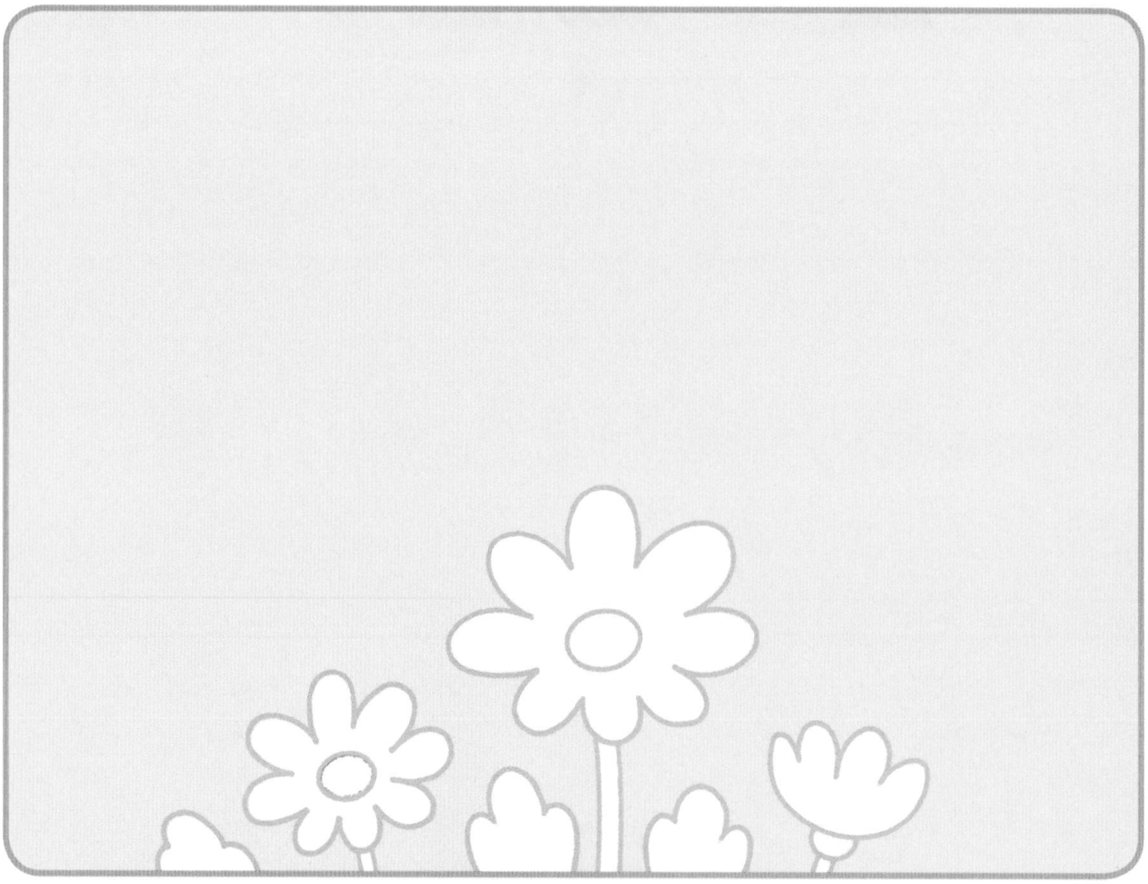

6 Completing Scenes

Level Two

Name

Date

To parents
As your child progresses through these activities, he or she may start to rely less on the samples and more on his or her own creativity.

■ Look at the sample. Then trace the gray lines in the picture below.

sample

■ Trace the lines. Then color.

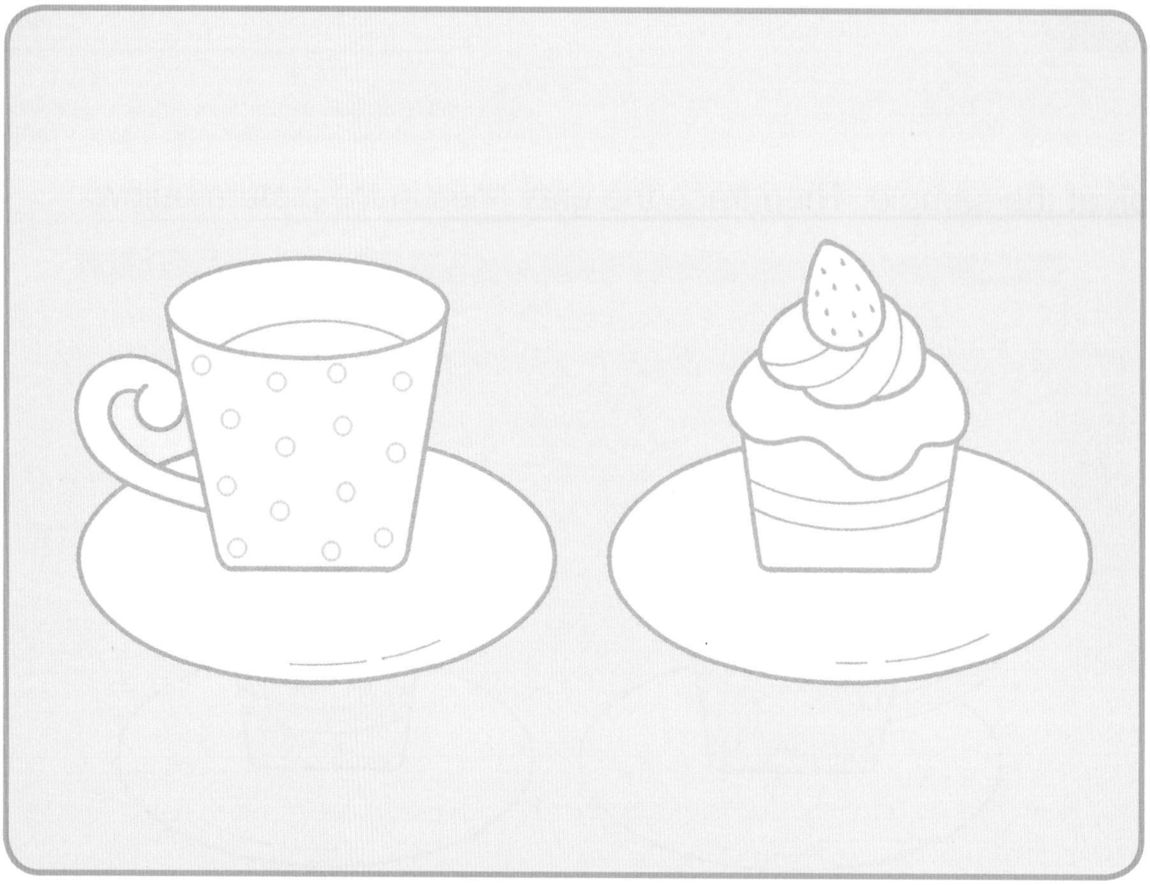

■ Draw a cup and cake that are different from the sample. Trace the lines. Then color.

7 Completing Scenes

Level Three

Name

Date

To parents
When your child has finished, ask your child to describe the decorations he or she has drawn.

■ Look at the sample. Then trace the white lines in the picture below.

sample

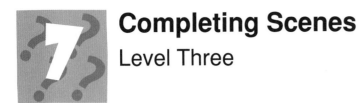

■ Trace the lines. Then color.

■ Draw three decorations that are different from the sample. Trace the lines. Then color.

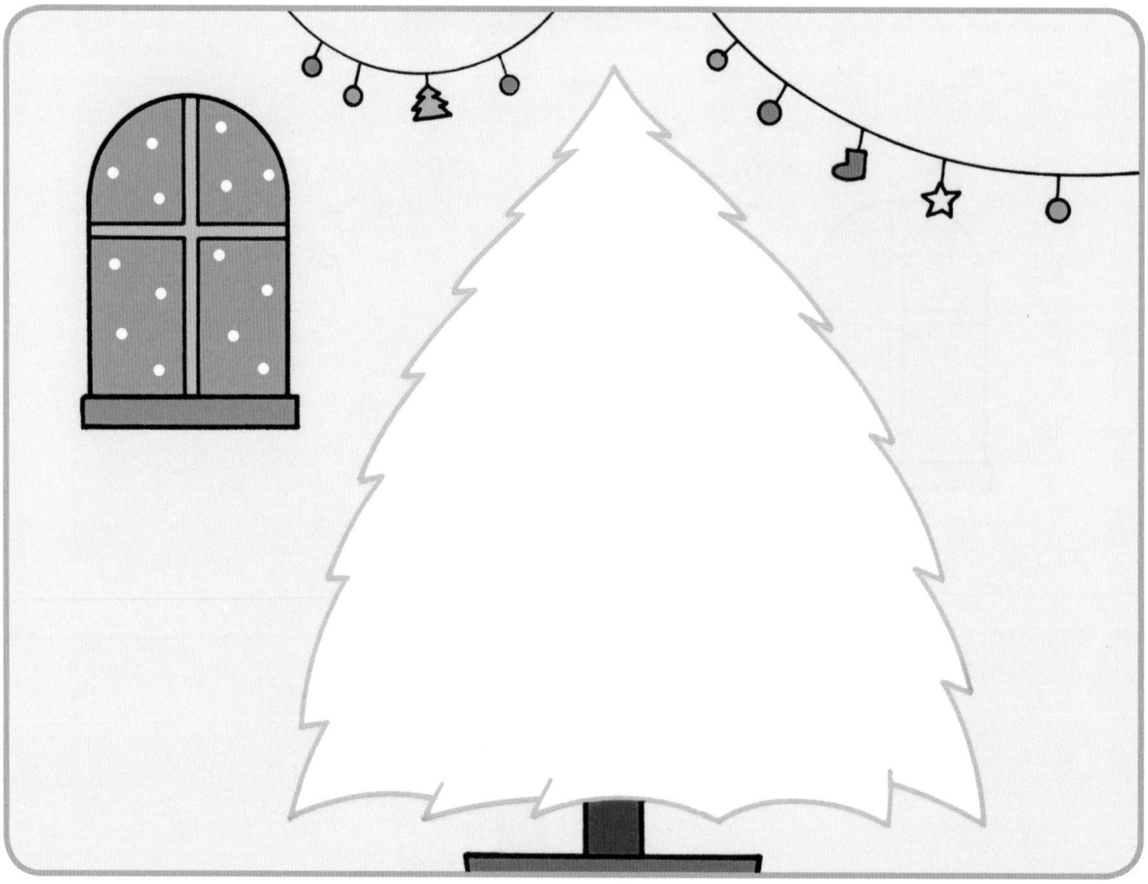

8 Completing Scenes
Level Four

Name

Date

To parents
Offer your child a lot of praise for his or her drawing. This will help build your child's confidence in his or her creative abilities.

■ Look at the sample. Then trace the gray lines in the picture below.

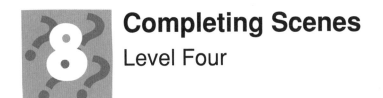

■ Trace the lines. Then color.

■ Draw three animals that are different from the sample. Then color.

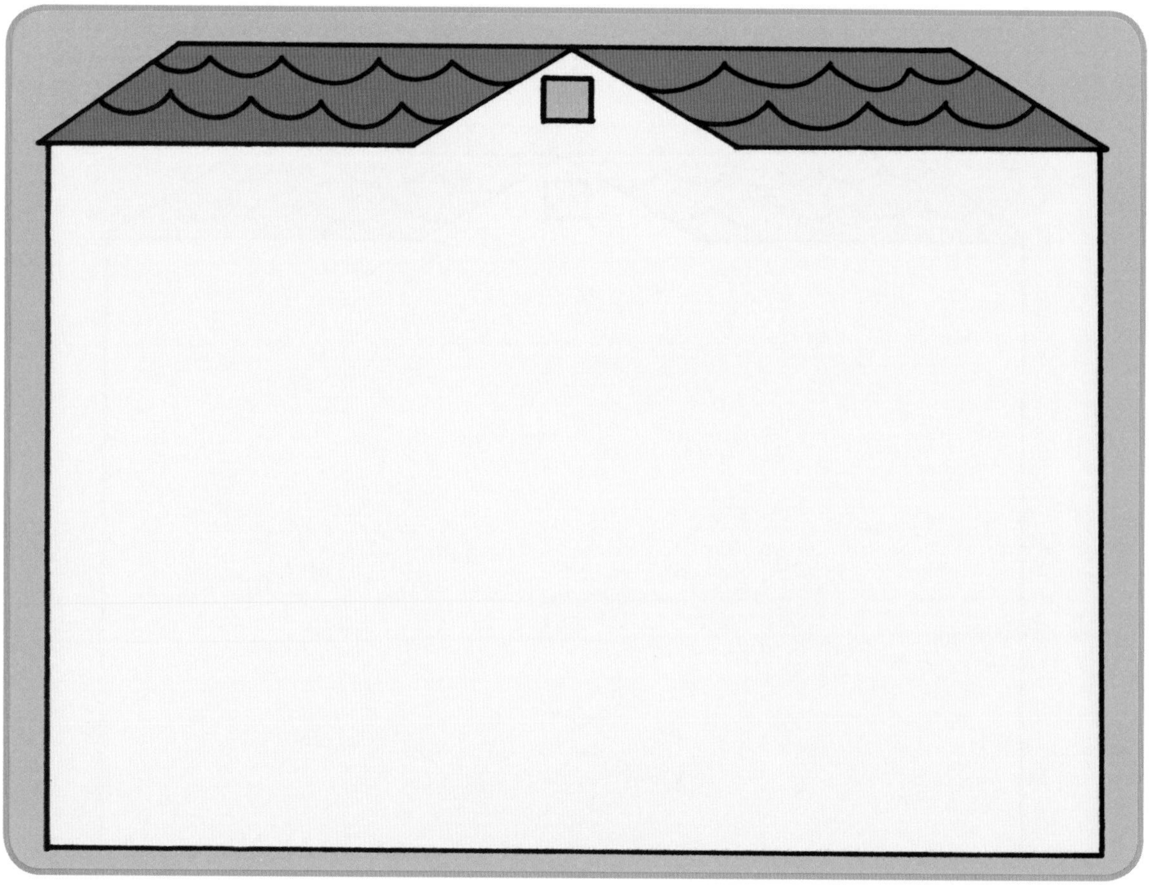

9 Creative Drawing with Samples

Level One

Name

Date

■ Look at the samples. Draw a beard or mustache on the face. Then trace and color.

To parents
Your child can copy one of the samples or draw something different.

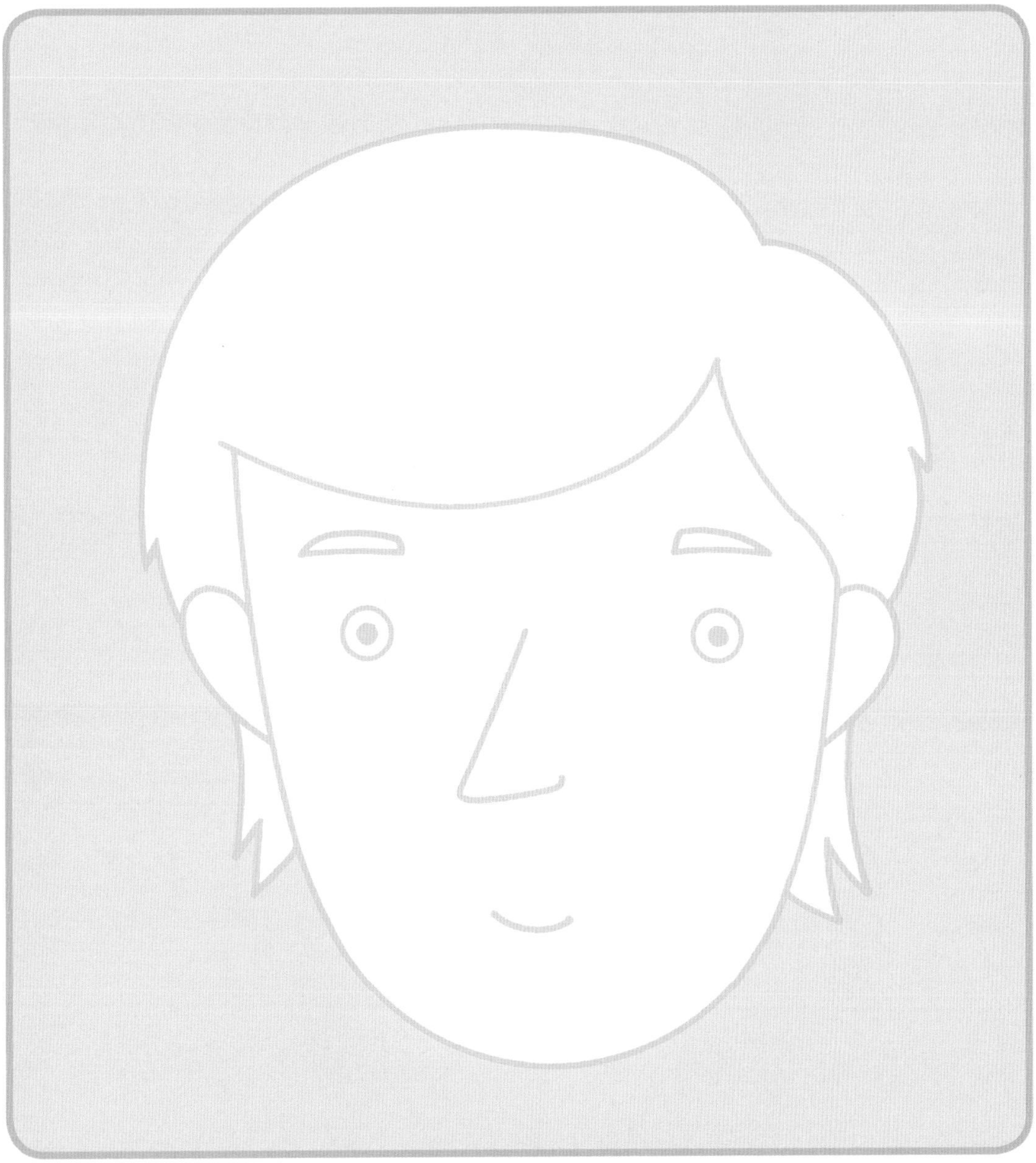

■ Look at the samples. Draw hair on the head. Then trace and color.

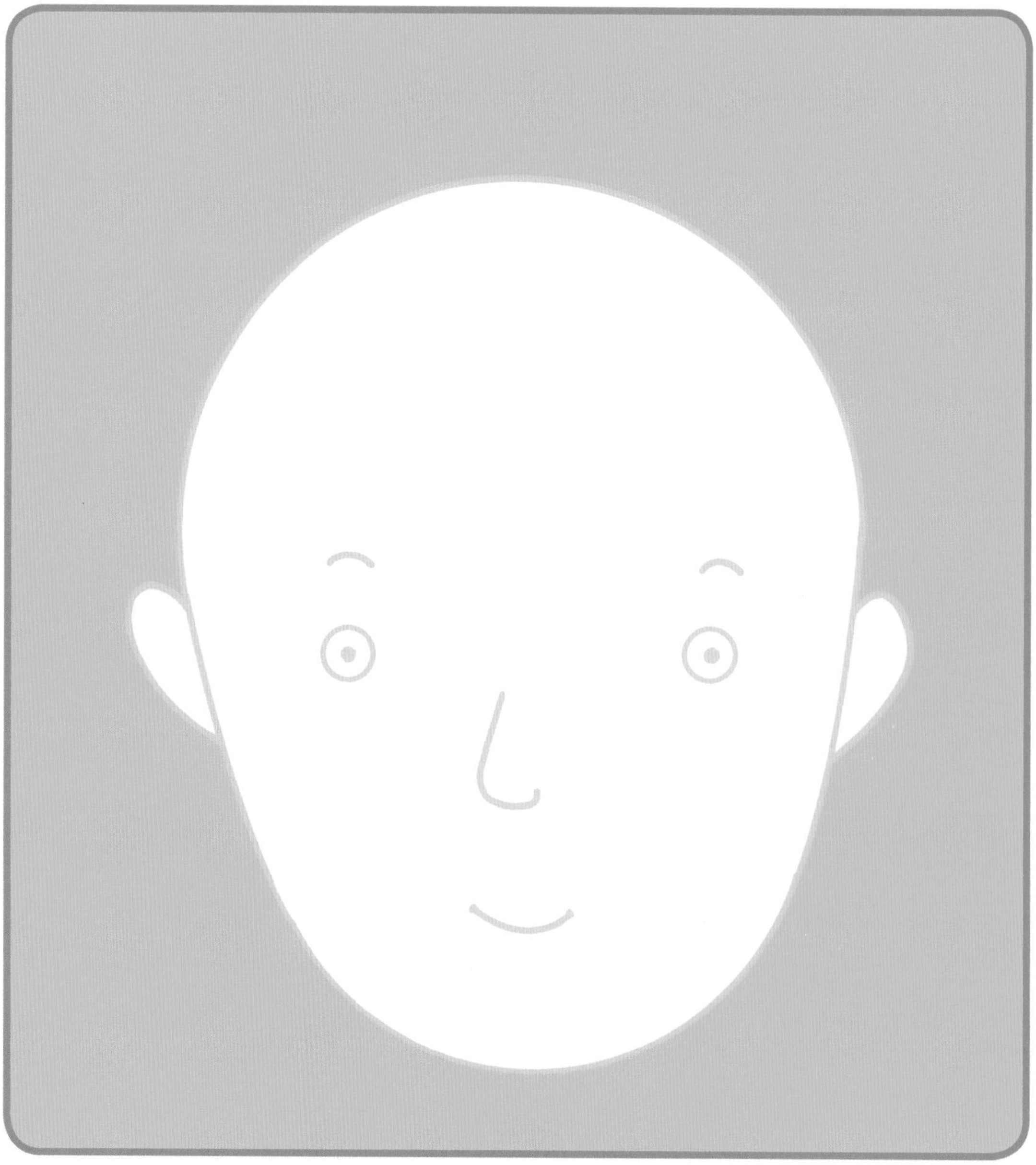

10 Creative Drawing with Samples

Level Two

Name

Date

To parents
If your child has difficulty, encourage him or her to use the samples as a guide.

■ Look at the samples. Draw hair on the head. Then trace and color.

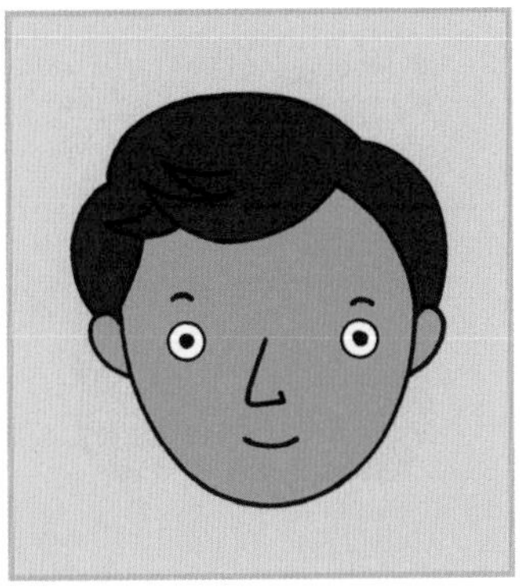

■ Look at the samples. Draw ribbons on the hair. Then trace and color.

11 Creative Drawing with Samples

Level Three

Name

Date

■ Look at the samples. Draw a baseball cap on the head. Then trace and color.

To parents
Your child's drawing does not need to look like the samples. The samples are provided only as a model.

■ Look at the samples. Draw a pattern on the skirt. Then trace and color.

12 Creative Drawing with Samples

Level Four

Name

Date

To parents
Offer your child a lot of praise for his or her drawing. This will help build your child's confidence in his or her creative abilities.

■ Look at the samples. Draw a pattern on the shirt and pants. Then trace and color.

■ Look at the samples. Draw a pattern on the dress. Then trace and color.

13

Creative Drawing with Samples

Level Five

Name

Date

To parents
From this page on, your child can choose his or her favorite illustrations from the sample.

■ Look at the sample. Then draw and color three piles of blocks of your choice.

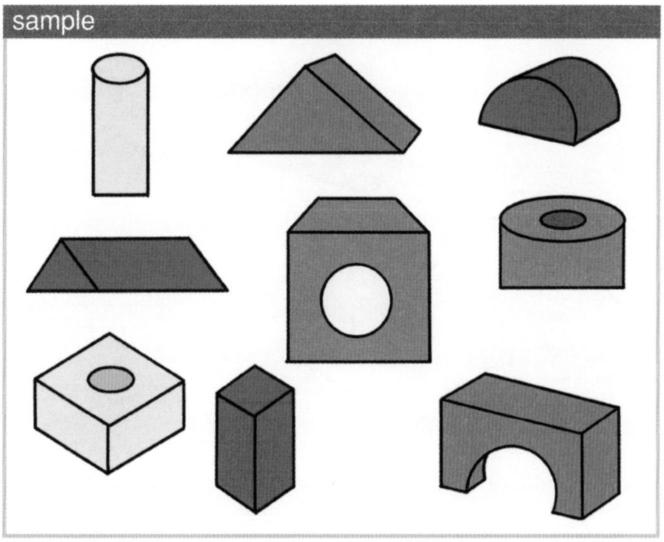

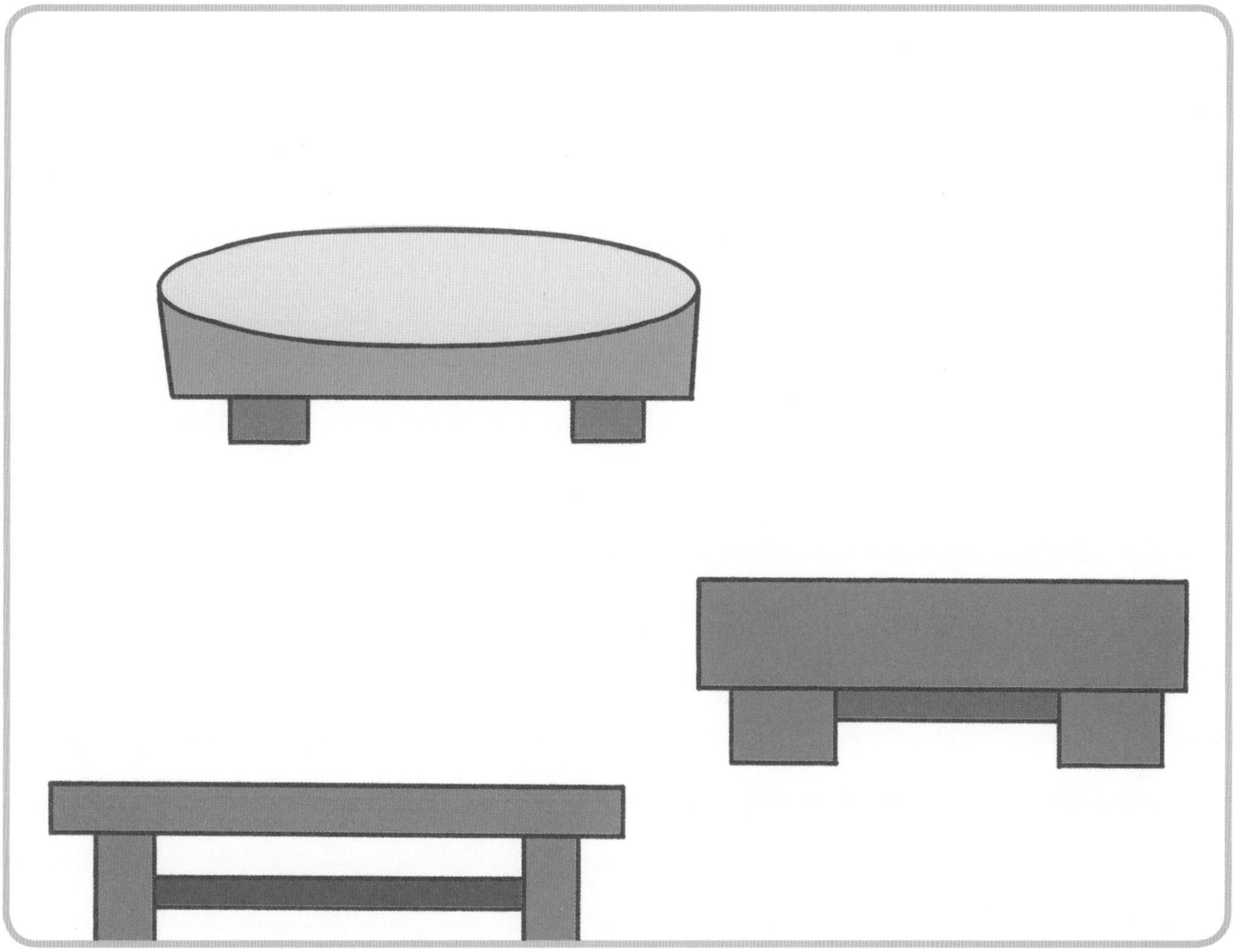

■ Look at the sample. Then draw and color three cakes of your choice.

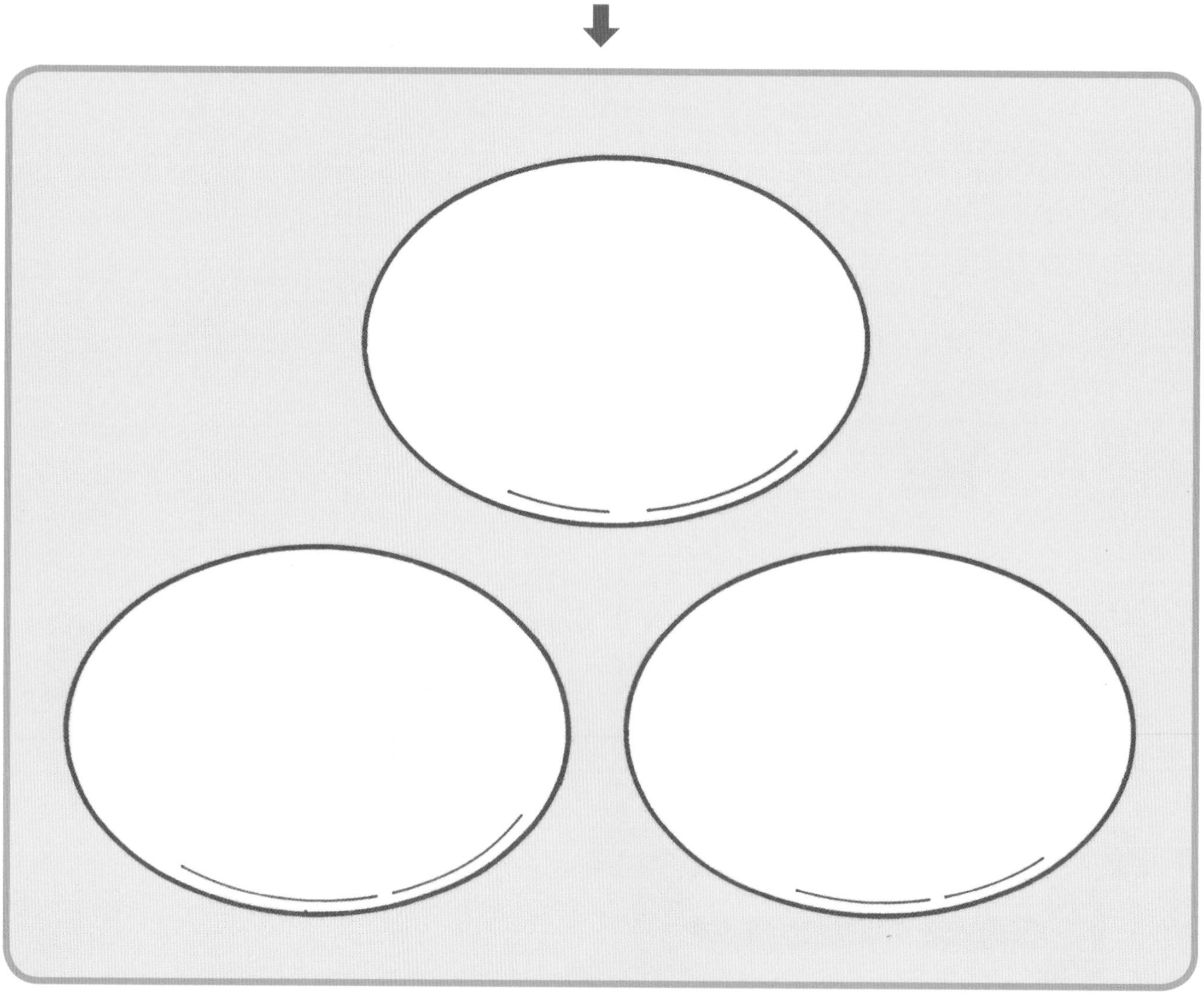

14 Creative Drawing with Samples

Level Six

Name

Date

To parents
It is okay if your child wishes to use different colors from those shown in the sample.

■ Look at the sample. Then draw and color three flowers of your choice.

sample

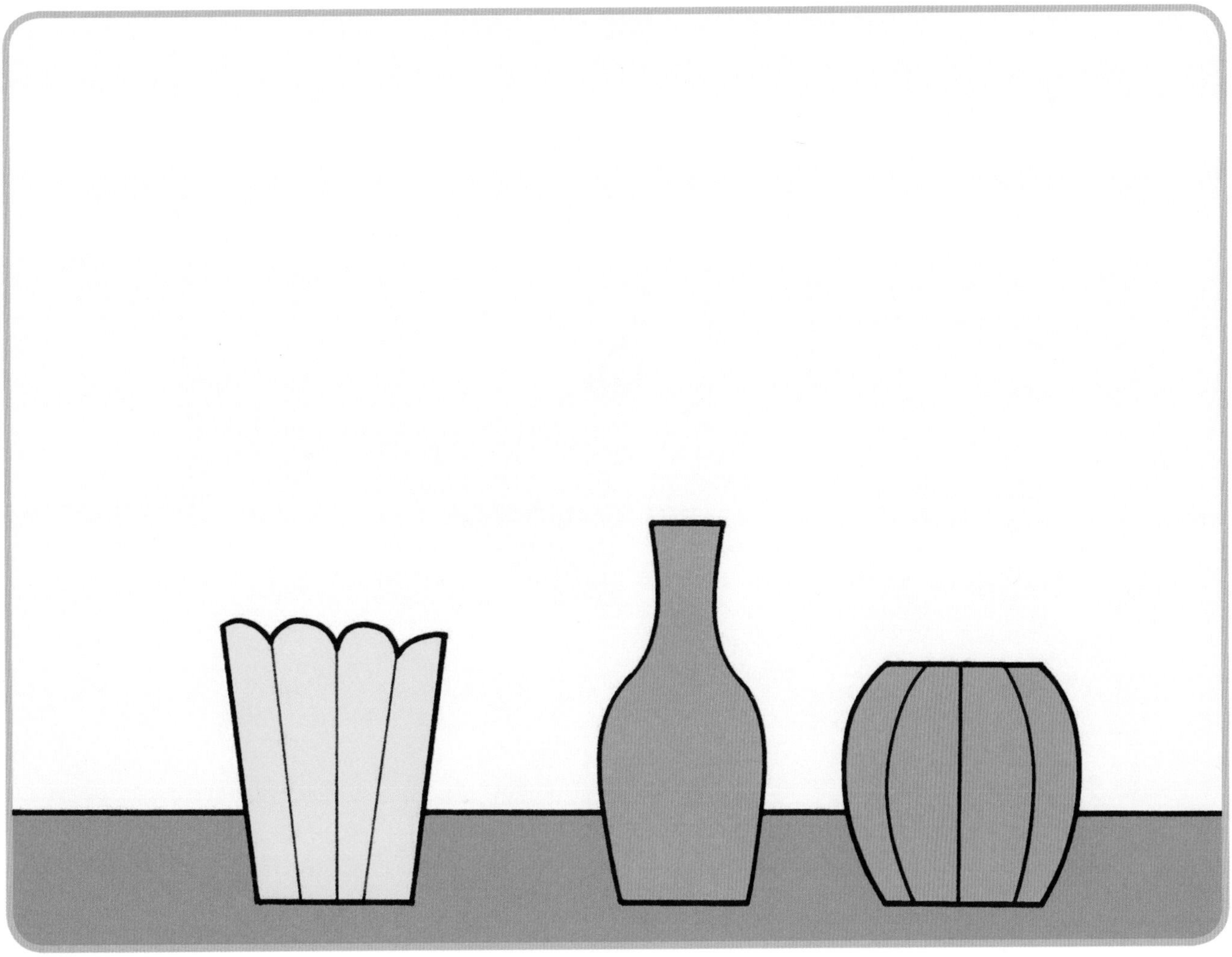

■ Look at the sample. Then draw and color three toy cars of your choice.

sample

15 Creative Drawing with Samples

Level Seven

Name

Date

To parents
If your child has difficulty choosing which insects to draw, you can ask your child to pick his or her favorites.

■ Look at the sample. Then draw and color three insects of your choice.

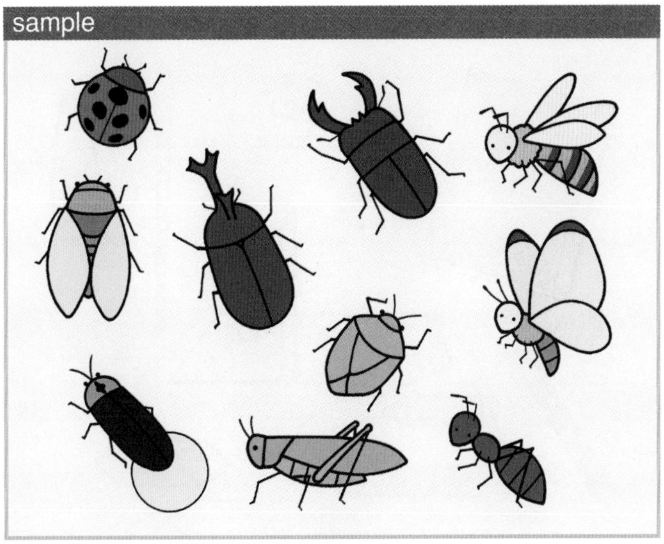

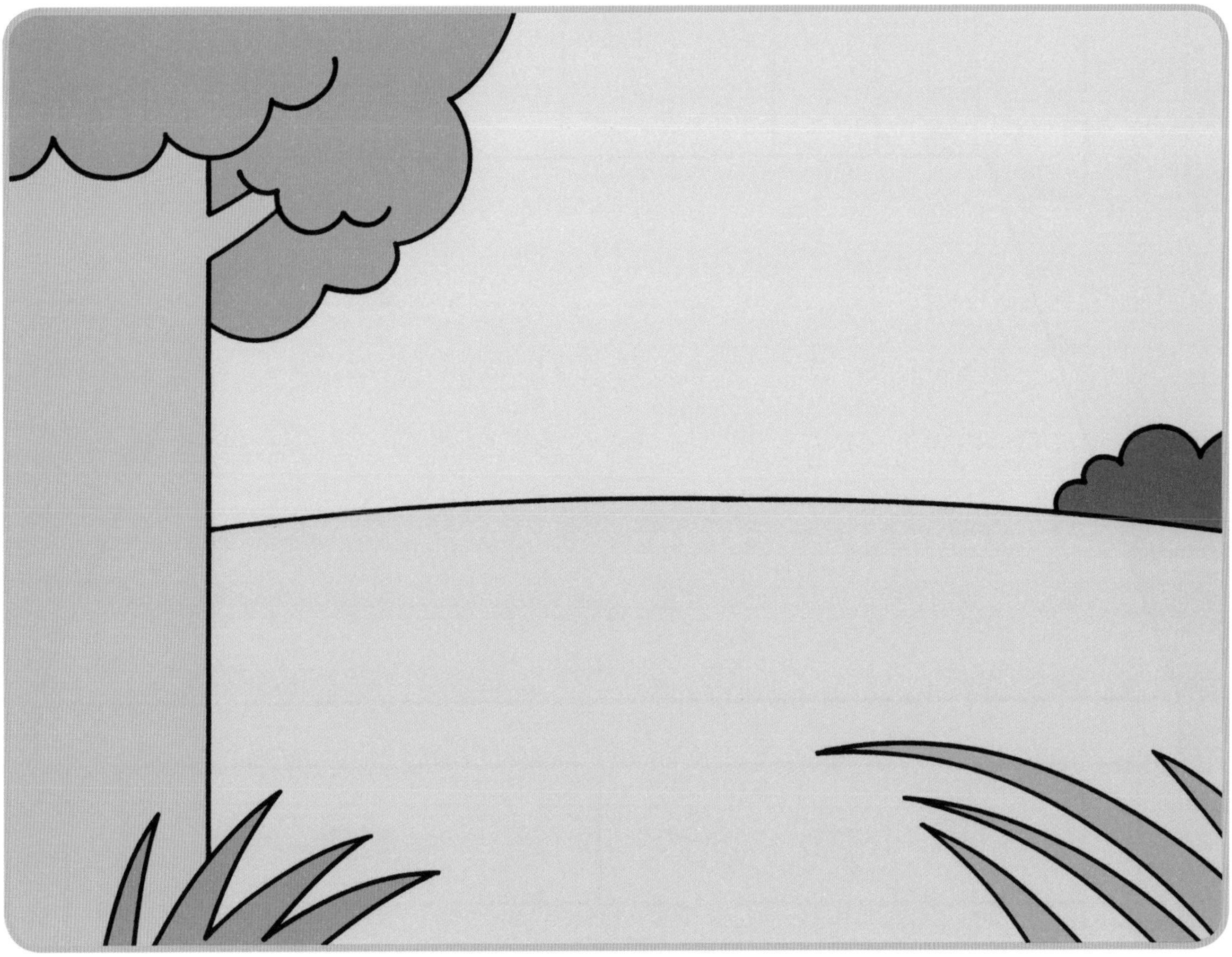

■ Look at the sample. Then draw and color three items of your choice.

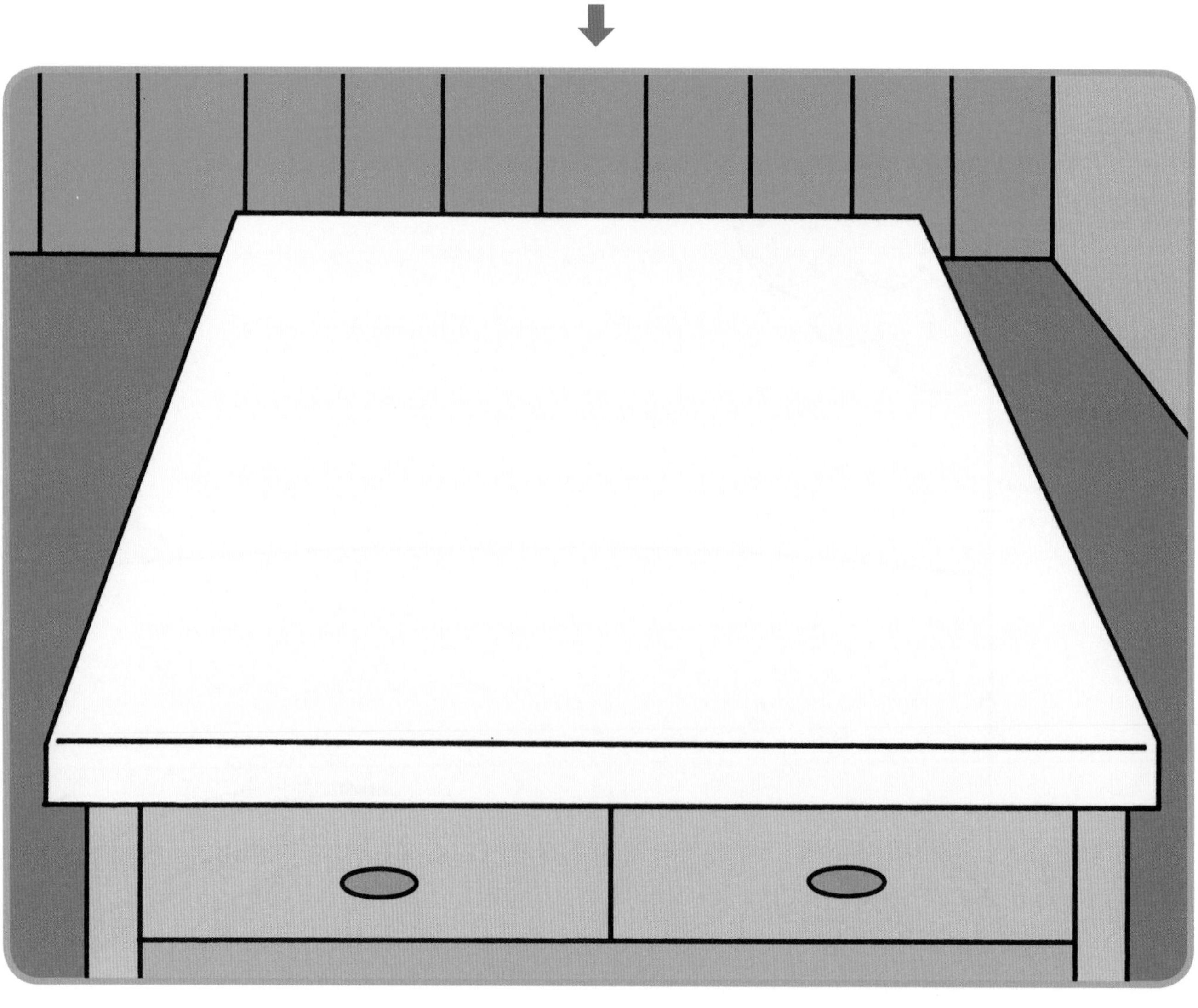

16 Creative Drawing with Samples
Level Eight

Name

Date

To parents
When your child has finished, ask your child what he or she likes best about his or her drawing.

■ Look at the sample. Then draw and color three fish of your choice.

■ Look at the sample. Then draw and color three baby animals of your choice.

17 Creative Drawing with Samples

Level Nine

Name

Date

To parents
Encourage your child to enjoy completing the scene by drawing and coloring.

■ Draw and color food on the plates. Then complete the scene as you like.

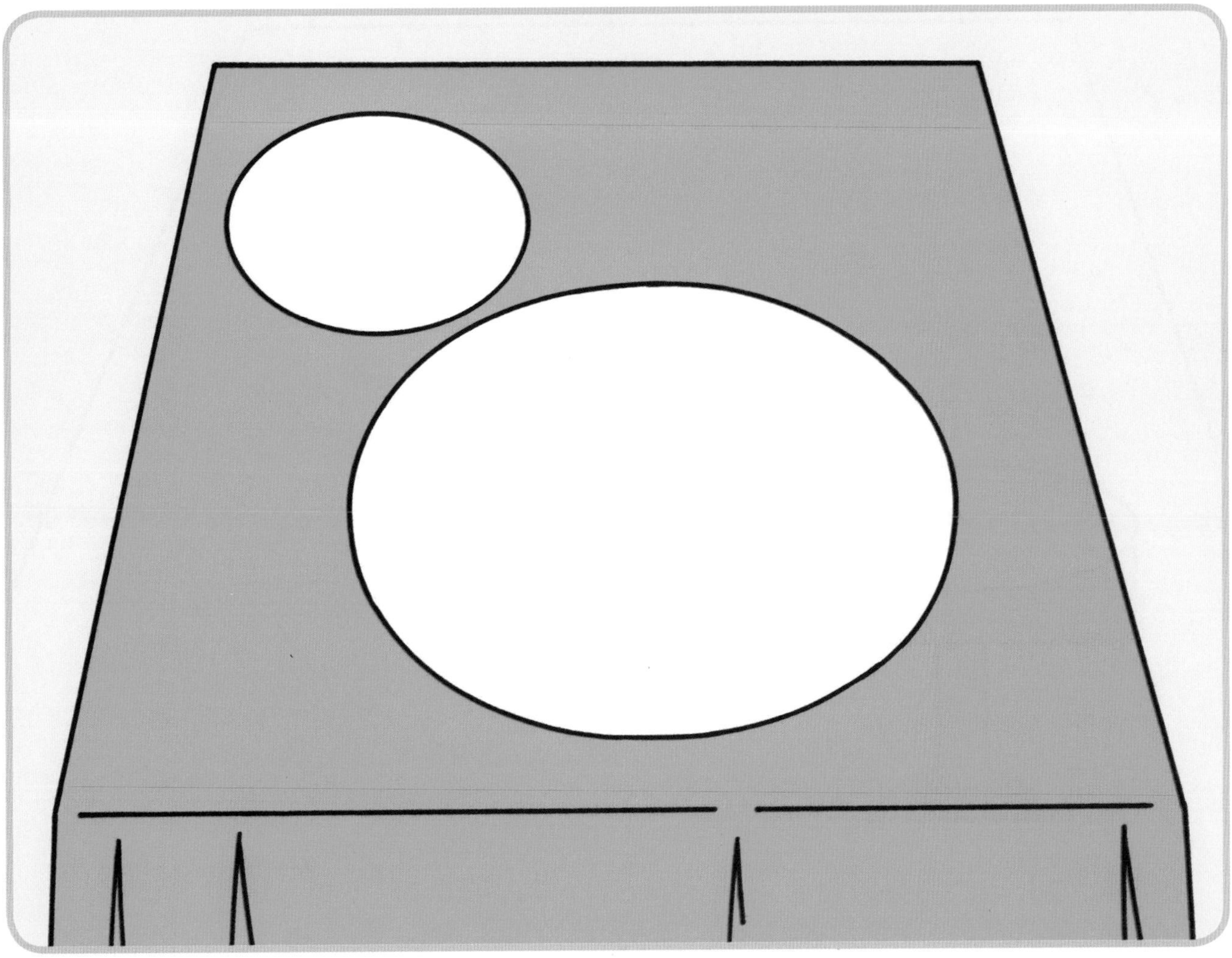

■ Draw and color toys in the room. Then complete the scene as you like.

samples

18 Creative Drawing with Samples

Level Ten

Name

Date

To parents
The sample pictures are examples only. Your child does not need to copy the samples.

■ Draw and color animals behind the fences. Then complete the scene as you like.

samples

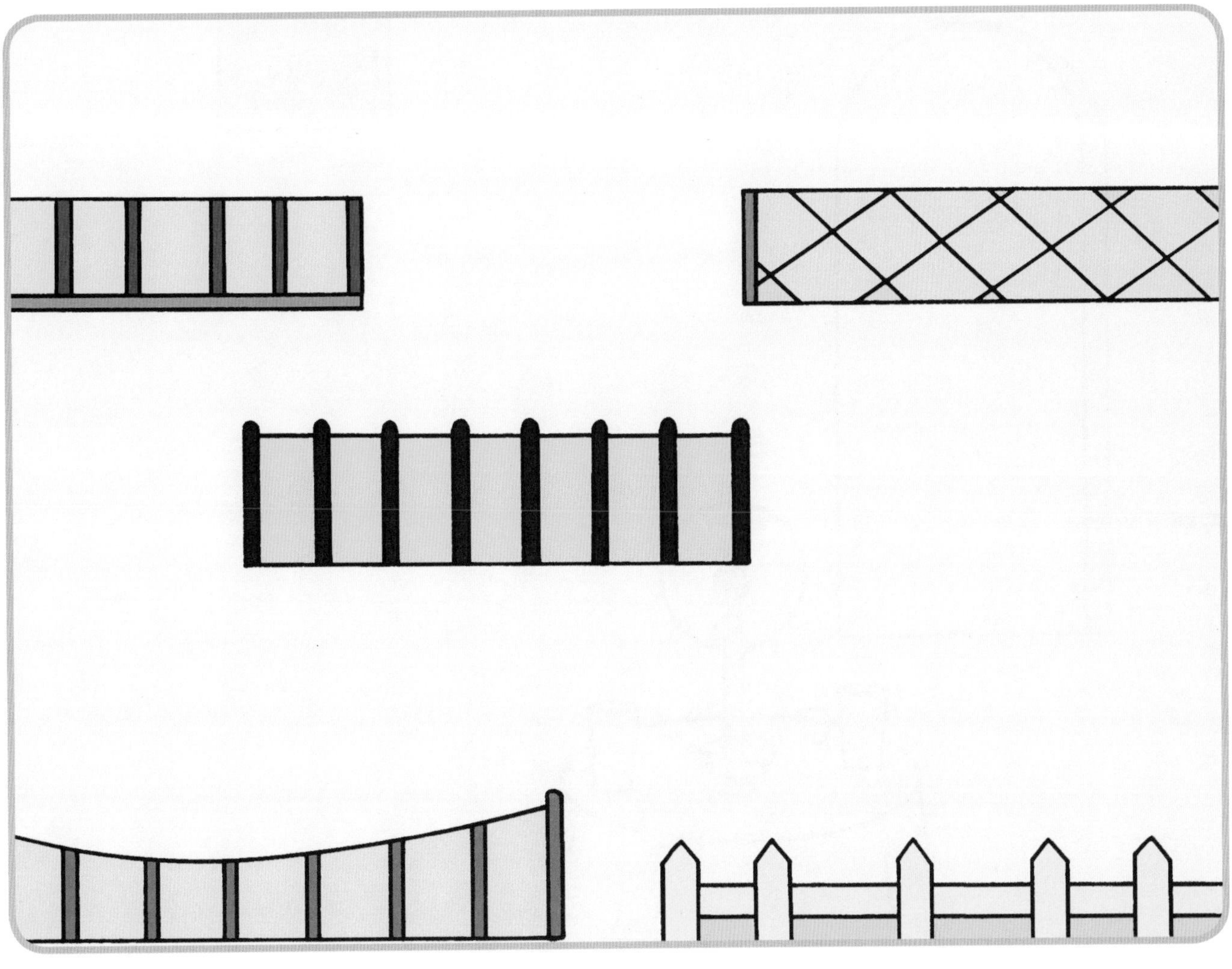

■ Draw and color ghosts and monsters in the party room. Then complete the scene as you like.

19 Creative Drawing with Samples

Level Eleven

Name

Date

To parents
Guide your child to create a scene by drawing and coloring.

■ Draw and color items in the bedroom. Then complete the scene as you like.

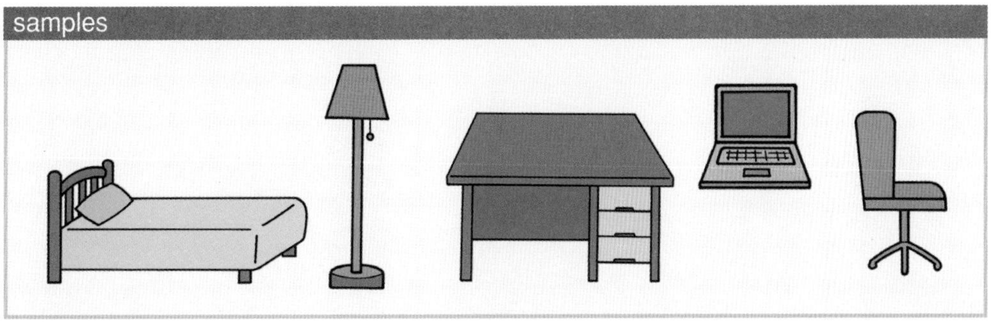

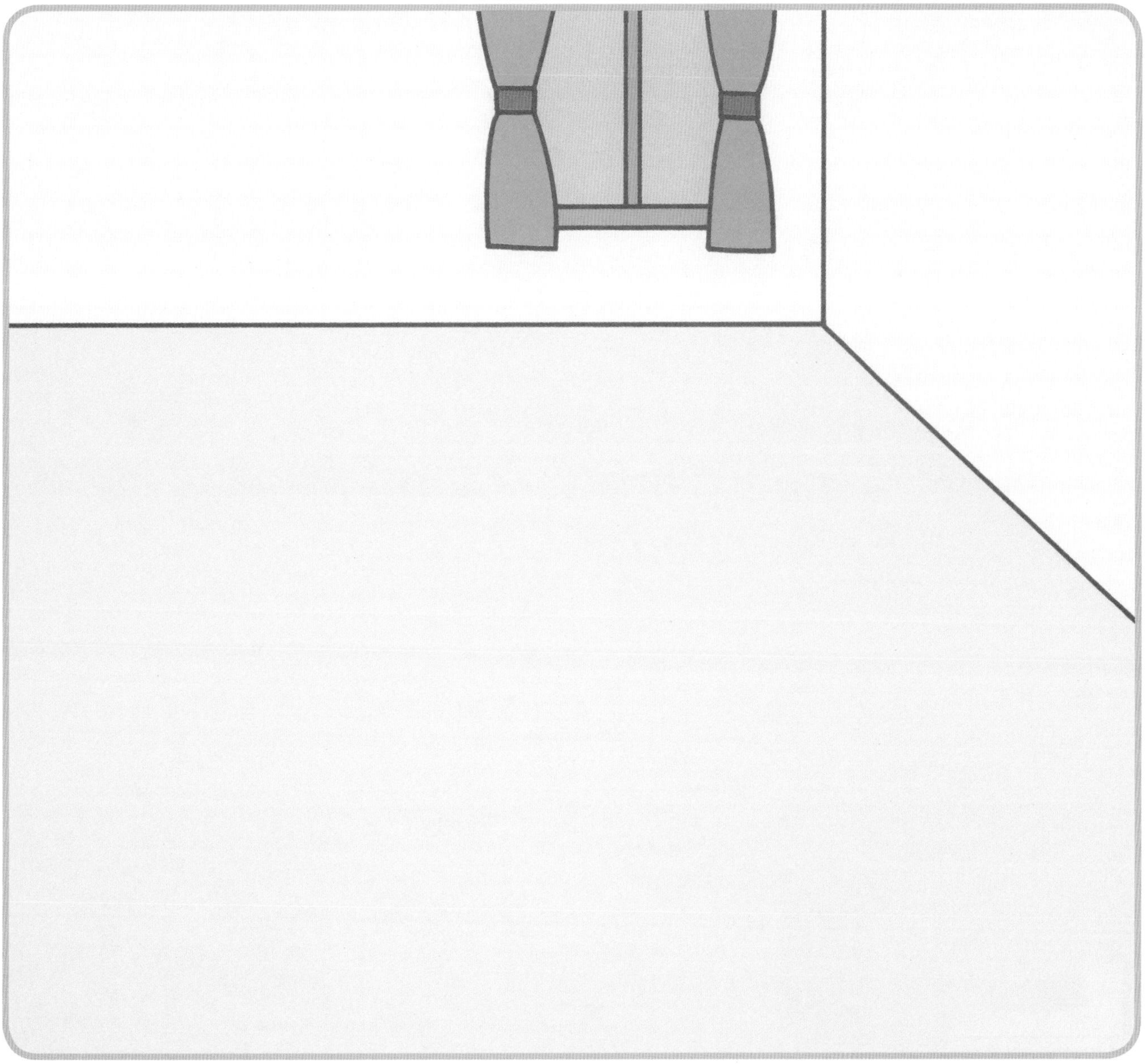

■ Draw and color cars on the highway. Then complete the scene as you like.

samples

20 Creative Drawing with Samples

Level Twelve

Name

Date

To parents
Offer your child a lot of praise for his or her drawing. This will help build your child's confidence in his or her creative abilities.

■ Draw and color birds and aircraft in the sky. Then complete the scene as you like.

samples

■ Draw and color plants and animals in the jungle. Then complete the scene as you like.

samples

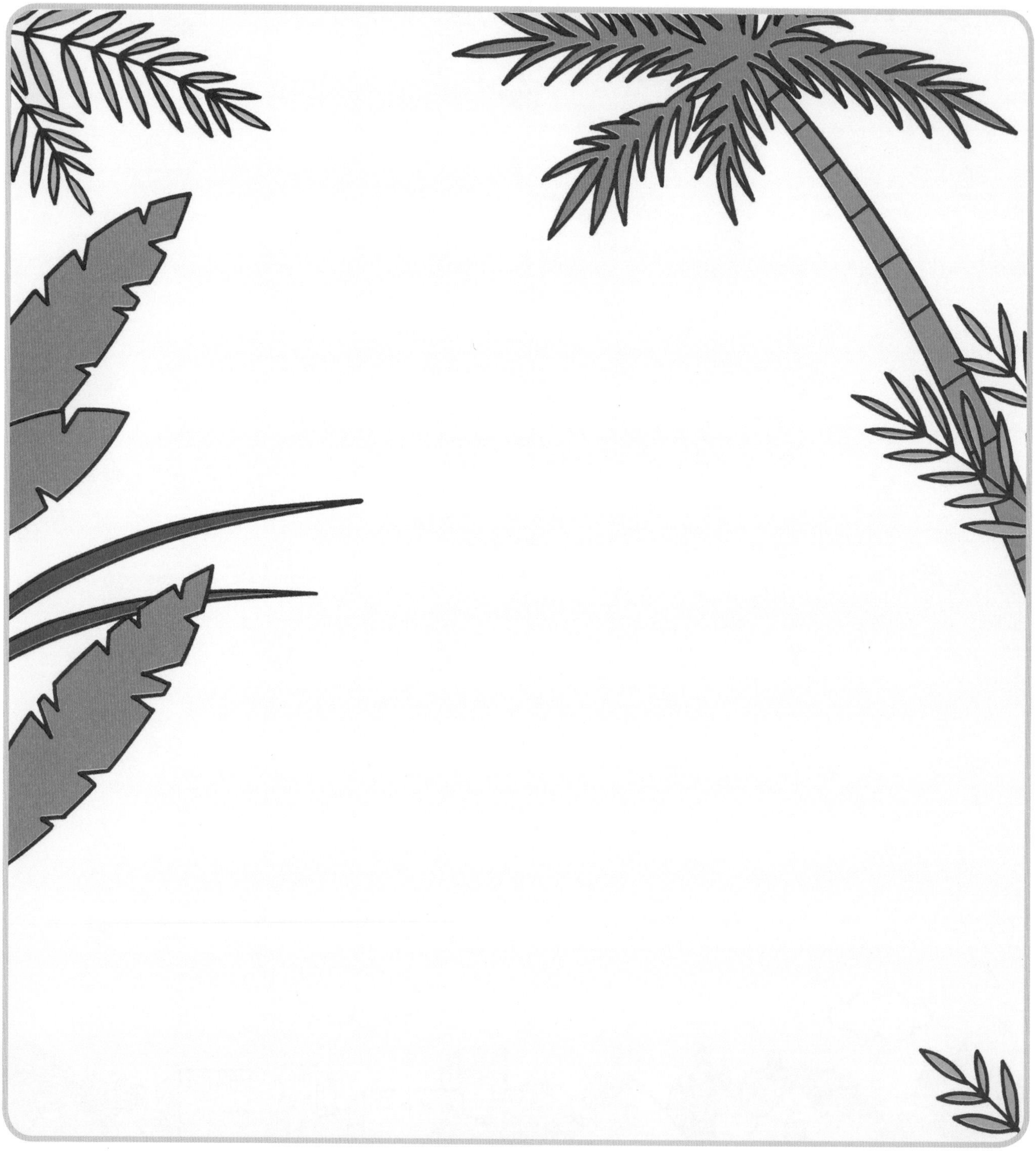

21 Creative Drawing
Level One

Name

Date

■ Draw and color fireworks in the sky.

To parents
From this page on, no samples are provided. You may wish to read the directions out loud to your child. For this page, crayons work best for drawing fireworks.

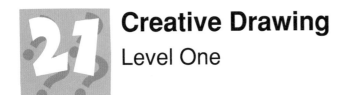

■ Draw and color a field of flowers.

22 Creative Drawing

Level Two

Name

Date

■ Draw and color animals in a fish tank.

To parents
Your child can draw and color the background if he or she wants.

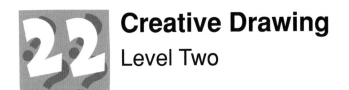

■ Draw and color fashion models in a fashion show.

23 Creative Drawing
Level Three

Name

Date

To parents
Guide your child to draw and color a picture related to the topic.

■ Draw and color people and buildings in a city.

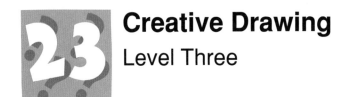

■ Draw and color stormy weather on a mountain.

24

Creative Drawing

Level Four

Name

Date

To parents
If your child has difficulty, ask your child to first describe what he or she wants to draw.

■ Draw and color children playing outside on a winter day.

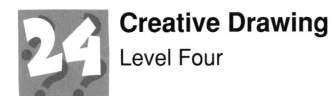

■ Draw and color an amusement park.

25 Creative Drawing with Sample Pictures

Level One

Name

Date

■ Draw and color a dog. You can use the sample pictures to help you.

To parents
From this page on, two photographs are provided as samples. Your child does not need to try to copy the samples. Also, your child can draw more than one animal if he or she wants.

■ Draw and color a cat. You can use the sample pictures to help you.

26

Creative Drawing with Sample Pictures

Level Two

Name

Date

■ Draw and color a rabbit. You can use the sample pictures to help you.

To parents
Your child can draw and color the background if he or she wants.

■ Draw and color an insect. You can use the sample pictures to help you.

27 Creative Drawing with Sample Pictures

Level Three

Name

Date

■ Draw and color a bird. You can use the sample pictures to help you.

To parents
Your child does not need to complete an entire scene. It is okay if your child just wants to draw and color an animal.

■ Draw and color a bird. You can use the sample pictures to help you.

28 Creative Drawing with Sample Pictures

Level Four

Name

Date

■ Draw and color an ape. You can use the sample pictures to help you.

To parents
When your child has finished, ask your child to describe what he or she has drawn.

■ Draw and color a flower. You can use the sample pictures to help you.

29 Creative Drawing with Sample Pictures

Level Five

Name

Date

■ Draw and color an animal. You can use the sample pictures to help you.

To parents
Encourage your child to enjoy drawing and coloring.

■ Draw and color an animal. You can use the sample pictures to help you.

30

Creative Drawing with Sample Pictures

Level Six

Name

Date

■ Draw and color an animal. You can use the sample pictures to help you.

To parents
Offer your child a lot of praise for his or her drawing. This will help build your child's confidence in his or her creative abilities.

■ Draw and color an animal. You can use the sample pictures to help you.

31

Creative Drawing

Level One

Name

Date

To parents
From this page on, neither samples nor background colors are provided. You may wish to read the directions out loud to your child.

■ Draw and color your favorite food.

What is your favorite food?

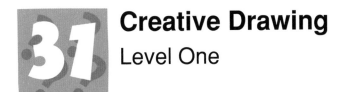

■ Draw and color your favorite animal.

What is your favorite animal?

32

Creative Drawing

Level Two

Name

Date

To parents
Guide your child to draw and color anything he or she wishes, as long as it fits the topic.

■ Draw and color your favorite flower.

What is your favorite flower?

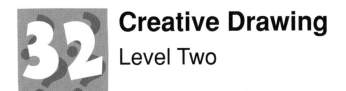

■ Draw and color your favorite kind of vehicle.

What is your favorite kind of vehicle?

33 Creative Drawing

Level Three

Name

Date

To parents
When your child has finished, ask your child what he or she has drawn. Talk about the book with your child.

■ Draw and color your favorite moment in a book.

What is your favorite moment in a book?

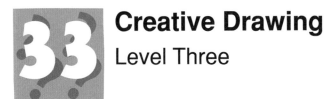

■ Draw and color your best friends.

Who are your best friends?

34 Creative Drawing
Level Four

Name

Date

■ Draw and color your family.

To parents
If your child has difficulty, have him or her describe each family member before drawing.

Ask your family to be your models!

■ Draw and color your favorite activity.

What is your favorite activity?

35 Creative Drawing

Level Five

Name

Date

To parents
When your child has finished, ask your child what he or she has drawn. Talk about the summer activity with your child.

- Draw and color one exciting thing you did last summer.

What was one exciting thing you did last summer?

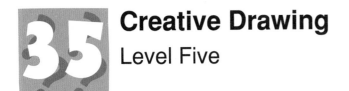

■ Draw and color your favorite memory of Halloween.

What is your favorite memory of Halloween?

36 Creative Drawing
Level Six

Name

Date

To parents
If your child has difficulty, reviewing the previous pages may help him or her get ideas.

■ Draw and color the best meal you have ever had.

What was the best meal you have ever had?

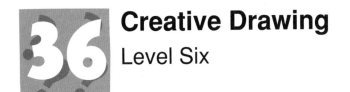

To parents
This is the last exercise of this workbook. Please praise your child for the effort it took to complete this workbook.

■ Draw and color your favorite memory from a family trip.

What is your favorite memory from a family trip?

Drawing Imaginary Creatures
Level One
Look at each sample. Then trace the lines in each picture below.
Trace the lines. Then color each picture.
Trace the lines. Draw the eyes, nose, and mouth. Then color.
243
244
pages 243 and 244

Drawing Imaginary Creatures
Level Two
Look at each sample. Then trace the lines in each picture below.
Trace the lines. Then color each picture.
Trace the lines. Draw the eyes, nose, and mouth. Then color.
245
246
pages 245 and 246

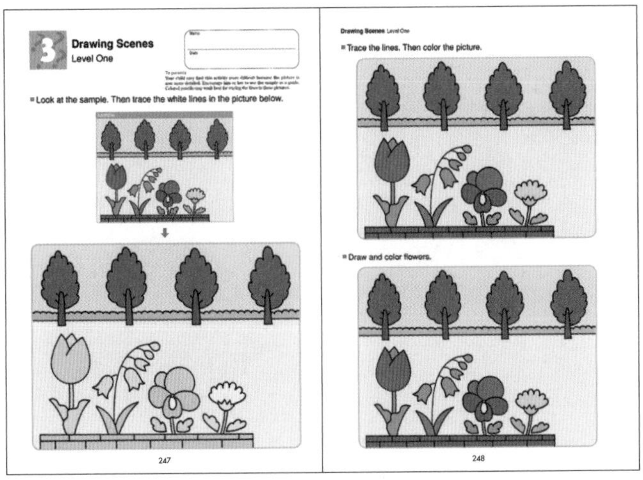
Drawing Scenes
Level One
Look at the sample. Then trace the white lines in the picture below.
Trace the lines. Then color the picture.
Draw and color flowers.
247
248
pages 247 and 248

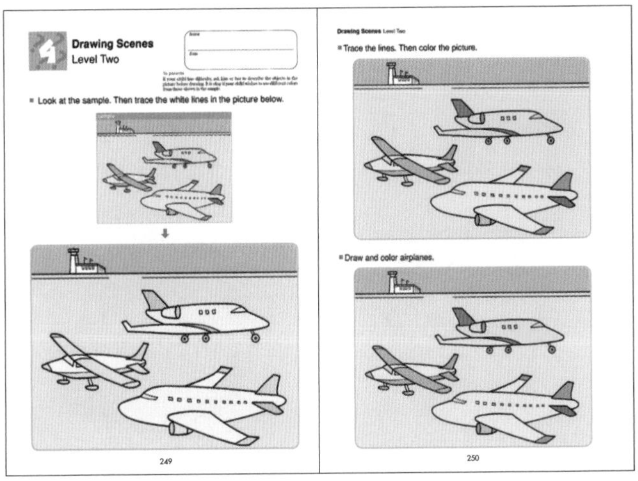
Drawing Scenes
Level Two
Look at the sample. Then trace the white lines in the picture below.
Trace the lines. Then color the picture.
Draw and color airplanes.
249
250
pages 249 and 250

Completing Scenes
Level One
Look at the sample. Then trace the white lines in the picture below.
Trace the lines. Then color the picture.
Draw two butterflies that are different from the sample. Trace the lines. Then color.
251
252
pages 251 and 252

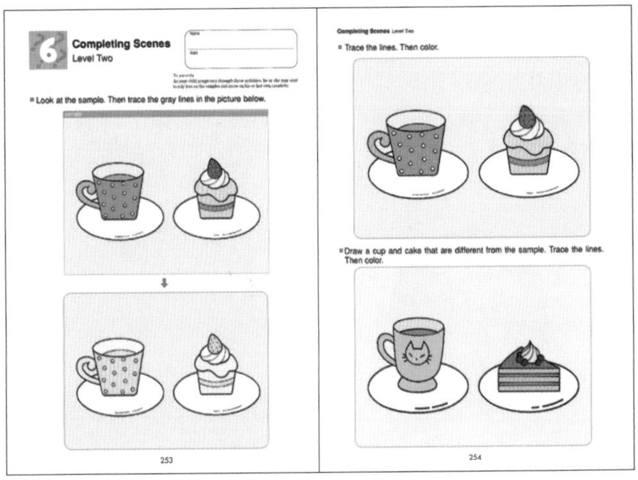
Completing Scenes
Level Two
Look at the sample. Then trace the gray lines in the picture below.
Trace the lines. Then color.
Draw a cup and cake that are different from the sample. Trace the lines. Then color.
253
254
pages 253 and 254

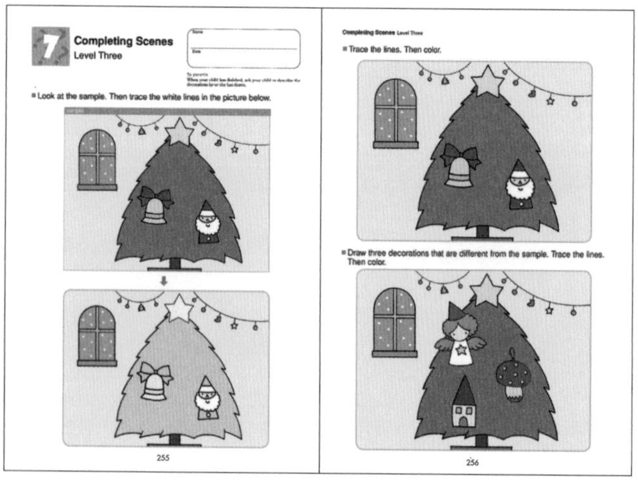
7 Completing Scenes
Level Three
■ Look at the sample. Then trace the white lines in the picture below.
Completing Scenes Level Three
■ Trace the lines. Then color.
■ Draw three decorations that are different from the sample. Trace the lines. Then color.
255
256

pages 255 and 256

8 Completing Scenes
Level Four
■ Look at the sample. Then trace the gray lines in the picture below.
Completing Scenes Level Four
■ Trace the lines. Then color.
■ Draw three animals that are different from the sample. Then color.
257
258

pages 257 and 258

9 Creative Drawing with Samples
Level One
■ Look at the samples. Draw a beard or mustache on the face. Then trace and color.
Creative Drawing with Samples Level One
■ Look at the samples. Draw hair on the head. Then trace and color.
259
260

pages 259 and 260

10 Creative Drawing with Samples
Level Two
■ Look at the samples. Draw hair on the head. Then trace and color.
Creative Drawing with Samples Level Two
■ Look at the samples. Draw ribbons on the hair. Then trace and color.
261
262

pages 261 and 262

11 Creative Drawing with Samples
Level Three
■ Look at the samples. Draw a baseball cap on the head. Then trace and color.
Creative Drawing with Samples Level Three
■ Look at the samples. Draw a pattern on the skirt. Then trace and color.
263
264

pages 263 and 264

12 Creative Drawing with Samples
Level Four
■ Look at the samples. Draw a pattern on the shirt and pants. Then trace and color.
Creative Drawing with Samples Level Four
■ Look at the samples. Draw a pattern on the dress. Then trace and color.
265
266

pages 265 and 266

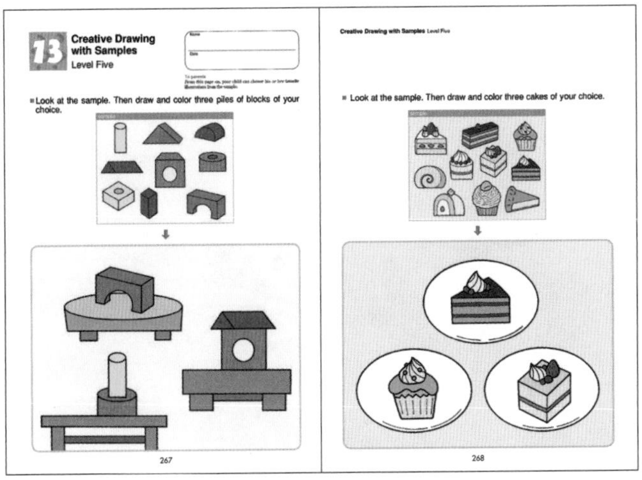

13 Creative Drawing with Samples Level Five
Look at the sample. Then draw and color three piles of blocks of your choice.
267
Creative Drawing with Samples Level Five
Look at the sample. Then draw and color three cakes of your choice.
268

pages 267 and 268

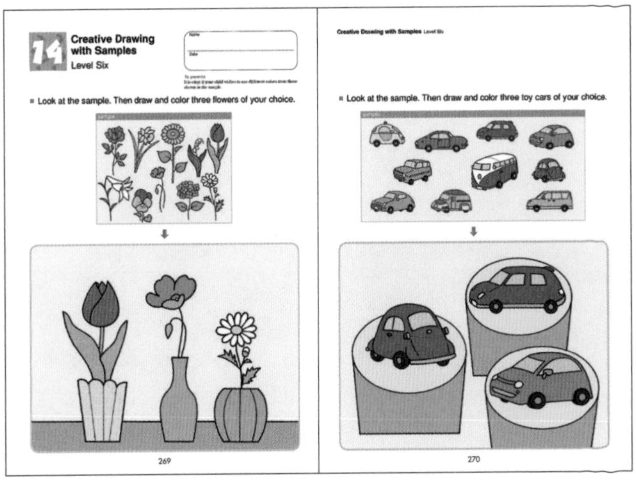

14 Creative Drawing with Samples Level Six
Look at the sample. Then draw and color three flowers of your choice.
269
Creative Drawing with Samples Level Six
Look at the sample. Then draw and color three toy cars of your choice.
270

pages 269 and 270

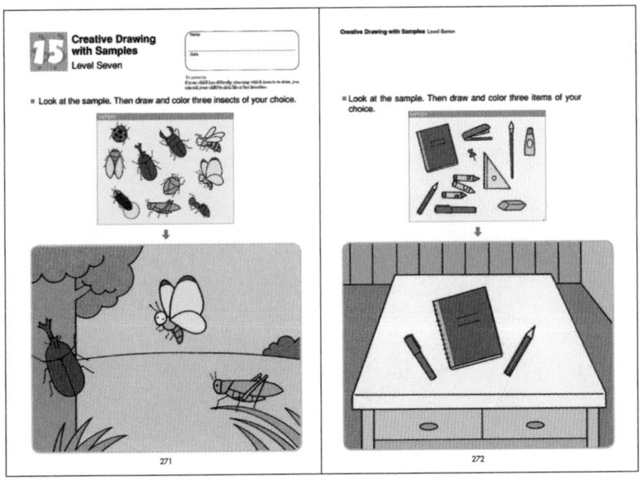

15 Creative Drawing with Samples Level Seven
Look at the sample. Then draw and color three insects of your choice.
271
Creative Drawing with Samples Level Seven
Look at the sample. Then draw and color three items of your choice.
272

pages 271 and 272

16 Creative Drawing with Samples Level Eight
Look at the sample. Then draw and color three fish of your choice.
273
Creative Drawing with Samples Level Eight
Look at the sample. Then draw and color three baby animals of your choice.
274

pages 273 and 274

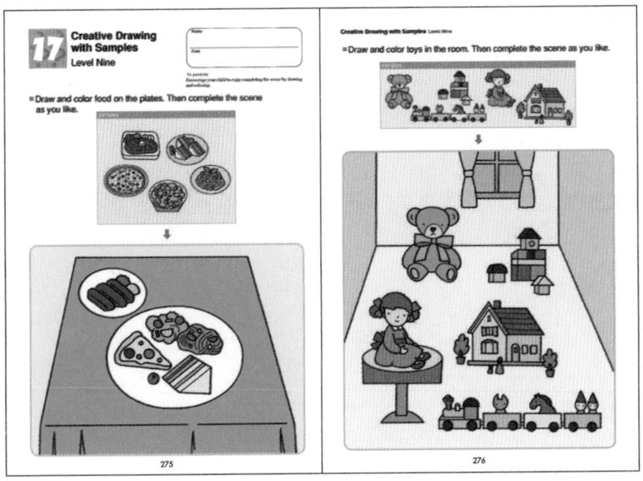

17 Creative Drawing with Samples Level Nine
Draw and color food on the plates. Then complete the scene as you like.
275
Creative Drawing with Samples Level Nine
Draw and color toys in the room. Then complete the scene as you like.
276

pages 275 and 276

18 Creative Drawing with Samples Level Ten
Draw and color animals behind the fences. Then complete the scene as you like.
277
Creative Drawing with Samples Level Ten
Draw and color ghosts and monsters in the party room. Then complete the scene as you like.
278

pages 277 and 278

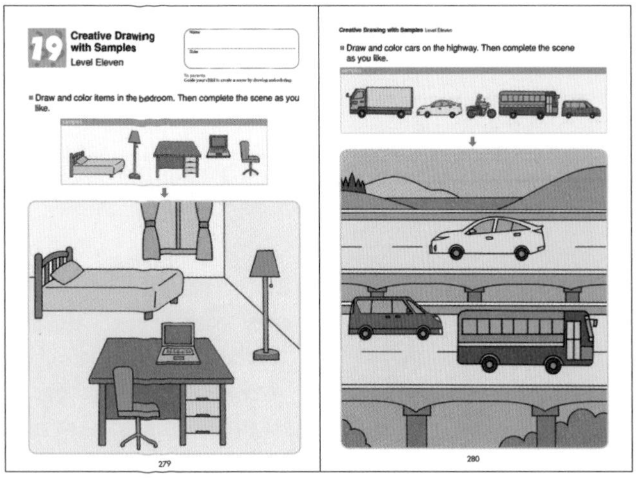
19
Creative Drawing with Samples
Level Eleven
Draw and color items in the bedroom. Then complete the scene as you like.
Draw and color cars on the highway. Then complete the scene as you like.
279
280

pages 279 and 280

20
Creative Drawing with Samples
Level Twelve
Draw and color birds and aircraft in the sky. Then complete the scene as you like.
Draw and color plants and animals in the jungle. Then complete the scene as you like.
281
282

pages 281 and 282

21
Creative Drawing
Level One
Draw and color fireworks in the sky.
Draw and color a field of flowers.
283
284

pages 283 and 284

22
Creative Drawing
Level Two
Draw and color animals in a fish tank.
Draw and color fashion models in a fashion show.
285
286

pages 285 and 286

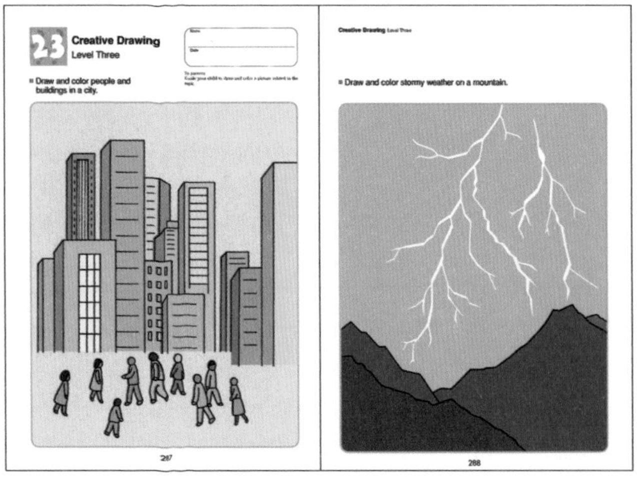
23
Creative Drawing
Level Three
Draw and color people and buildings in a city.
Draw and color stormy weather on a mountain.
287
288

pages 287 and 288

24
Creative Drawing
Level Four
Draw and color children playing outside on a winter day.
Draw and color an amusement park.
289
290

pages 289 and 290

pages 291 and 292

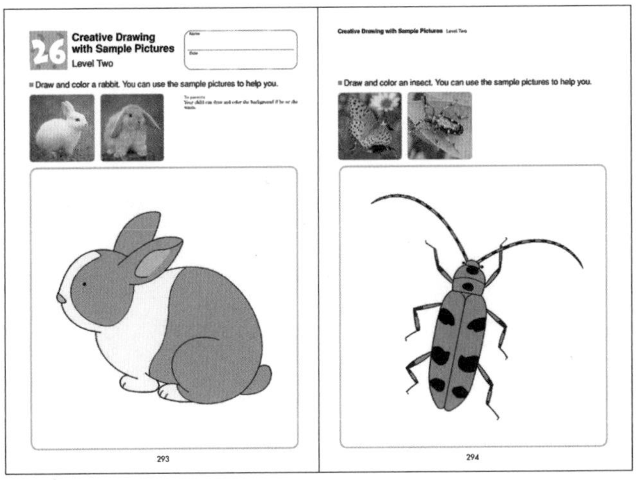

pages 293 and 294

pages 295 and 296

pages 297 and 298

pages 299 and 300

pages 301 and 302

pages 303 and 304

pages 305 and 306

pages 307 and 308

pages 309 and 310

pages 311 and 312

pages 313 and 314